"Don Locke's book is a tender yet unflinchingly gritty portrayal of small-town life in the sixties. Courageously and creatively told in the fresh and true voice of a precocious young boy, this tale brings the emotions and events surrounding a turbulent time to life. Highly recommended."

—ANNETTE SMITH, author of *A Bigger Life* and *A Crooked Path*

Also by Don Locke:

The Reluctant Journey of David Connors

A Novel

THE SUMMER *the* WIND WHISPERED MY NAME

DON LOCKE

NAVPRESS

NAVPRESS⦿

NavPress is the publishing ministry of The Navigators, an international Christian organization and leader in personal spiritual development. NavPress is committed to helping people grow spiritually and enjoy lives of meaning and hope through personal and group resources that are biblically rooted, culturally relevant, and highly practical.

For a free catalog go to www.NavPress.com
or call 1.800.366.7788 in the United States or 1.800.839.4769 in Canada.

NAVPRESS and the NAVPRESS logo are registered trademarks of NavPress. Absence of * in connection with marks of NavPress or other parties does not indicate an absence of registration of those marks.

ISBN-10: 1-60006-153-2
ISBN-13: 978-1-60006-153-0

Cover design by The DesignWorks Group, Charles Brock
Cover image by Veer
Author photo by Michael Christman
Creative Team: Jamie Chavez, Reagen Reed, Darla Hightower, Arvid Wallen, Kathy Guist

This novel is a work of fiction. Names, characters, places, and incidents are either the product of the author's imagination or are used fictitiously. Any resemblance to actual events, locales, organizations, or persons, living or dead, is entirely coincidental and beyond the intent of either the author or publisher.

Unless otherwise identified, all Scripture quotations in this publication are taken from the King James Version (KJV). Also used is the HOLY BIBLE: NEW INTERNATIONAL VERSION® (NIV®). Copyright © 1973, 1978, 1984 by International Bible Society. Used by permission of Zondervan Publishing House. All rights reserved.

Published in association with Jill Grosjean, Jill Grosjean Literary Agency.

Library of Congress Cataloging-in-Publication Data

Locke, Don, 1949-
The summer the wind whispered my name : a novel / Don Locke.
     p. cm.
  ISBN 978-1-60006-153-0
1. Neighborhood--Fiction. 2. Nineteen sixties--Fiction. 3. Racism--Fiction. 4. Race relations--Fiction. I. Title.
PS3612.O248S86 2008
813'.6--dc22
                                        2008005371

Printed in the United States of America

1 2 3 4 5 6 7 8 9 10 / 11 10 09 08

For Mom and Dad, who provided me with a wonderful childhood. And for Morgan and Graham and Garrett, who gave me the joy and privilege of sharing in theirs.

On one occasion an expert in the law stood up to test Jesus. "Teacher," he asked, "what must I do to inherit eternal life?" "What is written in the Law?" he replied. "How do you read it?" He answered: "'Love the Lord your God with all your heart and with all your soul and with all your strength and with all your mind'; and, 'Love your neighbor as yourself.'"

"You have answered correctly," Jesus replied. "Do this and you will live."

But he wanted to justify himself, so he asked Jesus, "And who is my neighbor?"

LUKE 10:25-29 (NIV)

CONTENTS

PREFACE

Until recently my early childhood memories weren't read-ily available for recollection. Call it a defective hard drive. They remained a mystery and a void — a midwestern landscape of never-ending pitch-blackness where I brushed up against people and objects but could never assign them faces or names, much less attach feelings to our brief encounters.

But through a miraculous act of divine grace, I found my way back home to discover the child I'd forgotten, the boy I'd aban-doned supposedly for the good of us both. There he sat beneath an oak tree patiently awaiting my return, as if I'd simply taken a day-long fishing trip. This reunion of spirits has transformed me into someone both wiser and more innocent, leaving me to feel both old and young.

And with this new gift of recollection, my memories turn to that boy and to the summer of 1960, when the winds of change blew across our rooftops and through the screen doors, turning the simple, manageable world of my suburban neighborhood into something unfamiliar, something uncomfortable. Those same winds blew my father and me apart.

One

ROUTE 666

With a gentle shake of my shoulders, a kiss on my cheek, and the words *It's time* whispered by my mom, I woke at five thirty in the morning to prepare for my newspaper route. Careful not to wake my older brother, Bobby, snoozing across the room, I slipped out of bed and stumbled my way into the hallway and toward the bathroom, led only by the dim glow of the night-light and a familiarity with the route.

There on the bathroom floor, as usual, my mother had laid my clothes out in the shape of my body, my underwear layered on top. You're probably wondering why she did this. It could have been that she severely underestimated my intelligence and displayed my clothes in this fashion in case there was any doubt on my part as to which articles of clothing went where on my body. She didn't want to face the public humiliation brought on by her son walking out of the house wearing his Fruit of the Loom undies over his head. Or maybe her work was simply the result of a sense of humor that I missed completely. Either way, I never asked.

Mine was a full-service mom whose selfless measures of accommodation put the men of Texaco to shame. The fact that she would inconvenience herself by waking me when an alarm clock would suffice, or lay out my clothes when I was capable of doing so myself, might sound a bit odd to you, but believe me, it was only the tip of the indulgent iceberg. This was a woman who would cut the crust off my PB&J sandwich at my request, set my toothbrush out every night with a wad of Colgate lying atop the bristles, and who would often put me to sleep at night with a song, a prayer, and a back scratch. In the wintertime, when the wind chill factor made the hundred-yard trek down to the corner to catch the school bus feel like Admiral Perry's excursion, Mom would actually lay my clothes out on top of the floor heater before I woke up so that my body would be adequately preheated before stepping outside to face the Ohio cold. From my perspective my room was self-cleaning; toys, sports equipment, and clothes discarded onto the floor all found their way back to the toy box, closet, or dresser. I never encountered a dish that I had to clean or trash I had to empty or a piece of clothing I had to wash or iron or fold or put away.

I finished dressing, entered the kitchen, and there on the maroon Formica table, in predictable fashion, sat my glass of milk and chocolate long john patiently waiting for me to consume them. My mother, a chocoholic long before the word was coined, had a sweet tooth that she'd handed down to her children. She believed that a heavy dusting of white processed sugar on oatmeal, Cream of Wheat, or grapefruit was crucial energy fuel for starting one's day. Only earlier that year I'd been shocked to learn from my third grade teacher, Mrs. Mercer, that chocolate was not, in fact, a member of any of the four major food groups.

Wearing a milk mustache and buzzing from my sugar rush, I walked outside to where the stack of *Tribunes*—dropped off in my driveway earlier by the news truck—were waiting for me to fold them.

More often than I ever cared to hear it, my dad would point out, "It's the early bird that catches the worm." But for me it was really those early morning summer hours themselves that provided the reward. Sitting there on our cement front step beneath a forty-watt porch light, rolling a stack of *Tribune*s, I was keenly aware that bodies were still strewn out across beds in every house in the neighborhood, lying lost in their dreamland slumber while I was already experiencing the day. There would be time enough for the sounds of wooden screen doors slamming shut, the hissing of sprinklers on Bermuda lawns, and the songs of robins competing with those of Elvis emanating from transistor radios everywhere. But for now there was a stillness about my neighborhood that seemed to actually slow time down, where even the old willow in our front yard stood like one more giant dozing on his feet, his long arms hanging lifeless at his sides, and where the occasional shooting star streaking across the black sky was a confiding moment belonging only to the morning and me.

From the porch step I could detect the subtle, pale peach glow rise behind the Finnegans' house across the street. I stretched a rubber band open across the top of my knuckles, spread my fingers apart, and slid it down over the length of the rolled paper to hold it in place. Seventy-six times I'd repeat this act almost unconsciously. There was something about the crisp, cool morning air that seemed to contain a magical element that when breathed in set me to daydreaming. So that's just what I did . . . I sent my homemade bottle rocket blasting above the trees and watched as the red and white bobber at the end of my fishing pole suddenly got sucked down below the surface of the water at Crystal Lake, and with my Little League team's game on the line, I could hear the crack of my bat as I smacked a liner over the third baseman's head to drive in the go-ahead run. Granted, most kids would daydream bigger—their rockets sailed to the moon or Mars, and their fish, blue marlins at least, were hooked off Bermuda in their yachts, and their hits were certainly grand slams in the bottom of the ninth to win the World Series for the Reds—but my dad always suggested that a dream should have its feet planted firmly enough in reality to actually have a chance to come true one day, or there wasn't much point in conjuring up the dream in the first place. Dreaming too big would only lead to a lifetime scattered with the remnants of disappointments and heartbreak.

And I believed him. Why not? I was young and his shadow fell across me with weight and substance and truth. He was my hero. But in some ways, I suppose, he was too much like my other heroes: Frank Robinson, Ricky Nelson, Maverick. I looked up to them because of their accomplishments or their image, not because of who they really were. I didn't really know who they were outside of that. Such was the case with my dad. He was a great athlete in his younger years, had a drawer full of medals for track and field, swimming, baseball, basketball, and a bunch from the army to prove it.

It was my dad who had managed to pull the strings that allowed me to have a paper route in the first place. I remember reading the pride in his eyes earlier in the spring when he first told me I got the job. His voice rose and fell within a wider range than usual as he explained how I would now be serving a valuable purpose in society by being directly responsible for informing people of local, national, and even international events. My dad made it sound important—an act of responsibility, being this cog in the wheel of life, the great mandala. And it made me *feel* important, better defining my place in the universe. In a firm handshake with my dad, I promised I wouldn't let him down.

Finishing up folding and banding the last paper, I knew I was running a little late because Spencer, the bullmastiff next door, had already begun to bark in anticipation of my arrival. Checking the Bulova wristwatch that my dad had given me as a gift the morning of my first route confirmed it. I proceeded to cram forty newspapers into my greasy white canvas pouch and loop the straps over my bike handles. Riding my self-painted, fluorescent green Country Road–brand bike handed down from my brother, I would deliver these papers mostly to my immediate neighborhood and swing back around to pick up the final thirty-six.

I picked the olive green army hat up off the step. Though most boys my age wore baseball caps, I was seldom seen without the hat my dad wore in World War II. Slapping it down onto my head, I hopped onto my bike, turned on the headlight, and was off down my driveway, turning left on the sidewalk that ran along the front of our corner property on Willowcreek Road.

I rode around to where our street dead-ended, curving into Briarbrook. Our eccentric young neighbors, the Springfields, lived next door in a house they'd painted black. Mr. and Mrs. Springfield chose to raise a devil dog named Spencer rather than experience the joy of parenthood. Approaching the corner of their white picket fence on my bike, I could see the strong, determined, shadowy figure of that demon dashing back and forth along the picket fence, snarling and barking at me loudly enough to wake the whole neighborhood. As was my custom, I didn't dare slow down while I heaved the rolled-up newspaper over his enormous head into their yard. Spencer sprinted over to the paper and

pounced on it, immediately tearing it to shreds—a daily reenact-
ment. The couple insisted that I do this every day, as they were
attempting to teach Spencer to fetch the morning paper, bring it
around to the back of the house where he was supposed to enter
by way of the doggy door, and gently place the newspaper in one
piece on the kitchen table so it would be there to peruse when
they woke for breakfast.

Theirs was one of only two houses in the neighborhood that
were fenced in, a practice uncommon in the suburbs because it
implied a lack of hospitality. Even a small hedge along a property
line could be interpreted as stand-offish. The Springfields' choice
of house color wasn't helpful in dispelling this notion. And yet it
was a good thing that they chose to enclose their property because
we were all quite certain that if Spencer ever escaped his yard,
he would systematically devour every neighborhood kid, one by
one. The strange thing was that the picket fence couldn't have
been more than three feet high, low enough for even a miniature
poodle to clear—so why hadn't Spencer taken the leap? Could it
be that he was just biding his time, waiting for the right moment
to jump that hurdle? So I was thankful for the Springfields' inepti-
tude when it came to dog training because it allowed me to buffer
Spencer's appetite, knowing that whenever he did decide to make
his move, I would most likely be the first course on the menu.

The neighborhood houses on my route were primarily ranch
style, third-little-pig variety, and always on my left. On my left
so that I could grab a paper out of my bag and heave it across my
body, allowing for more mustard on my throw and more accuracy
than if I had to sling it backhand off to my right side. This technique also helped build up strength in my pitching arm. I always
aimed directly toward the middle of the driveway instead of

anywhere near the porch, which could, as I'd learned, be treacherous territory. An irate Mrs. Messerschmitt from Sleepy Hollow Road once dropped by my house, screaming, "You've murdered my children! You've murdered my children!" Apparently I'd made an errant toss that tore the blooming heads right off her precious pansies and injured a few hapless marigolds. From that day on I shot for the middle of the driveway, making sure no neighbors' flowers ever suffered a similar fate at my hands.

I passed my friend Mouse Miller's house, crossed the street, and headed down the other side of Briarbrook, past Allison Hoffman's house—our resident divorcée. All my friends still had their two original parents and family intact, which made Mrs. Hoffman's status a bit of an oddity. Maybe it was the polio scare that people my parents' age had had to live through that appeared to make them wary of any abnormality in another human being. It wasn't just being exposed to the drug addicts or the murderers that concerned them, but contact with any fringe members of society: the divorcées and the widowers, the fifty-year-old bachelors, people with weird hairdos or who wore clothing not found in the Sears catalogue. People with facial hair were especially to be avoided.

You didn't want to be a nonconformist in 1960. Though nearly a decade had passed, effects of the McCarthy hearings had left some Americans with lingering suspicions that their neighbor might be a Red or something worse. So everyone did their best to just fit in. There was an unspoken fear that whatever social dysfunction people possessed was contagious by mere association with them. I had a feeling my mom believed this to be the case with Allison Hoffman—that all my mother had to do was engage in a five-minute conversation with any divorced woman, and a week or so later, my dad would come home from work and out of the blue announce, "Honey, I want a divorce."

Likely in her late twenties, Mrs. Hoffman was attractive enough to be a movie star or at least a fashion model — she was that pretty. She taught at a junior high school across town, but for extra cash would tutor kids in her spare time. Despite her discriminating attitude toward Mrs. Hoffman, my mother was forced to hire her as a tutor for my sixteen-year-old brother for two sessions a week, seeing as Bobby could never quite grasp the concept of dangling participles and such. Still, whenever she mentioned Mrs. Hoffman's name, my mom always found a way to justify setting her Christian beliefs aside, calling her *that woman*, as in, "just stay away from *that woman*." Mom must have skipped over the part in the Bible where Jesus healed the lepers. Anyway, Mrs. Hoffman seemed nice enough to me when I'd see her gardening in her yard or when I'd have to collect newspaper money from her; a wave and smile were guaranteed.

I delivered papers down Briarbrook, passed my friend Sheena's house on the cul-de-sac, and went back down to Willowcreek, where I rolled past the Jensens' vacant house. The For Sale sign had been stuck in the lawn out front since the beginning of spring. I'd seen few people even stop by to look at the charming, white frame house I remember as having great curb appeal. Every kid on the block was rooting for a family with at least a dozen kids to move in to provide some fresh blood.

A half a block later, I turned the corner and was about to toss the paper down Mr. Melzer's drive when I spotted the old man lying under his porch light, sprawled out on the veranda, his blue overall-covered legs awkwardly dangling down the front steps of his farm house. I immediately stood up on my bike, slammed on the brakes, fish-tailed a streak of rubber on the sidewalk, dumped the bike, and rushed up to his motionless body. "Mr. Melzer! Mr. Melzer!" Certain he was dead, I kept shouting at him like he was only asleep or deaf. "Mr. Melzer!" I was afraid to touch him to see if he was alive.

The only dead body I had touched up till then was my great-uncle Frank's at his wake, and it was not a particularly pleasant experience. I was five years old when my mom led me up to the big shiny casket where I peered over the top to see the man lying inside. Standing on my tiptoes, I stared at Frank's clay-colored face, which I believed looked too grumpy, too dull. While alive and kicking, my uncle was an animated man with ruddy cheeks who spoke and reacted with passion and humor, but the expression he wore while lying in that box was one that I'd never seen on his face before. I was quite sure that if he'd been able to gaze in the mirror at his dead self with that stupid, frozen pouting mouth looking back at him, he would have been humiliated and embarrassed as all get out. And so, while no one watched, I started poking and prodding at his surprisingly pliable mouth, trying to reshape his smile into something more natural, more familiar, like the expression he'd worn recalling the time he drove up to frigid Green Bay in a blizzard to watch his beloved Browns topple Bart Starr and the Green Bay Packers. Or the one he'd displayed while telling us what a thrill it was to meet Betty Grable at a USO function during the war, or the grin that always appeared on his face right after he'd take a swig of a cold beer on a hot summer day. It was a look of satisfaction that I was after, and was pretty sure I could pull it off. Those hours of turning shapeless Play-Doh into little doggies and snowmen had prepared me for this moment.

After a mere twenty seconds of my molding handiwork, I had

successfully managed to remove my uncle's grim, lifeless expression. Unfortunately I had replaced it with a hideous-looking full-on smile, his teeth beaming like the Joker from the Batman comics. Before I could step back for a more objective look, my Aunt Doris let out a little shriek behind me; an older gentleman gasped, which brought my brother over, and he let out a howl of laughter, all followed by a flurry of activity that included some heated discussion among relatives, the casket's being closed, and my mother's hauling me out of the room by my earlobe.

But you probably don't really care much about my Uncle Frank. You're wondering about Mr. Melzer and if he's a character who has kicked the bucket before you even got to know him or know if you like him. You will like him. I did. "Mr. Melzer!" I gave him a good poke in the arm. Nothing . . . then another one.

The fact is I was surprised when Mr. Melzer began to move. First his head turned . . . then his arm wiggled . . . then he rose, propping himself up onto an elbow, attempting to regain his bearings.

"Mr. Melzer?"

"What?" He looked around, glassy-eyed, still groggy. "Davy?"

I suddenly felt dizzy and nearly fell down beside him on the porch. "Yeah, it's me."

"I must have dozed off. Guess the farmer in me still wants to wake with the dawn, but the old man, well, he knows better." He looked my way. "You're white as a sheet—you okay, boy?"

Actually I was feeling pretty nauseated. "Yeah, I'm okay. I just thought . . ."

"What? You thought what?"

"Well, when I saw you lying there . . . I just thought . . ."

"That I was dead?" I nodded. "Well, no, no, I can see where that might be upsetting for you. Come to think of it, it's a little upsetting to me. Not that I'm not prepared to meet my maker, mind you. Or to see Margaret again." He leaned heavily on his right arm, got himself upright, and adjusted his suspenders. "The fact is . . . I do miss the old gal. The way she'd know to take my hand when it needed holdin'. Or how she could make a room feel comfortable just by her sitting in it, breathing the same air. Heck, I even miss her lousy coffee. And I hope, after these two years apart, she might have forgotten what a pain in the rear I could be, and she might have the occasion to miss me a bit, too."

Until that moment, I hadn't considered the possibility of the dead missing the living. Sometimes when he wasn't even trying to, Mr. Melzer made me think. And it always surprised me how often he would just say anything that came into his head. He never edited himself like most adults. He was like a kid in that respect, but more interesting.

"You believe in heaven?" I asked Mr. Melzer.

"Rather counting on it. How 'bout you?"

"My mom says that when we go to heaven we'll be greeted by angels with golden wings."

"Really? Angels, huh?"

"And she says that they'll sing a beautiful song written especially for us."

"Really? Your mother's an interesting woman, Davy. But I could go for that—I could. Long as they're not sitting around on clouds playing harps. Don't care for harp music one bit. Pretty sure it was the Marx Brothers that soured me on that instrument."

"How so?"

"Well, those Marx Brothers, in every movie they made they'd be running around, being zany as the dickens, and then Harpo—the one who never spoke a lick, the one with the fuzzy blond hair—always honking his horn and chasing some skinny, pretty gal around. Anyway, in the middle of all their high jinks, Harpo would come across some giant harp just conveniently lying around somewhere, and he'd feel obliged to stop all the antics to play some sappy tune that just about put you to sleep. I could never recover. Turned me sour on the harp, he did. I'm more of a horn man, myself. Give me a saxophone or trumpet and I'm happy. And I'm not particularly opposed to a fiddle either. But harps—I say round 'em up and burn 'em all. Melt 'em down and turn them into something practical . . . something that can't make a sound . . . that's what I say."

See, I told you he'd pretty much say anything. I don't think that Mr. Melzer had many people to listen to him. And just having a bunch of thoughts roaming around in his head wasn't enough. I think Mr. Melzer chattered a lot so that he wouldn't lose himself, so he could remember who he was.

"Yeah, well, anyway, I figure I'll go home when it's my time," he continued. "Just hope it can wait for the harvest, seeing as there's no one else to bring in the corn when it's time."

As far back as I could remember, Mr. Melzer used to drag this little red wagon around the neighborhood on August evenings, stacked to the limit with ears of corn. And he'd go door to door and hand out corn to everybody like he was some kind of an agricultural Santa.

"Do you know I used to have fields of corn as far as the eye can see . . . way beyond the rooftops over there?"

I did know this, but I never tired of the enthusiasm with

which he told it, so I didn't stop him. About ten years before, Mr. Melzer had sold off all but a few acres of his farmland to a contractor, resulting in what became my neighborhood.

"I still get a thrill when I shuck that first ear of corn of the harvest, and see that ripe golden row of kernels smiling back at me. Hot, sweet corn, lightly salted with butter dripping down all over it . . . *mmm*. Nothing better. Don't nearly have the teeth for it anymore. You eat yours across or up and down?"

"Across."

"Me too. Only way to eat corn. Tastes better across. When I see somebody munching on an ear like this"—the old man rolled the imaginary ear of corn in front of his imaginary teeth chomping down—"I just want to slap him upside the head."

I was starting to run very late, and he noticed me fidgeting.

"Oh, yeah, here I am blabbering away, and you got a job to do."

"I'll get your paper." I ran back to my bike lying on the sidewalk.

"So I see nobody's bought the Jensen place yet," he yelled out to me.

I grabbed a newspaper that had spilled out of my bag onto the sidewalk, and rushed back to Mr. Melzer. "Not yet. Whoever does, hope they have kids." I handed the old man the newspaper.

"Listen, I'm sorry I scared you," he said.

"It's okay." I looked over at a pile of unopened newspapers on the porch by the door. "Mind if I ask you something?"

"Shoot."

"How come you never read the paper?"

"Oh, don't know. At some point I guess you grow tired of bad news. Besides, these days all the news I need is right here in the neighborhood."

"So why do you still order the paper?"

The old man smiled. "Well, the way I see it, if I didn't order the paper, I'd miss out on these splendid little chats with you, now wouldn't I?"

I told you you'd like him. I grinned. "I'm glad you're not dead, Mr. Melzer."

"Likewise," he said, shooting a wink my way. When I turned around to walk back to my bike, I heard the rolled up newspaper hit the top of the pile.

Two

THE BEST LAID PLANS
OF MOUSE AND MEN

Once a week I rode my bike into town and paid a visit to Ben Franklin's Five and Dime. Though I was saving up money from my paper route and weekly allowance to buy a new bike (I had my eye on a Schwinn Black Phantom, $79.95 at Hendee's Bike World), I would spend at least a portion of my profits on rolls of caps and baseball cards.

Just below our tree house in the shade of a massive oak tree, on my knees with my heels tucked beneath me, I leaned over a piece of plywood, scraping the gun powder from a roll of caps with my pocket knife. If my mom had known that I was playing with a knife, she might have thrown one of those dreaded conniption fits that she always threatened to have. If she'd known that I'd stolen the knife from Rugen's Hardware store while old man Rugen had his back turned, she certainly would have just fallen over dead on the spot. Her diagnosis for cause of death: failure as a parent. But she didn't know and she wouldn't find out, because while the neighborhood was basically owned and operated by our parents, the vacant field that stretched out behind the row of houses on Briarbrook Road was the world that belonged solely to the kids on the block. Oakfield is what we called it, named simply for the giant oak tree that stood majestically in its midst, a good fifty yards away from civilization.

With long grass concealing garter snakes and housing grasshoppers and crickets, and a long, meandering creek filled with crayfish and frogs that we'd catch and release for sport, Oakfield may as well have been located somewhere in a distant countryside rather than in the suburbs. The far perimeter of Oakfield was lined with maple trees that enclosed it from the civilized world. The best thing about the field was that when we'd ride our bikes down the dirt pathway of the vacant lot on Briarbrook and cross the makeshift bridge over the ditch that bordered the hundred or so undeveloped acres, we became transformed. No longer was I Mr. and Mrs. Connor's youngest son or Bobby's kid brother — I became Davy, my own person, responsible for my own life, independent and exempt from the rules and regulations set down by my parents, having escaped beyond the force of their magnetic field. That's not to say that my conscience didn't follow me out there, or that I didn't do battle with my own personal Jiminy Cricket on a regular basis when engaging in wrong behavior. But Oakfield was a place where you could try out your wings and be the kid you always suspected you really were, rather than the one your family expected you to be. You could test out language that you heard older boys use, but had never dared speak yourself, words that back at home would have drawn gasps and looks of horror, not to mention the threat of a Palmolive sandwich served up by your mother. Out in Oakfield, around your peers in your private wilderness, those same words sounded grown-up and rebellious and cool.

On this particular summer afternoon Sheena was seated high above me on the edge of the tree house porch, her long stick legs hanging over, bending down at a right angle out of red bermuda shorts, and swinging back and forth in an unconscious show of contentment. Our old red floral carpetbag rested against the wall. "I do not like them, Sam I am. I do not like green eggs and ham," Sheena said. She was looking through the lenses of her pink cat's-eye sunglasses, reading Dr. Seuss out loud to her Raggedy Ann doll that sat beside her, slumped against the tree house wall. This was the kind of thing that drove us guys nuts, especially Mouse.

Wearing his bent-up old blue Chicago Cubs cap with the white C peeling off, Mouse looked up from setting an empty Dr Pepper bottle on top of a flat rock and shot a disgusted look in my direction, as if I were responsible for Sheena's acting way too girlie to justify her hanging out with us. "Does she have to do that?" he asked.

A couple years older than me, Mouse, whose real name was Daniel Miller, was one of those kids who becomes your friend not by choice, but only because he's about your age and he lives in the neighborhood and you couldn't avoid him if you wanted to. So you wind up hanging around with him, wishing he were cool so that you could improve your own sadly sub-par level of coolness, but always knowing he was really a jerk. He had moved to Ohio from Chicago a couple years earlier, and all he ever did was talk about how great Chicago, Illinois, was (the Cubs in particular) and how lousy Glenview, Ohio, was (the Reds in particular).

If you're wondering why they called him Mouse, the answer is I don't know. And I suppose I should have, but I never did ask why that was his nickname. I can tell you this—he didn't have big ears or a pointy nose or an extraordinary appetite for cheddar or limburger.

None of the guys wanted to have to put up with dolls in our tree house, much less have to listen to Sheena reading a kid's book out loud to them as if the freckled, pigtailed doll could actually hear Seuss's silly rhymes. You can't really blame them. But since Sheena, who was my age, was basically responsible for the tree house's even being there, we were forced to make allowances. You see, it was Sheena's dad, Mr. McGuire, who decided it would be safer and more fun for his daughter and all of us if he built a tree house up in the oak. So early one morning during the previous summer, Mr. McGuire had backed his blue pickup truck full of lumber into the field and gone to work with a handsaw, hammer, and bucket of nails. By the end of the day, an impressive pine tree house, with three windows and a small balcony, sat comfortably in the broad, strong arms of the great oak, looking very much at home. The ladder that ran at a slight angle alongside the trunk leading up to the tree house made for a safe and easy climb.

Even though the Fourth of July was still a long way off, we had taken a break from our usual field games of cowboys and Indians and turned our collective attention toward fireworks and the pleasure found in blowing things up. Personally I loved everything about fireworks, and firecrackers in particular. I loved the colorful packaging, the smell of gunpowder before a fuse was lit, and the smell of sulfur after detonation. I loved the sounds they made, the drama of the timing of the explosions, and the way the blasts would startle your heart no matter how prepared you might be. And then there was the element of danger. It was thrilling—the chance that something could go terribly wrong.

But in our little town fireworks were illegal. Fortunately caps were not. And so we started buying rolls of caps from the dime store, not as faux ammunition to load in our cap guns but to use as a resource for producing our own firecrackers and bottle rockets.

While Mouse prepared for a test launch by attaching a two-inch long homemade firecracker to the head of a punk with some Scotch tape, I continued with my own job of extracting the gunpowder from a roll of caps for future flights.

Cap scraping was a delicate process that took a steady hand and a keen eye, a procedure comparable only to that of brain surgery. Patience and precision were the key skills when deftly manipulating the point of the pocket knife as if it were a surgeon's scalpel. We'd meticulously tear open the thin layer of red paper that sealed the precious tiny packets of gunpowder at quarter-inch intervals. We'd then proceed to lift off the thin membrane, exposing the dark gray powder. Next, we'd skillfully scrape the small load of gunpowder off the roll and onto the waiting piece of typing paper to join forces with the huge mound of powder that had already been collected through the same process. And the trick was to perform this surgery without allowing the friction of the act to cause the gunpowder to ignite, resulting in a flash explosion. A blast early in the process wasn't a big deal, but every time you'd drag your small pile of gunpowder over to the more substantial pile, the possibility of a dangerous situation existed. But it was okay. Because we loved danger. We loved living on the edge. Unfortunately it was the edge of stupidity. Pure and simple, we were idiots to do this sort of thing.

We were fools to store the gunpowder we'd collected in empty aspirin bottles and to cut newspaper pages into squares the size of Bazooka Bubble Gum comics, and to dump various amounts of gunpowder in a row onto that newspaper, and to then roll it up and seal it with a dab of Elmer's Glue. We were also crazy to soak short pieces of string in glue and roll them around in gunpowder to create a less-than-perfect fuse, which we then inserted into the ends of our rockets and firecrackers.

It was a lengthy, tedious process to complete the assembly of even one firecracker, but when you watched your firecracker explode or bottle rocket shoot up into the air, the result was more rewarding, knowing you had created the moment with your own hands rather than having simply purchased some commercially manufactured fireworks like the Black Cat brand off the black market. Still, that doesn't excuse the stupidity of it all. Have I made that clear?

"Geronimo!" This was the voice of Mouse letting out his famous battle cry, signaling he was about to launch a bottle rocket.

"Oh, let me light it!" Sheena yelled down from her perch. Sheena talked a good game, always coming off like this courageous little tomboy in an attempt to meet with our approval, but she didn't fool anyone. At the time there was almost nothing that Sheena *wasn't* afraid of. She just wasn't about to admit it. And I was fine with that. My concern was that someday her mouth would convince her brain that it was okay to take a big risk and she'd wind up regretting it.

"No way, shrimp," I answered before Mouse had a chance to agree. She dropped the Seuss book into her doll's lap and shimmied down the ladder where her patiently waiting, tail-wagging dog, Sunny, greeted her with sloppy kisses and barks.

Sheena was the little sister I never had—so I needed to protect her. I set my knife down and bowed the paper with the gunpowder on it, funneling the powder that I'd collected down into the aspirin bottle. Sheena walked over to Mouse, who sat cross-legged next to the empty soda bottle sitting on the stone launching pad.

"Come on! You guys never let me!"

"Forget it. It's a man's job," I said.

Mouse inserted the rocket into the Dr Pepper bottle, the fire-cracker head and fuse sticking out of its top. "You let me light it or I'll tell your parents that you both play with firecrackers and matches and knives and that you smoke cigarettes and talk dirty," Sheena said. Mouse just laughed and pulled a book of matches out of his pocket and tossed them at her feet. "If it means that much to you," he said, "go ahead." Sunny saw it as a game and made a playful pounce toward the matches, but Sheena grabbed him by the scruff of the neck and pulled him away.

"Go get your steak," she said to him, referring to the red rubber chew toy in the shape of a T-bone steak that lay near the base of the tree. But instead of obeying his master, the golden retriever mix sat down on the spot, anxious to watch the drama unfold. Sheena looked over at me. "I wanna do this."

"I think we should let her do it," Mouse said, surprising both of us.

"Fine. Go ahead and blow your head off. See if we care," I said.

Sheena hesitated for a moment, then bent down and snatched the book of matches off the ground. Mouse walked around behind her and sat down on a large root that extended several feet from the trunk of the oak. Sheena began walking toward the bottle rocket and then stopped. "It's a pretty big one, isn't it?"

"You think this one's big," Mouse said, "wait till you see the rocket Davy and I are going to blast off on the Fourth. It's gonna be five times the size. When that baby sails across the sky, it'll light up the whole neighborhood. So, yeah, go ahead, simp, light it. Unless, of course, you're afraid."

"I'm not afraid!" Sheena flipped open the matchbook cover, but her red PF Flyers were still stuck about four feet away from the rocket.

"I knew a little kid once—" Mouse began.

"Yeah, sure you did," Sheena said, knowing he was about to make up some outrageous story, as was his habit. She began walking toward the rocket again, out from the cool shadow of the oak into the sunlight to the launching pad, a circle of dirt about four feet in diameter, with a perimeter of boulders, beyond which were patches of dry, trampled grass.

"Like I was saying, there was this little kid I knew who was lighting one of these handmade rockets like this one and nobody knows exactly how it happened, but—"

"Shut up, Mouse," Sheena said.

"It blew off the whole side of his face. Took a team of doctors to sew it back on. It's a fact."

Sheena stopped in her tracks. "Shut up!" She walked right up to the bottle rocket and stared it down. You could see her building up the nerve to light it.

"And now he has to drink his sodas with a straw . . . through his nose," Mouse added.

Sheena spun around toward Mouse. "You are so full of it!" She turned back around to the job at hand, squatting down in front of the bottle rocket, one knee resting on the dirt. She lifted the cover from the matchbook, methodically selected a red-headed match, and tore it away from its row of cardboard clones.

Meanwhile, Mouse eased himself up off the root, looked over at me, and raised his index finger up to his mouth requesting my silence and confidence.

As Sheena closed the matchbook cover in preparation to strike, Mouse silently crept up directly behind her. Sheena struck the match; it lit on the first try. She leaned forward and, delicately holding the lit match between her fingers, slowly and carefully eased it toward the tip of the fuse, her body poised for a hasty retreat once the sparks began to spit. The match flame was only an inch at most away from the bottle rocket when Mouse cupped his hands on either side of his mouth, leaned right up over Sheena's crouched back, and shouted, "Boom!"

"Aaaaahh!" Sheena cried out, startled off her feet and onto her butt as if Mouse had pulled an invisible rug out from underneath her. The match flew from her hand.

Mouse roared with laughter, and, as cruel a joke as it was, I have to admit that I found Sheena's reaction pretty amusing. Sitting on her rear end, she was red-faced and furious, almost in tears. Sunny was barking at the commotion.

"That's not funny!" Sheena said, springing to her feet. As Mouse turned toward me for my reaction, Sheena charged, blind-siding him with a gangly tackle that sent him sprawling to the dirt.

Mouse's laughter turned to anger, and he battled back. "Hey, cut it out!" Every ounce of Sheena's lean muscles struggled to hold Mouse to the ground in hopes of getting in at least one punch, but her efforts were short-lived. At a few inches taller and a good deal heavier, Mouse easily managed a reversal—flipping her over onto her back amidst a small cloud of dirt and pinning her down by her wrists on either side of her head. He sat down on top of her, straddling her belly and leaning over her face, while her entire body wiggled, her legs kicking in all directions in a futile attempt to escape his hold.

"Stop squirmin'!" he said. Sunny misinterpreted her situation as play, so he danced around the pair, wagging his tail and continuing to bark.

"Get off of me, jerko!" she said.

"No problem, but first you need to say *uncle*."

"I won't," Sheena exclaimed.

"Well, you know what I'm going to have to do then, don't cha?"

"Don't you dare. Davy!"

Now what Mouse was about to do to Sheena was one of the more disgusting little measures of torture to be found in his vast arsenal of methods to get the enemy to talk. I hesitate even to describe the details of this technique for fear you will be so offended that you set this book down and never pick it up again, that you will just let it lie there on your coffee table collecting dust until a friend of yours notices it and asks you what it's about and you simply roll your eyes and say, "Hawking a loogie—can you believe it?"

And that's just what Mouse did. Sitting upright like a cowboy on a bronco, while still pinning the helpless little girl to the ground, he arched his neck, lifting his head, and inhaled an extended snort of air through his nose in such a way to call up the substantial wad of phlegm that he always seemed to have stored in bulk in the reservoir found deep down the recesses of his throat. The sheer sound of this nasal mining process, similar to that of a slowed-down audio of an attacking wild boar—I'll give you a moment—would send shivers down the spine of a potential victim, which I'm sure was Sheena's reaction, as she bucked harder to free herself.

"Davy, get him off of me!"

I mumblety-pegged my knife into the ground. "Hey, Mouse, come on—let her up."

Instead Mouse leaned forward, steadying his mouth directly above Sheena's face as she turned from side to side to avoid the impending gross-out. "She needs to learn a lesson, Connors." Mouse said in a voice garbled by the introduction of mucus into his mouth. "She can't just jump somebody whenever she feels like it. Last chance . . . *say uncle*."

"I won't," Sheena stubbornly responded.

Mouse began working his weapon around in his mouth, molding it into shape. His lips puckered and from his mouth he ever-so-slowly released into view a soft, yellow-tinted, bulbous loogie about the size of your average cat's-eye marble.

Turning her face away, Sheena let out a little shriek, but her eyes remained glued to the loogie. Her body became very still. With superb control Mouse began to slowly, meticulously lower the gleaming spit wad farther and farther down toward Sheena's smooth cheek, its long, thick salivary tail extending from his lips. I'd seen Mouse execute this particular kind of torture on kids before, and never once had he made the mistake of losing control of his object of torture. But the considerable size of this loogie begged the question—was the consistency of his saliva sufficiently dense enough to hold the weight? Make no mistake, as with every magician, there was high drama in the act, knowing that there was always a small margin of error that would result in the pretty lady really getting sawed in half, the man bound in locks and chains actually drowning in the water tank, or, in this case, Sheena winding up wearing a snot puddle on her face, producing a gross-out moment so intense as to scar her emotionally for the rest of her days. It was mesmerizing. I couldn't look away. I could almost hear the drum roll as the loogie dripped its way down, lower and lower on its tenuous thread to within an inch of Sheena's nose, where it hung, suspended for what seemed like an eternity while Sheena's eyes doubled in size and then suddenly — *shooooop* — Mouse sucked that snotball back up into his mouth like a yo-yo on a string. Though you could question the manner in which Mouse used his gift, there was no denying that he possessed a truly amazing talent that every kid admired.

"Say uncle or the next one drops." With no immediate response, Mouse began lowering another loogie, the bigger, uglier brother of the one we'd just seen.

"I'll tell my brother, Terry, on you! Davy!" Sheena pleaded.

"Leave her alone, Mouse." I started in their direction with the intention of shoving Mouse off of her, but then, in the short patchy dry grass a few feet beyond them, it caught my eye.

"Fire!" I screamed. Flames were flaring up, crackling and quickly spreading from where Sheena had accidentally dropped the match. As Mouse turned his head toward the small blaze, his world record–size loogie immediately fell and splattered right onto Sheena's closed lips. She muffled a scream, and Mouse leapt to his feet and squared off with the flames in a Greco-Roman wrestling pose, like he was going to somehow grapple the fire out. I ran past the moaning and spitting Sheena and started stomping around the edge of the three-foot wide ring of fire, trying to contain it before it had a chance to spread any farther. I could almost feel the soles of my hightop Keds melting to my arches, as flames shot up alongside the cuffs of my blue jeans, scorching my legs.

"Get some water," I yelled out to anyone and everyone. But Mouse just stood there, his panic having turned him into a statue, and Sheena, on her knees, was too busy wiping her face with her T-shirt sleeve and alternating between spitting and gagging. And then there was Sunny, who was proving he was no Lassie. Timmy's dog would have found a bucket, filled it up in the nearby creek, and dumped it on the fire herself, but Sunny just sat there, dumb as a rock. Finally Mouse came to life and ran over to join me in the frantic dance. I was motivated by fear to smother the fire at any cost. Running the risk of sustaining third-degree burns paled in comparison to facing the disappointment and anger in my parents' eyes after having to confess to them that I was partially responsible for accidentally burning down the entire field, and possibly the neighborhood. So I danced and high-stepped a little quicker and watched the flames eventually lose the battle and die down.

Sheena had finally stopped spitting and wiping and was sitting quietly, petting Sunny the wonder dog, looking off to the side. I plopped myself down on the ground, feeling fortunate and relieved, knowing how close we'd come to a real disaster. Mouse was equally shaken as he stood over the charred grass, searching with the tip of his toe for any surviving embers to kill. He looked over at Sheena. "Way to go, spaz."

Sheena just kept patting Sunny, her face now turned completely away from us.

"This is all your fault," Mouse added. If it was anyone's fault, it was Mouse's, and I should have said something to that effect right then and there, but I didn't. "Why don't you and your dolly go play with the other girls?"

Sheena never said a word, never turned around, just stood up and walked over to the tree, climbed the ladder and disappeared into the tree house, leaving Sunny to lie down at the base of the trunk.

"Man, you just don't know when to shut up, do you?" I said to Mouse.

"Yeah, well, maybe you should join her," he said.

In a way I already had. I was a chameleon when it came to adapting to the feelings of others, proficient at turning blue when people around me felt melancholy themselves, for example. This was especially true when it came to Sheena. The mood to scrape caps had passed, so I took a walk down to the creek.

At its narrowest part, a casual step could get you to the other side of the stream, and at its widest, a brave leap. I sat down on the bank. The early summer had the cool, clean water rushing along the bed at a decent clip. I selected a fat green grassy reed on the ground in front of me, plucked it, and positioned it between my thumbs as I cupped my hands. As I blew through the small space between my thumbs, the reed vibrated until it created a clear-sounding, single sax-like note. There was something about sitting under a summer blue sky, blowing my handmade reed instrument, and listening to the babbling of a brook that was so peaceful it could just absorb my tension and remind me that life was good.

Sheena had her own way of renewing herself. The sound of a music box melody began tinkling down from the tree house through the leaves; I'd expected to hear it even before I did. Brahms's Waltz in A-Flat Major. It was a magical music box—for one thing, Sheena was the only one who could manage to make it operate. Whenever Sheena grew sad or got upset about something, she'd climb up into that tree house, grab our old carpetbag, pull out the music box with the cherub angel on top, and listen to that tune over and over. A few minutes later she'd reappear, completely rejuvenated, like nothing had even happened. You'd think you had to be about a hundred years old to enjoy that kind of classical music, but she did. There was a mystical connection between Sheena and that music box from the moment we found it in the field.

It was June the previous year when the two of us had walked single file through Oakfield, in waist-high grass and wild flowers, down a narrow, matted pathway with honeybees, dragonflies, and startled grasshoppers impeding our progress. We were nearly at our destination—the railroad tracks, where we'd hoped to turn a penny into a copper pancake—when Sheena first heard the melody. Without speaking a word about it, she stopped in front of me, then veered off the pathway and into the field.

"Where you going?" I asked, but she didn't respond. I followed her for maybe ten yards before I began to hear it too. The tinkling music grew clearer and more audible until we found ourselves standing over a spray of black-eyed Susans. As we bent down and spread apart the yellow wildflowers, we uncovered an old red floral carpetbag. It was partially open, and cream-colored cotton clothing flowed out of it like a wave, as the delicate music grew louder. The moment we both squatted down to examine the bag, the music inside slowed and then stopped like a cautious cricket—as if it knew we were closing in on it.

"What is it?" Sheena asked.

"Some sort of bag," I replied.

Three weeks earlier, in the middle of the night, a train had derailed not far from there, and although personal belongings were retrieved from the wreckage, somehow this bag must have eluded recovery. We looked down at the carpetbag, then at each other, knowing we'd found a treasure.

I slowly spread open the top of the bag wider and began pulling out what appeared to be a nightgown, when a snake sprang out toward me, mouth wide open.

"Aaaaah!" we both yelled.

The green snake struck my silver Roy Rogers belt buckle, knocking me over with the impact of surprise and temporarily stunning itself. A few seconds later it slithered away, disappearing into the grass, and Sheena and I composed ourselves enough to continue our investigation of the bag. I spread the nightgown out over the matted grass and tipped the bag, allowing the contents to tumble safely onto it. Out came a cameo brooch, a pearl necklace, a silver bracelet, a wooden egg, and a bundle of pastel blouses and other clothing. I unfolded the blouses, which still retained a hint of a sweet perfume, and uncovered the gilded, porcelain music box with the charming little figure of the cherub on top, her arms reaching toward the heavens with her palms turned up, and her peaceful expression looking skyward as well. Considering the adventure the bag had apparently encountered, it was a miracle that the figurine was completely intact—no clipped wings, no missing fingers.

"It's beautiful," Sheena said, picking it up and looking it over. "It's the most beautiful thing I've ever seen. She called to me."

"What?" I asked, snatching the egg and twisting it open.

"The angel . . . with her music. She called to me with her music."

Common sense and reason explained that the most likely scenario involved the snake sliding its body up against the lever of the music box, engaging the gears and initiating the melody, but I didn't suggest that idea to Sheena. The look of wonder on her face was too appealing to remove it.

The sense of wonder is not something you want to mess with, not something you want to deny someone simply because you believe you know better, because you suspect you know what really happens to the doves when the magician makes them disappear. So with Sheena I kept my mouth shut.

Besides, you so seldom get to see the expression of wonder flash across someone's face in real life that it would be a pity to deny either of you that pleasure. Excitement and surprise—those expressions are a dime a dozen, right? But the look of wonder is a rare occurrence, a fleeting moment of enormous value, that precious commodity of your youth. You search the eyes of the elderly and notice something's missing, and you just can't put your finger on it. And then you look deeper and realize what it is: the sense of wonder . . . vanished with time, vanished with the doves.

Sheena located the key along the side of the music box, gave it a few twists, pushed the lever, and the song began to play again.

There was a certain mystery to that carpetbag that became the collect-all for our toys that we liked to store up in the tree house. It had come into our lives in such a magical way, never belonging to one of us more than to the other.

"Davy!" A rejuvenated Sheena called out from the doorway of the tree house. I called back, and she climbed down the ladder and, with Sunny, walked through the tall grass to where I was sitting by the creek. Mouse had taken off, leaving the three of us. We had been sitting alongside the running stream for no more than a minute when we heard the sound that jumpstarts the heart of every kid.

The constant growling of lawn mowers, the hissing lawn sprinklers, the spattering laughter of kids throughout the suburban neighborhood . . . they were all emblematic sounds of my childhood summers, but the jingling of bells on the front of the Good Humor truck as it puttered down our street was the signature sound of my childhood.

Sheena and I jumped to our feet and ran back to the oak tree where our bikes were parked. "I'll give you five," I said, and counted out loud while she hopped onto her bike and took off down the dirt path and across the bridge.

The mere ringing of those chimes always sent me into a state of frenetic motion, knowing I had a limited window of opportunity to drop whatever activity I was doing, locate one of my parents, preferably my mom, convince her once again that ice cream would not spoil my dinner, finagle some change, and sprint to the wonderful white truck.

When Sheena, Sunny, and I arrived, Jack, dressed in his white jacket, pants, and hat outfit, was finishing up serving Jimmy Dumpkins, our pudgy ten-year-old friend. Seeing as he needed Jack's services the way a junkie needs crack, Jimmy could always be counted on to be the first kid on the block to reach the truck, assuring me the time to place my order before Jack lost patience and pulled away in search of the next customer.

"Thanks, Jack," Jimmy said, as he received his ice cream bar and crammed it into his mouth nearly before he'd removed the wrapper. "Hey, guys," he garbled in our direction. "What's up?"

Sheena and I greeted Jimmy, then turned our attention to Jack.

"The usual, Davy?" Jack asked.

"Please," I said. Jack reached his arm into the misting freezer compartment without looking and brought out a Fudgesicle covered with a layer of frost and handed it to me. I forked over my two nickels, and he casually inserted them into his silver coin changer on his belt and said, "Thanks."

As I sat there with Sheena and Jimmy on my front lawn, sucking on my Fudgesicle, looking out across the neighborhood, I was content. I was a happy kid growing up in a friendly, nurturing, quiet place, and even though I had nothing else to compare it to, I believe I knew I was lucky to be there. What I didn't know was how soon that idyllic life of mine would change.

Three

FATHER GLOWS BEST

While my mom was in the kitchen preparing dinner, I was lying on the couch in the living room, pounding a baseball into my glove while stoically watching the Three Stooges on our Philco. As the three of them continually poked, prodded, slapped, and insulted each other, I kept thinking about how close we'd come to burning down the field earlier. What was strange, though, was that my ankles didn't feel the least bit burned, and even my pants showed no evidence of being scorched by the fire. I considered how this could be and came up with two possible scenarios. Maybe, unbeknownst to me until that very day, I was actually a superhero named Flameboy who was impervious to fire. I wasn't positive of all of my superhero abilities, but was certain that I was a friend to animals and, of course, a defender of truth, justice, and the American way. But I suspected true superheroes knew in their hearts that they were meant for more than an ordinary life, while I sensed mine would never exceed Walter Mitty status.

The second scenario may have been equally as far-fetched. My mother had suggested on several occasions that I had a guardian angel watching over me at all times who prevented me from serious harm. I always found this concept—that someone was watching my every move—rather unnerving, knowing that many of those moves were less than angelic in nature. On the other hand, having an invisible friend to keep me from falling off roofs, crashing my bike into cars, and incinerating myself *was* sort of handy, not to mention pretty cool. At that moment I wasn't so sure that I could commit to an angel, but I was willing to believe in a Casper the Friendly Ghost sort of companion. I decided to call him Newton after my favorite fig cookie.

While Moe, Larry, and Curly took a break, a favorite commercial of mine came on TV. I'd seen it dozens of times, and it intrigued me each time. Standing on a pier in front of a serene, picturesque lake, a big, friendly man wearing a white cowboy hat pointed right at me, saying, "You lookin' for great fishin' action? You lookin' to land the big one? Well, then, you need to get yourself on out here to Fisherman's Dude Ranch, where we guarantee you'll have the fishin' experience of a lifetime." And then he'd proceed to show clips of satisfied customers of all ages landing these gigantic fish. Pulling in a big fish would be a welcome change from the puny perch or bluegill that I'd usually catch at Crystal Lake with the family, but I was just as interested in the chance to spend the day alone with my dad. I'd asked him several times if we could go, but his busy work schedule was such that he'd always reply with, "Well, let me see what I can do."

The show was wrapping up; Moe was feeding Curly cheese to keep him from freaking out after having seen a mouse, when from behind me I heard the wooden kitchen screen door slam shut and my dad's loud, enthusiastic voice, "Attention, Connors family members . . ."

I turned around and saw my dad, carrying his briefcase and a long cardboard cylinder, enter the kitchen through the side door. "How'd the show go, dear?" my mom asked, greeting him with their routine peck on the lips.

"Smooth, as usual. Dinner smells great," my dad said, and then immediately, "All right, everybody, family meeting! Everybody in here right now."

My father liked being in charge, having control over his wife, his kids, his universe. So it was appropriate that he was employed as a director of TV shows for our local station in Cincinnati. Because he would always deliver a running critique of the camera work whenever we watched TV shows as a family at night, I got the impression he'd prefer living out in Hollywood, directing the likes of Cary Grant or Elizabeth Taylor rather than working in a small pond like Cincinnati on *Two-Ton's Tree House Show*.

There were a lot of kids' shows around at the time, but I was proud that my dad directed *Two-Ton's Tree House*, even though I had begun to outgrow it. Most other kid shows had some goofy, well-mannered host unconvincingly dressed up like a cowboy or a railroad engineer or a clown, and they'd talk about dreadfully dull, unfunny things and then show you a bunch of old cartoons that always involved screwball animals whacking each other over the head with large mallets. But Two-Ton Trzcinski was different. First of all, he was, as his name suggests, an enormous man with virtually no neck to speak of, and long, greasy black hair that he combed straight back on his equally enormous head. Upon first inspection he was an unlikely role model for a kid. But unlike the other kids' show hosts, Two-Ton didn't waste your time teaching you things like how to floss, or that Z stands for zebra. Instead he was there to entertain you. He didn't wear a costume, maybe because they couldn't find one big enough to fit him, but more likely it was because he didn't need a gimmick to entertain kids. He could perform sleight of hand magic tricks, illustrate wonderfully goofy cartoon characters on his big drawing pad, was an excellent teller of jokes, and could dance a little soft-shoe. He was the consummate entertainer, the Sammy Davis Jr. of the kiddie set.

Though it was never explained how he managed to climb up there, Two-Ton lived in a spacious tree house, where he would be visited by an assortment of woodland creatures such as Stupid Cat, who, true to his name, had little common sense, and was always getting stuck up in the tree, but who, ironically, would quote Confucius and Abraham Lincoln. And then there was Sidney, a wacky squirrel with a bad case of mange and a severe lisp, who would stash acorns in his cheeks and tell hilarious jokes while cracking nuts with his magic nutcracker.

Inevitably during the show, one of the little woodland creatures would ask Two-Ton some probing question, such as *Where do babies come from* or *Why do skunks stink*. Two-Ton would waddle over to his vintage upright piano, spin the top of his old-time, claw-footed piano stool, plop his big rump down, and cheerfully say, "I'm so glad you asked." And then he'd proceed to sing and play some catchy little ditty he wrote that may not have completely addressed the question, but was silly and funny and entertaining enough that you didn't really care if he ever answered it or not.

This was always my favorite part of the show, because he would start all his songs out slowly and quietly, then gradually build up the intensity so that by the last chorus, he'd be pounding on those piano keys, his long black greasy hair dangling down over his face, his cheeks dripping with sweat, screaming out the lyrics like Little Richard. It was shocking for a kid my age, living in the conservative Midwest back then, to see an adult carrying on this way. It was just so inappropriate. Maybe that's why I loved it. And when other kids whose dads had regular jobs—like mailman or accountant—learned that my dad directed *Two-Ton's Tree House*, I also loved the attention and admiration I received by just being my father's son.

I got the chance to meet Two-Ton. And though I know it might be more interesting if I told you that he was this crass, alcoholic pervert of some sort, in truth he was really a very gentle, sweet man. When I went down to the TV station and my dad introduced me to him, Two-Ton took me onto the set and showed me around. He was even bigger in real life. And at his considerable size, you'd think Two-Ton would lumber about with a cumbersome gait, but he was actually quite light on his feet. Once I got over the initial fear of his immense size and the remote possibility of his accidentally squishing me to death, I thoroughly enjoyed his company.

On his show he was always grabbing handfuls of cherries out of his coat pocket and offering them to Stupid Cat and other visitors to his tree house, so I was thrilled when he asked me, "Hey, want some cherries?" It was like I was on the show. He reached into his pocket and pulled out a couple, holding them in front of me by their stems. "Because, you know," he began, and then, just like on his show, he broke into song. "Life is just a bowl of cherries, so live, and laugh at it all." And he let out a belly laugh as he handed me the cherries and I popped them into my mouth. When I had finished scraping off the sweet pulp with my teeth, I took those two pits and stashed them in my pocket as a souvenir. Can you imagine what a thrill that was for a little kid?

Two-Ton said I should always listen to what my dad has to say because "he's a smart man who cares" about me, and then he actually took the time to sit me down next to him at the piano as he tried out a new silly song he'd written about eating worms covered in chocolate. The best part was when he had finished the song, he asked my opinion of it. He also autographed a drawing of a donkey that was used on the show, signing it, *To my new pal, Davy. Your buddy, Two-Ton.*

A couple days later, when my mom was emptying the pockets of my pants in preparation of washing them, she came across the two cherry pits. Instead of throwing them away, she asked me if I'd like to plant one of them. So in the fall we'd dug up an area of dirt at the corner of the backyard, stuck a pit in the ground, and covered it up. In the spring there appeared a sapling, and a year later, a small tree.

Not long after I'd met him, our entire family was invited over to his apartment for a real Polish dinner cooked by him and his wife, Janis, who would sometimes appear on the show as the owner of Stupid Cat. In retrospect it seems sort of sad that someone who was so in touch with kids didn't have any kids of his own. We all had a great time singing polka songs and playing games, doing magic tricks, and eating enough kielbasa and sauerkraut to stuff a horse. But what I remember most about the evening was that when we sat down to eat, Two-Ton mentioned that he and Janis had recently given their lives to the Lord, and he hoped we didn't mind if he said a blessing before the meal. So with our consent Two-Ton offered a prayer from the heart, thanking God for the company of our family and for the many blessing in their lives.

I entered our kitchen about the same time my sister, Peggy, entered from the hallway. Wiping her hands on her apron and fixing her eyes on the cardboard cylinder, my mom asked my dad, "Is that what I think it is?"

"Depends what you think it is, pumpkin," my dad said with a wink. "Hi, kids. Where's Bobby?"

"Hey, Dad, when can we go to Fisherman's Dude Ranch?" I asked.

My dad pried the top off one end of the cylinder and pulled out a long, rolled-up piece of cobalt blue paper. "I'll see what I can do, sport."

I told you he always said that. I won't lie to you.

"Bobby!" my father yelled out to the air. "Where's your brother?" he asked me, like I should know. He scooted a bowl of fruit off to the side of the table and began to unroll what looked like some kind of architectural drawing.

"What's that?" Peggy asked.

My dad called out one more time for my brother, but only got as far as "Bah—" before Bobby sauntered in from the hallway, reeking of Old Spice and dressed in his standard blue jeans and white T-shirt. He'd most likely spent the last hour or so in the bathroom staring at his reflection, working his metal comb and dab of Brylcream through his long brown hair, shaping and styling the shiny strands into just the right form of delicate swoops and swirls to replicate the coif of every pop singer of the day: Bobby Rydell, Frankie Avalon, Bobby Darin . . . teen idols or, as my father would call them, shower singers because of the reverb used to make their vocals sound on key. But my brother had another reason for molding his hair to fall like a wave crashing over his forehead, one that had nothing to do with style.

My dad greeted my brother with the same scowl he'd been flashing him for some time. "Thanks for honoring us with your presence," my dad said caustically, as he placed a banana and three apples on the corners of the blueprint to keep it from rolling back up. As was the case of late, whenever my brother and dad were in the same room, the same vicinity, in fact, there was this tension, an underlying animosity that they held toward each other, expressed with gritted teeth, dagger glares, and, on my dad's forehead, a purplish vein that would appear out of nowhere, swelling until you were certain it would burst open right then and there. I didn't understand the change that had taken place between the two of them, why there was apparently nothing my brother could do that would meet with Dad's approval. It had been a long time since I'd heard my brother call our dad "Pop" and an even longer time since I'd heard my dad call my brother any name in a manner that wasn't filled with anger.

Waving her hand in front of her twitching nose, Peggy looked over disapprovingly at Bobby standing next to her. "You smell like Dad."

"Shut up," Bobby said below the radar.

"Did you hear that?" Peggy asked. "He told me to shut up. Wash his mouth out with soap!"

"Sorry, but I've got to go," said Bobby.

"Go? Go where?" my mom asked.

"I'm meeting some guys down at the diner," Bobby said.

"Some guys, huh?" Peggy said suspiciously in a nasal tone, her nose pinched shut. "You're not going to let him go, are you, Dad?"

"But dinner's almost ready," Mom said. "I made meat loaf just for you."

"Sorry, Mom, but I'm late already."

As my brother took a stride toward the door, my dad caught him by the short sleeve, stretching it out of shape. "Hold on. This meeting concerns the whole family, and your mother took the time to make your favorite meal, so you're not going anywhere."

"But they're expecting me."

"They can wait," Dad said in a tone that meant business.

Peggy smiled at Bobby, content that he wasn't getting away with something. My dad turned his attention back to the blueprint, spreading it out flat with the palms of his hands. His attitude suddenly shifted from annoyed to cheery. "So what do you think?"

We all stared down at the technical drawing with its straight white lines, unexplainable angles, and numbers all over the place. "What is it?" I asked.

"It's a hole in the ground for our backyard," Bobby said with attitude.

"We're getting a swimming pool?" Peggy asked excitedly.

"No, honey. It's a bomb shelter," Dad explained.

"But that's nothing like a swimming pool," Peggy said.

"No. It will shield us from fallout," said Dad. "Capable of accommodating a family of five quite comfortably and able to withstand up to a one-hundred megaton bomb. It's equipped with a thirty-centimeter concrete shielding that will reduce gamma ray exposure by a factor of one thousand percent."

He reeled off these facts like we were supposed to be impressed, but he may as well have been speaking Martian.

"Oh, Robert, I don't know," my mom said with a sigh, sitting down at the table.

"I don't understand," Peggy repeated with a vacant gaze.

"It's to protect us, sweetheart," my father said.

"Against what?" Peggy asked.

"Good question," Bobby said.

My dad gave Bobby a cross look, then looked beyond Peggy toward the living room and pointed. "Against that man."

Peggy and I turned around and witnessed Nikita Khrushchev on the TV, pumping his fist into the air, blabbering about something. I knew who Khrushchev was, to a point. I was aware that he was an angry, overweight Russian leader with a nasty mole on his face. I knew he had something to do with a cold war, presumably one fought in a place with a lot of snow. And I also knew that he'd promised us, "We will bury you," which, for me, fell under the category of "If you can't say something nice, don't say anything at all," a phrase first spoken by Thumper then repeated endlessly by my mother. But I had no idea what we had done to upset ol' Nikita to make him dislike us so much.

"He is a maniacal, power-hungry imbecile!" my dad continued.

"But dear, what would something like this cost?" Mom asked.

"What does it matter what it will cost? You can't put a price on protecting your loved ones." It sounded like that line might have been a direct quote from the salesman, but my dad delivered it with a freshness and sincerity that made it very convincing.

"Think you might be overreacting a little?" Bobby asked.

"I do not! These Russians are godless animals who would find no greater pleasure in life than to obliterate us with atomic bombs so they can take over the world."

"Oh, I don't believe they're all godless, Robert," said Mom.

"This is really too much," Bobby said under his breath. "Can

I go now?"

"No, you can't," Dad said. "This is important."

"Dad, the guy's a goofball. He's just a loudmouthed jerk who's full of BS if you ask me."

"Well, I didn't ask you, and what do you know about it, anyway?" Dad said. "You're sixteen, for crying out loud! You think just because you're old enough to drive a car now that you have a handle on foreign affairs? I got news for you, buddy, when it comes to real life, you're still in diapers. Not until you've been out there in the real world for a while will you be able to see how naive you are right now. I served in the army! I was there to defend the freedoms that this great country was founded on, freedoms that you take for granted. I am an American, and I will not stand by and let some fat, pinko-commie bully intimidate me!" He turned toward me. "Right, sport?"

"Right," I replied.

I was hoping my brother would keep his mouth shut, but he wasn't about to. He looked our dad dead in the eyes and said, "All Khrushchev wants to do is scare you . . . and by the looks of these plans, he's already succeeded."

There was a moment of silence, the calm before the inevitable storm, for which all of us, including Bobby, emotionally braced ourselves. Nobody in the family had ever dared challenge my dad's authority on anything. But instead of blowing up, my dad simply looked down at the plans and said calmly, "Anyone who doesn't understand the severity of the matter . . . well, he's way down in my book."

Bobby remained for a moment, looked over at my mom, and then took off out the door. "Bobby, wait," my mom said, starting after him, but he was long gone. She stood there for the longest time just looking out the screen door.

My dad composed himself, turned toward me, smiled, and said, "*You* think this whole bomb shelter thing is a good idea, don't you, sport?"

Did I? Though on the surface the idea of a bomb shelter located in our backyard scared the crud out of me, on a deeper level I remember thinking that it actually might be a good one for a couple reasons. We'd been having those duck-and-cover drills at school for some time now, and I never quite understood them. For one thing it didn't seem like something we needed to practice. Squatting under our desks was about as challenging as swallowing. I didn't see the point. I knew how to do it. It wasn't hard. And, in retrospect, what kind of protection was a three-quarter-inch of plywood going to give me anyhow? Yes, it could support my sixty-five pounds if I sat on it, but against a forty-megaton bomb I was pretty sure it would be as useful as a substitute teacher. With a shelter in my yard you wouldn't catch me ducking and covering when the real alarm went off. I'd be out the door and safe in my bomb shelter before I could catch sight of any mushroom clouds. I had no intention of sticking around for an atomic blast. I'd seen the B-movies. I'd read the comic books. It was a well-known fact that exposure to radiation could turn a normal individual into a mutated monster freak—usually something with additional appendages and an appetite for mayhem, not to mention murder. Or it could convert you into something that could glow and shoot sparks from his fingertips. Radiation could turn the average size person into a fifty-foot woman or an incredible shrinking man. I'd seen those movies, and I had no intention of growing past six feet tall, much less shrinking into oblivion, thank you very much.

And although Khrushchev didn't look like a friendly man, maybe Bobby was right. Sure he had the bomb, but would he really use it, knowing that we'd just return the favor and bomb him back? This wasn't two kids facing off with squirt guns, and it wasn't even Marshal Dillon in some showdown out in front of Miss Kitty's saloon. No one was going to win this war, so what made us think someone was crazy enough to push that red button? Still, a bomb shelter in the backyard would make a great fort.

"Yeah, I guess," I responded.

"Finally, somebody with some insight." Dad playfully spun my army hat around backward on my head and began rolling up the blueprint. "Then it's done."

"Maybe we should talk this over more," my mom said, turning away from the door.

"Well, you need to talk fast—the workers are scheduled to start digging on Monday."

"Robert . . ."

Dad walked over and kissed my mom on the cheek. "Trust me on this one, hon."

"Now I want all of us to keep a low profile on this. Don't tell anyone what we're building," Dad said.

"I can't tell my friends?" Peggy asked.

"No. No one can tell anyone," said Dad.

"That stinks," Peggy said. "Why not?"

"If word gets out that we have a bomb shelter and the bombs start falling, we'll have every last Tom, Dick, and Harry trying to break down our shelter door."

"But what if someone asks us about the hole in the yard?" I asked.

"He's right. People are bound to ask," Mom said. "Maybe it's not such a good idea after all."

"Well, we'll just tell them that we're building . . . I don't know . . . a wine cellar. Yeah, that's it . . . we've developed a taste for fine Italian wines, and we're building our very own wine cellar."

"I can't lie to my friends, Rob. Besides, you don't even like wine," Mom reminded him. "As a matter of fact, you haven't had a sip of alcohol in ten years."

"Well, I'll take it up again, okay? We'll buy bottles and bottles of the stuff and leave it lying around to show people that we are, in fact, wine connoisseurs and are building, yes, a wine cellar in our backyard."

This was all starting to sound a little insane. My dad grabbed the ball out of my glove, his voice reflecting the pleasure of how well the meeting had gone from his point of view. "Okay, then. Hey, what do you say we toss a few before dinner?"

"Yeah, sure," I said.

"I'll get my glove."

Usually my mom didn't argue with my dad on matters. He was a more articulate debater, did his homework, and so it was generally a short amount of time into such a discussion that she would give in. Maybe she really thought he knew best, or maybe she thought getting her way wasn't worth the confrontation it took. I could see it more clearly in her eyes this time—the resignation as she turned her attention back to her dinner preparation, stirring the potatoes and repeatedly thumping the stem of the spoon against the rim of the bowl to loosen the remaining glob of starch. I felt lousy for her—her voice silenced even earlier than usual, before it could even offer up a decent challenge.

The family sitcoms of the 1950s and '60s have been accused

of being unrealistic, but one of my favorite shows, *Father Knows Best*, was very authentic in portraying family dynamics. The three Anderson kids—the eldest daughter, Betty, aka Princess; Bud, the only son; and the youngest child, Kathy, aka Kitten—all seemed like real kids with real problems that I could relate to. They fought with each other just like I did with my brother and sister.

Failings and shortcomings were generally the problems with which the kids usually dealt, and when they'd find themselves unable to handle those issues, they'd always turn to their dad, Jim Anderson, possibly because they needed to justify the title of the show, but maybe because that's how it really was back then for most families. Or at least the way we all wished it to be. Mr. Anderson was a gentle man who smoked a pipe, wore patches on the elbows of his corduroy sport coat, and doled out wisdom to his children with calm sympathy. Over the span of only a minute or two, Mr. Anderson would manage to make the kids see the error of their ways and just how to solve the crisis. I didn't find my parents quite as accessible as Jim and Margaret Anderson. In fact I found my dad, especially, to be quite the opposite.

Maybe part of the problem involved the fact that there was an unspoken limit to the depth to which my relationship with my dad could go when I was a boy. Most of the time it was difficult to know what he was thinking, much less what he was feeling. And I think my dad liked it that way. It was safer territory. Less vulnerable. He didn't dare let down his guard or reveal to the boys he was trying to raise into responsible adults any of his shortcomings, doubts, or fears. He was the undisputed head of the household, the rock, the one everyone counted on to make the important decisions—but not someone you could go to with problems.

And though my mom was a loving and caring woman, when I found myself frightened or with genuine kid concerns, her reaction was always, "Don't be silly, monsters don't live under your bed." Or "Don't be silly, you won't be kidnapped by flying monkeys." The expression *don't be silly* seemed to preface all her advice, leaving me not with assurance but, if anything, with an impression that my feelings didn't matter or at least weren't taken seriously. Yet as it was with all her enabling habits toward me, her manner of downplaying the importance of any of my concerns was still a show of her love for me. She just couldn't turn it around on herself and see how she was dashing my feelings. She could only see that she was deflecting my fears, and hoped that would be enough.

So as time went by, I found myself growing jealous of the Andersons, wishing Bud would show up at my door and invite me to be adopted by his family, so that when I needed someone to turn to, I'd have a parent who would sit down with me, listen to my problems without saying, "Don't be silly," someone who would share invaluable wisdom from his own experience with a sincere empathy and, preferably, wrap up my dilemma in less than a half an hour.

Four

HIDE-AND-GO-PEEK

Summer dinners with the family were shorter in duration than meals during the rest of the year. My meat and potatoes and vegetables were gobbled up in a matter of minutes so I could scamper outside to join the rest of the neighborhood kids for games. But the games didn't take on real magic until our long, distorted shadows faded into the veil of dusk, turning the neighborhood into a land of enchantment and mystery.

In the middle of the street where Willowcreek dead-ended into Briarbrook, a triangular island split the road in two. Surrounded by loose gravel, the island was covered with grass and a few evergreens. Aside from supporting the street signs, the pole that stood directly in the middle of the island often served as a base for our Wiffleball games and also provided us with a home base for most other neighborhood games such as SPUD and—my favorite—hide-and-go-seek.

With a flashlight firmly grasped in one hand and his face buried in the crook of his arm that leaned up against the street sign pole, Jimmy Dumpkins began to count. "One-Mississippi, two-Mississippi!" With that we were off—about ten squealing neighborhood kids sprinting in all directions away from the island, off into the night in search of a hiding place.

"Three-Mississippi!" Jimmy yelled out. I was tearing down my street, passed my house on my right, considered for a moment ducking under the willow limbs and climbing up its trunk . . . but continued on.

"Four-Mississippi!" The Cunninghams' Buick was parked at the curb in front of their house, and I circled around it for a second, thought better of it, and continued across the front lawns, looking for just the right spot.

You see, the thrill for me was not so much in the ability to sneak back to the road sign to tap the pole and declare to the world that I was "Home free!" but in the possibility of getting caught. The closer I came to being found, the closer I came to peeing in my pants, which was, of course, the true measure of any kid's excitement level. Even being discovered and tagged was more exhilarating than not getting caught at all.

At "five-Mississippi" I heard a second voice not far behind me. "Davy! Wait up!" I looked over my shoulder and saw Sheena chasing after me. I tried to wave her off, but she continued to gain on me.

"Six-Mississippi!" I passed the Jensens' For Sale sign and turned up the driveway heading for the corner of their house.

"Seven-Mississippi!" I stopped at the far side, turned around, and saw Sheena running up to me, out of breath.

"Find your own hiding place," I said.

"I don't want to. I want to hide with you. Come on; it'll be fun."

It wasn't that it would be fun; it was that it would be less terrifying for her. Jimmy—who was at "nine-Mississippi" and by now surely peeking out from between his fingers to gain an unfair advantage—was famous, once he'd found you, for screaming out "Got you!" at the top of his lungs so you just about leaped out of your skin. Sheena was trying to minimize that reaction.

We heard the barely audible call of "ten-Mississippi! Ready or not, here I come." Sheena curled around behind me and waited in the shadows as I peeked out from around the corner of the house. She couldn't stand the suspense. I slapped a mosquito on my arm and Sheena jumped a foot. For some reason spraying myself with insect repellent before going out only seemed to make me more attractive to the little buggers. With the moon half full, I couldn't actually see Jimmy, only make out the flashlight beam shining in all directions as he decided on a route to take.

"Which way's he going?" Sheena asked. "Is he coming our way? Tell me. Tell me!" As the flashlight beam began stretching out from only four houses away, it was clear that Jimmy was headed our way.

"Here he comes," I informed her. With that she let out a little squeak, like I'd stepped on a baby doll. "We need to hide better," I suggested. I rushed over to a nearby double-hung window, pushed up on the frame, and lifted it open.

Sheena jumped up just high enough to support her weight on her arms on the outer window sill. "Help me." I gave her a leg-boost up, and she tumbled inside. A moment later I climbed in, landing feet first on the hardwood floor. The living room was completely vacant of furniture. Without curtains on the windows, we could see across the room, out the far window where shafts of light from Jimmy's flashlight were dancing around, briefly illuminating trees and lawns, moving closer to us every moment.

Shadowed by Sheena, I crossed the room, knelt down in front

of the window, and peered out. "What's the dealeo?" she asked. "Do you see him? Is he here?"

Jimmy had either suddenly chosen to stalk a different victim, or had turned off his flashlight in preparation for a surprise attack. Just then we heard what sounded like a window opening somewhere in the back of the house, possibly in the kitchen. "Davy!" Sheena shouted in a whisper. I grabbed her hand and led her back across the floor and into the front hall closet.

I closed the door behind us all but a crack as we eased ourselves down on the floor, the faint aroma of mothballs in the air.

We could hear footsteps now. Sheena's body was leaning up against my side, nearly knocking me off balance. "He knows we're here," she said. I covered her mouth with the palm of my hand. As the footsteps entered the living room, I swear I could hear her heart beating. Or was it my own? It seemed silly to be getting so worked up about it—I mean, it wasn't like we were being stalked by some creature from the black lagoon or the wolfman. It was just Jimmy, for crying out loud—a kid whose most terrifying feature was his unruly red hair. And then I realized something: Either Jimmy had grown another pair of legs or he had brought someone with him. There were just too many footsteps to account for. And then we heard a voice say, "I'm starting to like this place." It was a girl's voice, one that I couldn't quite place until . . . a familiar smell wafted through the crack in the door. *Old Spice.*

"You don't think it's creepy anymore?" This voice I definitely knew. This voice I'd heard almost more often than my own, every day, at the dinner table and in my bedroom. My eyes had adjusted to the dark just enough to see Sheena's eyes widen at the recognition of my brother's voice.

"Not as long as I'm with you," his girlfriend, Nancy, answered.

They crossed right in front of the door, and we leaned back deeper into the closet shadows. I eased my hand off Sheena's mouth. It seemed odd that I didn't hear anything out of them for the next thirty or so seconds, and I was even considering just walking out of the closet to reveal us when I leaned forward and was able to peer through the crack in the door to see the couple.

There, with just enough backlight from the half-moon filtering into the room, I witnessed my brother kissing Nancy McGee. I'd never seen him make out with a girl. It was weird and interesting.

At this point Sheena shoved me aside so that we both had a view of the proceedings. I was embarrassed for her until I noticed how fascinated she seemed by the sight. There were times in Oakfield when it was just the two of us, and Sheena had actually tried to chase me down to kiss me, but I always managed to elude her. I hoped Nancy wasn't giving her any ideas.

"It's not too dark in here for you, is it?" Bobby asked in a sweet tone that I'd never heard coming out of his mouth before.

"No, it's perfect. Just like you," Nancy replied. "Besides, the moon always shines a little brighter when I'm with you."

I had to cover my mouth to keep from laughing out loud. Sheena rolled her eyes. Maybe I shouldn't have been so critical. I mean, what did I know about romance? My hormones were not yet capable of raging. For me the main difference between boys and girls was in the length of their hair and their penmanship.

Continuing to smooch away, Bobby and Nancy wrapped their arms around each other up and dropped down to their knees. I wondered if ol' Nancy would be quite so anxious to lock lips with him if she'd known that he'd replaced the stones in his rock collection display with scabs of various sizes and shades of brown peeled off of different body parts, and substituted formal labels such as *topaz* and *quartz* with handwritten ones that said things like, *Elbow, Summer of '56, bike accident, oozed neat puss.*

I also wondered if she'd be quite so googly-eyed over this dreamboat of hers if she knew that late at night while lying in the bed across from me, Bobby had the habit, a hobby, really, of naming his farts as he birthed them. He would actually create names on the spur of the moment based on their varied and distinct personalities. I thought it was an admirable talent. With a certain amount of pride and formality, he'd broadcast them out loud, as if he were announcing the names of arriving royalty at a fancy ball. For instance, he might name a short, cute one "Sweet Sue," or if he ripped a high-pitched squeaker, he might call out, "Welcome, Whistling Jack," while for a booming, multi-layered one, Bobby might announce, "Alexander the Great." And even though I'd be trying to fall asleep, it made me crack up to hear him call out these names. At times like these the big difference in our ages didn't seem to matter, and I was thrilled that he cared enough to include me in his crude madness, to allow me to be his audience of one.

You might wonder if I was concerned about how far Bobby and Nancy's passion might escalate, but the truth is I wasn't really aware of one's ability to reach second or third base outside of the actual game of baseball. As far as I knew, hitting singles were all any couples ever hit. Since sex education was limited in the movies, and entirely off-limits to TV, radio, and educators, this left it up to my parents to reveal the mystery of the birds and the bees to me. Unfortunately my parents were neither ornithologists nor were they good with intimate details of private matters, so, like many of my peers, I was left in the dark to work things out in due time.

It looked like I could pick up some pointers just by watching my brother. Nancy pulled away for a moment and just stared at my brother. She brushed aside the wave of Bobby's pompadour that hung down over his forehead, revealing his red birthmark that always reminded me of the shape of West Virginia.

Bobby immediately reached up to whisk her hand away. "Don't," he said in a whisper. But she grabbed hold of his hand, held it for a moment, and lowered it.

"Hey," she said, "It's okay, Bobby. It's okay." She sounded like a mother comforting her child during a lightning storm. It was kind of nice of her. I could tell by Sheena's smile that she thought so, too. Slowly, delicately, Nancy began to run her fingers through his hair, brushing the pomp part of his pompadour aside again to expose the birthmark to the light. Maybe the closet was running out of air, because I was suddenly finding it difficult to breathe. Even from across the room, peeking through the crack in the closet door, I could tell how uncomfortable my brother felt at that moment, how vulnerable he was as he turned away from Nancy.

"I love your birthmark," she said in a breathy tone.

"Don't say that," Bobby said.

"But I do," Nancy said. He slowly turned back and faced her again. She leaned forward and planted a kiss directly on it. "Know why? Why I love your birthmark?" He shook his head. "For the same reason I love your ears." With that Nancy playfully kissed his right ear, making him scrunch up his neck and laugh. "And the same reason I love your chin." She gave him a loud smacking kiss on his chin. "Same reason I love your pointy nose." She gently kissed him on the tip of his nose and pulled her head back and looked directly into his eyes. "I love all those things about you . . . because I love you." She leaned in and gave my brother a kiss so passionate that it literally knocked Bobby over onto the floor.

Wow, I thought. Sheena must have had a similar reaction because right then I felt it: a smooch on my cheek that tipped me off balance, my elbow bumping up against the side of the closet wall with a *thud*.

"What was that?" Nancy said.

I grabbed hold of Sheena's arm, keeping her whole body from moving. I didn't dare look out the door. If Bobby caught us now, he'd surely smother me to death with my own pillow later that night.

"Nothing. It was nothing," Bobby said, determined not to break the mood.

"Bobby, somebody is here."

She was right, but we weren't the ones that she was referring to. Voices growing in volume could be heard right outside the front door. Was it Jimmy? I could hear Bobby and Nancy scramble to their feet. A key was inserted into the front door lock. The shadows of my brother and his make-out partner rushed past the closet doorway and out the back door. The front door to the house opened and several footsteps entered the room. A moment later the overhead light filled the living room.

"Oh, this is lovely," a mature woman's voice said.

A shaft of light lit up a vertical streak on Sheena's worried face.

"It *is* nice, isn't it?" another woman's voice added. "The house was built only seven years ago, and as you can see, the owners have done a great job of keeping it up."

Footsteps, at least three pair, started shuffling along in all directions. "There are many built-in features throughout the house, such as these decorative bookshelves."

"How long has it been on the market?" a baritone voice asked.

"A few weeks now. The owners have already found another house out of state, so they're very motivated to sell."

The floor creaked, and a shadow fell across the crack in the door. Heavy footsteps walked closer to our hiding place and stopped right in front of the door. Suddenly the door swung open, and Sheena and I found ourselves looking up at a big man staring down at us with mild surprise on his face. "Do these come with the house?" he asked.

I immediately noticed two things about this man. He wasn't mad at us, and he was dark-skinned. A woman came into view alongside of the man to have a look. She just smiled down at us and laughed. She was likewise a Negro. Everything seemed to be going pretty smoothly until the real estate agent poked her face into the picture, a face that was neither expressionless, nor smiling, or even pleasant to look at.

"What in the world are you two doing in there?" She was not pleased. "Get out of there this instant!"

Sheena looked like she was going to cry as we crawled out of the closet and headed straight out the front door. "Now, *shoo!*" the agent said, showing us the way out. It was nice to get out into the cooler night air again.

I wasn't that familiar with Negroes. I don't believe any lived in our town. Of course, I knew them from watching sports; Wilt Chamberlain and Frank Robinson were a couple of my favorites. There were entertainers—Nat King Cole and Chuck Berry and

Johnny Mathis, whose Christmas songs dominated our record console at Christmastime—and I'd seen Martin Luther King Jr. on TV quite often lately.

But those examples were all bigger-than-life people who I admired from afar. Real Negroes, ordinary people with darker skin than my own, were not a part of my life. I hadn't actually met one until that moment.

"Ollie, ollie, oxen free!" Jimmy's voice called out and we all made our way back to the island. Stretching the evening out to its limit, Jimmy, Mouse, Sheena, and I strolled around the neighborhood while waiting for our calls to come home. Mouse was still plenty annoyed with Sheena. They hadn't spoken a word to each other since the fire.

We told the two guys about the couple we'd met looking at the Jensens' house while we were hiding. I'd made Sheena promise not to tell anybody about our seeing Bobby making out with Nancy, and so far she'd kept her word. I was worried if she told, it would eventually get back to my brother and he'd let me have it with the popular knuckle sandwich. But worse than the pounding he'd give me would be the silent treatment that followed. I didn't need something like this to widen the gap in our relationship.

Jimmy unwrapped a slab of Bazooka Joe bubble gum and tossed it into his mouth. He turned the inside of the wrapper toward an upcoming streetlight in an attempt to make out the comic. He giggled. "That Bazooka Joe . . . what a funny guy. Question though . . . why does Mort wear his red sweater over his mouth?"

"That's a stupid question," Mouse said.

"It's stupid 'cause you don't know the answer," Sheena said.

"I know the answer. Mort does it just to be cool," Mouse said.

"Oh," Jimmy replied, his jaw really working over the gum. "But the thing is I don't know how anyone can even understand what he's saying with that thing over his mouth."

"Maybe they just read the bubble over his head," I said.

"Oh," Jimmy said, satisfied. "*Oh*, I get it. It's a joke. That's funny, Connors." He forced a laugh.

A flood of light from an open garage fell across the four of us as we walked past the Borkowskis' house. Standing there in his usual spot alongside his old blue Ford with the hood propped open, his head buried in the engine, was Vern Borkowski, tinkering, tapping away at some piston or engine part that was preventing his prized possession from running smoothly.

I didn't really know much about Mr. Borkowski. The main thing I did know was that he wasn't anything like my dad. He was usually decked out in his blue work overalls, looking like he had lost a grease fight. His face was broad and asymmetrical, and reminded me of the *Dogs Playing Poker* painting that hung in Mouse's den. He keenly resembled the cigar-smoking bulldog that is cheating by passing a card under the table. Mr. Borkowski always had a big stogie clamped down between his teeth — sometimes lit, sometimes not, but seemingly always half-smoked, never long, new, or fresh. He'd work that nasty thing back and forth to either side of his mouth like he just couldn't get comfortable with it. My dad smoked cigarettes, but never cigars. Cigars stunk. Borkowski stunk. Even standing out on the sidewalk, I swear I could smell him, like a combination of smoke, gasoline, and trash — that's how he smelled. Bad. And I guarantee he didn't care one bit. In fact it wouldn't surprise me if he were proud of that smell. He liked putting people off. I wondered how his wife could put up with it. They didn't have any kids, and it was probably a good thing for all possible parties involved.

Mr. Borkowski lifted his head out from under the hood and looked in our direction. He turned to the side, pinned shut one nostril with his finger, and shot a snot rocket out onto the floor of his garage. Lovely, eh? He went back to work.

"So they have any kids?" Mouse asked.

"Who?" I answered.

"The people who looked at the house," Mouse said.

"Oh, no. Not with them. They seemed pretty nice, though. Didn't get mad at us or anything."

We passed through the garage light and back into the darkness and continued making our way around the corner. About waist-high in front of us, a firefly momentarily turned on its chartreuse light. Mouse immediately began stalking it, and when it showed itself again, he snatched it out of the night air.

"Hey, leave it alone!" Sheena said.

Mouse slowly opened his hand to get a look at the bug but found he had accidentally squashed it. As the firefly's glow began to dim, he flicked it off his palm.

"Murderer," Sheena said.

"Boy, how'd you like to go through life with your butt lightin' up every few seconds?" Mouse asked.

Jimmy, a few steps ahead of us, turned around, and began walking backward. "Oh, there's a good idea . . . yeah, let's draw even more attention to my big butt."

"What do you expect? You eat like a pig," Mouse said.

Jimmy blew a bubble that immediately popped. "Yeah, well, not anymore. My mom says I have to go on a diet. She says no more Good Humor bars and no more banana splits from the Dairy Queen. Do you believe that? I will die without ice cream. You might as well just take me out into the field and shoot me, because—"

"Jimmy!" Mouse yelled out. "Don't move!"

Jimmy stopped in his backward tracks and stared at the three of us. He immediately knew the error of his ways. Slowly turning his head to the side in the direction of the Goswellers' house, he realized that he had just crossed their property line. He froze in fear.

"Hold your breath and don't look at it!" Mouse instructed him. Jimmy closed his eyes, quickly took a deep breath, held it, and jerked his head forward, away from the big old two-story Victorian house. The wrought-iron fence that surrounded the property was thick with roses sporting thorns long enough to pierce all the way through your hand. The house itself was covered in ivy.

Mouse looked down at his feet and inched his way toward Jimmy's outstretched arms, until his toes nearly reached the fluorescent green painted line that streaked unevenly across the sidewalk—a line that Mouse had badgered me into spraying a couple months earlier with a can of my own paint.

"Closer . . . closer," Mouse instructed. He reached across the property line, grabbed Jimmy by the front of his striped shirt, and yanked him back across the line. Relieved, Jimmy collapsed in a heap onto the safe side of the sidewalk.

"Thanks, man. I thought I was a goner," he said.

"You know, this is getting way out of hand," I said. "It's childish."

"No, it's not," Jimmy said.

"It's *just* a house," I assured them.

"Is it? Is it really, Davy?" Sheena asked, obviously quite sure that it wasn't *just* a house.

"Yeah, well, tonight I'm not doing it," I said. "I'm not running like some idiot, and I'm not holding my breath either."

"You have to," Sheena said. "You just have to."

"What, are you crazy, Connors?" said Mouse. "You have a death wish of some sort?"

"There's no proof," I said defiantly.

If you haven't noticed by now, Mouse was an inventive sort. An expert fabricator. He'd managed to create a mystery about this house over a short time with such an effortless, convincing twist of his tongue that we all got swept away in the undertow of his fantasies. And he never backed down from his exaggerations. Part of the problem for me was that whenever I did ask my mom or dad about the Goswellers' house, they found a way to avoid the subject, lending credence to the possibility of some monstrous activity going on over there.

"No, you're right, Davy. There's no proof. So go ahead and just walk on by."

Jimmy sprang to his feet. "What are you talking about? Don't do it, Connors."

I wasn't sure what Mouse was up to, but I knew it was something screwy. Mouse pulled a tennis ball out of his back pocket and began bouncing it on the pavement.

"Go ahead, Davy. I dare you." He rolled the tennis ball down the sidewalk so it stopped in front of the Goswellers' house. "Just take your sweet time and walk down there and pick up the tennis ball and try to bring it back, and when little Drake's evil force suddenly sucks you into that house and steals your soul, then we'll have our proof."

Sheena grabbed onto my hand. "Don't do it, Davy."

"The Goswellers have lived here for — what? — three months now, and just 'cause nobody's ever seen the kid, you think he's some kind of monster."

Casually turning away from the group, Mouse said, "I've seen Drake-ula."

"The kid's name is Drake, and you have not!" I said.

"When did you see him?" Sheena nervously asked.

"A couple days ago. You know how the Goswellers' fence backs up to Oakfield? Well, I saw him through a knothole."

"What did he look like?" Jimmy asked, his voice cracking on the word *look*. "I'll bet he was ugly — real ugly. Was he ugly?"

Mouse spun around rather dramatically. "He was hideous! His eyes were twice the size of ours."

"Oh, come on," I said.

"And he was all hunched over like this." Mouse did his best Quasimodo. "And his skin was covered with these awful bumps and open cuts and sores that oozed out this greenish yellow stuff that looked like what you puke up when you're real sick and can barely barf anymore. And he made this horrible sound."

"What kind of sound?" Sheena felt compelled to ask.

Still crouched over, Mouse began making a quiet gagging sound as he moved in toward Sheena. "Gggggkkk . . . gggkkk." As he got louder and more intense, Mouse began circling around Sheena until finally he let out an enormous roar, "Aaaarrrgghhh!"

Sheena shrieked.

"You are so full of it," I said.

"I don't think he is full of it," Jimmy said. "You know

the reason Drake and his parents had to leave their old neighborhood?"

Apparently unable to stop herself, Sheena asked, "Why?"

"Because a bunch of little kids in their neighborhood started turning up missing," Jimmy explained. Sheena looked concerned.

In a voice and delivery that would have made Vincent Price proud, Mouse added, "I guess they didn't . . . hold their breath."

"Where did you hear that?" I asked Jimmy.

"From Mouse, here."

Before I could say, *It figures*, classical piano music began emanating from the Gosweller house. We all turned in unison to look.

"What's that?" Sheena asked.

"You've never heard it before?" Jimmy asked.

"No," Sheena said.

"That's old lady Gosweller," Mouse said.

"It's so pretty," Sheena said.

"She's, like, a professional piano player or something," Mouse said.

"I think she played Carnegie Hall," Jimmy said. "Every night at exactly nine thirty she sits down and plays some long-haired number like that."

"Yeah," added Mouse, "every night. Most people think she's practicing, but I know better. She plays to keep ol' Drake-ula from going completely mad. It's a fact."

It's not that I actually believed any of what Mouse was saying, but I couldn't explain away the chill that ran down my spine. We were all standing around for a moment saying nothing, just looking at each other, then over at the house. All at once the four of us took a collective deep breath, held it, and began racing down the sidewalk past the Goswellers' place. Sheena beat us all to the other side, where we bent over to catch our breaths.

"You can thank me later," Mouse said to me. I didn't want to thank him later or anytime. I wanted to prove that a monster didn't exist beyond that black wrought-iron fence, behind that ornate house exterior, and I had an idea exactly how to do that.

While Sheena and the other kids had met their curfews and gone home, I sensed I still had a few minutes before I heard my dad's whistle to come in, so I laid down on our backyard hammock to search out the Little Dipper. I heard the tapping of typewriter keys coming from the house: Framed by the kitchen window and lit up by a red-shaded table lamp, my mom sat with her perfect posture, pecking out a little one-note ditty on her Underwood manual, her eyes fixed on her Bible as it lay open on the table.

I knew what she was up to. She was preparing for an annual family tradition that ushered in the beginning of summer almost as much as the end of the school year did: On the second Sunday of every June, we celebrated my mom's own personal holiday creation—Gospel Flight Day, or as we kids called it, Balloon Day.

A few days before the event my mom would type out verses from the Bible, guidelines for life, selected as the spirit so moved her at the moment. Expressed in courier elite on three-by-five index cards were Scriptures such as "Every way of a man is right in his own eyes: but the Lord pondereth the hearts" or "Blessed are they that mourn: for they shall be comforted." My siblings and I would hole-punch one end of each card, then scissor-snip short strands of red yarn, symbolizing the blood of Christ, thread them through the holes, and tie them off like a shoelace. Early Saturday morning my dad would make a trip down to Rugen's Hardware and rent a helium tank. Working as a family, we'd inflate exactly twenty-seven colorful balloons, one for each book of the New Testament; then we'd tie the loose ends of the yarn to the nubs of the balloons. One by one, Bobby, Peggy, and I would pick out a balloon, read the attached Scripture out loud, release it to the wind, and follow its shrinking progress skyward until we only imagined that we could still see it.

Though my dad would help my mom with the event, it was definitely her show. Sometimes I thought that my dad got involved just so he could help justify to my mom his inevitable long stretches of staying home from church.

My mom was a shy woman whose timidity carried over into the sharing of her faith outside the family. I don't think she was ashamed of it — she just preferred to witness by the way she lived her life. She may have felt guilty about her lack of boldness. So the idea of sharing the gospel anonymously with complete strangers on Balloon Day was the perfect solution for her inability to verbally carry out the Great Commission.

I often wondered at the end of Balloon Day if anyone ever really found the balloons or if they just gradually met a desolate and lonely fate, shrinking up into a sad, shriveled latex blob in a vacant field, or wrapped around a telephone wire somewhere, having lived short, unfulfilled lives. Could their lives have been better served as decorations for a kid's birthday party or as ammunition for some frantic, fun-filled water balloon fight? The unexpected, explosive impact of a water balloon hurled at some unsuspecting kid, dousing him in a drenching shower to the shrieking pleasure of all eyewitnesses was my personal idea of a balloon's life well-lived.

I'd once suggested to my mom that we turn the flip side of the index cards into self-addressed postcards to find out who it was that actually found the card, where they were from, and to even get their reaction to the verses. Maybe more than a hundred miles away, a man standing weak-kneed on the twenty-eighth–story ledge of a skyscraper at night while conjuring up the courage to step off would see the surreal image of a pale yellow balloon with a red tail, lit by the moonlight, sailing in his direction . . . right there above his head . . . within his reach . . . and purely out of curiosity he'd snatch the card that hung twisting and dangling like bait on a hook. With trembling hands he'd read the words—"Ask, and it shall be given you; seek, and ye shall find; knock, and it shall be opened unto you: For every one that asketh receiveth; and he that seeketh findeth; and to him that knocketh it shall be opened." And the man would weep openly, and a spark of hope would ignite in his heart, and he'd fall down to his knees and surrender his life to Jesus on the spot. Weeks after we had sent it flying off into space, the postcard would boomerang back, showing up in our mailbox, and my mom would sit down at the kitchen table and read of how the life of that desperate man on the ledge had been changed by a yellow balloon, the word of God, and her act of kindness; I'd watch from a distance as she'd weave her fingers together, bow her head, and silently give thanks to God for allowing her the privilege of being his good and faithful servant.

But my mom claimed that attaching a return address to the card would only show a lack of faith on our part—the fact that we would need confirmation of positive results would only suggest that we might somehow doubt God's ability to deliver those cards into exactly the right hands at exactly the right hour. To me that seemed like a faith both frightening and unattainable, reserved for saints and such. It sounded like a faith that I might not even want to be capable of possessing.

By the time my father whistled for me to come in, I'd forgotten about looking for the Little Dipper. After I got ready for bed and lay there waiting for my parents to come in to say good night, I looked over at the empty bed across the way where my brother would crawl in a while later. As was my habit, I gazed over at the large floral patterns that covered the curtains on the window above my brother's bed and searched for faces among the petals and leaves.

I'd just located a crossed-eyed woman with a long, pointy nose and cocker spaniel ears when my mom walked into the room. "Sleepy, Davy?" she asked, sitting down on the bed. I nodded. "Have you said your prayers already?"

She always asked me this question, and I always answered no. Not because I didn't remember to say them—I just preferred she was there when I did. After we prayed I turned over and my mom lifted up my pajama top and scratched my back for a while, humming a tune as she did. When she finished, I turned over and pulled down my pajama top. "Bright and early," she said, and then gave me a kiss on the cheek.

My dad showed up moments later, gave me a kiss on top of the head, and delivered his patented line—"Night, night, sleep tight, don't let the bed bugs bite"—even though we both knew I'd outgrown it a while ago. "Good night, sport," he added before hitting the light switch, and the two of them slipped out of the room, leaving me in the dark.

I don't know if you noticed it or not, but back in 1960 the words *I love you* were not allowed to be exchanged between parents and their kids. It was an unspoken rule, especially as it applied to fathers and sons.

It wasn't as though I thought my dad didn't love Bobby or me. He did plenty of stuff for me—helped coach my Little League team, took me to Reds games, dragged his push mower out into Oakfield and sweat bullets in an attempt to cut down the foot-long grass into the shape of a diamond on which my friends and I could play baseball. And he never turned down a request to play catch with me. It should have been obvious to me that my dad loved me, since true love is really defined by actions rather than words. But for some reason it just wasn't enough.

As kids we didn't know it, but back then parents had a code for conveying those words. When my mom tucked me into bed and gave me a little peck on the cheek, or when my father said the night-night rhyme, this was actually code for "I love you." When my dad would haul me up on his shoulders and parade me around, or give me horseyback rides to bed, or when he'd just walk past me and casually muss up my hair and call me *kiddo*, he was saying "I love you."

Also, it was imperative back then that fathers not hug their boys. Daughters, like Peggy—Dads could hug all they wanted, smothering them until the stuffing came out of them, sitting them on their laps and kissing them on the cheeks. But if a dad embraced his sons, it might make them soft, might even have some lasting developmental effects detrimental to the psyche that could very easily turn their boys into sissies, or worse, homosexuals—a term never spoken out loud in 1960 for fear the mere utterance might somehow trigger the conversion process.

There were other acceptable forms of code for fathers to say, "I love you," most of which involved physical actions that demanded a response, such as playfully shoving or pushing. My dad could tickle me under my armpit or squeeze the fleshy part right above my knee, resulting in nearly uncontrollable laughter that seemed to please him. This was allowed. He couldn't kiss my brother or me anywhere near the face, but he could playfully grab us and place his open mouth on the back of our necks and blow hard, his vibrating lips creating a fart-ish sound that gave us wonderful chills down our spines and produced giggles galore. It was code. And when my dad *really* wanted to express his love, he would tackle us to the floor and begin wrestling—*roughhousing*, my mom called it, and she'd tell us not to do it for fear "someone's going to get hurt." But we seldom listened to her because we knew it was an excuse to get close to one another, to share an acceptable embrace that we both needed.

So back in 1960 fathers all over the country were forced to muss up their sons' hair, trap them in headlocks, and wrestle them to the ground—when I'm sure they just wanted to hug them, to safely wrap them up in their big arms and hold them close, and recall the first time they cradled their perfect baby boy in their arms. And knowing that they could never love anyone more than they did their son at that moment, I'm certain fathers could not help but whisper, "I love you."

So we grew up wondering if our parents really loved us, relatively certain that they did, but never positive about it. And I don't know how you feel about this, but it would have been nice back then to have the codebook—or a magic decoder ring, for that matter. It would have been better yet if someone had just told my mom and dad that no one would get hurt, no damage would be done to their boys if they would just say those three words occasionally, and that, in fact, they couldn't say it too much . . . so that the question in our minds would never have the chance to linger into adulthood.

Five

THE LEAKY BALL

Tony the milkman waved to me as he drove by in his truck. I sat on the porch step folding the last few papers for the morning route. Tony was one of a long list of home delivery men whose services were quickly dying out—a list that included the baker, the laundryman, and the Fuller Brush man, from whom my mother felt sympathetically obliged to purchase a brush with each visit, leaving us with a closetful of useless brushes.

Riding past the Jensens' house, I noticed a gentleman in a suit hammering away on the For Sale sign. I eased on my brakes in front of the property to watch. It certainly seemed like an odd time of the day to be doing this. He finished his work, and stepped away, revealing a second sign that read Sold angled across the first. He began to walk toward his station wagon parked in the driveway.

"Hey!" I called out, but he kept walking. "Excuse me!" I called out louder. Reluctantly he stopped and drooped his head and shoulders like he'd heard me the first time but chose to ignore me. I couldn't help but notice that he was wearing a pair of sunglasses, even though the sun had yet to rise. "Do they have kids?" I asked.

"Two," he said, confirming it by flashing the victory sign.

Great! This small bit of information was enough to elevate my mood by a good fifty percent, and I pedaled on down the sidewalk, tossing papers and whistling, which I couldn't remember ever having the ability to do before.

Two kids, I thought. This could change everything. Were they boys? Girls? One of each? Were they my age? At least one had to be close to my age, right? Yeah, a boy, and maybe he'd be cool. Maybe he'd become my very best friend and we'd hang out together, and he'd love baseball as much as I did, and maybe he'd have the same desire to blow things up, and maybe he wouldn't be a big phony like Mouse or wimpy like Jimmy. I mean, Sheena was nice and all, and we had fun together, and she was one of the few people I knew who ever really listened to the things I had to say, but a guy friend . . . this was going to make the summer special.

Later that afternoon we rounded up players for one of my favorite games. In our neighborhood the sound of a bat smacking a ball was not the familiar rich crack produced when horsehide collides with maple. It more closely resembled the slap of a ruler on your school desk when your teacher was trying to bring you back from a daydream. This was partly because when we played baseball, rather than getting our butts slapped with a belt for shattering a neighbor's window with a hard ball, we chose to use a Wiffle ball—a large, white, hollow plastic ball with eight oblong holes in it—one of the greater inventions of the twentieth century. No doubt neighbors appreciated our choice of balls as well.

Wiffleball was the suburbs' sanitized version of street baseball, employing a thin yellow bat made of hard plastic instead of one made of wood. The playing field was the middle of the street with condensed foul lines extending onto the neighbors' front lawns.

From day to day during the summer we would move our field up and down the street to keep up with our neighbors' complaints.

Other than the fact that it was an easier game to play than hardball, the main advantage to playing Wiffleball was that the only real equipment you needed was a bat and a ball—no helmets, no gloves. Even the bases were usually improvised, generally consisting of whatever was close at hand: a hat, a sweatshirt, or even a scrap of corrugated cardboard with a rock on top of it to keep it from blowing away. On this particular day first base was an elm tree located on the Finnegans' front lawn. Trees were always a little tricky when it came to using them as bases, especially first base. It was important, as the hitter, not to watch the path of the batted ball for too long, or you'd wind up with a concussion.

We had some difficulty locating a second base for this game, but managed to recruit Mouse's little brother, Joey, who was actually quite content to just sit there in the middle of the blacktop road and pop tar bubbles in the asphalt with a little stick. We thought it best not to actually step on him, so we made the rule that we simply had to touch the top of his head to be safe at second.

Third base was a big boulder that sat on our property, placed there by my dad, who had decided that our yard would look fabulous decorated with big white rocks placed at ten-foot intervals around the curving perimeter of our property. My dad believed that all of nature could be improved with a coat of paint, making him an especially dangerous man with a spray can in his hand. He preferred embalming dead things almost always in semi-precious metallic colors. For instance, if he came across a bunch of cattails in a creek somewhere, he wouldn't give it a second thought to cut them down, bring them home, spray paint them gold, and stick them in a big vase and declare it to be decorator art. One time he found a branch that had fallen off a tree. He stripped its leaves, spray-painted it silver, dangled little white lights all over it, and hung it on our dining room wall. I'm not kidding. I guess it was the artist in him that compelled him to do it, but it drove my mom nuts and embarrassed us kids to no end when friends would drop by for dinner. The day my hamster, Fred, died, my dad had a wild look in his eyes that worried us all, but nothing ever came of it.

"Ducks on the pond, Davy," Jimmy called out to me from Joey—second base—as I stood beside an old tennis shoe that we were calling home plate. There were five of us on each team that day, typical of our games. Concealing the Wiffle ball behind his back, Mouse prepared to pitch to me. Sheena, who was a surprisingly good athlete considering her affection for dolls, was playing a shallow left field in my front yard. Though the holes in the Wiffle ball provided the pitcher with an obvious advantage, I was pretty sure that if I got a decent pitch to hit, I could drive it over her head.

"It'd be just our luck they turn out to be a couple females," Mouse said in response to my telling him about the new neighbors.

"Just pitch the ball," I said impatiently.

"Three and two on the batter, Davy Connors . . ." As he stared in at me, Mouse began his usual play-by-play banter. "Miller looks in to get the sign . . ." Actually the catcher, a little kid named Arty, wasn't giving Mouse any signs. His glasses were so thick he was lucky he could even locate Mouse.

"Here's the windup and the pitch!" Mouse fired the ball right at my head. It broke sharply down and over the plate. I took a vicious cut, but only managed to get a piece of the ball, topping it onto the ground in foul territory behind the shoe, where Arty eventually tracked it down. "Connors is fooled by the pitch, but stays alive."

"Strike him out, Mouse!" Sheena shouted from left field, having forgiven him for the loogie episode. Arty tossed the ball back to his battery mate.

"With the game on the line, Miller appears calm out there," Mouse started up again. "Look for the pitching ace to throw Connors his special, super-duper dark one . . . Here's the windup and the pitch . . ."

I was looking for the changeup, and I got it. The Wiffle ball floated out of Mouse's hand, headed in slow motion toward the middle of the plate. I waited . . . and waited, and took a wicked, free-swinging cut, connecting dead on. The ball sprang off my yellow bat, sailing deep to left field. As I started for first base, I saw Sheena take one, two steps back before she stopped and watched the ball carry deep over her head, beyond my property and over the picket fence into the Springfields' yard. From my vantage point I could only hear Spencer's vicious attack on the ball, like someone had tossed him a T-bone steak or a newspaper. As I touched the trunk of first base, I slowed into my home-run trot. Heading toward Joey, I looked over at Sheena, who stood a safe distance away from the picket fence, just staring at the spectacle of Spencer's rage.

"And that's the ball game," Jimmy shouted out in celebration.

"Your turn to buy the next ball, Connors," Mouse said, his arms folded in dejection.

After the game Sheena and I rode our bikes around the block. Mr. Melzer flagged us down and asked if we wanted to harvest some strawberries and take them back to our moms. We spent a good hour picking strawberries and collecting them in the baskets he gave us. When I gave the basket to my mom, she was so delighted that she called Mr. Melzer on the spot to thank him.

Because my brother had to get up early to start his caddying job at the Elmwood Golf Club, he climbed in bed about the same time that I did, so I decided to take this opportunity to do some brotherly bonding. But what subject could I bring up that would keep him from responding with *Shut up and go to sleep, nerdo*? It couldn't be too personal, like *So what's it like to kiss Nancy?* or too bland, like *Are you looking forward to caddying tomorrow?* I decided on middle ground. "That Mrs. Hoffman's a pretty nice lady, isn't she?"

He turned over toward me, clearly annoyed, and said tersely, "What?"

I knew I was in trouble already. I had to present the subject in a more stimulating manner. "What I mean is, when I collect money from her, she seems nice. And she smells good, too, don't you think?"

There was a long pause, leading me to believe the conversation was about to come to an abrupt end, and then he softened and said, "She smells okay."

"Is she a good tutor?" I asked.

"Her hair smells very good."

Not really the answer to my question, but okay . . . I could run with it. "Yeah, I've noticed that too, when she hands me the money for the paper. Her hair smells like . . ." I couldn't think of a single decent description. As it turned out, I didn't have to.

"Trees," Bobby said.

Trees? I thought. *Really?*

"She smells like the outdoors," he went on. "Sort of fresh, like springtime. I think she uses Prell."

Okay, this wasn't bonding—this was just weird. "I wonder why she got a divorce," I said.

"I don't know. But he must have been some kind of idiot."

It took me a moment, but it finally dawned on me: My brother had a little crush on his tutor. He had a crush on our neighbor, Allison Hoffman. I had no idea. I wondered if Nancy was aware of this. We both fell asleep soon after that. And even though it wasn't as much fun as when he named his gaseous releases, I enjoyed it.

Six

THE COLOR OF MONEY

The aroma of barbecued meat was beating out that of freshly cut grass for my attention as I sat with Peggy at our small, round aluminum patio table in the backyard, drinking a Coke. This Saturday we stared at the large hole in the spot where our family normally played badminton or croquet. It was beginning to sound like *not* a very good trade-off to me — safety from possible nuclear holocaust over fun and games. The cement foundation had been partially laid, leaving ominous iron rods sticking out of concrete blocks everywhere, giving the hole a less-than-hospitable appearance.

My mom approached with a plate full of lettuce and tomato and onion slices and set it down on the blue and white checkered vinyl tablecloth. She looked over at my dad, who was standing across the yard next to the barbecue, stacking the cooked burgers onto a plate while talking to Mouse's dad, Pete Miller. Blue smoke swirled around their heads.

I'd never heard Mr. Miller and my father actually carry on a conversation, and yet they had been jabbering away out of earshot as long as it took to cook those burgers. Mouse's dad worked for a lumberyard—maybe even owned it, I wasn't sure. But when Sheena's dad decided to build that tree house, Mouse's dad didn't help out at all, didn't even contribute any wood to the project. I still couldn't understand that.

"Anybody seen Bobby?" my mom asked.

"No, but I bet I know where he is," I said, like it was a secret of some sort.

"Where?" Peggy asked.

"None of your beeswax," I replied.

"He's not being tutored by that woman today, is he?" my mother asked.

"That *woman*?" Peggy said. "You mean Mrs. Hoffman?"

"You should have seen what she was wearing in her garden the other day." My mother shook her head. "It's unhealthy to reveal that much skin. Aside from just being downright immoral."

"So why does Bobby get out of eating with the family and I don't?" Peggy asked Mom. "It's not really fair. And you know what else? He told me he wasn't going to help out with Balloon Day in two weeks."

"I expect the entire family to participate in Gospel Flight Day. And it's not in two weeks; it's next Sunday."

"What?" Peggy began. "I promised Betty I'd go up to the lake with her family next weekend."

"You'll have to tell her no."

"I can't," Peggy said. "Besides, I'd rather go up to the lake."

My mom sat down at the table. "I don't ask much of you kids. The least you can do . . ." Her voice trailed off in disappointment.

"I'll be there," I said. "It's fun." It wasn't really that much fun anymore, but it was what my mom needed to hear.

Gazing over at the immense concrete hole in the ground, my mom said, "That thing scares me." Then she looked at us as if she hadn't meant to say it out loud.

We all watched as Mr. Miller walked off between the houses and my dad finally crossed the yard toward us. He set the plate of blackened burgers and burned buns on the table and sat down, looking like someone had died. Mom looked at the food, then at Dad. "I didn't realize Pete was such a fascinating conversationalist."

Peggy delicately picked up a charred patty with her fingertips and peeked at its equally scorched bottom side. "I'm sorry, but I can't eat this," Peggy said.

My dad remained in mourning.

"Have you convinced Pete yet that it's a wine cellar?" Mom asked. I don't think my dad heard a word either said.

"Rob?"

"It seems we have some new neighbors," said Dad.

"The Jensen house?" Mom asked.

"Yeah," he murmured.

"Good," Mom said. "I hate to see a house sit empty like that. Davy, will you do the honors?"

I closed my eyes and folded my hands. "Come Lord Jesus, be our guest, and may thy gifts to us be blessed. Amen." Mom and Peggy followed with their own amens, but my dad was silent.

"There's just one problem," my dad said softly, stabbing the smoldering burger with his fork and dragging it onto his bun.

"Oh, I forgot the salt and pepper," said Mom. "Davy, could you get it please? What did you say, dear?"

As I went to fetch the salt and pepper, I heard my dad speak up. "With the neighbors . . . there's a problem."

"They don't have any kids, do they?" Peggy asked disappointedly.

"I don't know," said dad, slightly annoyed.

"I hear they have two!" I shouted from the kitchen door.

"What ages?" Peggy shouted back.

I returned to the table, "I'm not really sure, but I hope—"

"What does it matter?" my dad erupted, surprising us all.

"Rob! What's wrong?" Mom asked.

"I'm sorry. It's just that . . ."

"What? What's the problem, dear?"

Dad spread his fingers out and slowly placed his hands down on either side of his paper plate like he was attempting to prevent the table from lifting off the ground. Then with a deadly serious expression, he panned our faces and said, "It's a family of Negroes." He then patiently waited for our reactions.

"Oh. Could you pass the potato salad, Peggy?" asked Mom.

By the dumb look on my dad's face, I could see he was completely thrown by his wife's passivity. Leaning toward Mom, he enunciated, "Honey . . . they're colored."

"Yes, I am aware what the word *Negro* means, dear."

"Wow," Peggy said. "Colored kids . . . that's cool."

My dad looked at my sister like she'd just asked him to explain Einstein's theory of relativity.

"They must have been the people Sheena and I saw," I said.

"Who? When?" he asked.

"Last week. Wednesday night. We were . . . well, we kind of ran into some people who were looking at the house."

"At night . . . they were showing the house at night. That figures," Dad said. "So let me see if I understand this, Davy. You *knew* that there were coloreds looking at the Jensen house, and you didn't tell us?"

"I didn't know it mattered," I said.

"It doesn't, Davy," Mom said, biting into her hamburger.

"Look, Ruth . . . let's be realistic here. You know I'm not a prejudiced man. In fact who's my favorite entertainer?"

"What?" Mom asked.

"My favorite entertainer—who is it?" Dad repeated.

"I don't know . . . Jimmy Stewart?" Mom guessed.

"No."

"Frank Sinatra?" Peggy said.

"No! Who do I always say is the most talented performer alive today?"

"That's easy," I said. "Sammy Davis Jr."

"Bingo!" said Dad. "Sammy Davis Jr., a Negro man who also happens to be Jewish, and only has one eye to boot. And down at the studio, Ralph, the colored maintenance guy—nice man. I like him. In the service I knew plenty of coloreds and had no problem with them. In fact I like most coloreds that I've met. So this is nothing personal. I'm not a bigot, you know. . . . It's just that you need to understand the financial ramifications of something like this. This house of ours—it's not just a home, it's an investment. If this colored family moves in, our property value and everyone else's in the neighborhood will be affected. In fact it's a guarantee that they will plummet."

"What do you mean, Dad?" I asked.

"I mean when we decide to sell this house, we will lose money."

"Are we selling the house?" Peggy asked, concerned.

"No, honey. Look, Rob, maybe it shouldn't be only about money," Mom suggested.

"What? What fantasyland are you living in? When we bought the house it was about money. We just refinanced to help send Peggy to college. And in a couple years when it's Bobby's turn, chances are we're going to have to borrow on the equity in this house again."

"But why will our house be worth less money?" I asked.

"Because people . . . white people . . . won't want to live in a neighborhood where colored people live."

"Why not?" I asked.

"Yeah, this isn't Little Rock. I wouldn't care," Peggy added.

"And neither would I, pumpkin, but some people would," Dad said. "And when the cost of housing drops, even more coloreds will move here, until pretty soon —"

"Robert, maybe you're overreacting," Mom suggested. "We don't know for sure what will happen years down the line. Besides, this whole thing might just blow over."

"You think so, Ruth? Pete told me that the Wheatons have already decided to put their house on the market."

"You're kidding. I haven't heard anything about it," said Mom. "Well, that's not right."

"No, I agree. That's *not* right," Dad said. "And I personally refuse to just sit by and be bullied out of my own house."

This was starting to sound a lot like the Khrushchev scenario. "What are you going to do, Dad?"

"All I can do to keep them out."

"Rob . . ." my mom began, as if she would challenge him.

"What, dear?"

"Nothing," she said, and took a drink of Coke.

All the excitement of having new neighbors was being squelched by my dad, and I didn't like it. But maybe he knew more than I did. I had hoped to go to college someday too, and I didn't want to lose that opportunity just because some new family moved into the neighborhood, regardless of what color they were.

Seven

LET'S PLAY TWO

A warm breeze rustled the leaves of the oak tree as it blew on through. Mouse and I sat across from each other at the base of the tree, once again scraping caps with our pocketknives. Jimmy was off to the side, blowing pink bubblegum bubbles while spinning his Duncan yo-yo, trying his hardest to pull off the complex rock-the-baby maneuver. Humidity, the weather we lived with, made my white T-shirt stick to my body.

"So when are they supposed to move in?" Mouse asked.

"I don't know. Soon I guess." I noticed that the pile of gunpowder was pretty enormous. "Your pile is getting a little full there."

"My dad says that niggers only want to move into white neighborhoods to start trouble," Mouse announced.

Now you may find this hard to believe, but I couldn't ever remember hearing the word *nigger* before, except when my grandma would produce a bowl of Brazil nuts or those small, licorice babies made from a humanoid-shaped mold. But somehow, in the manner and context in which Mouse said it, the word took on an ugly sound.

"Why would they want to do that?" Jimmy asked, his string

tangling up in a wad.

"How would I know?" Mouse replied, his eyes focused on his knife scraping the cap membrane. "My dad said it's just in their nature. It's a fact."

Suddenly with a bright flash and a *whooosh!* a small explosion blew up in Mouse's face. He flew backwards onto the dirt, grabbed his hand, and curled up in a fetal position, screaming at the top of his lungs. "Aaaahhh!"

I sprang to my feet, dumping my small piles of gunpowder onto the ground, and ran over to his side. "Mouse! You okay?"

"My hand! My hand!" he yelled, spinning away from Jimmy and me. He looked down at his hand. "Aahhh!" He began running in circles on the ground, like Curly of the Three Stooges when he needed cheese. "My fingers! My fingers! I've blown off my fingers!"

Mouse leapt to his feet and ran right up to Jimmy, sticking the back side of his hand, minus the middle two fingers, right in front of his face. Jimmy's eyes grew huge and his mouth let out a long and loud, "Aaahh!"

Mouse immediately composed himself and flipped up the two missing fingers, which he'd been concealing in his palm. "Oh, there they are," he said calmly. Mouse smiled and then broke into laughter.

I was relieved to see that Mouse still had all his digits in place. Jimmy, on the other hand, was not so forgiving. "You jerk, Mouse!" he said. But Mouse couldn't stop laughing. "Yeah, you're a real panic!"

"Whatsamatter? Can't take a joke?" Mouse said.

"As far as I can see, you'd be doing those colored kids a favor if you didn't play with them," Jimmy replied.

"What? So *you're* planning on playing with them?"

"I might. Why not?" Jimmy asked, attempting to unknot the yo-yo string.

"'Cause they're colored, and 'cause we're not. Right, Davy?"

"Oh, I don't know," I said.

"My dad said your dad doesn't want any coloreds moving in around here either," said Mouse.

"Yeah, well, no, he doesn't want them moving in here, but—"

"See," Mouse said, turning to Jimmy. "Nobody except you likes their kind."

"That's a lie!" Jimmy said, about as emphatically as I'd ever heard him speak. His face was turning candy apple red.

Mouse marched right up to Jimmy and poked him in the chest. The yo-yo fell from his hand, still attached by its string to his finger. I was sure that it was only a matter of moments before I had to relive the loogie scene, this time with Jimmy playing the role of the tortured victim. "You callin' me a liar, Dumpkins?"

"I *am*," Jimmy said, the words coming out a pitch higher than he probably had hoped. But he didn't back down. "You *are* a liar." Jimmy's face was so red I thought his head might explode. He slipped the looped yo-yo string off his forefinger and let it drop to the ground.

"So who besides you likes coloreds?" Mouse asked.

"*You* do," Jimmy said.

Mouse's striped T-shirted chest inflated. "Take it back, chubby!" He shoved Jimmy so hard he nearly lost his balance.

"I won't. And don't call me chubby. I'm stocky. And you *do* like coloreds."

"Take it back or I swear I'll—"

"You'll what?" Jimmy said, showing courage I never imagined him capable of. I could see him clenching his fist. He wanted to punch Mouse's lights out. We all did from time to time, but Jimmy was too smart for that. He knew that landing a punch anywhere on the surface of Mouse's face would only mean immediate retaliation — resulting in loose teeth, bruising of facial tissue, a bloody nose, and an evening of lying down and moaning.

Suddenly it dawned on me where Jimmy was going with all this. "He's right, Mouse. You *do* like Negroes."

"What?" As a confused Mouse turned toward me, Jimmy saw his opening. He lunged forward, took a wild swipe, and snatched Mouse's Chicago Cubs hat right off his head.

"Hey, gimme that!" Mouse said. Jimmy turned around, clutching the hat to his stomach with both hands. Mouse wrapped his arms around Jimmy's jiggling belly, trying to retrieve his hat, but Jimmy's girth provided a necessary shield as he fumbled with the inside of Mouse's cap. Mouse spun Jimmy around and tried to pry the hat from his hands, and when Jimmy wouldn't let go, Mouse reared back and popped him one right on the nose, sending Jimmy straight back down onto his butt. Holding his crumpled Cubs cap in his hand, Mouse stood over Jimmy, whose left nostril was dripping blood onto his upper lip and down his chin.

With a flushed face and eyes tearing up, Jimmy held out a 1958 Topps baseball card toward Mouse. It was Chicago Cubs shortstop Ernie Banks. "What about him?" Jimmy shouted out.

Mouse just stood there, disarmed.

"Ernie Banks, *Mr. Cub!* You keep his card under your hat for good luck. You met him outside Wrigley Field. You told me he was nice. You told me he smiled at you when he shook your hand and asked who your favorite team was. And he gave you his autograph right here on this card." Jimmy pointed out the auto-graph for emphasis. "You said it was the best moment of your entire life. What about *him*?"

Mouse looked over at me with a smart-aleck grin on his face, probably killing time until he came up with a good answer. "What *about* him?" he responded coolly.

"He's your favorite player in the world," Jimmy said. "He's colored, and you like him, right?"

"That's different."

"Why?" Jimmy asked, like he really wanted to understand.

"Because he can hit forty homers in a season. Because he was the National League's Most Valuable Player last year. Because he's *Mr. Cub.*"

Jimmy remained on the seat of his pants just looking completely baffled. "So if Ernie Banks decided to move across the street from you tomorrow, that would be okay with you?" he asked.

"Yeah."

"Why should that be any different?" Jimmy asked.

Mouse reached down and grabbed the card from Jimmy. "Just is." He reinserted the baseball card back under the front of his hat, snapped the cap back onto his head, and walked off in the direction of his house.

I walked over to Jimmy. He grabbed hold of my extended hand, tipped up to his feet, and dusted himself off. "I don't get it," he said to me, shaking his head.

I wasn't sure I was *getting it* either, so I needed to turn to a wiser voice.

It was early afternoon when I rode my bike over to Mr. Melzer's farmhouse. I hadn't seen him earlier when I delivered his paper. The front door was open so I knocked on the screen door, and waited. The heavy mesh screen made it difficult to view what was going on inside, but I saw no signs of life.

"Mr. Melzer?" No one answered. I had a bad feeling about the whole thing and decided to look around back. As I turned the corner of his house, I spotted him lying on his back in his vegetable garden among the heads of lettuce.

"Mr. Melzer!" My walk—through his yard and under the clothesline littered with clothespins—turned into a run. He wasn't moving. I ran up and looked down on him. His eyes were open and staring up into the sky; his expression was one of total peace.

Then he shifted his focus onto me. "Davy! How are you, boy?" He'd done it to me again, and I waited for my heart to find its rightful, calm place in my chest.

"You okay?" I asked. "Did you fall?"

"I'm fine. I just tripped. Never trust a head of lettuce. They look innocent enough, but given the chance, they'll sneak up on ya every time."

"Can I help you up?" I asked.

"Nah, that's all right. I considered getting up a while back, but then I just found the view so dang pleasing . . . I didn't see the point." He looked back at the white clouds in the sky like he was viewing them for the first time. "Cumulonimbus . . . who could design a better cloud? Come see for yourself."

I looked back at my bike on the walkway to the farmhouse. His request seemed sort of crazy to me.

"Odd," Mr. Melzer began. "Seems the less time I have to spend in this world, the more time I find myself taking to look it over. Maybe not so odd, after all." He looked over at me. "Trust me — they look different from down here."

I had no deadlines, no place to be, so I lay down in the soft brown soil, a row of lettuce between the two of us. I looked up at the sky, but it didn't look much different to me than it had any other day of my life. Summer skies were beautiful, and I'd always loved the way those big puffy white clouds would float across the sun, casting the shadows of passing giants on the landscape as I played ball, flew a kite, or just lay on my rooftop daydreaming.

"Such a simple idea," Mr. Melzer began.

"What's that?"

"Well, you've got this blue sky . . . and you add clouds and suddenly you've got a view that is never exactly the same . . . ever. So there's no growing tired of it. So simple an idea, and yet . . . incredible."

I had never considered that. "Did you hear about the new neighbors?" I asked.

"Yep. Seems to be stirring the pot up pretty good 'round here."

"It's just that it's got everybody acting so weird about it."

"Change can be a scary thing. Take that cloud up to the left there, about ten o'clock." The old man pointed a knobby finger up to the sky. "The one that juts out to a point. What's it look like to you?"

"Don't know. A duck maybe," I suggested.

"Really? A duck. I see more of a giraffe."

"No, see the little tail there?" I said, pointing.

"Oh, yeah, with its bill open?"

"Right," I said.

"Okay. Yeah, I see it," Mr. Melzer said. "So, anyway, just when you think you've got your cloud figured out to be looking like a duck . . . sure enough, the wind picks up, and it starts changing shape, and pretty soon you don't know what the heck it is. A dog? A turtle? Who knows?" The old man fell silent for a moment. "People are like that too. Just when you think you know them, the slightest breeze will blow and they start showing you a whole new side. And it can be scary . . . lonely . . . confusing. And you just wish you had your old duck back again."

"My dad says our house will be worth less money if this new family moves in."

"Might very well be the case. When it comes to money matters, a man's gotta have foresight, that's for sure." He smiled at me across the lettuce. "Then again, the way I see it, we're born into this world with nothing, we die with nothing, and in between, we're just borrowing stuff. This land isn't really my land. Oh, I have a piece of paper that says it is, but really I'm just a steward."

"What's a steward?"

"Well, it means that I'm just watching over it, taking care of it until I'm gone, until someone else takes over."

I knew he was trying to be helpful, but to be honest, he wasn't. I needed something more concrete than clouds and ducks and stewards to help me figure this thing out. He could see that as well. "One thing I do know for sure is that worrying about it won't change it. I spent a lifetime worrying about my crops. Would the weather be too dry, too wet, would bugs or an early frost wipe out all my profit? But all that worrying didn't change a thing."

"It just scares me. I feel like something bad's going to happen, you know?" I said.

"Challenge them, Davy. Look those fears of yours straight in the eyes, and chances are they'll turn tail and run."

That's all that was said on the matter. And maybe more than all the words and folksy analogies, it was just passing the time with Mr. Melzer as we watched the clouds float by that did me the most good, that put me the most at ease.

Staring up at the sky, Mr. Melzer sighed. "Old Mark Twain was right on the nose when he said, 'One must wait until evening to see how splendid the day has been.'"

Eight

IT WAS A DARK AND RAINY NIGHT . . .

Originally the four of us had planned to go down to the Coronet Theater, but neither Jimmy nor Mouse was willing to join us if the other was going, so Sheena and I were dropped off by her mom to see the movie *13 Ghosts*.

As you can imagine, Sheena was not thrilled with the idea of spending ninety minutes sitting in the dark, attempting to control her bladder while being terrified. But, as usual, she never came out and said so. Instead she justified her reluctance by explaining that she just thought the whole idea of being frightened as a form of entertainment was, in her words, "silly." And to be honest, I never quite understood it myself. I just enjoyed it.

We stood at the back of the line of people waiting to buy tickets at the fancy art deco ticket booth that sat out in front of the Coronet Theater. "So what's the dealeo? Do we really have to see this stupid movie?" Sheena asked me.

"I thought you wanted to see it."

"No. You were the one who wanted to see it. I was the one who thought it would be dumb."

Inside the Now Playing display case outside the theater, the movie poster read *13 Ghosts in Illusion-O!* in typical drippy lettering, indicating that this particular movie was going to be scary—the drippier the lettering, the scarier the movie. Titles for the scariest movies were nearly indecipherable. Just inside the poster's meandering border, high-contrast images of ghoulish-looking fiends in menacing poses emerged from a black background. Sheena read the tag line out loud: "'Thirteen times the thrills! Thirteen times the screams! Thirteen times the fun!' Thirteen times the *stupid*, if you ask me," she said, folding her arms across her pink mohair sweater.

"If you're too afraid to see it, we don't have to see it," I said.

"I didn't say I was afraid. I said it was going to be stupid."

I suppose I was looking forward to getting scared out of my wits partly because I knew the experience wasn't real. I knew I wouldn't be taking those ghosts home with me. I was also aware that this wasn't the confrontation that Mr. Melzer had suggested. But still I felt I needed an escape from those things in my life that really did scare me: the feeling I'd get in my lungs when Bobby and my dad were together in the same room, the anger in my dad's voice when he spoke of Khrushchev or the neighbors that he'd yet to meet, the way Mr. Borkowski would clear his throat and then spit onto the ground. Without a good explanation for it, I even found myself growing fearful over the way my mom would occasionally stand in the kitchen, her hand on her hip, just gazing out the screen door at nothing in particular.

As we walked into the lobby, a girl usher dressed in a trim

burgundy outfit handed us "ghost viewers" that resembled 3-D glasses, although they weren't wearable. A one-inch strip of red acetate ran across the top of the cardboard holder, while a blue strip was encased just below it. In this way both eyes would look through the same color filter at the same time.

The story line of the movie dealt with a Dr. Zorba who had died and left his spooky mansion — which, of course, contained a hidden fortune — to his broke nephew, Cyrus. He also conveniently left behind a special pair of goggles that allowed Cyrus and his family to view the ghosts who threatened their lives. Only a slightly ludicrous concept in my opinion. The Illusion-O gimmick was that when the Zorba family put on the goggles to see the ghosts in the mansion, the audience would know it was time for us to look through our ghost viewers, enabling us to see the apparitions. Looking through the red acetate would make the ghosts appear, while looking through the blue would make them disappear — which was pointless, because not looking through either color would also make them invisible.

After we found our seats near the center of the theater, Sheena escaped back out into the lobby and returned with a big carton of salted, buttered popcorn, with a root beer for her and a Coke for me. The lights dimmed, and Sheena started scarfing down that popcorn. I could tell she was nervous. By the time the Zorba family finally got around to putting on the goggles, the popcorn was gone. With her legs tucked beneath her, Sheena leaned up against me, her face hidden behind the empty carton as the audience buzzed in anticipation of a ghost sighting. I held my viewer up to my eyes and . . . there they were . . . *ghosts*. But it wasn't like they were jumping out at the audience or anything. In fact they weren't threatening at all. They just hung around the mansion looking grim.

Sheena spent the rest of the movie clutching my sleeve, more afraid of what she *might* see than she would have been if she'd allowed herself to view the lame ghosts.

By the time we had exited the theater, it had turned dark and a bit breezy. "That was pretty cool, don't you think?" I asked.

"It was stupid just like I said it'd be. Those ghosts looked so fake."

"How would you know? You never even looked through the viewer."

"Did too."

A car horn honked, and I spotted my brother parked across the street in his green 1950 Studebaker Commander convertible. Sheena and I ran across the street and climbed into the backseat. I could tell right away that this was an inconvenience for his girlfriend, as she sat cuddled up against Bobby, not acknowledging our entrance by greeting us or turning around. "Any good?" my brother asked.

"What?" I asked.

"The movie, nerdo. Was it any good?"

"It was okay, but it wasn't scary," Sheena butted in.

It felt pretty cool stretched out in the backseat of my brother's car listening to Bobby Darin on the radio singing "Somewhere beyond the sea, somewhere waitin' for me . . ." The warm summer night wind swept into the backseat and whipped Sheena's ponytail around like it was alive. I held on to my army hat just in case.

With cigarettes dangling from their lips and the sleeves of their white T-shirts rolled up, teenage boys with cocky laughs and animated bodies were out and about in number, strutting down both sides of the main strip that ran through town or hanging halfway out of their hot rods, in various stages of repair, scoopin' the loop. Perky young girls with big eyes, red lips, and goofy giggles, hair curled up tight to their heads from their Lilt home permanent kits, followed the boys, all searching for the heart of Saturday night.

The beat of rock-and-roll shouted out at us from every passing car like buckshot—the Everly Brothers harmonizing about Cathy's clown, the Ventures' electric guitars maxed to reverb limit, delivering the pulsating rhythm of "Walk, Don't Run," and Ray Peterson belting out his passionate plea to tell Laura he loved her as he lay dying from a stock car crash during the race in which he'd hoped to win enough money to buy ol' Laura a wedding ring. Back then you couldn't have the radio on for long before hearing some teenager sing about his dead significant other—his teen angel or his Patches or his Laurie. With the likes of Brando, James Dean, and Elvis setting the tone, it was a passionate time for teenagers, and although I was not yet a member, I could imagine the possibilities. This could be nice, leaving behind all the childish attitudes of the Mouses and the Jimmys of the world. In a few years I'd be the one driving and maybe Sheena would be there leaning up against my shoulder in her pink mohair sweater.

But for now there I was, rolling down the road, a part of it all, on display with my older brother for everyone to see. The opportunity seldom arose for me to hang out with Bobby, and now here we were, practically on a double date. I didn't want it to end.

"What do you say we stop off at the Dairy Queen for a dip?" I asked him.

"Do you mind, Nancy?" Bobby asked politely.

"Isn't it enough we had to pick them up? Do we have to babysit them now too?" Nancy said in a snotty tone.

Sheena had just endured an evening of terror, scrunched up in her theater seat, deflecting hideous ghosts with an empty popcorn box. She was in no mood to be condescended to by some teenage hussy.

"You don't need to babysit anybody," she shot back.

"I suppose we can go there if you want," Nancy whined to Bobby. "It's just that you promised me we could spend some time alone tonight."

"Yeah, why don't you go do that," Sheena said. "Maybe you should go over to the Jensens' place."

I glared at Sheena, hoping to derail her intentions. Nancy slowly turned her head around toward the backseat and said, "What did you say?"

"Oh, I'm sorry. I forgot," Sheena began. "The Jensen place is sold now. Guess you'll have to find some other place to —"

"Hey, I could go for a banana split, how about you guys?" I interrupted.

Nancy turned back around, leaned toward Bobby and frantically whispered something into his ear.

"Oh, of course not!" Bobby said. "She doesn't know what she's talking about."

"Oh, look at the moon, Davy." Sheena pointed up to the nearly full moon poking out between the clouds. Then in a breathy voice she added, "Whenever I'm with you, the moon *always* shines a little brighter."

Nancy looked like she was about to vomit. "You did tell him!" she screamed. "I can't believe you did that!"

"No, I didn't! I swear," Bobby said. "I don't know how—"

"Let me out!" Nancy said, laying butt rubber over toward the passenger door. "This is so sick!"

"Nancy, wait!" Bobby said.

"Pull over! Now!" she demanded.

My brother did as he was ordered, and Nancy kicked open the door, sprang out, and slammed it shut.

"Nancy—please—wait," Bobby said, but Nancy was already well down the sidewalk. He peeled rubber as he drove off, and I knew I was in for it. He was leaning back over the front seat, screaming at us. "Thanks a lot! You really know how to screw things up."

"Yeah, well, I don't like her anyway," Sheena said out the side of her mouth.

"But I do! Why don't you just keep your mouth shut, you little brat!"

"Hey, leave her alone," I said, somewhat surprised to find myself defending her.

We pulled up to a red light, and Bobby turned around. "Nancy's right. I don't know why it's my job to haul you two twerps around in the first place!"

"Then just forget it! I don't need you to drive me home!" Sheena jumped over the side of the car into traffic and ran off toward the sidewalk. People were bailing out faster than on the *Titanic*. The light turned green.

"Sheena, stop!" I said.

I started to go after her, but Bobby caught me by the arm. "Let her go."

A '57 Chevy behind us blared its horn, and I sat back down in my seat, watching Sheena disappear down the sidewalk. How a few words and a couple minutes could change an evening.

Bobby and I drove home without so much as a word between us. A storm was brewing; the wind picked up considerably, and I sat there fretting about Sheena walking home alone. The following day I discovered I'd had good reason to worry.

Apparently at first Sheena skipped briskly along. But the rustling leaves on the maple trees that lined the sidewalks shifted and swirled in unpredictable, reckless waves, and impatient clouds conspired to banish the moon from the night sky. Both these changes in the evening's weather unnerved her enough to knock the bounce right out of her skip, but it was the purple flashes of lightning streaking across the western sky, accompanied by distant rumblings like disgruntled giants, that added a measure of urgency to her gait.

Without slowing her pace, Sheena picked up a branch she found beside a tree along the parkway, broke off one of its twiggy extremities, and stripped it of its foliage. A bolt of lightning split the clouds just above and beyond the rooftops of the houses ahead. "One-thousand-one, one-thousand-two, one-thousand-three, one-thousand-four, one-thousand—" she whispered before the sky crackled then boomed close enough to send its sound waves through her heart. She whipped her stick in front of her like a foil, battling the night, providing an added sense of security.

The sidewalks were desolate now except for a high-heeled lady across the street yanking at her little white poodle's leash as she informed him he'd spent enough time sniffing a particular patch of grass. Then the lady was on her way, leaving Sheena once again alone.

About the time she got to our neighborhood, the clouds succeeded in obliterating the moon, while the lightning flashes and thunderclaps were now only one-thousand-one away from meeting up. She could smell the rain.

She decided to sing and belted out, "It was a one-eyed, one-horned, flyin' purple people eater" just to challenge the night, just to prove to the darkness and its accomplices that she was not about to let them intimidate her. Boldly she began singing about this hideous creature that dropped out of the sky, refusing to allow her voice to waver one bit.

A block later she felt raindrops and saw them spattering the sidewalk, shiny under the streetlights. Just then a large branch from a box elder gave way to the wind, crashing down in a soft heap right in front of her. Sheena shrieked, dropped her weapon, hurdled over the low end of the branch, and began jogging down the walk. Every few seconds a bolt of lightning lit up the sky, thunder crashing simultaneously now, shaking the ground beneath her fleet feet.

Then the heavens opened, and a torrential rain fell and blew in sheets, soaking her pink mohair sweater and obscuring her vision. She ran faster. A huge German shepherd leaped out of nowhere, banging its front paws up against a rattling gate, barking ferociously. Sheena spun around with a scream, forced onto the parkway, believing it was Spencer. It was not. It was a dog she'd never seen before, and for a moment she felt as though she was in a different town altogether. She took off running in a full-out sprint down the sidewalk again, hoping her direction was still homeward.

With her ponytail dripping like a garden hose behind her, she rounded a corner and recognized Mr. Melzer's farmhouse. She was almost home. A metal trash can blew over in the wind and crashed onto the drive, sending empty cans and bottles spilling out onto the pavement. The lid spun off and began rolling on its edge down the drive toward the street.

There was a small imperfection in the sidewalk, a nearly insignificant dip in the surface, but it was enough to suddenly cause Sheena to stumble, her feet slipping out from beneath her. She went sprawling forward, her exposed knees taking the brunt of the fall as she scraped them on the cement. She lay there beaten, her cheek flat against the damp pavement, the rain pelting the side of her face while her heart raced. She opened her eyes and saw a glistening black wrought-iron fence inches away. Through the wet bars and the intertwined, twisted rose bushes with their deadly thorns, Sheena could see the Gosweller porch light. Unfazed by the burning of her bloody knees or scraped elbows, but panicked by the presence of real horror, she scrambled to her feet and started away from the house, but found that she couldn't move. Something was pulling her back toward the house. She opened her mouth to scream, but nothing came out. Drake-ula had stolen her voice, and her soul would certainly be next.

Sheena lunged forward a second time, but once again she was jerked backward. Her lungs were deflating—the air being sucked out through her back. With one final attempt she charged forward, a clap of thunder overhead masking the ripping sound of her pink mohair sweater, the blinding light releasing her body from the monster's gripping force. Her breath returned in the form of a scream as she immediately bumped into a dark figure.

"Sheena, it's okay. It's me," I said.

For a moment she tried to run from me, but I wrapped one arm around her while covering her up with my umbrella. "Aaahhh!" she screamed.

"Sheena! It's okay! It's okay. It's me, Davy."

She looked up, soaking, shaking, eyes glowing. "Davy, oh, Davy!" She wrapped her arms around me. "Did you see it?"

"What? See what?"

"Him! Drake! It was awful! He tried to pull me in! He tried to take my soul."

I attempted to comfort her. "*Shh*. It's okay, squirt. You were just caught on something, that's all."

"No! No! It was him! It was Drake! I know it!"

I could feel where her sweater was ripped in back. "No, see . . . your sweater's torn. It was just a branch or something."

"You don't believe me." She tried to pull away from me. "I want to go home."

I kept my arm wrapped around her while covering her from the falling rain with the umbrella, and walked her down our sidewalk. Silently she continued shaking. I noticed light coming from Vern Borkowski's open garage. Veiled behind a yellow curtain of dripping beads of water falling off the open garage door, several men from the neighborhood stood around Vern's car, sharing a smoke and a drink. At first I ignored it, but then something caught my attention. It was laughter. One laugh in particular. It belonged to my father. Miscast among that group of men, my father stood holding a beer in his hand and smiling.

Unnoticed, we kept walking. I escorted Sheena to her doorstep, where I said good night. She thanked me for rescuing her from Drake, and I didn't argue with her. I was too tired, and besides, I was preoccupied with the unsettled feeling in my gut, a residue of fear. Not fear from any of the thirteen ghosts or from how my brother would treat me tomorrow or from the storm or the Goswellers' house. This was a fear of the sound of my father's laughter that night.

Nine

GOSPEL FIGHT DAY

Sunday morning paper routes were exhausting due to the sheer size of the paper and the additional copies, since some people subscribed exclusively to the Sunday edition. By the time I had finished up, I would have gone back to sleep if it weren't for the smell of bacon sizzling in the kitchen and my promise to my mother that I'd go to church. Wearing her red chenille bathrobe and a smile, she greeted my return with, "How'd it go?"

"Fine," I replied.

"You know what today is, right?" Mom asked with as much enthusiasm as she could muster up.

I did know. It was Balloon Day, and it seemed inevitable that it would wind up a disaster. The punching of holes in the index cards and attaching of red yarn to the cards, which they'd done earlier in the week, would be the extent of my siblings' participation in Balloon Day, and it made me feel surprisingly lousy. It had become a holiday I looked forward to because there was no pressure about giving or receiving gifts, no disappointment like at Christmas, when that one special gift you had hinted about to your parents for months ended up missing under the tree. It was just a time when the family got together and laughed. A time when my mom glowed for an entire day. I wondered if this was the beginning of the end for Gospel Flight Day.

As I walked into the bedroom to get my clothes for church, Bobby was carrying his own set of clothes, apparently headed for a shower. He ignored me as we passed, then closed the door, quickly turned around, dropped his clothes, and locked his arms around my chest from behind, pinning and squeezing me, and not letting go.

"Hey!" I shouted.

"How did she know?" he asked.

"What are you *talking* about?"

"You know, what Sheena said . . . about the moon and all . . . How'd she know?"

"Lucky guess?" I suggested.

He squeezed tighter and lifted me off the floor. "Tell me!"

"All right, all right—first let me go!"

He released his grasp, and I turned around to face him. I knew if I told him the truth he'd be embarrassed and probably never speak to me again, so I said, "Sheena told me that she was walking by the Jensens' house the other night when we were all playing hide-and-go-seek, and she overheard Nancy saying it . . . through the window, I guess."

"You didn't hear it?"

"No."

"You didn't see anything?"

"No . . . I didn't hear anything. I didn't see anything. I wasn't even there." I suppose I lied my share when I was a kid, and I'm not saying it was a good thing to do, but you've got to admit this was a little white lie that was beneficial to all.

Bobby didn't say anything else, just picked up his clothes and walked out of the room. And that was okay. Although I wished I could have told him the truth about us hiding in the closet and asked him exactly what that was like—kissing a girl and all, and feeling that way. And I would have asked him what he was thinking when Nancy brushed away his hair and kissed his birthmark. I would have liked to have known that. And I know it's unreasonable to think this way, but that's the brother I was hoping for—one who would have shared that information. I'm not sure what kind of brother he was hoping for, but I was more certain than ever that I wasn't it.

When I entered the kitchen, my dad was sitting at the breakfast table in his T-shirt and boxer shorts, eating scrambled eggs and bacon, while Mom wiped down the stove. A helium tank rested up against the wall, and several balloons of various colors had their heads pressed up against the ceiling.

"I swear the realtors are intentionally pushing this escrow through before any of us has a chance to take legal action against this family," my dad said.

"Hey, honey," Mom said to me. "Want some eggs?"

"Sure," I said.

"'Morning, sport," my dad said.

"'Morning."

"Did you hear me, dear?" Dad asked my mom.

"Yes, I did," my mom said, cracking a couple of Grade A's into the skillet. "But I don't really think the Bufords are breaking any laws by moving in here."

"The *Bufords*? You know them by name already?" he asked.

"I heard it from Audrey. Tom and Charlene Buford."

"And Pete tried to get a hold of the Jensens down in Florida," my dad said, "but they aren't returning his calls."

"The Jensens have the right to sell their house to whomever they want," said Mom. She poured me a glass of orange juice.

"Why do you insist on doing that, dear?" Dad asked.

"Doing what?" she asked.

"Why are you always siding against me on this issue?"

"Dear, render unto Caesar what is Caesar's, etcetera, etcetera, etcetera."

"Who's Caesar? And why are you quoting from *The King and I*? What does that even mean?" he asked.

"It means I don't believe we should attempt to exclude anyone from our neighborhood based on the fact that their skin tone is slightly darker than our own. Have you noticed our daughter lately?"

"What are you talking about?" he asked.

"She rubs baby oil all over her body and lies out in her bathing suit in our backyard trying to get the sort of look that you seem to have a problem with."

"I don't have a problem with a look," said Dad. "And it's not that I have a problem with this family personally. I just don't understand why anyone would want to move in where they aren't welcome."

"Oh, they'll be welcomed, dear. In fact there are several of us women who have already signed up to serve as a welcoming committee."

"You're kidding, right?" Dad said.

"No, I am not. You know those delicious chocolate chip cookies I bake from scratch that you love so much? Well, they won't be for you this time."

"I forbid you to do it, Ruth," Dad said. "You are my wife, and

I forbid it."

"Robert . . . you can do all the *forbidding* you want, but shortly after the Bufords arrive, I will be there with a basket of cookies in hand."

"Ruth! Don't do it! Don't make me quote Scripture!"

"I'm sorry, I didn't know you knew any." That might have been the first sarcastic comment ever to exit my mom's mouth, and I couldn't help but laugh. Both my parents glared at me, and I composed myself.

"The Bible says somewhere in Corinthians . . ." my father began. "It says that wives are to submit to the authority of their husbands."

My mom yanked off her apron. "You're right, Rob. The Bible does say that. And by the way, it's Colossians 3:18. It also says to love your neighbor as yourself. And as soon as you're ready to do that, I'll start submitting." Mom threw the apron down on the table and turned to me. "Get a move on, or we'll be late for church." As she exited the room, my dad looked at me and pretended not to be upset.

"Once they move in, if you don't want me to play with them, I won't," I said.

"Well, let's hope it doesn't come to that," he said.

After I got dressed and was ready to go, I walked into the kitchen, where my mom, wearing a flowered dress and holding her purse in her hand, was looking out the screen door. "We about ready?" I asked her.

"Do you have any idea why Sheena is standing in our backyard staring into the bomb shelter?" I walked over next to my mom and saw Sheena, dressed in her church clothes, doing exactly that.

I joined Sheena outside. "What are you doing here?"

"I don't know. I didn't sleep too well last night," she said.

"Because you got your sweater caught on the Goswellers' fence?" I asked.

"No, because Drake tried to take my soul." She shivered. It was then that she told me the frightening details of her walk home the night before. "I don't like being scared like that. I don't like being scared at all."

"So why don't you do something about it?"

"Like what?"

This was my chance to actually have a positive effect on Sheena, maybe to make up for all my bad influences. I had to think of something clever to say. No, more than just clever . . . it needed to be wise. "Maybe you should challenge them, Sheena. Look those fears of yours straight in the eyes, and chances are they'll turn tail and run." I had tried my best to make it sound like I came up with it on my own, but she looked at me a bit skeptically, knowing she'd never heard me use an expression like that.

"Thanks, Davy. Maybe I'll do that." Then she turned and looked down into the cement foundation. "What's the dealeo with this thing? What's it going to be again?"

"A wine cellar—" I said.

"—'cause it looks a little like a bomb shelter."

"No, it's a wine cellar."

"If it *was* a bomb shelter," Sheena said, "and we were being attacked by the Russians, would you let me come in?"

"Yeah, you can come in. Hey, listen, you want to come over after church? We're going to have our Balloon Day. I know my mom would like it if you joined us."

"Yeah, maybe. I'll ask my mom if it's okay."

"Great."

"We're ready to go, Davy," my mom called out from the kitchen door. "Hello, Sheena."

"Hello, Mrs. Connors."

"Then I'll see you later," I said.

"Okay." Sheena turned and ran back toward her house.

My mom taught Sunday school during the school year, but in the summers we all attended church together, including my father, when he could get out of bed. I liked that. For one thing, I didn't care for Sunday school. I wasn't the brightest biblical scholar, and there were just too many names and stories between those covers to keep straight. I was never very clear on the chronology of the whole thing. I knew Adam and Eve came first, but after that it was anyone's guess. And Christmas didn't help. As far as I knew, Santa was the third member of the Trinity.

I was clear on a few things: David knocked Goliath out with a slingshot, Jonah got eaten by a whale, and Noah built this huge boat where two of every animal got on board before it rained for forty days and forty nights. Those were the classics that held my attention. But the one thing that bothered me about all three stories was that God spoke to the starring characters. I found it unnerving that God would pick out three ordinary people and not only speak to them but give them employment, as it were. I worried that one day he might speak to me, but at least up until then, he'd kept quiet.

On the drive to church, I sat in the backseat with my brother. Though I didn't miss my usual job of keeping my brother and sister apart, I did miss the fact that Peggy wasn't there. And although she could be hard on me, usually when I felt lousy about something, she was the one in the family who'd pick up my spirits simply by listening to whatever it was that I had to say. As we started down the driveway, Bobby continued to act like I was personally responsible for ruining his love life. Meanwhile, he had no idea of the trauma he'd caused Sheena by not letting me chase after her and walk her home.

My parents' new-neighbor debate continued as a stubborn silence by both parties. I was beginning to feel like something horrible might happen to me, maybe to all of us, if I had to endure even one more block's worth of silence and was, therefore, relieved when my dad finally turned on the radio. He reached into his coat pocket and took out his little box of Sen-Sens, slid open the lid and popped a couple in his mouth. "Anyone want a Sen-Sen?" he asked. My mom and brother passed on his offer, but I grabbed the box and shook a few of the tiny licorice squares onto my tongue. This small gesture by my dad was enough, at least temporarily, to make the world right again for me.

Ten

BREATH OF HEAVEN

When we got home from church, I changed out of my fancy clothes and into my blue jeans and white T-shirt. My brother took off somewhere, possibly to beg Nancy's forgiveness. I became an only child, eating at the kitchen table with two parents who were still silent. The manner in which Mom chomped down on her cream cheese–filled celery stick made clear her disappointment in her family's unwillingness to participate in her self-proclaimed holiday. Her munching became even more intense when Dad announced, "You know, I'm not feeling all that well. I think I'll lay down for a while."

"You *are* going to help launch the balloons, aren't you?" Mom asked.

"Why don't you go ahead and start without me," he said, getting up from the table, slowly rubbing his hand on his stomach and shuffling out of the room like his death was at hand. Mom's lot in life was one of sacrifice, continually, effortlessly swapping the service hats that she wore for the benefit of her family: the entertainer, the chef, the maid, the butler, the nurse, the teacher. She performed to a full house without applause, without acknowledgment or compliment, and maybe mostly without appreciation. And now on the one day when her desire was to bring her family together to indulge her in a little spiritual celebration, they scattered. I wasn't any better. It just so happened that I really enjoyed watching things fly, helium balloons among them. We could have just as easily attached library cards to the ends of those balloons, and I would have shown up just to watch them rise and sail into oblivion. But just when it appeared that my mom was ready to take a butcher knife to those balloons and curse the dregs she'd been forced to share her house, her life with, Sheena showed up at the front door with a rookie's eagerness to participate in the event. Mom's spirits lifted dramatically.

Sheena's family was Catholic, so I wasn't so sure her parents would allow her to partake in our peculiar Gospel Flight Day. I didn't know a lot about Catholics. I did know that some guy named Kennedy was running for president, and it seemed to be a big deal that he was a Catholic.

Most everything I knew about Catholics came from one particular time when I was invited to go downtown to church with the McGuires. Entering the massive and ornate building with its vast open space was an overwhelming visual experience as our footsteps quietly echoed down the aisle. Dramatic shafts of dusty yellow light shown down on row after row of bulky wooden pews from beautiful, tall stained-glass windows decorated with vibrant images of Jesus and Mary and the saints. Rising up behind the congregation were the columns of giant golden pipes of a colossal pipe organ. Swallowed up by the cathedral, my first thought was *God must be here.*

Sheena pointed out something that looked like a wooden phone booth along the side of the sanctuary and explained how mysterious and dark it was inside and how people confessed their sins to a disguised individual through a screen door and were then forgiven and told to recite prayers as their penance. That information threw me into a small panic, believing I might be required to do the same during the service. But when she assured me that I wouldn't have to, in my relief I started coming up with all the sins to which I would have had to confess. Lying came to mind first, followed closely by stealing, and swearing and belching in public, although I wasn't so sure the last one made the list. I kept adding things until the list got so long and I felt so lousy about myself that I sort of wished I was in that booth blurting out all this stuff so that someone could just tell me that I could say a few prayers and I'd get a fresh slate.

During the service we spent a lot of time kneeling, and when the priest, decked out in an elaborate costume, opened his mouth and began speaking/singing, I had three thoughts. Initially I wondered, *What planet is he from?* When Sheena leaned over to inform me that he was speaking Latin, my second thought was, *My, aren't all these people smart to understand Latin!* And when I learned that the majority of the congregation didn't understand Latin, my third thought was . . . *Huh?* But even with that handicap in communication, a sense of holiness was conveyed.

In past years the middle of the backyard had served as the launch site for our balloons, but because that spot was now covered with a large mound of dirt excavated from the bomb shelter hole, we needed to choose another locale. The previous night we'd briefly considered moving the launching to the front yard, but mom feared it might become too much of a spectacle for the neighborhood to handle. So we settled on the corner of our backyard away from the possibility of any entanglements with trees.

While my mom cleaned up the lunch dishes, Sheena and I carried out into the backyard two large bouquets of lively, colorful balloons, banging their heads against one another while they mumbled something about their possible freedom. We had fewer hands than in previous years to contain the balloons as they waited for their individual launchings, so I improvised a solution. Though it was the electronic age of Maytag and Westinghouse and GE, my mother remained mysteriously uncommitted to the larger appliances, still preferring to wash her dishes by hand and hang her family's wash on a clothesline to dry in the fresh, clean air. That currently vacant clothesline ran along the side of our backyard, making it the perfect tether for our balloons. Sheena and I attached them by clipping wooden clothespins to the yarn just above the index cards, securing them on the line until their time of glory arrived.

A gentle wind, a clear sky, and temperatures in the upper seventies with a typically high humidity level provided ideal flight conditions for Balloon Day.

The row of twenty-seven evenly spaced balloons—with alternating color theme, Sheena's idea—waved gently like a line of choreographed ballerinas, their three-by-five slippers spinning and pirouetting in the warm breeze. My mother walked out of the back door, so pleased at the site that she continued to smile even while she skirted the bomb shelter excavation site. For the moment I'd chased away her gloom, and it felt good.

My mom briefly explained to Sheena why we held this annual

event and then proceeded to offer up a commissioning, of sorts, for the line of balloons. "Heavenly Father, we commit these balloons into your service, that their message of your Word might reach ears willing to hear, hearts soft enough to care, and minds open enough to surrender their own will to yours. And we ask these things in the name of your son, Jesus Christ." Then she turned to me and asked, "You want to lead us off, Davy?"

And so I made my way over to the clothesline, reached up, and slid the wooden pin off of the first balloon in line. I walked over and stood a few feet away from where Mom and Sheena sat on metal patio chairs, cleared my throat, and read the card out loud like I was announcing the Reds' starting lineup.

"Judge not, and ye shall not be judged: condemn not, and ye shall not be condemned: forgive, and ye shall be forgiven. Luke 6:37." Then I simply let go of the card and it rose straight up, tagging along for the ride up into the blue.

The three of us watched the balloon sail away for about thirty seconds, and then Mom said, "Sheena, would you like to read one?"

Sheena skipped over to the clothesline, where she craned her neck and peered over her pink cat's-eye sunglasses to scan the line of tethered balloons above her, shopping for a preferred color. The once-gentle zephyr had now become agitated, transforming the line of ballet-dancing balloons into boxers, bobbing and weaving as they dodged invisible punches. And the graceful footwork of the cards that hung down just below the line now danced like Sugar Ray. Sheena stood on her tiptoes, reached up, and grabbed hold of the card attached to a red balloon and pulled on it until the line stretched down far enough for her to reach the clothespin and pop it off. Grabbing the balloon around the throat to control it, she walked back and stood a few feet from where we sat waiting. The blue sky was losing ground to a bank of muddy-green clouds that were passing overhead in time-lapse photography fashion. I detected concern on my mom's face when she glanced up at the neighbor's treetops arching over.

Sheena stood at attention, holding the three-by-five index card in front of her face while the balloon above her head battled to free itself. The wind tossed her voice and her ponytail in all directions as she began to read, "Verily I say unto you, Except ye be converted, and become as little children, ye shall not enter into the kingdom of heaven." She continued to stare at the card as if rereading it for comprehension.

Most of my mom's choices for Scriptures were generally directed more toward offering up advice rather than ultimatums, so it surprised me when Sheena read this particular passage quoting the rebel Jesus. "Read the book and Scripture number too," I called out over the whistling wind.

"Oh, right. Matthew 18:3," Sheena added.

"Good, Sheena," said my Mom. But instead of releasing the balloon, Sheena just stood there staring at the card as the wind picked up even more, swirling around the mound of dirt, blowing it in our faces. "You can let it go now," Mom said over the whirl of the wind and the rush of leaves on nearby trees.

"But what does it mean?" Sheena called out.

"It means . . ." My mom sheltered her eyes from the dust and debris that were lifting off the ground around us and thought about it for a second. "It means you need to feel . . . your heart needs to be open and loving like that of a child if you want to go to heaven."

"But I already am a child," Sheena called out, squinting her eyes from the dust and struggling to hold onto the balloon.

"So you are," Mom yelled back. This simple response seemed to satisfy any concerns Sheena might have had, as she said, "Oh, okay," and raised her red balloon up above her head . . . and let go. It shot up into the air, darted back and forth before being swept away in the direction of the swiftly moving clouds. I looked up at the green sky, certain I'd soon be spotting a tornado, and it scared me. I'd seen *The Wizard of Oz* often enough to know the kind of damage a twister could do. Life was getting interesting enough without adding the threat of flying monkeys.

As my mom stood up, leaves and dirt and scraps of newspaper began lifting off the yard all around us, swirling about, building momentum until it grew into a dust devil that spun in a funnel reaching twenty feet into the air. The small twister blew right past us and circled the clothesline. One after another, clothespins began popping off the line in all directions, lifting the balloons skyward in a whirling mass as we watched in stunned silence. A moment later the tornado of wind dissipated, and the group of balloons were released from its hold to drift higher . . . floating away into the distance, looking like some unsolvable connect-the-dots puzzle. The three of us kept our squinting eyes on the pattern of colors. I thought for sure Mom would be disappointed that her Gospel Flight Day was spoiled, but when we scampered back into the house, she was smiling. She swept her hair away from her face, looked out the window, and said, "Boy . . . I guess the Lord was in quite a hurry to send those Scriptures on their way."

"He certainly was," Sheena agreed.

I stared at them, hesitant to admit that I must have been missing something. This was the kind of faith that Sheena had just read about out loud, the kind she sent up into the sky for the recipient to consider, the faith of a child that apparently both my mom and my friend possessed—but not me. While they saw the breath of God come down and blow those twenty-five balloons free to find his seekers, I simply saw a freak dust storm roll on through. The door to the kingdom of heaven was standing wide open to them, but was about to slam closed in my face. I was a child. Why didn't my faith come as easily?

I remembered my mom showing me how to catch snowflakes on my tongue a couple years earlier, standing out in our backyard knee-deep in snow. She suggested to me that each snowflake was a piece of Jesus and that when I caught one on my tongue it would melt and slide down my throat and into my chest, where it would transform my heart into one that could understand God and his mercy. I remember wanting to believe that it was true then, and I wanted to believe her again now as I stood searching the sky for any remaining sight of the balloons.

Eleven

TEN CENTS A DANCE

I hated Tuesday nights, and not because there was nothing on TV except maybe *The Rifleman*, which I didn't get to watch much anyway because my brother and sister preferred *The Many Loves of Dobie Gillis*. No, it was the night of the week when I had to collect newspaper dues from customers. To add to the general displeasure of the chore, my father made me wear my suit coat and tie to do it. He explained to me, "It adds a touch of professionalism that will benefit you in the future." I had yet to understand how.

It was an uncomfortable situation, walking into somebody's house and trying to act like an adult. Some customers had enough foresight to just leave the two-twenty-five, plus the occasional tip, in an envelope in the doorway for me, but most would swing open the door and greet me with, "That time again, already?" or "Who are you and what do you want?"

I never knew what to expect when I entered. I could find some businessman working on his third martini, unable to locate the money, or some woman dressed totally inappropriately (use your imagination).

Sometimes there were complaints. One time a lady who must have been a teacher handed me back a Sunday edition covered with red circles marked all over the place: "You see these? What kind of a paper are you running that you can't keep from making spelling and grammatical errors?" Like I was Perry White, for crying out loud.

On this particularly warm night one of the customers I had to collect from was Mrs. Winklemeyer on Sleepy Hollow Road. As I walked up to her screen door and rang the bell, I could hear a radio playing some jazzy swing music from the forties. "Be right with you," she called out. Drying her hands on the front of her apron, Mrs. Winklemeyer swept grandly into the room in one of her zillion long, flowing dresses, looking like she was going out for an evening of dancing.

"Oh, Davy, hello. That time again? Come on in."

As she leaned forward to open the screen door for me, I got that familiar whiff of her hair, which—although it had the consistency and general shape of cotton candy stuck up there on her head—smelled like insecticide. Always looking as though she had just returned from the beauty parlor, Mrs. Winklemeyer's hair was a shade of brown that I don't believe exists in the natural world of follicles. Despite her overly made-up face, she was one of my nicest customers. But it's true—while her face might have been suitable for viewing at a funeral, it looked a bit out of place among the living. And the sad thing was that she had no one around to tell her to lay off the rouge. My mom had mentioned something to me about Mrs. Winklemeyer's husband dying in a car accident a few years back, though I never remembered seeing the man.

As I entered the dimly lit room, Mrs. Winklemeyer's cats

scattered like cockroaches from a light. Mr. Bergen, a big, fat, long-haired thing, was the only one who would stick around for my visits. She had about a dozen cats all named Mr. or Mrs. Something or other, all named after old celebrities. Not a Whiskers or a Boots in the bunch. Mr. Bergen, named after Edgar because his mouth barely moved when he meowed, immediately began rubbing himself back and forth against my pant leg and throwing his voice.

"Oh, leave him alone, Mr. Bergen," Mrs. Winklemeyer said in a voice usually reserved for toddlers, but then did nothing to discourage the feline. Cats were city animals. I preferred dogs, like Sheena's Sunny. He was cool, friendly—you knew where you stood with him at all times. He was not a bit moody. But cats, they made me nervous. Something about the look in their eyes always suggested that at any moment they could leap at your throat, take a bite out of your jugular, and then stroll away like nothing had happened.

Mrs. Winklemeyer turned around toward me—spun is more like it. Whenever she turned her body even a little bit, her dress would be set in motion and swish around. "Have a seat over there on the couch while I round up some money," she said, untying her apron. I had learned over the past few months that the length of my stay at Mrs. Winklemeyer's house during collection night was directly proportionate to the amount of tip I received; the longer I remained, the bigger the tip. Usually it came to about thirty cents, and she always paid me in dimes, saying, "Now, don't go spending it all in one place," like it was some kind of a fortune that I could spread around town. So I sat down on the couch and tried to make myself comfortable.

But it wasn't easy. The place smelled worse than usual: stuffy and heavy. A veritable potpourri of bad odors circulated around the room as Mrs. Winklemeyer spun aimlessly about, a wave of cat urine followed by a wave of hair spray, followed by a wave of mothballs, colliding with a breeze of leftover pot roast. I took short breaths in hopes of not inhaling so much as to trigger involuntary gagging, which would result in my insulting the woman, surely causing a scene, and possibly losing my tip. Maybe my visit wouldn't be a complete loss if I could get her to lend some perspective to the new neighbors. I just needed to introduce the subject without sounding like a jerk.

"Here, have some candy while I get my purse," she said, sliding the usual cut-glass dish of assorted hard candy over to me. You could tell the stuff had been sitting out for months, maybe years . . . the pieces had melted together like a modern sculpture. Who knows how many flies had licked it—or worse? In fact there were two flies slowly buzzing around the coffee table like they were already half-dead. Apparently they hadn't been warned by fellow insects and had ventured too close to Mrs. Winklemeyer's hair, and were now paying the price. But I couldn't be impolite; my mom had hammered good manners into me, so I broke off a piece of butterscotch that was stuck to one of those lousy-tasting orange candies that nobody likes, and I thanked her.

On the table next to me sat a stuffed white game bird covered by a big glass dome. It was a lovely bird with long plumage, but I couldn't help but have an intense, irrational desire to uncover it so the bird could somehow be resuscitated and fly off to somewhere that didn't stink.

"I'll get you some milk to go with the candy," she said, pirouetting on her toe at the kitchen doorway, and before I could say, "No thanks, ma'am," she had disappeared into the kitchen. I stashed the butterscotch in my pocket. Usually if you didn't break your molars on her candy, you'd have to chew a hundred bites minimum in order to grind it down into a consistency that you'd be able to pinch down your throat with the half a glass of milk she'd usually offer you, served in dainty little porcelain teacups with blue flowers all over them—like she was entertaining your Aunt Mildred or somebody.

I looked over at a familiar art print hanging on the wall. It was a little girl with gigantic sad eyes peering over a fence with her cat, which sported equally humongous eyes. These prints by the artist Keane—of depressing-looking kids with big weepy eyes—were becoming sort of the rage at the time. Why anyone would want dreary images of despondent-looking kids stuck on their walls was beyond me.

Mrs. Winklemeyer spun back into the room with a couple of those silly teacups I was talking about, half-full of milk.

"Here you go." The thing was . . . she returned too soon. It was just a sense I had of how much time it would realistically have taken her to fetch the teacups from the cupboard, open the fridge, pour the milk, put it away, find a tray to set the cups on, and bring them into the living room. She set the tray down on the coffee table next to a couple dead flies.

"Thanks," I said, pretending to still be chewing on the butterscotch. I took a sip of milk from the teacup. She sat down across from me. The way I figured, considering the time it took her, she'd have had to set out the tray with the teacups in the kitchen before I even arrived. It wasn't bad enough she was spinning around in her dance dresses to some outdated, big band songs on a big console radio, or hanging pictures of sad kids all over her walls—she was looking forward to a visit from the kid who delivered her newspaper. I might have been the highlight of her evening. It was depressing as all get out. At that moment I didn't want a tip. I didn't want to stay a second longer, and yet I wasn't moving. Where were her kids, I wondered? Her family? Why weren't they eating the stupid butterscotch candies and shooting the breeze with her? Someone besides me should have been there with her. Someone who really cared.

She was asking me about school when she suddenly jerked her head like she heard a burglar. "Do you hear that?" she asked. Then she started nodding her head in rhythm to the upbeat swing tune that had come on the radio. I think it was called "In the Mood."

"What?" I asked.

"That rhythm, those horns? Glenn Miller." She closed her eyes for a moment as if she could see the music in her head. Then her eyes popped open, she looked straight at me, and said, "Let's dance."

"What?"

"You can't just sit on your hands when a song like this presents itself. Come on, it'll be fun."

I could think of several things it might be, but *fun* was not one of them. *Awkward, terrifying, humiliating*—these were all excellent words that accurately described what my experience of dancing with Mrs. Winklemeyer might be like. "I don't think so," I answered politely.

"Oh, come on, don't be a stick in the mud. I won't bite."

I wasn't certain of that. "I don't really know how to dance," I informed her.

"Nonsense. Everyone knows how to dance. Come on."

She grabbed my hand and yanked me onto my feet. She took

hold of my other hand and started shifting her hips back and forth, alternating dipping her shoulders up and down and swaying her head to the music. I stood there motionless, *terrified*, as Mr. Bergen watched smugly from his perch on the back of the couch.

"Just close your eyes and feel the music. Go ahead, close them."

I closed them. I didn't feel the music as much as I felt self-conscious of holding her hands. She must have used the gentle dishwashing detergent that they advertised on TV because her hands were surprisingly soft for an older woman. And yet, holding her hands felt creepy.

"Okay, keep them closed . . . feel the music." All I could hope was that when I opened my eyes I'd find myself home, safe in my bed. "Feel it?" she asked.

"I guess," I said.

"Relax your body a little." I tried, but my muscles were too tense. "Okay, start moving a little, any direction . . . there are no rules here, David."

I felt like I was drowning in raging rapids, and I could either try to swim for shore—by running screaming from the house, which was my instinct—or give up the struggle and float downstream. I decided to try what she suggested and let my muscles ease. I could feel them taking up slack on my bones as I began to ever so slightly sway with the music.

"That's it, that's it," she said with encouragement. "Now open your eyes and just watch me and do what I do." I watched Mrs. Winklemeyer begin moving my arms around while her feet stepped in every direction to the beat of Glenn Miller. "Go ahead, just start moving with the music."

I took a deep breath and began trying to emulate her move-ment. Ol' Glenn's tune was so upbeat and catchy that soon it actually became difficult for me not to move my body.

"That's it. Just like that," she said. I looked down and suddenly my feet were not my own. They were acting crazy, jumping around all over the place, and the thing was . . . it felt okay. In fact it felt surprisingly *fun*. Mrs. Winklemeyer pulled me forward, then rocked me back, then pulled my hand over my head and spun me around. My tie flew up and smacked me in the face, but that was okay too. It felt good, so I spun her right back and that dress of hers finally got the chance to swirl about with enthusiasm and style and purpose. It had found the liberation that it had sought from the moment I'd entered the house. With eyes closed, Mrs. Winklemeyer tossed her hair to the side, smiling and laughing like she was a kid on some kind of carnival ride. For the next couple minutes I couldn't smell her insecticide hair or see the weepy-eyed kids on the walls anymore, and I didn't care about the candy sculpture or the flies. All of it was consumed by the music and the motion. And then the song ended abruptly and both of us slowly wound our bodies down while we laughed at the sheer exhilaration of the experience. A slow song came on the radio, and I plopped back onto the couch.

Mrs. Winklemeyer finally did get around to fetching her purse, and when she did, she offered me a dollar tip, not ten dimes, but a bill. I refused it several times, but she insisted. I said good-bye and walked out her door. On the way home my legs continued on their own to display occasional fits of dance. And then I realized I never *did* ask Mrs. Winklemeyer how she felt about the colored family moving in. With the tune still popping around in my head, I couldn't help but feel that she wouldn't have minded one bit.

Twelve

DRAKE-ULA MEETS THE MOMMY

I looked at my watch again: 9:25. Jimmy and Mouse were already five minutes late meeting us.

"I don't like it," Sheena said. "Why are we here anyway?" The two of us were standing on the sidewalk in front of the Gosweller house, on the safe side of the florescent green line.

"Why won't you tell me what's in the bag?" she asked for at least the third time. I was carrying a paper bag from the A&P, the contents of which, I hoped, were going to alleviate some unfounded fears and bring some much needed reality to the imaginations of my three friends.

"Finally," I said, spotting Mouse and Jimmy walking across the street toward us.

"So what the heck's this all about?" Jimmy asked as he approached.

"Yeah, what's with all the mystery, Connors?" Mouse added. "And what's with the bag?" Typically he tried to snatch the bag from me, but I pulled it away in time.

"He won't tell," Sheena said.

"Well, you keep talking about what a freak Drake is and all . . ." I said. "So I thought maybe you'd want to try to prove it."

"Prove it?" Mouse said. "I told you how hideous he looked. What more proof do you need?"

I opened up the bag and pulled out my dad's black-and-white Polaroid camera. "A photo," I said.

"Wow! Is that a Poloroid camera?" Jimmy asked.

"A photo?" said Mouse. "You want to take a picture of old Drake-ula? Yeah, right."

"Don't be stupid, Davy," Sheena agreed and chuckled.

"You got some kind of a death wish?" Jimmy said.

"And even if you were able to get near enough to take his picture without dying, his image wouldn't show up on the film," Mouse said. "It's a fact. Yeah, that's really rich, Connors." He laughed. "You want to take a picture of Drake-ula."

"No," I said. "*I* don't want to take his picture. I want *you* to take his picture."

Mouse stopped laughing. I handed him the camera. "Here. Here's your chance to prove that all the stuff you said about him is true. His mom's going to be busy playing the piano pretty soon, right?"

"So?" Mouse said.

"So while she's playing, you sneak in—"

"Hey—I ain't sneakin' in anywhere," Mouse said.

"You sneak in, take a picture of Drake, and sixty seconds later we'll know exactly what he looks like," I said.

Mouse jammed the camera back into my gut. "No way! He'll suck my soul."

"He will. He will," Sheena said. "He tried to do that to me."

"And then he'll stare at me with fire in his eyeballs until, you know, my body explodes—*kabluey!*" Mouse said, his arms panto-miming an explosion. "He does that, you know."

"No, I don't know," I said. "And I'm really tired of you scar-ing everybody with your ridiculous lies. You can't just go around making stuff up," I said.

"They aren't lies!" Mouse said.

Just then classical piano music began to emanate from the Gosweller house. We all turned to look.

"Prove it." I tried handing the camera back to Mouse.

"I'm not the one who doesn't believe," said Mouse, pushing the camera back to me.

"You're too young to die, Davy," Jimmy said, dead seriously.

"Oh, I wouldn't worry. He's too chicken to do it," said Mouse.

"He's not afraid of anything," Sheena blurted out on my behalf.

"Not even that I might be telling the truth?" Mouse asked.

From the moment I had conceived this idea, I realized that it might come down to this, and I was prepared to go it alone. I looked over at the Gosweller house and then at Sheena. "Don't do it, Davy," Sheena pleaded. I draped the camera strap over my head, took a deliberate step across the green line, scaled the black iron fence and leaped off the top rail, clearing a rose bush and landing gently on the lawn.

I could hear Mouse say to Sheena, "Your boyfriend's a brave kid. A dead kid, but a brave kid."

"He's not my boyfriend," she replied.

As the piano music continued, I crept along the side of the big old house, through an archway trellis whose fragrant vines of jasmine helped conceal me from any eyes that might be peering down from the windows. As I slipped through the yard, crouching along the side of the massive, winding porch like an infantryman sneaking up on the enemy, I had no sense of being drawn in by any evil force. I was only compelled by a need to understand what I didn't understand. And yet for some reason I had to remind myself it was only a rose bush that had Sheena thinking Drake's force had taken hold of her.

Approaching the steps leading up to the kitchen's small, well-lit porch and wooden screen door, I wondered if maybe I was actually rooting to see the hideous monster kid that Mouse had seemingly invented, or something more innocent and benign as I had assured my friends was the case. The Polaroid would be my ghost-viewer. I just needed to lift it up in front of my eyes and see — not a celluloid apparition, but the real flesh-and-blood truth. My objective was not to have to sprint across the sidewalk in front of the Goswellers' even one more time or see that look of fear on Sheena's face again.

On previous nights I'd estimated the length of Mrs. Gosweller's little piano solo, so I knew I had to pick up my pace. Fortunately when I entered I could hear the concerto, or whatever it was that she was playing, transitioning into another movement, picking up steam and building volume, so I took that opportunity to open the screen door, which, predictably, creaked like crazy. Easing the door closed behind me, I stepped into the spacious, dimly lit, uncluttered kitchen, pots and pans hanging overhead. I literally tiptoed through until I entered a formal dining room, lit only on the far wall by a couple elephant head sconces with small bare bulbs sticking out of the upturned trunks.

The air was filled with the smell of flowers. One long stride past the potentially squeaky hardwood floor onto a giant Persian carpet that lay under the dining table found me positioned to investigate a long dark hallway that led to the foyer. There was no sign anywhere of any little monster. I took a few cautious steps down the hallway runner when the right side of the wall opened up to a large, step-down living room. Every note from Mrs. Gosweller's music furiously bounced off its walls, demanding my attention. I squatted down at the heavy oak trimmed entry-way to peer around the corner and shifted my focus to the dark figure profiled at the baby grand piano across the room. Just then, headlights from a passing car shone through the lace curtain on the bay window, casting a wide band of light on the face of the pianist. A young boy, his eyes closed and his head jerking side to side with the frantic rhythm, sat at the piano, his fingers dancing across the keys like a madman's. The light swiftly slid across his features and then faded.

Every hair on my body stood on end, but not out of fright. It was Drake. I knew it immediately. I couldn't wait to lift the camera up and click his picture, run back out of the house, through the yard, hop the fence, tear the photo from the camera, and cram it in front of Mouse's face, but I was too mesmerized by both the revelation and the sheer energy of the music to move.

With my hands shaking, I finally managed to raise the camera up and frame my subject up as best I could in the dark. My finger searched along the top of the camera until it found the button and settled on top. As I began to press down, a hand suddenly grabbed the back collar of my shirt, snapping my head back. The camera's flash lit up the room. With an upward thrust I was nearly lifted off the ground and then dragged backward down the hallway, the front of my collar choking me as I stumbled all the way into the dining room, trying to position my dragging feet beneath me. With the music still playing in the background, I landed on my back on the Persian rug and looked up to see Mrs. Gosweller's upside-down face smiling at me.

"What in the blazes you think you're doing?" she roared at me. "You wretched brat!"

I spun around on the carpet to face the tall, imposing lady staring down at me, her eyes on fire and her mouth — now right side up — clearly not smiling at all.

"Get up! Now!" She was nearly hysterical.

I got myself to my feet, scared to death. "I'm sorry. I didn't mean . . ."

Reminiscent of my own mother's technique, Mrs. Gosweller grabbed me by the earlobe and tugged, leading me into the kitchen to a phone on the counter.

"What are you going to do?" I asked. She released custody of my lobe, picked up the receiver, stuck her finger in the zero slot on the phone, and dialed.

"I'm calling the police. You nasty kids!"

"What? No. Please, don't." I could see the headline: *Davy Connors Disappoints Parents Again*. I'd been taught to respect my elders, but the woman had to be stopped. I poked down the receiver peg on the phone, disconnecting her.

"What do you think you are doing?" She was so mad that spit was accompanying her every word. "How dare you break into my house! What is your name, young man?"

"Look, I'm really sorry, I am," I said. "It's just — "

"Your name!" she demanded.

"What?"

"Your name! What is your name?"

"Davy. It's Davy Connors. But don't call my parents. Please. Just let me explain."

"There's no explanation for this outrageous behavior. You! You are the sick ones! I see you kids looking in our yard—running past our property! Just leave us alone!" Mrs. Gosweller grabbed my arm and dragged me through the kitchen.

"But you don't understand," I said. "I didn't know. I mean there are these stories going around about your son—"

"My son is none of your business!" she said, opening the screen door. "Now get out!" She actually pushed me out the door, and I fell down the stairs and onto my butt, the camera sailing off over my head. I had so much to say to her—so much to ask, but she wouldn't give me a chance, and it was starting to irritate me.

"But the music—he's amazing!"

"My family will not stand for this invasion of our privacy!"

"But we didn't know—"

"This neighborhood has no right to treat my son like a monster!"

"Well, then, maybe you shouldn't keep him locked up like one!" I blurted out of frustration. If you thought she was mad before, my candor lit her up like a Brahma bull.

"Get off my property this instant!"

She made a threatening move in my direction, like she was going to punt me, so I quickly rose, grabbed the camera, and took off in the direction of the front of the house. My three friends were just where I left them.

"Look, he lives!" Mouse said gleefully.

"Davy! You okay?" Sheena shouted. "We heard yelling."

They still didn't move from behind the green line as I walked through the front gate. "Did you get it? Did you get the picture?"

Jimmy asked.

"He was repulsive, just like I said, wasn't he?" Mouse said.

Sixty seconds were long up. As I approached the threesome, I yanked the photo out of camera by its tab and peeled apart the positive paper from the negative, revealing the developed photograph. I glanced at it.

"Let me see; let me see," Jimmy said, while Sheena grabbed the sides of her head and scrunched up her face, hesitant to be subjected to a gruesome image. I crossed the fluorescent green line and handed the photo off to grabbing hands.

"Here's your monster," I said, and walked on down the street toward home.

"I don't get it," Jimmy said, as the three of them analyzed the photo.

What Jimmy and others didn't get was that the image on the scrap of paper they held wasn't Drake at all. The distorted, anguished face that stared back at them was that of Mrs. Gosweller.

Walking home beneath the clear, starlit night sky, I couldn't stop thinking about the kid at the piano. Drake-ula had been replaced by a boy whose life was equally as mysterious and bizarre as Mouse's made-up story. In some ways I wished I'd never entered the house.

Thirteen

A CUP OF JOE TO START THE DAY

It couldn't have been a more beautiful morning. Even the Springfield's dog, Spencer, seemed to be in a better mood than usual, his bark sounding more joyous than his usual nasty *woof.* When I tossed the paper over his head, I honestly thought this would be the day he'd retrieve it in one piece. But as I rode by, I heard the snarling and gnashing of teeth as he once again tore the news of the day to shreds. Apparently the training was not going well.

It was shortly after I'd delivered the *Tribune* halfway down Willowcreek that I pushed back on my breaks at the sight of the Jensens' house. I stopped my bike directly in front of the place and couldn't quite comprehend what I was seeing. The golden morning light behind me lit up the front of the white house enough to reveal black spray-painted graffiti, phrases, and symbols covering nearly every available space on the face of the otherwise charming cottage-style home. As I stood there straddling my bike, the words became more defined. There was that word again, the one

Mouse preferred using when describing the new family that he had yet to even meet: the N-word. There were other sentiments, some just as nasty, some I didn't even understand completely, but the most popular saying was *Niggers go home!* In some cases the word was spelled with an *a*. There were symbols, too. Swastikas of all sizes blemished the wood siding. I felt weak in my knees and sick to my stomach.

As an orange moving van rolled down Willowcreek and pulled up to the curb in front of the house, I pedaled across the street but stopped on the sidewalk, not ready yet to continue on my route. I watched as a canary-yellow Cadillac drove in my direction, slowed down as it passed the moving van, and pulled into the driveway of the Jensens' house. My stomach began to knot.

At first no one got out of either vehicle. Then the man who had said, "Do these come with the house?" slowly got out of the driver's side of the car, never taking his eyes off his new house. He strolled around to the passenger side of the car, where his wife emerged. He motioned for the boy and the girl in the backseat to stay put. Then he wrapped his arms around her as she broke down in tears. She buried her face in his chest, and he slowly turned his head and scanned the neighborhood, his eyes stopping and fixing on the only other person in sight.

As he continued to stare in my direction, a feeling began to overtake me, the same feeling I'd experienced when I was caught stealing a pack of Dentyne gum at the A&P, or when my second grade teacher, Miss Berger, caught me copying off Becky Anderson's math paper, or when my parents discovered that I'd lied about not shooting my Wham-O slingshot at a bird. It was shame and guilt that I was feeling. But this time I wasn't sure exactly what it was that I'd been caught doing. I wasn't the one who spray-painted those words. Still, the feeling was there in the pit of my stomach. I wanted to get on my bike and ride away to another neighborhood, any neighborhood but mine. But I had responsibilities, so I slowly slung my leg over the seat, climbed aboard my bike and rode down the sidewalk, throwing newspapers onto driveways nearly unconsciously.

Finishing up my paper route, I glided up my driveway, dismounted from my bike and leaned it up against the garage door. A family had recently discontinued delivery of their paper, leaving me with one extra remaining in my canvas bag. As I walked toward the kitchen door, I stopped by the trash can, removed the lid, and tossed the newspaper in. I just about got to the kitchen door when I stopped. I turned back and stood directly in front of the trash can, afraid to take a second look inside. I considered walking away, but instead I lifted the lid off the can again. There among the newspapers, empty soup and vegetable cans, and other assorted trash, lay four cans of black spray paint.

When I entered the house through the kitchen door, my mom was sitting at the table in her robe, reading the newspaper and drinking a glass of orange juice. "Good morning again. The paper swears it's going to rain, but it's clear out there, right?"

"Yeah," I said.

As I suppose most moms do, mine had a built-in sensing device, able to detect even the smallest trouble in her children by hearing the slightest inconsistency in our intonation. "How'd the route go?" she asked.

"Okay, I guess."

"What is it?" she asked.

I was hesitant to tell her for fear I'd get emotional about the whole thing, but I knew it was better she hear it from me than from one of the gossipy neighbors. I sat down at the kitchen table beside her.

"Davy, what happened?"

"Nothing . . . it's just that . . . somebody painted on the Jensens' house."

"What do you mean?"

"I mean somebody spray-painted on the house. Words . . . bad words."

"What?" she said, more upset than I'd seen her in a while.

"All over the front of the house," I said. Mom got up from the table like she was going to walk right outside and take a look, but then she sat back down. "I was there when they arrived."

"Who?"

"The new neighbors."

"Oh, my Lord. They saw it?"

"Yeah. The moving van was there and everything."

"Oh, those poor people," my mom said. "Those poor people."

"Who do you think did it?" I asked.

"I never would have guessed anyone in this neighborhood would be capable of such a thing."

I was afraid to ask my mom if she thought my dad might have had anything to do with it. "Do you think that maybe . . ." I couldn't bring myself to say it.

"Maybe what?"

"Good morning," said my dad, appearing at the kitchen doorway dressed in his robe.

"'Morning, Rob. Coffee?" Mom asked.

"Yeah. Please. Need something to lift these eyelids."

My dad sat down across from me at the kitchen table and filed through the newspaper. He yawned as Mom got up and poured him a cup of coffee. I kept an eye on my dad the way I used to look at my brother when I knew he was lying to our parents about something.

"How'd the route go, sport?" he asked, with relative disinterest.

"Our new neighbors' house . . ." Mom began as she served my dad his cup of coffee. "Somebody spray-painted all over it."

I watched for his reaction, his body language, his eyes, something to indicate that he may or may not have been involved in the graffiti handiwork. He lifted the cup up to his mouth, blew across the steaming surface of his coffee and set it back down, and didn't say a word. He set the newspaper back down on the table.

"Rob, did you hear me? Davy said that the Bufords' house is covered with bad words," Mom said.

"Now you can't tell me that you're surprised at this reaction, Ruth," said Dad as he dumped a teaspoonful of sugar into his coffee.

"I'm sickened by it. I'm ashamed to be a part of this neighborhood today."

"Ruth . . . they should have known people would react like this."

"What?" Mom said. "*I* had no idea anyone would react like this! How can you predict such hatred? I'll bet Vern Borkowski was involved. What about Pete? Do you think he's capable of such a thing?"

"I don't know, dear."

Never once did I get an indication that my mom ever even considered my dad to be a possible participant. Looking for subtle evidence to the contrary made me feel so uneasy that I excused myself, saying that I had to do some work on my bike, when the truth was I couldn't spend another moment in that room searching for a flaw in my hero.

I rode over to Mr. Melzer's house to deliver the news. It was good to find him wide-awake on the porch, sitting in his rocking chair, having watched the sunrise. In greater detail than I had done with my mom, I described to him how the Bufords arrived with the moving van and how Mrs. Buford broke down in tears when she saw her new house covered in racial slurs.

When I was finished with my retelling of the story, Mr. Melzer just sat there, rocking back and forth, not saying a word for the longest time. It was as if he hadn't heard a word I'd said. Finally he got up and walked around to the side of his house, down his dirt driveway to the back of his house. I followed him. He disappeared into his old garage for a few minutes and came out with a gallon paint can dangling from each of his hands and a couple brushes tucked under his arm. He walked up to me, set the paint down, and handed the brushes to me. He still didn't say anything. Then he picked up the cans and marched down his driveway, me following behind. Even though I knew where he was headed, I felt compelled to ask, "Where are we going?" He didn't even turn around.

Once the Jensen house came into view on our right, Mr. Melzer's steps slowed as he eyed the house. His shoulders slouched. He looked down at his shoes and took a couple deep breaths. He looked back at me, and I swear it looked as if he was going to cry. He straightened up and began down the sidewalk again, turned ninety degrees at the walkway and up to the front porch, where the screen door filtered what sounded like a heated discussion between Mr. Buford and his wife. She was saying something about wanting to go back home, something about the old neighborhood.

I worried that Mr. Melzer might be making a bad decision as he set down the paint cans and rapped his old knuckles against the screen door. Mr. Buford looked from his position in the kitchen through the living room to see Mr. Melzer standing outside on the porch, while I hid behind him. "What now?" I could hear Mr. Buford say from the other room. His wife wiped her cheeks and followed her husband out to the living room.

Mr. Melzer turned around to me and said, "Wait here." I moved off to the side, feeling very conspicuous standing there out in front of the house.

"Yes?" Mr. Buford said suspiciously to the stranger at his door.

"My name's Joe Melzer. I live in the farmhouse down the street a ways."

"Yes. Well, we're awfully busy right now," said Mr. Buford. "If you'll excuse us—"

"But if I could just have a minute of your—" Mr. Melzer began.

"Maybe you could come back another time," Mr. Buford said as he began to shut the door. Mrs. Buford circled around her husband and caught the door before it closed.

"I'm sorry . . . what can I do for you today, Mr. Melzer?" Mrs. Buford asked.

"Well, I couldn't help but notice—" Mr. Melzer began again.

"Wait." Mrs. Buford opened the screen door, much to the dismay of her husband. "Please, won't you come in?

Mr. Melzer entered the living room. "Thank you." Mr. Buford

turned his back on Mr. Melzer as he entered.

"I'm Charlene Buford, and this is my husband, Tom." I looked through the screen door as Mr. Melzer reached out and shook Mrs. Buford's hand while her husband remained facing away.

"Nice to meet you both," said Mr. Melzer. "As I was saying, I couldn't help but notice that your house has several . . . several *unpleasant* words on it . . ."

Mr. Buford turned back around to Mr. Melzer. "Look, buddy, I don't know what this is all about, but I suggest you—" Mrs. Buford grabbed her husband's arm, indicating he should calm down.

"I remembered I had a couple gallons of white paint left over from when I painted my barn last year," Mr. Melzer continued. "So if you'd like, I could start in on the job right away."

"You mean paint our house?" Tom Buford asked.

"The cans are out there on your porch. I just need—"

"I appreciate the offer, Mr. . . ." Mr. Buford began.

"Melzer. But please just call me Joe."

"But I think we can handle it on our own," Tom Buford said. "Thank you anyway." He began to show Mr. Melzer to the door, but Mrs. Buford took her husband aside. "Tom! Tom, he wants to help."

"I know, dear, but we don't need to rely on—"

"You know," Mr. Melzer interrupted, "some of the folks around here, well, they were a little concerned when they heard a colored family was moving in." The Bufords turned toward their new neighbor. "They thought it might lower the standard of the neighborhood. I laughed and said they were crazy. But when I walked down here this morning and took a look at what some of those neighbors have done to your house . . . well, I realized I was dead wrong. They've lowered it considerably."

Mr. Buford folded his arms looking almost disgusted. "And exactly how much might this job be costing me?"

"You're in luck. I just happen to be having a special this week—first two coats of paint are free."

"Out of the question," Mr. Buford said. "I wouldn't feel right unless I paid you something."

"Tell you what. I haven't had many real home-cooked meals since my wife, Margaret, passed on a couple years ago . . ."

"Say no more, Joe," Mrs. Buford said. "Once we get settled in, I'll be happy to cook whatever your preference might be."

"Thank you, Charlene," Mr. Melzer said.

Mr. Buford reached out and shook Mr. Melzer's hand. In a soft but detached tone, he said, "Mrs. Buford and I appreciate this."

Through the bedroom window I saw the Buford boy and girl looking out in my direction. My concern was that they might make their way outdoors. Introductions were something that I wasn't ready for, so in a cowardly fashion I decided to slip away, back to Mr. Melzer's house where I retrieved my bike and rode around for a while. I traveled down to Ben Franklin's Five and Dime, where I bought a couple new Wiffle balls and a rubber snake to scare Sheena with. As I handed the cashier the money, I pictured Mr. Melzer walking out of the Bufords' house and not finding me there on the porch. Had he expected me to help him with the painting?

I'd always thought of Mr. Melzer as a kind man, but this act of generosity toward the Bufords was more than I'd expected. Although, I don't know what I'd expected, really. The door could have been slammed in his face, but it wouldn't have mattered because he felt he was doing the right thing. Even when I did know what the right thing was, sometimes it scared me to do it. I'm not sure why. Maybe because I feared it might set some kind of precedent and all the fun would be sucked out of my life. Maybe I feared that if I became some kind of saint, nobody would like me and I'd have no friends. And yet . . . I considered Mr. Melzer my friend even though he was a few hundred years older than me. I wondered if, as he dipped his brush in the paint can and spread a coat over the N-words, he'd be thinking I had let him down.

Fourteen

THAT STILL, SMALL CHOICE

The midday sun glared down from directly overhead as a group of about eight of us — including Sheena, Jimmy, and Mouse — played a leisurely game of Wiffleball in the street in front of my house.

None of us, not even Mouse, could help but be distracted by the sight of Mr. Melzer balancing on a ladder painting the Jensens' graffiti-covered house down the block — and by the continuing response of the neighbors. All morning long, folks had been popping their heads out of their front doors like gophers, walking halfway down their driveways (some still in their PJs or robes), just to see with their own eyes the atrocity they'd heard about — most likely over early morning phone calls. Some would pick the newspaper up, open it right there, and pretend to be reading an article while casually glancing down the block or across the street to the house covered with the angry, ugly words. There was no bigger news story to be found anywhere within those pages of newsprint; the headline was right there on our own block that day.

Only one neighbor had demonstrated the audacity to venture down to the actual scene of the crime. Allison Hoffman's demeanor was such that when she had strolled more than half-way down the block, I was certain that she was going to go the distance and prance right up to the Bufords' door. But when she got a good look at the remaining words, the swastikas, the damage done not just to the house but to the Bufords' dreams of a new beginning, she put her hand up to her mouth, turned away, and headed back home. It was as if someone in that house had died and people were giving the family their space, their time to grieve in private. The question was—would my neighbors ever have the guts or compassion to walk down to where their old friends the Jensens once lived and offer their condolences to the replacement family?

Breakfast table conversations that morning must have been passionate. Hate crimes weren't a subject that you could easily dismiss with talk of weather, not something you could swallow with an extra glass of OJ, not a fence you could sit on without losing your balance and falling to one side or the other. And yet balancing seemed to be exactly what my father had done. It frightened me.

Traffic on our block became so heavy that we grew tired of calling time-out to let cars pass and were forced to move our game around the corner onto Briarbrook. Most cars would simply slow down as they passed the house, but some actually stopped and gawked like they were at the zoo or something. A blue Ford Fairlane pulled up in front of the house, and a guy poked his head out of the passenger side and took a photo with a big old camera, then drove off. I was hoping he was only an idiot and not some photographer from a newspaper. No one should have to experience the humiliation of having their new house defaced like that, much less have a lasting image of it plastered all over the newspapers for everybody to glare at while they ate their breakfast.

I had spotted a police car in front of their house earlier in the day that remained for a short period of time. I wondered if the cops had planned on dusting the outside of the place for fingerprints or looking for footprints around the house like the detectives on *77 Sunset Strip* would do. Would an investigation turn up the responsible parties? And what about the location of the weapons used to intimidate the family, to discourage and dishearten? Would the cops be looking for them? For me the most critical piece of evidence as to who might be implicated in the crime, aside from the cans I found in the trash, was the fact that Vern Borkowski never came out of his house that morning. It was almost noon, and he still hadn't walked out to pick up his newspaper. It lay there, exactly where I had thrown it, growing anxious to be read.

It felt sort of funny, immoral actually, to be outside having fun on the same day and just down the street from where the crime had occurred, pretending that it was just another perfect summer's day in the neighborhood. Not that I was really having that much fun. My stomach had been twisting its way into a knot all morning long. Mouse hadn't offered up much of an opinion concerning what had taken place. With all his previous racist rants, I wondered if his insides were numb to the offense.

While Sheena and I waited our turns to bat, she asked, "So who do you think did it?"

"I don't know and I don't care," I answered. It was true that I didn't know, but a lie that I didn't care. And Sheena knew that.

There were a dozen questions that ran through my brain, but the only real question I had been avoiding dwelling on was the one Sheena asked next.

"You think maybe your dad had anything to do with it?"

"What?" I said, looking at her with disdain. "Are you crazy?"

"Well, the way Mouse said that his father said that your dad said—"

"Yeah, well, Mouse doesn't know what he's talking about."

The truth was I hadn't stopped thinking about that possibility since I first spotted the spray cans lying in the trash. It was one thing to understand the logic behind my dad's assertion that the new neighbors moving in might possibly have negative economic ramifications, but quite another to imagine that he was insensitive, immoral, and violent enough to partake in such a heinous act.

Sheena slammed a base hit down the right-field line just beyond Mrs. Hoffman's front yard, stretching it into a double, landing her at the sign pole in the island that stood for second base. As I came up to bat, I noticed that Sheena kept looking off to the side and behind her. Finally I spotted what had caught her attention: The two Buford kids had walked down the street and were now sitting on one of those big white rocks on my front lawn. Their presence didn't sit well with Mouse, as his whole attitude transformed into one of continued annoyance.

After Mouse had delivered a couple pitches to me, Sheena yelled, "Time out!" Then she just stepped away from the street sign and made a beeline for the new kids.

"Hey, where you think you're going?" Mouse yelled out.

Sheena ignored him. She walked right up to the boy and girl and said, "My name's Sheena—you want to play with us?"

"Hey, what are you doing? We're in the middle of a game here!" Mouse shouted out.

Jimmy walked in from his position at shortstop, and I walked over to join Mouse as the other players began to congregate around us. We all watched as Sheena led the Buford kids over. They both had slim, athletic bodies. The boy was about my height, with a tight nap of hair and a naturally engaging smile. His sister kept her eyes on the ground as she twisted her black pigtails.

"Hey, everybody, this is Hank and Amelia," Sheena said, like she was introducing her new best friends. "They'd like to play."

"Yeah, well, you see, we're sort of in the middle of a game here," Mouse said, cocky as all get-out.

"So we'll start a new one," Jimmy said over Mouse's shoulder.

"Maybe I don't want to start a new one," Mouse said. "*You* don't want to start a new game, do you, Connors?"

I should have answered right away, but I didn't.

"Fine, then they can join this one," Sheena said, determined to make it work. "Who do you want—Hank or Amelia?"

"Neither," Mouse said. "This game is over. Let's go, Jimmy," he said, walking away. But Jimmy didn't follow him. Only Arty and one other kid did.

"New game, Mouse," Sheena said. "Davy and I and Hank and Amelia will stand you and everybody else."

"Yeah, right. That's so funny I forgot to laugh," Mouse said, continuing to walk away.

"Six innings, if we lose, I'll buy you each a Good Humor," I said. Jimmy perked up and Mouse and Arty turned back around. I pulled several dollar bills out of my wallet and waved them in the air.

"And if you win?" Mouse asked.

I looked over at Sheena. She shrugged. "If we win . . . we win, that's all," I said.

Mouse converged with the others, huddling up for a conference. A moment later they broke the huddle and Mouse said, "You're on, Connors."

Had my parents known that I had put a wager on the game, they would have been very unhappy. But adding gambling to my long list of vices didn't seem to bother me as much as it should have. Maybe it was because I felt it was the only way for all of us to give Hank and Amelia a fair shake.

With Hank's initial appearance at the bat, he found Mouse's first several pitches all sailing toward the vicinity of his head, forcing him to duck and dodge. But with each wild pitch, Hank just took another practice swing and flashed his great smile back at Mouse, which seemed to infuriate him all the more. I wondered where the source of those pitches came from, why Mouse felt an anger toward the Bufords that I didn't. I wondered if maybe there was an element of racism that was justifiable, a reason why there were white folks who still considered Negroes to be less than their equals, something other than the color of their skin that made them legitimate victims of bigotry—because the mere fact that their skin was darker than my own wasn't enough for me to view them as inferior.

There were never any walks allowed in our games, and so Hank was still smiling out toward Mouse even after the sixth wild pitch. From his position at shortstop, Jimmy yelled in, "Hey, the sooner you give him something to hit, the sooner I get some ice cream." The next pitch was very hitable, and that's just what Hank did, whistling a line drive right back past Mouse's ear into center field. Hank flew around the fire hydrant on the Emorys' property that served as first base and headed for second.

Jimmy was there to cover the base. "We've got him!" he yelled out to Arty in center field, but Arty mishandled the ball and it rolled a few feet past him. Hank reached out his left hand, caught the sign pole in midstride, and swung his body around it, heading for third base.

"Go! Go!" Sheena shouted. Mouse could see that no one was stationed at third — an old catcher's mitt on the Morgans' front lawn — so he ran over to cover it as Jimmy finally received the relay throw from Arty and fired the ball at him. Unfortunately the ball, Hank, and Mouse all arrived at third base simultaneously. Hank collided with Mouse, sending the latter airborne off the base onto the grass where he rolled over one and half times, his Cubs hat sailing off his head and the ball coming to rest nearby.

Hank, knocked on his butt, scrambled safely back to third base. Amelia, Sheena, and I stood behind home plate cheering for him.

Hank dusted off the knees of his grass-stained jeans, raised his hand and called for time-out. He walked over and picked Mouse's Cubs hat off the grass. He noticed the baseball card that had fallen out nearby, and so he picked that up, too. As Mouse crawled over and retrieved the stray ball, Hank walked up to him and looked down at the Ernie Banks baseball card.

"He's some player, isn't he?" Hank said, sticking the card back into the cap and handing it to Mouse.

Mouse stood up and shoved the ball into Hank's chest. "No times. You're out."

Hank was confused. "What?"

"No times," Mouse repeated. "We never said okay. You're out."

"That's not fair," Hank said. "That's not how we play back in my neighborhood."

"Yeah, well, maybe you should go back to your neighborhood," Mouse said, taking a step closer to the colored boy. But instead of arguing with Mouse, Hank simply smiled at him and jogged over to join the rest of us.

The game continued for another half hour or so. Mouse just looked for opportunities to harass Hank or his sister, and I must admit I didn't make much of an effort to come to their aid. Amelia proved that she was an excellent athlete, coming through with impressive plays, but Hank was a better baseball player than any of us. Out in center field he managed to run down every fly ball that came anywhere near him, much to the dismay and frustration of Mouse.

The game was on the line in the bottom of the final inning when I made a pitching blunder. I grooved a floater to Mouse. With a considerable breeze blowing behind him, Mouse swung halfway off his heels, the ball exploding off the bat, shooting over the second base street sign, over Willowcreek, sailing deeper and deeper out to center field. Hank glided back, onto the corner of our property, but the ball just kept carrying until Hank ran out of real estate, finding himself backed up against a fence. A white picket fence. Spencer's fence. The ball dropped out of the sky beyond Hank's reach, falling into the Springfields' yard.

As Mouse rounded the fire hydrant, celebrating, none of us thought to consider the fact that Hank was new in the neighborhood and that he wasn't aware of some of the rules. Rule number one: You never enter Spencer's yard. Ever. It wasn't until Hank opened the Springfields' front gate and jogged into the yard to retrieve the Wiffle ball that a collective panic took place.

"Hey! No! Get out! Hank! Get out of there!" Sheena, Jimmy—everyone shouted. We all began a sprint toward the fence, while I noticed that down the block, the Good Humor truck had turned onto our street, though he wasn't ringing his bells.

As I approached the fence I could see Hank lifting up an evergreen bough by the porch, searching for the ball. Oblivious to our panic, Hank stood up, raising the ball into the air. "Here it is; I got it," he said.

"Hank, you gotta get out—there's this dog—" No sooner had I said the words than the beast tore around the corner of the house, growling ferociously. The dog and the boy caught sight of each other at the same time, and both froze in place. We all leaned over between pickets, our bodies taut with the anxiety of the moment.

The white ice cream truck continued rolling down Willowcreek in our direction. Hank apparently had ferocious devil dogs back in the neighborhood he came from, too, so he knew enough to remain still as Spencer, the fur on the back of his neck standing straight up, let him have an earful. The Good Humor truck, still silent, parked right alongside the triangle behind us, but no one made a move for ice cream. No one even seemed to take notice of it.

While Spencer continued his relentless barking, his quivering, curling upper lip revealing his dagger teeth, Mouse quickly ran over to the Springfields' gate and pulled it shut.

"What are you doing?" I snapped at Mouse.

"Saving our butts. You want him to eat us all?"

Suddenly Spencer decided he had been patient long enough, and he charged toward Hank—but then stopped no more than three feet away and took an even more menacing stance. He leaned forward on his haunches, threatening a violent attack with his throaty snarling and barking. Knowing that her brother was in real danger, Amelia took off running in the direction of her house. It was then that Sheena quietly, impulsively made her way over to the gate.

"Hey! Where are you going?" I asked, alarmed.

I could hear the engine of the ice cream truck turn off, and I turned around to see the Good Humor man dressed in his white pleated outfit step down from his white truck and walk in the direction of the picket fence. It took me a moment to realize that it wasn't Jack, our regular Good Humor man. I didn't recognize this man at all.

Sheena slowly unlatched the gate and pushed it open. "Don't move, Hank," she said. He didn't. "And don't look directly at him either," she added. He didn't. Sheena closed the gate behind her.

"Sheena, get out of there," Jimmy advised.

The Good Humor man walked up to the fence and just stood at the gate, watching as Sheena took a few cautious steps into the yard. Spencer took a step in Sheena's direction and stopped, now dividing his attentive barking between Sheena and Hank. Sheena looked right at the dog and said, "Spencer! Spencer! Stop it!"

"Oh, that should work," Jimmy said sarcastically.

I leaned over the fence and started banging on it with my fist in an attempt to draw the dog's attention away from Sheena. "Spencer! Spencer! Over here, boy!" Others joined in doing likewise. But Spencer already had his two victims in mind.

Then Sheena knelt down to his level. "Spencer! It's okay. It's okay. Hank is new here. He didn't know not to come into your yard." It was as if she were talking to her Raggedy Ann, but I was sure that the dog would not be as patient as the doll.

"The dog does not understand English," Jimmy said. "Just get outta there."

"Spencer!" Sheena started up again. "Hank is going to go now."

Hank eyed Sheena with skepticism. "I am?" he said.

"Yes. Just start walking toward the gate."

"Bad idea, simp," Mouse said. "Real bad idea."

Hank took a step in the direction of the gate, but Spencer took a step of his own toward Hank, continuing to threaten with his vicious barking. Hank looked over at Sheena, questioning her decision.

Then Sheena did something strange. She turned her head around slowly and stared at the Good Humor man standing still by the gate.

"What's she doing?" Mouse asked.

"What's she looking at?" someone else asked.

Sheena looked over at me for a moment, then turned back around and said to Hank, "Drop the ball." Hank wasn't so sure. "Go ahead. It's okay. Drop the ball for Spencer."

Hank squatted down slightly, eliciting more intense barking. With his eyes fixed on the ground, Hank gently tossed the ball in front of the bullmastiff. Spencer immediately stopped barking.

"Now you're going to let Hank walk away, right, Spencer?" The dog remained silent.

"Okay, now will you get out of there?" I begged her.

"No. Everybody just walk away," Sheena said.

"What?" Jimmy said, confused.

"Just leave," she demanded.

I refused to leave, and as everyone else reluctantly backed off, Mrs. Buford and Amelia came running down the sidewalk in our direction.

"Go ahead, Hank. Now."

Hank slowly began taking small, shuffling steps toward the gate. Spencer's ears drooped back, and he lay down with the ball resting between his enormous front paws. As Hank unlatched the gate and passed through, the Good Humor man stepped aside, allowing Hank to walk right into the waiting arms of his mother. "It's okay, baby," she said to him.

Spencer calmly looked over at Sheena, who remained in a squatting position. "Good dog, Spencer. Good boy. There's nothing to be afraid of now," I could barely hear her say to the dog. "They're gone. They're all gone." Spencer watched as Sheena stood up, turned, and calmly walked out of his yard, closing the gate behind her. Then he picked up the ball and trotted around to the back of the house.

As I joined Jimmy and Mouse, I could see Mrs. Buford walk up to Sheena, bend down, and brush the side of Sheena's hair as if to say thanks.

"That girl is nuts," Mouse said. "Wouldn't catch me risking my life for some—"

"So I guess I owe you guys some ice cream," I said.

"Guess you do," Mouse said.

I looked over to where the Good Humor truck had been, but it was gone. "Where'd he go?" I asked.

"Where'd who go?"

"The truck. The Good Humor man. I didn't see him leave."

Jimmy looked at his watch. "Maybe you're seeing things.

What time is it?"

I looked at my watch. "One o'clock."

"Trust me, I know. Jack doesn't show up anytime before two. That's right about the time my stomach starts growling."

"Stop messing around. He was just here," I said. "You saw him, right?"

"Hey, you tryin' to get out of this?" Mouse asked. "'Cause we won that game fair and square, so—"

"No, I'm telling you the truck was right here. The guy was standing right there at the gate. You saw him—I know you did."

"Hey, you better be out here when he shows up! I expect a Dreamsicle, and no telling my mom, either," Jimmy said.

Perplexed, I watched the two of them walk off. I just didn't understand what motivation they'd have for lying.

After she'd thoroughly thanked Sheena for her part in rescuing Hank, Mrs. Buford and her two kids walked off toward their home. As they passed, Hank gave me a wave good-bye, and I nodded. Sheena remained by the picket fence for a few seconds before walking over to me. "Hey," she said.

"Hey," I returned, as if nothing extraordinary had occurred.

"You were right," Sheena said.

"About what?" I asked.

"When I saw him standing there, shaking, with Spencer ready to kill him, I knew I had to face it. I just knew it. So I walked in there like there was nothing to be afraid of."

"So what was I right about?"

"About not being afraid of stuff—about facing your fears. You were right."

"No, I wasn't. You could've wound up as Spencer's lunch."

She looked confused. "What?"

"You heard me. It was stupid, what you did."

"But you said—"

"I don't care what I said. You didn't see any of the rest of us risking our lives just for some colored kid." I'm not sure why I said it like that. I was just mad, that's all, and I wanted her to know it. I wasn't even sure what I was so mad about. It was something. Something that escaped me—it just came out. Maybe I was jealous that she was the brave one—she was the one who performed in the clutch in a way that I knew I would never be capable of. "Don't be looking for some kind of pat on the back from me," I said defiantly.

She stared off across the street at nothing in particular. "I thought you'd be proud of me," she said in a voice smaller than her own. "I thought that you'd be glad that I was okay."

The truth is I was proud and relieved. I worried about her from the moment she pushed open the gate and walked into Spencer's yard. But I didn't tell her because I couldn't. I just stood there—an arrogant, stubborn, insensitive dope.

And the thing is, as you probably know, you don't get those moments back. Those bits of precious time when you wanted to say something to someone about how you really feel, how you really care. You want to unzip your heart for a second, but something stops you: the fear of embarrassment, of being vulnerable, the fear that if, God forbid, you commit to that feeling out loud it will change everything, and to change everything is too risky a thing to do. Even for a child. I wanted to be able to tell Sheena that what she did was not only admirable but that it was heroic. That I'd never felt prouder of her than at that moment. But those sentiments quickly got stuffed down, and the ones that rose up

in their place only addressed how insignificant her act of courage made me feel. Expressed like prods from a hot poker, my
words pained Sheena, though the scars that were to follow could
be found on both of us.

Sheena gazed at me with her big blue eyes, giving me one more
chance to redeem myself and speak the truth with love. But when
I didn't, she turned to walk away. She immediately turned back
around and kicked me in the shins. "I hate you, Davy Connors.
And he's not just some colored kid. His name's Hank. And he's
my new friend. And I think your father did do that horrible thing
to their house. And I think you know that, but you're just too
stubborn to admit it."

Right then and there she proved it: She knew me better than
anyone else, and knowing that should have brought me closer to
her. But it's difficult to feel close to someone who just kicked you
in the shins.

An hour later the Good Humor truck did show up on our
block, and I did buy members of the winning team ice cream
bars from Jack. I considered asking him if any other driver might
have come down our block earlier, but I didn't. I knew he'd say
no. Sheena didn't come out of her house for ice cream. In fact I
didn't see her for the rest of the day. I didn't like how that made
me feel.

Fifteen

THE DAY THE
EARTHWORMS
WOULD SPILL

Returning from my route the next morning, I found the workers showing up to continue turning our backyard into a shelter for World War III. I also found my dad loading up the trunk of our Studebaker Golden Hawk with a couple fishing poles, the tackle box, and a big net. "Ready to catch some whoppers?" he asked.

Was he talking about going to Fisherman's Dude Ranch?

Ironically, though all these weeks I'd been hoping to spend a day alone with my dad, after what had transpired with the Bufords' house, I wasn't feeling much in the mood to hang out with him. Not that I was convinced that he'd had something to do with defacing the house—but his attitude toward the new family had me at least wondering what I might not know about this hero of mine.

But my dad had promised we could go to Fisherman's Dude

Ranch someday, and—because Two-Ton Trzcinski had gone home sick the day before and was still out sick today—here we were on our way to my fantasy.

As we traveled the short distance to this lake in the suburbs, my mind was still on Sheena. The gloomy, threatening skies reflected my mood—I kept thinking about the things I *shouldn't* have said to her while we stood there in the street, and the words I *would* say to her, given a second chance. I was good at that: reliving scenes from my life over and over in my head until I'd rewritten them, not into perfection, but to a degree of satisfaction that would, in theory, help me to avoid making the same mistakes and eliminate similar regrets.

My dad lit up a cigarette, looked over at me, and smiled. "We're gonna have some fun, right, kiddo?" he asked. With mixed feelings I agreed.

There were only a couple cars in the blacktop parking lot when we pulled in. With nervous anticipation I stepped out of the car. We grabbed our rods and tackle box out of the trunk and walked through an opening in a split-rail fence onto a dirt pathway that led toward what looked like a log cabin.

I followed my dad beneath a tall, arching sign that informed us we were entering Fisherman's Dude Ranch. It was thrilling. The wooden sign portrayed a full-color illustration of a massive largemouth bass at the height of its breach out of the water, a black and yellow lure securely planted in the side of its mouth, jerking the fish's twisted, glistening body into flight. The taut line extended from the lure into the background where the excited angler balanced in his listing boat with his weight on his heels, his pole arching back over his shoulder as he battled to land his trophy-sized fish.

That was the kind of action I was hoping to experience that day. And I didn't mind waiting around—I was patient for a kid. I could stare down a bobber for a good half an hour without so much as a nibble before I'd start to get antsy. In fact I liked the anticipation of the strike. This day had all the makings of a perfect one, but only if I could cover up the single image of those spray cans in the trash with mental snapshots of our fishing day as it progressed.

As we walked up toward the cabin, we could barely make out the lake stretching out around and behind it, beyond a dense display of foliage. I followed my dad onto a long, narrow green porch and into the cabin, which I'm guessing was the *ranch* part of the Fisherman's Dude Ranch. I'm not sure why they called it a ranch, much less a *dude* ranch. After all, there were no horses or cows to be herded, no farmhands or anything remotely relating to cowboys except the hat that the smiley guy on the commercial wore. We walked inside. The man behind the counter also sported a cowboy hat, most likely against his better judgment.

"Good morning, folks! Welcome to Fisherman's Dude Ranch," he said.

"Morning," my dad said.

"My name's Buck. What can we do you for today?"

"Well, we thought we'd do a little fishing, Buck," my dad answered.

"That sounds like an excellent plan."

The two men continued with their stimulating banter while I took the opportunity to check out dozens of various, impressive petrified fish displayed on wooden plaques all over the paneled walls. On another wall hung a bulletin board plastered with candid photographs of people of all ages holding up the fish they had caught. Buck, if that was his real name, laid down some of the fishing rules, informing my dad that there was an initial fee to fish, which seemed odd to me. As my dad made the arrangements with the man in the cowboy hat, he opened up his wallet and shelled out a bunch of bills, and called over to me, "Night crawlers okay, Davy?"

"Yeah, fine," I answered with the confidence of a seasoned angler. But to be honest with you, I was never all that comfortable digging a big fat worm out of one of those little Chinese take-out food cartons full of soil and hooking him for bait. Night crawlers: Even the name sounded like a horror movie to me. I preferred fishing with good old processed American cheese. If it was good enough for me, it was good enough for them. My dad always claimed that worms didn't feel pain, but I think that was one of those you-have-to-lie-to-kids-about-this-for-their-own-good arrangements that parents all over the world made with each other. The fact was I'd never seen a worm *not* respond with what appeared to be nothing short of sheer agony when pierced with the pointy end of a fishhook. And I doubt the yellow puss and sticky, shiny substance that oozes out of them is likely a by-product of pleasure. Lanced with a giant spear, I'm sure I would react no differently, except I'd be much more vocal in my anguish.

"Yesterday they were biting pretty good right off the main pier," Cowboy Buck said. "I'd recommend you try there first."

"Sounds good," Dad said, like they were old fishing buddies.

"Grab a carton from the fridge, will you, son?" Buck asked of me.

On a nearby refrigerator a handwritten sign was taped on the door. It read Bait—Keep Door Closed.

I always found those kinds of mixed messages a little tricky. Maybe it was some sort of mental block for logic, but my first thought was, *Well, how in the world can I get the bait and keep the door closed at the same time? Is this a trick question? Is the man trying to be funny? Am I on* Candid Camera? Eventually my normal brain function returned to me, and I did open the door and grab one of the chilled white cartons by its two skinny little metal handles.

"Good luck out there, gentlemen," Cowboy Buck said as Dad and I walked out the door with our gear in hand. A crooked gravel pathway with tall wild flowers and giant ferns bordering either side led us about twenty yards before opening up onto the lake. It looked bigger on TV, but that was okay; its diminutive size created a more intimate setting. And though it was man-made, the lake looked very natural with several willow trees draped over its banks. Reaching alder limbs lush with leaves, cattails, and other reedy plants in the water reflected the calm morning. Lily pads speckled the shallow waters where several piers jutted out over the greenish-gray water. There were about seven small wooden rowboats, each a different pastel hue with a number painted on the hull, lined up on a sandy patch of shore. Looking around, I realized that the best part of the scenery was the fact that we had it to ourselves.

As we approached the bank, I noticed a couple of bleached fish floating on their sides along the shore, obviously dead. I was more impressed with the fact that they were pretty good-sized fish than I was concerned that they were goners. We climbed up three steps to the broad redwood pier where a wooden sign nailed to the first pylon warned, Do Not Release Fish Back into Lake. "Why can't we throw the fish back?" I asked.

"Well, I'm not sure. I guess they want to make as much

money as they can," my dad said. Stopping three-quarters of the way down the pier, I set the tackle box down on the planks.

"What do you mean?" I asked.

"Well, you have to pay for the fish you catch."

"Really? How much for a bluegill?" I asked.

"Depends how big it is. You pay by the pound."

I had no idea. This didn't sound like normal fishing to me. We opened up the tackle box, and my dad began helping me rig up my pole. With a hook already attached to my line, I grabbed a big red and white bobber out of the box. I pushed down the button on top of the bobber, threaded the filament through, and slid it down the line, assuring that the worm would do its dance of seduction about three feet beneath the water. Squatting down on one knee, my dad pinched a small, round, lead sinker onto the line below the bobber. Now was the moment of truth. Picking a juicy night crawler from the carton, dad shook loose the dirt from the worm's stretching body and laid it down on the pier. He flipped open his pocket knife and, without so much as a sympathetic sigh, chopped the fella in half, sending the worm into a spasmodic reaction, a pantomimed scream complete with mustard puss and the sticky stuff. Dad paused and looked over at me.

It was a look that said, *You're too old not to be baiting your own hook.* And I didn't want to let him down, so once the worm calmed down from the initial shock of losing the upper or lower half of its body, depending on your perspective, I picked it up, held it securely between my fingers, and carefully pierced it down the middle with the hook. Once again the worm was not thrilled, its body freaking out. "Good, now hook him again," my dad said. To prevent the worm from wiggling off, I punctured his body a second time.

"All right. Toss it in," my dad said.

"Aren't you going to fish?" I asked him.

"Let's just get you started."

I drew the plastic rod back over my head, across the pier, holding my thumb on the top of the reel. With an easy toss I snapped the pole forward over my shoulder. The reel spun, releasing the line, casting the jerking bobber in the air above me. It flew out away from the pier and plopped into the water, the three-foot leader snapping down onto the surface and sinking a moment later.

As soon as the lock on the reel clicked into place, my bobber was suddenly sucked below the water. "Hey, you got one," my dad yelled. And, boy, did I. My pole bent like crazy, the line dragging away beneath the surface, threatening to take me with it. This was no bluegill or sunfish.

"Easy, Davy, don't lose him." My dad got around behind me for support. "Okay, reel him in slowly."

I wasn't sure I could. The line was starting to dart all over the place while it continued to tug away with full force. For a few moments I feared the pole would be ripped right out of my hands. I pulled up on the pole with all my strength, dipped it down, and furiously wound the reel. After a couple more similar efforts, we could see the fish just beneath the surface, flitting side to side, its big, flat silver body flopping and flashing.

"There he is. He's a beaut!" my father said, while grabbing our fishing net. Dad got down on his knees, bent over the edge of the pier and dipped the net into the water.

I pulled back on the rod, drawing the fish up where it cut the water's surface and splashed onto its side, revealing itself at last—nearly mystical in nature and majestic in size and style.

"Bring 'im up, Davy." My dad slid the net underneath the fish and scooped him out of the water. "Got 'em? Good job, sport."

"What kind of fish is it?" I asked.

"A *big* fish," my dad said, grabbing my line and pulling the fish out of the net for a better look. The flat fish, whose dorsal fin rose and spread out along its spine, was one that neither of us could identify. "Four-pounder at least," he said enthusiastically.

After my dad had removed the hook, threaded the fish onto a stringer and lowered him back into the water, I rebaited my hook, ready to make my second cast. With a flick of my wrist, I sailed the bobber along with the other half of the first worm farther away from the pier. With a splash and a kerplunk, another fish, also enormous in size and power, struck immediately, gobbling up my little worm. I battled again, and with my dad's help brought it up onto the pier.

No more than ten minutes after we'd arrived, I had already caught two fish of considerable size. This was not a normal fishing day . . . no need for patience, no time to visit with my dad, no just sitting in a boat listening to the birds and the wind through the trees, no time out for a picnic lunch. Just *bam, bam*—two fish.

When we pulled in the second fish, my dad said, "Seems this is your lucky day." But something about the way he said it made me suspect that luck had nothing to do with it. With fishing there's always that chance you might not catch anything. But this wasn't fishing; this was shopping for fish. It was like being guaranteed to hit a home run each time I came up to bat in Little League. Where's the fun in that? Sometimes you need to strike out so that when you do hit a home run, it feels all that much more rewarding. Of course, I'm only speaking hypothetically, having never actually hit a home run in Little League.

"Maybe we should take a break," my dad suggested.

"A break? Why?"

"Well, the thing is, what with your pulling two pretty big fish in like this . . . well, it's gonna cost a bit. If we were allowed to throw some back, we could afford to stay longer."

"But we just got here," I said.

"I know, sport."

"So . . . why are they so easy to catch?" I asked him.

"I'm guessing it's because they overstock the lake."

"What do you mean?"

"I mean there's too many fish and not enough food. They're hungry, so when a worm drops in the water, it's gonna get eaten right away."

This may have explained the dead fish I'd seen earlier. "Why do they do that? Why do they put so many fish in here?" I asked.

"So people catch more fish, and they can make more money."

"But what about the fish?"

"Davy . . ." I could see my dad was beginning to lose patience with me, but I found the whole concept really perplexing.

"Doesn't anybody care about the fish?" I asked him.

Dad gazed at his overly sensitive child, pointed across the lake, and suggested, "Why don't we try fishing over there?"

We picked up our gear and walked halfway around the lake, mostly, I think, just to kill time. My first cast on the other side of the lake had the same result as the others. And the third fish was even bigger than the first two. "It's gotta be at least a five-pounder," my dad said unenthusiastically, doing the financial math in his head. We had no choice at that point but to pack up our gear and pony up the cost of our *lucky* catch.

"Have any luck?" old Buck asked as we entered the cabin. He knew we couldn't help but win out there on the lake, and it upset me that he had the nerve to ask. I'm not saying that it wasn't thrilling to reel those fish in. I'm just saying it wasn't normal. And it wasn't fair. Not for me, not for my dad, and not for the fish. The only one who came out ahead of the game was the *Ranch* part of Fisherman's Dude Ranch.

As the man behind the counter lofted the three fish we'd caught onto a big, metal scale, I strolled back over to the bulletin board. And though I stared again at all those people with their fish, this time I didn't see the photographs. All I could see was an image of all those fish in the lake trying to swim around but bumping into other fish because there wasn't enough room. I could see them all furiously competing for the same dinner. I could even visualize the normally congenial sunfish resorting to bad manners—pushing and shoving to get his mouth around some unfortunate water bug that had lit on the surface. It must have driven them all slightly insane. They were all crammed together in that pond for one reason—so that Buck, or whoever the owner was, could turn a healthy profit. Meanwhile the fish were suffering from claustrophobia and starving to death.

I once raised a goldfish for a while, and I made sure he was fed daily and that he had fresh water and a little ceramic castle to snooze in and lots of plants to make him feel good about his life. I started thinking that if I owned Fisherman's Dude Ranch, I'd be nicer to the fish while they were still alive. I'd treat them with respect and dignity, because they were the ones giving their lives so that I could make a decent living. They should at least live happy, comfortable lives before some worm enticed them into being caught and sold by the pound.

And that's when I figured it out. It all came down to . . . money. It was about money: making money or saving money at the expense of others—in this case, innocent fish. It didn't matter what was morally the right thing to do.

"Forty-five dollars and seventy-five cents," the cowboy said to my dad matter-of-factly. I could have been well on my way to buying the Black Phantom bike for that amount of money. The anxiety I was feeling over this whole experience was growing more and more intense by the second. My dad flipped open his wallet again as the man tugged on a roll of butcher paper on the counter and tore off a lengthy section.

I walked over to the refrigerator and stood in front of it, staring at that stupid sign again: Bait—Keep Door Closed! The idea of obeying rules didn't feel like a priority to me right then. I looked back across the room at my dad, once again removing bills from his wallet. Wrapping up our three costly fish in the brown paper, Cowboy Buck wasn't paying any attention to me either. I took a deep breath, grabbed the door handle, and quietly eased it open. I reached into the fridge with both hands, quickly grabbing hold of as many cartons of earthworms as I could manage, stacking them in my arms, up against my chest. I left the door open as I pretended to be invisible and shuffled toward the side door, not daring to look toward the cash register.

Just as I leaned my back up against the side door, I heard Buck's voice, "Hey, what are you doing there, son?" I didn't stop. I backed through the door and ran toward the pier as fast as I possibly could without dropping any of the cartons that jostled about in my arms. It felt like some picnic relay race as I sprinted toward the finish line.

I ran down the gravel path and just as I cleared the three

wooden steps leading to the pier, cartons filled with earth and worms began spilling out of my arms onto the dock.

"Hey! Come back here with those! Stop right there!" I heard the cowboy say in the background. I didn't look back. Surely my father thought his son had gone mad. I fell to my knees and dropped the remaining cartons down and ripped them open as fast as I could, dumping the worms, soil and everything, into the lake. Fish lips of all sizes appeared at the surface, causing it to stir and bubble up. Those lips began sucking down dozens of earthworms before they even had a chance to sink. I flung more worms farther away from the pier, and fish began leaping out of the water in utter joy at the opportunity of savoring a decent meal.

I could hear the hollow sound of boots stomping across the dock. When it stopped, I turned around and there was Cowboy Buck, standing over me with his hands on his hips, staring down at me with contempt. Dad caught up to Buck and stood beside him. But I didn't stop dumping cartons, not until the final worm had taken its first and last swan dive, as it were, into the lake. I wasn't sure why, but I was almost crying at that point.

Buck just shook his head, then turned to my dad. "You're going to have to pay for these—you know that," he said. My dad was surprisingly calm about the whole thing. I got up and ran past them both. "Crazy kid," I could hear the cowboy say as I hustled toward the parking lot.

Drops of rain gradually began pelting the rooftop as I sat in the back seat of our Studebaker, my eyes closed. I didn't want to relive the last fifteen minutes, or even attempt to rewrite them. I just wished I could somehow magically erase them from my history. But wishes and magic were a child's whimsy, and even though I'd just acted out in an immature fashion, I wasn't feeling much like a child at that moment, so I opened my eyes, preparing to face the consequences of my actions. Through the blurred windshield I could see Dad carrying the fishing poles, tackle box, and paper bundle containing the forty-five dollars and seventy-five cents worth of fish, marching toward the car, his head down. He was drenched from the rain, his black hair lying flat down his forehead. He circled around to the back of the car. I could hear him packing the gear into the trunk. The trunk slammed shut. I dreaded the ride home.

The driver's side door opened, and my dad slid in behind the wheel, closed the door, started the engine, and turned on the windshield wipers. He adjusted the rearview mirror so that his damp eyes were reflected toward me. "You okay, sport?"

At first all I could manage was a nod, then a whisper—a nearly inaudible, "Sorry."

He nodded back and in a monotone said, "Sometimes you gotta do what you gotta do." And there it was. For a brief moment my dad had become Jim Anderson. Bud's dad couldn't have said it better himself. Those few simple words brought me closer to my father than I'd felt in a long time.

He took out his little red box of Sen-Sens and offered them to me. I took the box from him and shook a couple of the little squares out onto my hand and tossed them into my mouth. I handed it back to my dad, and he stashed it in his shirt pocket again. "You can work off the money for the worms by mowing the lawn for a month," he added. He readjusted the mirror for the drive, shifted into gear, and we left Fisherman's Dude Ranch and the hope for a perfect day far behind.

On the ride home we didn't talk. It gave me time to try to sort out my feelings. But I was unsuccessful. All I could figure was that my irrational actions weren't really about the fish or the worms or the money. They were about something more—something I didn't understand then and don't fully understand even now.

With the rain continuing to fall, I was feeling melancholy —and yet every time I thought about those fish leaping out of the water, I had to smile. Hoping Sheena was still willing to listen to anything I had to say to her, I was anxious to tell her about those exuberant fish and looked forward to seeing her react with her own smile.

While I was lying in bed that night, waiting to fall asleep, my mom came into the dark room and sat down on the bed. She scratched my back and asked how the day went. I lied and said, "Good." Then out of the blue she said, "I know sometimes it doesn't seem like it, but your father means well. He's only looking to protect us."

"Against what?"

"I don't always know," my mother confessed candidly. "I'm not so certain he always does either. But he's your father, and you need to respect him."

Though I was afraid that she might make a big deal out of it, I asked my mom anyway: "Can a Good Humor man be an angel?"

"I don't see why not. The Bible says, 'Be not forgetful to entertain strangers: for thereby some have entertained angels unawares.'" She paused. "Do you think Jack is an angel?"

"No. Not Jack. I was just wondering anyway."

"Don't forget to say your prayers, okay?"

"I won't," I said.

Mom kissed me on the cheek and said, "'Night, Davy."

"'Night, mom."

She turned off the light and walked out of the room.

Prior to that evening it had never even occurred to me not to pray, not to give thanks, not to request health and happiness and various indulgences that I had no business asking for. After all, Mom had told me that God knows our requests before we even ask them, so what had been the point in asking them in the first place? Maybe I was a little upset with God, too, and I wanted to make that clear to him, to send a message his way that if he didn't start improving things in my life, he wasn't going to get my business. Blasphemous, I know. But all my relationships had become strained, and once I thought about it, I realized that all my problems started when the Bufords moved in. Since then my parents had begun arguing, my brother was more annoyed with me than usual, Mouse and I were at odds, I had jeopardized my friendship with Sheena, Mrs. Gosweller threatened to call the cops on me . . . and then there was this ongoing situation with my dad.

I decided to pray after all. But not the usual prayer. I wanted help understanding what was going on, and why, and what I should do about it. But more than all that, I wanted to know if God was even listening, if he did know my heart and how it was breaking, or if he cared about any of it. And so I asked for a sign. But I explained that I wasn't good at interpreting murky signs, so could he please make it clear and definite; something like a large rock falling from the sky and landing in my front yard would be sufficient. When I finished praying, I was feeling better already.

Sixteen

ANGELS UNAWARE . . . A SIGN OF WINGS TO COME

The next morning the rain had cleared out, having washed the exterior of the neighborhood clean. But like the fresh coat of white paint on the Bufords' house, an underlayer of filth remained concealed. I hadn't seen Mr. Melzer on my paper route, and wondered if he wasn't on his porch because he was upset with me for not helping him out. I was starting to burn bridges left and right.

Popcorn clouds decorated the blue sky above me as I sat out on the tree house porch. Occasionally the tree house was a refuge for me, rather than a place to play. I ducked inside its walls, grabbed the carpetbag, and sorted through some of its merchandise while waiting for my sign from God.

I pulled out my baseball and leaned back against a wall with my blue jeans — covered knees jutting up in front of me, tossing the ball against the wooden slats across from me and casually

snatching each rebound. This wasn't just any baseball; it was one
signed by Babe Ruth and had been given to me by my dad.

Yes, I know: A baseball with Babe Ruth's signature scrawled
across the sweet spot should surely be displayed under glass, away
from fresh air and direct sunlight to preserve it from those decom-
posing elements. But I didn't know any better at the time. Besides,
there was something about holding in my hands and actually
playing with the same horsehide ball that the Babe smacked out
of a ballpark that I found alluring.

I was hoping that the footsteps I heard on the ladder that
led up the side of the tree trunk weren't Mouse's, and that prayer
was answered: It was Sheena's face—wearing her pink cat's-eye
sunglasses and a smile—that popped up into sight just outside
the door at the top of the ladder.

"Hey," she said, in a light and airy tone that assured me that
I'd already been forgiven for our last encounter.

"Hi."

"Can I come in?" she asked politely.

"Sure."

Holding a brown paper bag, Sheena climbed up onto the
porch, stooped inside, and sat down across from me. "What's
that?" I asked nodding toward the bag.

"It's for you." She handed the bag over to me as I dropped the
baseball back into the carpetbag beside me. "My mom and I were
out shopping, getting some things for the new family's welcome
basket, and I saw this. I thought you'd like it."

I opened up the bag and slid out a Super Ace balsa wood
glider in its plastic package. Sheena was a giver. You could see her
love for giving gifts in her eyes.

"Thanks," I said.

"I remembered your last glider crashed pretty good, so I thought you'd like a new one."

"Yeah, thanks. It's cool," I said, immediately tearing open the plastic cover.

"Sorry we fought," she said.

"Me too."

"You were right—I was stupid to go into the Springfields' yard like that."

"No, you weren't stupid."

"Yeah, it was just dumb. If you hadn't told me to have Hank drop the ball—"

"What?" I said.

"To have Hank give Spencer the ball. If you hadn't said that to me, Spencer might have attacked us both," Sheena said.

"But I never said that."

"Sure you did. I heard you."

I thought back to the moment. "That's when you turned around, wasn't it?"

"Yeah. I never would have thought of doing that. You saved my life."

I didn't save her life. "When you turned around, who did you see?" I asked.

"Well, no one at first. Then I saw you."

She couldn't have missed the Good Humor Man standing there outside the gate. She looked right at him when she turned around. I was going to ask her if she saw him, but I didn't at first. It was between God and me. This was the sign I'd asked for; in fact, a sign he'd given me before I'd even asked for a sign. I thought the idea that God would send an angel dressed up like a Good Humor Man to rescue Sheena showed a certain sense of humor and good taste on his part. And the fact that I was apparently the only one privileged to view the angel gave me a moment of intimacy with God that I had never experienced in Sunday school or through silent prayer.

But then I realized I had no choice but to tell Sheena the truth. After all, if I knew that *you* had guardian angels helping *you* out, you'd want me to tell you, right? Cautiously, and with little inflection in my voice, I broke the miraculous news to her. "You have guardian angels watching over you."

"Yeah, I know," she said matter-of-factly.

"You do?" I asked.

"Yeah. So it wasn't your voice that I heard?" I shook my head. "So you saw my angel?" I nodded. "Guy or girl?" she asked.

"Guy."

"Wings?" she asked.

"Didn't see any."

"Was he handsome?"

"What does that matter?"

"I don't know. I just always pictured them as being handsome or pretty. You know, like Elvis or Sandra Dee."

"He was a Good Humor man."

"Really? Wow," Sheena said. "And I heard his voice."

"Yeah."

We were talking about the whole thing like it was not that big a deal to see or hear an angel, but it was. At the same time, it didn't surprised me that God would protect someone like Sheena. Truth is, I didn't believe that he would ever let anything bad happen to someone so good.

"Should we tell anyone?" I asked her.

"And have them think we're crazy?"

"But we know that we're not."

"Maybe that's good enough." She was right. "Booger promise on it?" she asked.

"Not this time," I replied.

The words "booger promise" alone are probably enough to spark your curiosity about the details of such a vow, but the explanation will have to wait for another time.

Carefully, so as not to crack it, I began to separate the perforated body of the glider from the thin rectangular sheet of balsa wood. "My dad and I went fishing yesterday," I said, changing the subject. And then I proceeded to tell her about my misadventures. Sheena was upset about the fish being crammed in the lake, and, just as I'd predicted, she got a big kick out of my kidnapping all the worms and feeding them to the fish. She even laughed when I described how they jumped out of the water for joy.

"I would have done the same thing," she said, and I believed her. "You want to fly it?" Sheena asked, seeing that I was just finishing up assembling the glider by inserting the airplane nose into the propeller casing.

We climbed down the ladder and walked a short distance away from the tree, where the wet wild grass had already been sun-bleached to a golden hazel, and took turns sailing the plane through the sky. While Sheena was winding up the propeller for another flight, I noticed a robin landing on a nearby sapling, bending the bough in an arch beneath its claws. I watched as it spread its wings and soared into the air, following it up and away, far above the tree house and onto an upper branch of the oak. Not more than two feet away from the bird, a blue oval object dangled on a red string. The morning sun in my face made it difficult to see.

"What are you looking at?" Sheena asked.

"Up there," I pointed.

It was a balloon. The morning breeze gently batted the dull, half-deflated balloon against the tops of leaves like it was playing a lazy game of paddleball. As we both stared at the object stuck up there, the identical notion came to our minds—this was most likely a balloon from Balloon Day that had second thoughts about making a long journey. I looked up at the balloon again, and could definitely see a card twisting from a piece of yarn below the balloon.

"You saw it first," Sheena said. "It's meant for you." She had obviously taken to heart my mom's preaching that the attached Scripture was intended exclusively for the finder of that balloon through a sort of divine intervention. Now that her theory had become personal, I found the concept frightening and thoroughly unreasonable.

"What if I don't want it?" I asked her.

"You have no choice. It's just going to stay up there waiting until you go get it."

She was right—just knowing it was up there would have driven me nuts in very short order. So I straightened my hat and began the climb, first back up to the tree house, then off its roof. The tree limbs were still plenty slick from the rain, and several times my sneakers slipped beneath me as I climbed higher through the branches toward where I believed the balloon to be. The limbs were becoming increasingly smaller as I balanced my way out toward where the more lush leaves billowed forth. Through a network of branches, and a myriad of leaves, I was finally able to get a view of the balloon. Lying out along the top of a branch at a forty-five degree angle, it was just out of reach.

"Careful, Davy," Sheena called from directly below. The

bough dipped and arched beneath me as I recklessly scooted farther out on the limb. Extending my arm out to its limit, I was able to curl my fingers around the red yarn that had wrapped itself around a fork in the branch. I pulled on it and the wrinkly, rubbery balloon followed, circling around the branch, batting against clusters of leaves, freeing itself. I scooted in reverse until I was in safe territory.

In retrospect, I realize it would have taken very little for that branch to break and for me to fall some twenty feet to the ground. My life was full of seemingly uneventful moments that could have just as easily led to tragedy. Was Newton—my own guardian angel—working overtime? Or was it just a roll of the dice that brought me down safe and sound? I can think of dozens of similar moments throughout my childhood alone, yet my life just continued on in a straight line to adulthood. And for me the question isn't why, but *for what purpose?*

I backtracked down into the tree house where Sheena sat waiting for me.

"So what's it say?" Sheena asked. I sat down beside her, held onto the balloon and yanked the card until it tore loose from the yarn. "Come on—read it," Sheena said, more anxious to have my direction revealed than I was.

Blurred from the rain, the inked letters were barely legible, and I took it slowly to get it just right. "Then said Jesus unto him, 'Go, and do thou likewise.'"

"What? That's all?" Sheena asked, puzzled and disappointed. "Here, let me see that." I handed her the card, and she held it up close to her face and began to read it. "'Then Jesus said unto him, "Go, and do thou likewise"' . . . that's all it says," she said. "But who did Jesus tell?"

"I don't know."

"And *do likewise* to what?"

"I don't know. It doesn't say."

"Well, that's just stupid," Sheena said. "Why did your mom copy that? Was she drunk?"

"What?" I asked, dumbfounded.

"Maybe she had too much wine to drink and didn't know what she was typing."

"My mom doesn't drink."

"Then why do you have a wine cellar again?"

"Look, maybe it doesn't mean anything."

"Of course it does." Sheena looked down at the card again. "Oh, it also says Luke 10:37. Maybe if you read what comes before it, you'll understand."

"I don't want to read what comes before it. The card should be enough."

"Maybe you should ask your mom."

"I don't want her to know I found it or she'll just get weird about it." This was more baffling than the bait sign at Fisherman's Dude Ranch. I took off my army hat, folded the card, and tucked it inside the lining in the front like a baseball card.

My disconnection from the verse left me feeling disappointed in Balloon Day. I hated to think that the other recipients all over the world were equally as confused. I may as well have been some guy in Paris finding a balloon and not being able to understand the verse because he can't read English. Or maybe there was some kind of cosmic mess-up, and I wasn't the one who was supposed to receive this message. Or maybe my mom was just deceiving herself into believing that God had his hand in this kind of thing. I didn't necessarily want to believe that, but that choice seemed to be most logical.

Seventeen

THE DAY TONTO LEFT THE LONE RANGER TO FEND FOR HIMSELF

According to my mom, involvement in the wives' welcoming committee for the Bufords' arrival into the neighborhood started out with *a strong head of steam*. But by the time the two of us walked out the front door with a basket full of goodies, we were joined only by Sheena and her mom, Audrey, who carried a chocolate angel food cake on a glass plate with a glass cover, and by Mrs. Merriweather, holding tightly to a geranium plant with a green bow attached to its terra-cotta pot. Not about to show up empty-handed herself, Sheena practiced twirling a brand-new plastic Wiffleball bat like a baton, while I was relegated to keeper of the new Wiffle ball, still in its box, both obviously gifts for the Buford kids. I had mixed feelings about the visit. On the one hand I genuinely wanted to get to know the neighbors better, but on the other I felt like I was betraying my dad.

Mom and Audrey, dressed in flowered summer dresses, high

heels, and with purses dangling from their arms, headed up our little parade, while Mrs. Merriweather kept step just ahead of Sheena and me. The lack of participation infuriated my mom, not a quality she often displayed. "I can't understand it," my mom began, "Alice, Myrtle, and the others . . . they all said they'd be happy to come along."

"Now I'm not saying this is what happened," Audrey said, "but sometimes husbands have a way of influencing their wives to do other than what we desire to do."

"We once had a colored lady come in and clean our house for a while when I was young," Mrs. Merriweather said, totally out of context. "Seemed very nice. Ethel was her name. Or was it Edith?" Mrs. Merriweather displayed a nervousness that manifested itself in the form of her not being able to shut up. "I believe that it's not only fair that the coloreds have the opportunity for a better life by moving from the cities to live with us whites in the suburbs, but I believe it's beneficial to both cultures."

We turned up the sidewalk toward the Bufords' house. Mr. Melzer had done such a good painting job that the house looked almost as if the crime had never occurred. But the five of us knew better, and we all gave the face of the house a good looking-over to see if we could detect some remaining sign of the evil act bleeding through. We approached the Bufords' porch, where the front door stood three-quarters open behind the aluminum screen door. Mom rang the bell.

Mrs. Buford showed up at the door in bermuda shorts and with a small red headband keeping her hair off her forehead. "Hello," she said.

"Good afternoon. I'm Ruth Connors, and this is Audrey McGuire."

"Hello," Audrey said.

"And Dorothy Merriweather," Mom continued.

"Hello, a pleasure to meet you," Mrs. Merriweather said, nearly curtsying.

"I'm Charlene Buford. It's good to meet you all."

"I'm sorry we're a little delayed in this gesture, but we just wanted to drop by and officially welcome you to the neighborhood," Mrs. McGuire said.

"Oh, well that's so nice of you all. The place is still a mess, but, please come on in," Mrs. Buford said, opening the screen door wide.

"Thank you. We promise not to stay long," Mom said. Sheena and I followed my mom into the living room. "We brought you a few gifts, nothing too fancy," Mom said, as she handed Mrs. Buford the basket filled with cookies, instant coffee, and other treats.

Sheena nudged me and nodded in the direction of the spot where we'd spied Bobby and Nancy making out. She briefly closed her eyes and made several quiet lip-puckering smacks. "Stop it," I advised her under my breath.

"Oh, how nice," Mrs. Buford said. "And is that angel food cake?"

"Freshly baked this morning," Sheena's mom said.

"Oh, my," Mrs. Buford let out a sigh that turned into a chuckle.

"And I brought you a geranium from my garden," Mrs. Merriweather said.

"Oh, it's lovely . . . my word," Charlene Buford said, obviously overwhelmed by the show of generosity. Her mouth suddenly did a downward turn, and she fixed her eyes on the floor and began to cry right there in front of us. "I'm sorry," she said, wiping her tears away. "This move has just been so difficult and . . . I just . . . I didn't expect this."

"It's okay," my mom said. I felt like she wanted to reach out and hug Mrs. Buford, but of course she didn't.

"We just want you to know that what happened to your house in no way represents the feelings held by the majority of the neighbors," Mrs. Merriweather said. Had she left it at that, her sentiment would have sounded perfectly sincere, but she felt obliged to add, "In fact most of us are just delighted that a Negro family has finally moved into our neighborhood."

There was a silence that followed that I swear lasted for five minutes before Sheena spoke up. "Davy and I brought something for Hank and Amelia." She held up the bat and pointed to the boxed Wiffle ball in my hand.

"Oh, and I believe you've already met Audrey's daughter, Sheena, and my son, Davy," Mom said.

"Yes, I have. Sheena was a brave little girl to rescue my son from that vicious dog. I'm very grateful. You know what — the kids are out in the back. Why don't you two go out there — I'm sure they'll be happy to see you."

Dressed in their bathing suits, Hank and Amelia were taking turns sprinting through and hopping over an oscillating sprinkler when we walked out into their backyard. When Hank and Amelia caught sight of us, they stopped and approached, their brown skin sparkling in the sun. We exchanged greetings, and then Sheena said, "We came by to bring you a new bat and ball."

"Why?" Hank asked, confused.

"Well, if you don't want them I can always take them back or feed the ball to Spencer for dinner," Sheena said. Amelia laughed.

"No, I'll keep it," Hank said with a grin, taking the box out of my hand.

A part of me still didn't want to like them. It was that part of me that looked hard for clues that might give indications of a lifestyle that justified distrust or scorn that could help explain my dad's real reasoning behind wanting them out of the neighborhood.

It was a bit of an awkward moment, and I felt like I had to say something. "So how do you two like it here?" I asked, like I was about thirty years old.

"I have my own room," Amelia said.

"And we never had a yard before," Hank said. "Dad said we could get a dog."

"Probably a beagle," Amelia said.

"Yeah, it'll be cool," Hank said, removing the ball from the box.

"Hey, and that Mouse guy," I said. "I know he seems like a real jerk—"

"He *can* be a jerk," Sheena chimed in.

"Yeah, he *can*, but once you get to know him better, it'll be okay. You'll see."

"Kind of like this neighborhood," Sheena said. "Once you get to know it, you'll like it here. I promise." With that Sheena felt compelled to inform Hank and Amelia about everything she knew relating to the neighborhood as if she were helping them cram for an exam. "Now the first thing you need to know is that some neighbors are nice and some are mean. The nice ones are . . ." and then she proceeded to list the neighbors in order from those most tolerant of children to the absolute meanest, Mr. Borkowski finding himself at the bottom of the heap.

"And come Halloween, you want to just stay away from the Morgans and the Taylors. And the Finnegans, they turn their porch lights out and pretend they're not home. We usually toss firecrackers in their gutters, don't we, Davy? Now the best candy comes from Mr. Melzer's house—candy apples or popcorn balls guaranteed. The Grahams usually hand out big candy bars, but steer clear of Mrs. Winklemeyer's house—don't even ask why, just do it." Sheena was a spectacle to behold as Hank and Amelia just stood there patiently, drying in the sun and politely nodding their heads.

Sheena continued acting as neighborhood advisor and guide on such subjects as who had the best and worst Christmas displays, who would and would not contribute money when you go door-to-door for UNICEF, whose yards displayed the best fall colors on their trees, the best place to go to view Fourth-of-July fireworks, best toboggan hill, nicest dogs, worst drivers, and kindest moms, and so on.

Finally Hank started getting fidgety, first flipping the ball from hand to hand, then tossing it back and forth with me. But this didn't deter Sheena a bit. For the next ten minutes she shared facts and fancy about our streets, which included giving away her secrets to Amelia as to which families were the most generous when it came to buying Girl Scout cookies. She told how all year long, old man Kelley on Briarbrook swears at kids to stay off his property, but then around Christmastime he floods his yard with the garden hose and turns it into a skating rink for everybody.

Amelia, Hank, and I were now batting the ball around but continuing to listen when Sheena said, "And then there's this kid, Drake, who we all thought—well, not Davy, but the rest of us—was some kind of a monster, you know, with horns and scaly green skin . . . he lives in the house on Briarbrook with the black fence that whenever we'd pass, we'd have to hold our breaths for fear he'd suck our souls. But turns out he's just this kid—this kid who's a little different, that's all. And when he sits in front of a piano, it's the weirdest thing—he turns into some kind of a Mozart. If you want, we can go over there tonight and listen to the music. It's really pretty."

"Sure, okay," said Amelia.

Sheena's face lit up as she told them about Oakfield and the tree house and the bottle rockets, and the carpetbag; how we found it and that we kept our most treasured possessions inside it. She described how last year the first snowfall of winter fell so softly in the middle of the night that no one even noticed until we all woke up to a beautiful white world that could have only been transformed by our dreams. And how we spent that entire day outside, rolling snowmen and sledding down the hill behind the Lincoln Elementary School, and catching snowflakes on our tongues until our hands and feet were frozen and every mom in the neighborhood drew a mustard bath for her kids. Sheena told them about all the fun street games we'd play on summer nights and how fireflies would appear out of the dusk like magic fairies, and how when it's time to come home at night all the neighborhood parents have a way of calling in their kids—with bells or special whistles or just calling out their names like they're lost boats at sea, and how hearing those calls gives you both a sad and a happy feeling.

Sheena chatted on so long that it easily could have turned into an embarrassing moment for her and for me by mere association with her, but instead it turned into something else. She had passionately described life in our neighborhood, almost like she was painting a picture that she had to get down on canvas before she lost the daylight. And her need to express this rich relationship with the neighborhood seemed to be as much for her benefit as it was for theirs; as if she needed, stroke by stroke, to express these slices of neighborhood life out loud and with a sense of urgency before they disappeared from her consciousness.

The significance of the landscape painting wasn't lost on me, having never considered all the elements as a whole before. It was a beautiful, inspired picture, simple and complex. And it was my life; one for which I should have been more grateful. And I couldn't help but consider at that moment how shallow my dad's concerns had been. Sheena's brushstrokes expressed the seasons, the places and faces and times and smells that were valued, the stuff that mattered, the experiences that helped define me. Like seeds carried by the wind into our garden, the Bufords' taking up residency would alter the scenery, but not diminish its worth. Hank and Amelia would add to the texture of the entire piece just as we all had mixed and blended ourselves onto its canvas. Their lives in the neighborhood would only increase its value as the landscape of my childhood.

When Sheena moved on to the subject of possible neighborhood employment opportunities, pointing out, "the best place for a lemonade stand is—" Amelia interrupted her with, "What's a lemonade stand?"

The question made Sheena flip. "You've never heard of a lemonade stand?" But before she could possibly suggest that we immediately set one up, we heard a loud shattering of glass coming from the house.

We ran through the back door, through the utility room, and into the kitchen where Mrs. Buford and my mom seemed to both be washing their hands at the sink, water streaming from the faucet.

"What happened?" Hank asked his mom.

"Nothin', sweetie. Why don't you and your friends go back out and play now. All right?" It was a universal misconception by parents that they could fool children into believing nothing was wrong when in fact something was. Mrs. Buford pretended to be calm, but none of us were buying it, so none of us were moving. I took a step closer to the sink, where I could see Mrs. Buford applying pressure to my mom's arm; blood was streaming down her wrist and spilling down the drain.

"Mom, you okay?" I asked.

"Yeah, I'm fine. You kids do as Mrs. Buford asked—go out and play."

Amelia walked over to her mom, leaned against her side, wrapping her arms around her waist. "We heard a crash. What broke?"

"It's nothing, Amy. We'll clean it up."

Despite the requests to the contrary, all of us kids remained, trying to piece together what had taken place. The kitchen opened up into the dining room, where we could see Mrs. McGuire peering out a broken window in front of the dining room table. Mrs. Merriweather sat motionless, with coffee cups and saucers, half-eaten cake, and shards of glass scattered on the table in front of her.

"Audrey, please stay away from there, okay?" Mrs. Buford called out over the sound of the running water. Sheena's mom walked away from the window and stopped at the entryway to the kitchen, where Sheena joined her.

"Probably just kids," Mrs. McGuire said. "Are you going to

be all right, Ruth?"

"Yeah, I'm fine. It's just a scratch."

"What happened, Mommy?" Sheena asked.

That's when Hank spotted the rock on the dining room rug. He tiptoed over and bent down to pick it up, but his mom stopped him. "Hank! You're barefoot, child. Just leave it, please." Hank did as he was told while Mrs. Merriweather continued to resemble a figure at Madame Tussauds.

"I'm so sorry, Ruth," Mrs. Buford said as she turned off the water.

"It's all right. It's not your fault," my mom said quietly with a smile.

"Hank!" his mom called out.

"Yes, ma'am?"

"There's some gauze and a bottle of iodine in a box on the bathroom floor. Please fetch it, son. And go around the other way."

Hank ran off through the utility room.

"We really should call the police," Mrs. McGuire said.

"No," Mrs. Buford said. "My husband doesn't want to involve them." Mrs. Buford looked down at the rock on the floor.

"I think it's pretty much stopped," Mom said, though I could still see blood seeping through the fingers on the hand that concealed the cut.

"I can't do this," Mrs. Merriweather solemnly admitted out loud to herself. We all turned toward her. "I'm sorry. I thought I could. I really did. But I can't. And so I have to go now." With that Mrs. Merriweather stood up, snatched her purse off the back of the chair, walked to the living room, turned back for a moment like she wanted to say something more, then turned and walked out the front door. No one said anything about it. We all just went back to attending to my mom.

"Amy, grab that towel over there on the stove," Mrs. Buford said. Hank returned with the box of gauze and bottle of iodine and set them on the kitchen counter. Mrs. Buford turned off the water, and took the towel from Amelia, saying, "Thanks, sweetie," and proceeded to dry off my mom's arm. Visible to all of us was an inch-long, splitting cut that ran up the inside of my mom's arm. The bleeding had subsided considerably, but blood still trickled out of the wound enough to make me feel her pain.

"Looks pretty deep. Maybe a doctor should take a look at this," said Mrs. Buford.

"No, it's fine," my mom said.

My mother wasn't much for running to the doctor at the first sight of blood. Once while playing in Oakfield, I made the mistake of stepping off a makeshift teeter-totter to attend to an untied shoelace. Unfortunately I bent over at the same moment Mouse chose to sit down on the opposite end. I watched the old gray plank rush toward my face, and I felt the rusty nail that was sticking out of it imbed itself in the fleshy space between my nose and my upper lip. I let out a scream so loud I'm sure that somewhere in outer space an alien's blood is curdling in reaction to it, even to this day. And even though the nail (did I mention it was rusty?) pierced entirely through to my upper gums, releasing a gallon of my own precious blood onto my favorite shirt, my mother made the determination that I was just fine and that a visit to Dr. Weston would not be necessary.

Mrs. McGuire picked up the bottle of iodine and handed it to Mrs. Buford, who unscrewed the black rubber top, squeezed the nub to draw up the liquid, and held it above my mom's arm.

"This may sting a bit." She dripped a few drops of the scarlet liquid into the cut. Mom winced. I winced. Mrs. Buford took the roll of gauze out of the box and began wrapping it around my mom's arm.

"My husband's going to love it when he gets sight of this," said my mother.

"Didn't want you comin' over?" Mrs. Buford concluded. Mom stared down at the white bandage and shook her head. "Well, it wouldn't have taken much for this to turn out a whole lot worse," said Mrs. Buford with glassy eyes as she looked over toward the dining room. "Maybe your man had the right idea."

My mom gently took hold of Mrs. Buford's hand, stopping it, for the moment, from further wrapping. She looked directly into the colored woman's large brown eyes and said, "This is exactly where I'm supposed to be. Right here. Right now."

Mrs. Buford's features softened. She began wrapping the gauze around my mom's wrist again. "My Tom . . . he's a good man. A stubborn man at times, but a good man. And a strong man. Me, I'm not so sure. Granted the good Lord has always provided strength for me when I was in need . . . brought me through some tough times, but this battle . . . I don't know . . . could be one we just aren't meant to fight."

Mrs. McGuire tore off a piece of cloth tape and handed it to Mrs. Buford. "Just know, you're not alone in this, Charlene," Sheena's mom said.

Mrs. Buford applied the tape to the gauze, securing its hold. "Thank you. Truth be told, I don't blame Mrs. Merriweather for runnin'. Not one bit. Similar feelings have filled up my head since the moment we arrived. Comin' over here like y'all did . . . Can't say if I was in your shoes I'd have done the same. Took guts."

I never thought of my mom as having guts. In so many ways she simply appeared to be my father's shadow. So when it came to heroics I always saw her more like a sidekick. Every cowboy had his sidekick: Roy Rogers had Pat Brady, the Lone Ranger had his faithful Tonto, the Cisco Kid had Poncho—and my dad had my mom. The job of the sidekick, aside from adding occasional comic relief, was to just make the hero look better by not acting nearly as brave. But after what Mrs. Buford said that day, I wasn't sure I could ever typecast my mom in that role again.

We stayed around to help the Bufords vacuum the dining room rug, and helped wash the dishes and found a piece of scrap cardboard and took scissors to it until it fit into the frame of the shattered window. Mrs. Buford took the rock and placed it in the center of the windowsill next to the broken window, in full view of all passersby.

I'm sure we all wondered exactly who might have hurled the rock through the window that day, but none of us ventured a guess, not out loud anyway. We knew that it wasn't just one person, or a person at all for that matter, but an attitude that shattered the windowpane and an attitude that spray-painted the house. And it was still out there in my neighborhood, hanging around like a fog bank with no intention of lifting anytime soon.

Was it fear that kept the other women in the neighborhood at home that day—to do laundry or dust furniture or wash and wax the kitchen floor until it sparkled and gleamed with their own reflection? And when each one caught a glimpse of her reflection, what exactly did she see—a woman content, at peace with herself, certain that she had made the right choice by staying home? Or a wife regretting she hadn't either stood up to the demands of her husband or more importantly, given in to the demands of her own conscience?

Later that day I kept riding my bike back and forth in front of Mr. Melzer's, hoping to catch sight of him. He finally stepped out onto his porch, saw me, and shouted out, "Got some cider . . . welcome to a glass if you want." He said it matter-of-factly, not like he really cared if I came in or not, and it hurt.

Inside the old farmhouse I sat down at a small table in the kitchen while Mr. Melzer grabbed a couple glasses from the cupboard and poured some cider for the two of us. I wasn't feeling comfortable around him and thought about telling him that the paint job on the Buford's house looked good, but I kept it to myself.

"You know, when I was your age," he began, as he sat down at the table with me, "I had this dog . . . a stray that wandered onto our property one day and my dad said we could keep him. Skitterish thing . . . mangy, with big brown eyes, but I loved that dog. We called him Scooter 'cause of the way he'd sometimes curl his tail 'tween his legs and scoot away when he was scared. My dad figured he must have been abused by his first owner. Anyway I was a shy kid . . . didn't have any friends to speak of, and this dog, well, he became my best friend. I mean, we did everything together . . . he even slept right there next to me on the bed at night. And one day I went into town with Scooter and there were these kids from school that I knew . . . kids that I wished were my friends, and they saw Scooter and thought he was the funniest looking dog they'd ever seen. And they started making fun of him, pokin' and proddin' him so that he'd scoot around, and they'd laugh. And so I started pokin' and proddin' him along with them. Then Scooter took one final look at me with those frightened eyes of his, and he took off running down the road. I was sick with grief. I ran home, hoping that ol' Scooter would be there waiting for me . . ." Mr. Melzer took a sip of cider.

"Was he there?" I asked.

"No. I told my dad that he just run off. I couldn't bear to tell him the truth of what I'd done. And that night . . . I don't believe I've ever prayed harder in my life. I prayed for that dog to come on back to me. The middle of the next day, I was just sitting on this tree swing out in front of my house, hating myself for what I'd done, when I looked up and there at the end of our property, Scooter was standing still, looking in my direction. I got off the swing, kneeled down, and called out his name . . . and that dog ran top speed into my waiting arms and licked my face until there wasn't a dry spot on it. And I'm not ashamed to say I cried. I didn't deserve it, but ol' Scooter had forgiven me, and it felt good. And from that moment on, I promised myself I would never do the wrong thing just 'cause it was the popular thing."

"I should have helped you paint the house."

"I'm not saying that. I'm just saying that's why *I* painted the house."

As we continued to drink the cider, I changed the subject and told him how the balloons just blew off the clothesline during Balloon Day, and how I snuck into the Goswellers' house and learned Drake could play the piano like a professional, and how I dumped all the worms into the Fisherman's Dude Ranch lake. I didn't tell him about how I danced with Mrs. Winklemeyer. But somehow we couldn't help but come back to the topic of the Bufords. When I told him that someone had thrown a rock through their window and how the glass cut my mom, the worried look on his face made me worried too.

Eighteen

INVASION OF THE MOMMY SNATCHERS

Throwing a gray, threadbare tennis ball against a wall may sound like the most basic and mundane of athletic exercises, but as a kid I always allowed my imagination to transform it into something grand. So after visiting with Mr. Melzer, there I stood on the far edge of my driveway facing the side wall of our house, the young pitching ace of the Reds' staff, my right foot planted on an old mitt, serving as the rubber. I wound up and hurled the ball against the red brick wall of our house, which, in turn, was the batter smacking it back at me. Now I was the shortstop back-handing the hot grounder, positioning myself and firing it on one hop against the wall so that it bounced up and sailed through the air on a line toward the first baseman, who was none other than me again. Striding in toward the throw, I stretched out my little hamstring to its limit and caught the ball just in time to beat the imaginary runner crossing the base. An entire nine-inning game—filled with diving stabs, leaping grabs, and game-saving plays—took place on a regular basis on my driveway, between a brick wall and a kid whose head was filled with too much fantasy for his own good.

While I was ranging to my left to snag a sharp one-hopper, my dad pulled into the driveway. He got out of our Golden Hawk, his tie hanging loose around his neck. With his briefcase dangling from his arm, he draped his sport coat over his shoulder and greeted me with, "Hey, sport." I acknowledged him with a nod but kept throwing the tennis ball against the wall. "Listen, the Reds are back in town next weekend if you're interested in taking in a game."

"Maybe," I said without looking at him.

"You okay?"

"Yep."

He stopped beside me and watched me throw. "We've probably got a little time before dinner. I'll grab the catcher's mitt—you can practice pitching some to me."

"That's okay. I'm just about done here."

Dad took a step over to me and playfully spun my army hat around backward on my head. It was all I could do to not immediately turn it back. "Come on, you could use the practice. Your first game's coming up pretty soon, right?"

He gave me one of those chummy, fatherly shoves I spoke of earlier. I knew it would lead to more roughhousing, which I was in no mood for, so I gloved the next rebound off the wall and took off for the house. "Gotta go, Dad."

"Why? What's the rush?"

I swung open the kitchen door and passed through the kitchen like a gust of wind. My mom was at the sink chopping up some carrots. "Hey, slow down. Dinner's in ten. Davy?" I turned the corner down the hallway, entered my bedroom, plopped down on the edge of the bed, and tossed my glove with the ball onto a nearby chair.

"Hi, honey," I overheard my dad greet my mom.

"Hi, dear," she returned.

"What's gotten into that son of yours?"

"Davy?"

"Yeah. He's acting sort of funny."

"Maybe you should ask him yourself."

"What's that supposed to mean?"

"Nothing. I just . . . nothing."

"What's that?" Dad had obviously spotted the bandage on my mom's arm. I stood up and walked over to my doorway, curious about his reaction.

"What's what?"

"On your arm. The bandage. Did you burn yourself?"

"Oh, no, it's just a little cut," Mom replied.

He must have grabbed a carrot off the butcher board and taken a bite, because he mumbled, "Chopping vegetables . . . dangerous work."

"Look, I'm not going to lie to you, Rob . . ."

"What? What are you talking about?"

"When we were over at the Bufords' house today with the welcoming committee —"

"You went over there?"

"Someone threw a rock through their dining room window and —"

"What?"

"A piece of glass must have —"

"That's enough, Ruth! Let me have a look at it."

"I'm fine."

"I told you not to go over there. You could have been seriously hurt."

"But I'm not."

"Well, you're not going back over to those people's house again."

I listened to the silence, waiting for it to end.

"*Are* you, dear?" my dad added.

I was tempted right then to walk down the short hallway and into the kitchen, knowing they'd most likely stop arguing if I showed up, but I also knew that things needed to be said—if not then, eventually.

"I'm worried about them," Mom finally said.

"They've brought these problems on themselves."

"No, they have not," my mom said emphatically.

"Their problems are not our problems," Dad said.

"Really? You really believe that? Then tell me, why is it affecting our lives?"

"What are you talking about?"

"You wonder why Davy is acting so strange. Maybe it's because he no longer recognizes his father."

"What? That's ridiculous! I haven't changed."

My mother lowered her voice. "Then maybe we never fully knew you," she said softly. "Because you scare me, Rob. Someone threw a rock into our neighbor's window today, and for all I know, with your attitude and the rhetoric you've been spouting around here, it could have been your doing."

"Listen, honey, I know you like to see the world through rose-colored glasses, but the fact is answers to some issues just aren't that simple. As head of this family, I do what I think is in the best interest of all of us."

"And we appreciate that, we do, but this is not a dictatorship —it's a democracy. And lately the more you try to bring this family together the more you push us away."

"Well, I'm sorry if I'm not the perfect father or the perfect husband." I could tell my father was getting mad.

"No one's asking you to be. All I know is that I feel myself disappearing a little more every day, and it frightens me. I wake up, look out my window, and wonder why on earth a group of men are digging a hole in my backyard——"

"We talked about that and——"

"No, we didn't talk about it, and that's my point. I'm not asking you to not hold the reins on this family. I'm just asking that you loosen them some . . . take a moment out of your life to see us . . . listen to us sometimes . . . give us a voice. Because if you don't, soon the rest of us will all wind up like Bobby."

"Meaning?"

"We'll tune you out, dear. We'll just tune you out. I'm glad I went over to Charlene's house today. And yes, I'll be going back. Someone threw a rock through their window, and as far as I'm concerned, it may as well have been our window."

I didn't hear my dad say anything more, so I ducked back into my room just in time to hear his heavy footsteps enter the hallway, then their bedroom, and the door slam shut behind him. I wasn't certain why, but I felt bad for him. It had something to do with his authority being undermined, his pride wounded, and I responded empathetically.

After a while I noticed the garage door had been raised and the two sides of the hood of my Dad's '53 MG were propped open. From my bedroom I could hear him tinkering around in there. And when it came time for supper, he was still out there.

On weekends or whenever Dad was home for dinner, we'd make a point of eating at the kitchen or dining room table, but otherwise we'd dine in the living room in front of the TV. But there we were—Mom, Peggy, Bobby, and I—sitting in the living room at the TV trays that we'd acquired from the S&H Green Stamp catalog after redeeming, like, a hundred books of stamps, eating our meatloaf, potatoes, and cooked carrots. We all stared at Malcolm Turner, a local newscaster, listening to his voice unnaturally rise and fall as he read the news from a stack of papers he held in his hands.

It was awkward, eerie even, to know Dad was in the vicinity but not eating with us. "Why isn't Dad eating with us again?" Peggy asked, having not been around to overhear the earlier confrontation.

"Apparently he's not hungry," Mom said. "I'm sure he'll grab something later."

But both my brother and sister could pick up the odd vibe that Mom was putting out. It was an alien mother that sat with us that night, a pod-mom whose body had been snatched and exchanged seemingly overnight. My siblings knew something was amiss, but neither were either bold or interested enough to investigate any further.

"We haven't seen much of Nancy these days," Mom said to Bobby.

"I hear she dumped him," Peggy blurted out.

"She didn't dump me," Bobby said. "We've just decided to play it cool for a while, that's all."

"She seems like a nice girl," Mom said.

Just as Malcolm Turner was signing off with a touching story of a kitten rescued from a drainpipe, I heard the spring on the kitchen screen door creek open and the door slap shut. We all turned our attention away from the scrawny, wet feline in the hands of his relieved owner and looked in the direction of the kitchen doorway. But my dad didn't appear. "Would you like me to warm up a plate for you, dear?" my mom called out.

"No, thanks," Dad's solemn voice came from the other room. "I can do it myself."

The three of us kids exchanged strained glances. As long as we had known him, our father had never taken it upon himself to warm up food of any kind except hamburgers and hot dogs on the grill. This was long before microwaves, when you actually had to place food in metal pots and pans and set them over an open flame on the stove, adjust that flame to an appropriate intensity, and then watch and stir the food so that it warmed sufficiently but didn't burn. It was a complicated ordeal to reheat food, a veritable science, one that we were sure my father had never studied or practiced. Something was definitely wrong here. A particular family dynamic was out of whack. The next move, of course, was my mom's, and we all stared in her direction waiting for her to rise and go to the aid of the helpless man she'd married, as she had done a zillion times before. And for a moment it looked like she'd do just that as she pushed her TV tray away and made a move to stand up. But she didn't. Instead her body relaxed, and she sank back into the chair. The three of us kids couldn't believe it: Mom was just going to let Dad burn his supper.

Nineteen

HEARTS FULL OF PASSION, JEALOUSY, AND HATE

I didn't really want to stick around for the kitchen blaze, so I finished eating and headed outside, where I hung out with Mouse and Jimmy for a while. Jimmy was playing in his front yard with one of those red plastic rockets that you fill with water, pump to build up pressure, then press a button and launch about a hundred feet in the air in, oh, about three seconds. If you aimed this toy at another kid within ten feet, you could take off his head, killing him instantly. Though the U.S. Military surely could have benefited from such a weapon, why it was sold as a toy at all was a mystery to children everywhere. Parents, on the other hand, seemed oblivious to the danger. Regardless, we took turns loading and pumping and retrieving the rocket, which would float down by means of a parachute. I was actually hoping Hank might come out and join us, but there was no sign of him, his sister, or of Sheena. Soon sending the rocket into the air lost its entertainment value, so I asked Mouse and Jimmy if they were interested in taking a trip to the batting cages in town.

As far as Little League went, I wasn't half bad in the field. Maybe it was all those hours of tossing the tennis ball against the wall. But when it came to batting, I was pathetic—I had such a lousy eye that I adopted the strategy of swinging at every pitch, hoping they'd be thrown down the middle of the plate. I could use the practice.

Jimmy passed, claiming his worn-out bike seat caused a lasting irritation on his butt cheeks if he rode for more than four blocks at a time. And Mouse said something about pitching machines being the first stage of robots taking over the world, and he'd have none of that. So I decided to go alone. Riding home to get my bat, I passed my brother sitting out front in his car, listening to the radio. When I came out of the house and rode down the driveway, Bobby called out, "Where you headed, little brother?"

"Batting cages."

"You want a ride?"

I skidded to a halt. Apparently the body snatchers had gotten a hold of my brother too, as his suggestion was totally out of character. I tried hard not to look too enthusiastic when I said, "I guess." I parked my bike and hopped into Bobby's convertible. Not only did he drive me there, but he took some cuts in the batting cage next to me too. He was a pretty decent player in his time, and offered some suggestions on how to improve my hitting by eliminating the hitch in my swing. After we'd exhausted our ability to swing a bat, we cruised through town with the music blasting, although the radio kept shorting out. Bobby would slam the palm of his hand against it, or fiddle with some other switches, creating a temporary fix. A defective car radio was a small price to pay for spending time with my brother. We talked about sports and girls, and he even told me a dirty joke about a farmer's daughter that I didn't understand at all, but laughed at nevertheless. The sky had grown dark by the time we approached the neon lights of the Dairy Queen for a shake. It was a great evening. This was the older brother I'd wished for, the older brother I'd searched for, but had caught only fleeting glimpses of. Maybe *this* was the person I was supposed to emulate, not my father.

"So you starting to like girls yet, or what?" he asked as we pulled up to a red light.

"Yeah, they're okay."

"Good. We'll have to double-date some time."

The Connors brothers on a double date . . . what could be cooler? I thought we were headed home when I looked out the window and realized that this wasn't a familiar route. "Hey, where are we headed?"

"I thought I'd stop by Nancy's to pick up a jacket I left there."

I wanted to say something cool, something contemporary that would make him think that I wasn't his little brother but his peer. I considered, "Man, daddy-o, it's really a drag that you and Nancy are splitsville." But it dawned on me that I'd never actually heard any teenager in real life talk like that. Only TV and movie teens used such phony lingo. So I simply said, "Sorry to hear you two split up."

"She didn't dump me," he shot back.

"I didn't say she did."

"We're just spending some time apart for a while, that's all."

I took off my army hat and began playing with the little medals that were pinned to it. Bobby looked over at the hat. "Why do you wear that old thing, anyway?"

"I don't know. I guess 'cause he gave it to me."

"That's not a real reason," he said, adding a discounting *tish*.

"Hey, at least he was an army hero. That's more than you."

"Some hero. He never even fought in the war. Did you know that? He never fought at all. Because he knew how to type, he just stayed back here in the States. Did you know that?"

I didn't know that and was disappointed about the revelation. "You don't like Dad very much, do you?" I asked straight out.

"Yeah, he's great. The man's a real prince."

Granted I was having my own issues with Dad, but I still felt the need to defend him. "What's your problem?" I asked.

"I don't have a problem."

"Then why do you hate Dad?"

"I don't hate him. I just think he's a racist and a bigot and . . . I don't know . . . we just don't connect, that's all."

"But he's your dad. I think it's against some kind of kid law not to like your dad."

"Yeah, well, I'm not a kid anymore, and you wouldn't understand."

"Why not? Because I *am* a kid?"

"Look . . . Dad's all right. But he just doesn't get me. You know? I used to look up to him . . . just like you do. When something got broke, he'd be there to fix it, you know. But somewhere along the way . . . I don't know . . . He stopped making sense to me. It's like this bomb shelter thing or the way he feels about the colored family. Anyway, he stopped having all the answers for me. I started coming up with answers of my own, answers that made more sense than his. And he didn't like that one bit. Still doesn't."

Neither of us said anything for a few blocks until he pulled up to the curb across the street from a two-story frame house. He left the car running and said, "I'll be right back." I looked out my side of the car at the neighborhood, then realized that Bobby hadn't gotten out of the car. I turned my head and saw him staring out across the street at the house. There, under a yellow porch light stood a teenage girl and boy. Caught up in some playful fondling of each other, the electricity of their laughter leapt across the street and paralyzed my brother. Bobby didn't look back at me. He just kept staring in the direction of the boy and girl, who were unaware of our presence.

My brother and I watched Nancy reach over and gently touch the boy's chin with her hand, while whispering words to him, words inaudible to us. She tenderly kissed the boy's chin. She then slowly placed her finger on the tip of the boy's nose. Again her lips whispered something as she leaned forward and kissed his nose as well. Bobby and I had both seen this routine before, though only one of us knew that to be the case. I felt an empathetic ache in my chest knowing what was coming next. Nancy raised her finger and laid it on the mouth of the boy. She leaned forward and replaced her finger with her mouth, passionately kissing the boy on the lips.

I didn't need my brother to turn around for me to know that he was destroyed. Having yet to experience similar rejection, I could only imagine exactly how he was feeling. Several phrases ran through my head as to what I could possibly say to him, but none sounded appropriate or intelligent or like they could make a bit of difference, so I just sat there pretending not to have seen what he'd seen. I fiddled with the radio dial, twisting it through a series of musical and vocal blips before settling on Rosemary Clooney singing some pop ballad.

"I'll get it some other time," Bobby said. He shifted into gear and we slowly took off from the curb. He was so busy inside his own head that he never even heard ol' Rosemary's voice until he'd driven several blocks. Finally he reached over and punched the radio button to a more contemporary channel.

Not long ago a stranger told me that hearts are bewildering things. She told me this at a time when mine was so tightly wrapped with layer after layer of insulation that I wasn't so much bewildered about it as I was indifferent. My brother's heart was anything but indifferent—not to Dad and not to Nancy. In the past I'd watched him share his heart with both and now had to watch it break. The insulation process was beginning.

The drive home seemed to take forever. Bobby pulled up in front of our house, and I grabbed my bat and got out. "You comin' in?" I asked.

"In a while," he said.

I shut the car door and said, "Thanks for taking me to the cages. It was fun."

He nodded and then laid a patch of rubber down the street. I was concerned about him, wondering where he was going and how he planned on dealing with his discovery.

The grass felt dry beneath my tennis shoes as I crossed the front yard toward the house. The flickering TV lit up the living room walls and Jack Webb's monotonous voice requesting *only the facts* escaped through the window screens, so I decided on an alternate entrance. When I'd walked around to the rear of the house, I looked over at the bomb shelter. I stepped down the several cement stairs into the now-completed concrete walls of the shelter. The full moon shone above me as I sat down against a wall that was still radiating warmth from the day's sun. I poked my finger up from beneath the brim of my army cap, leaned forward, tipped my head, and let the hat drop into my lap. I spun it around on my forefinger as a train whistle blew in the distance. My head had always felt comfortable under that hat. My mother's insistence that it be washed on a regular basis had caused it to shrink, allowing it to fit my head. It had been a good fit, but that night it felt small, tight. Maybe Bobby's inquiry as to why I wore it in the first place caught up with me. I'd always hoped someday to live up to that hat, but at that moment I felt that continuing to wear it would just be a lie. I jumped to my feet and flung it as hard and as far as I could—a UFO in flight, sailing through the night sky toward my house, spinning and humming as it climbed higher and higher, landing softly halfway up the roof.

Later that night I lay in bed in the dark, attempting to find faces in the big flowered patterns on the curtains above Bobby's bed while waiting for the sound of his car to pull into the drive. My anxiety over his tardiness resulted in my discovery of only ugly, evil faces on the drapes. The lime-green Day-Glo hands on the Bulova that lay on my nightstand informed me that Bobby's summer curfew of twelve o'clock had come and gone. Not long after, I heard the flip-flopping of my mom's slippers in the hall. The glass Mason jar on the kitchen ledge where my mom would deposit coins as payment for answered prayer each time my brother came home safely would not find a contribution in the morning. Her vivid imagination that envisioned Bobby's car turned over somewhere in a ditch or Bobby lying in some emergency room bleeding to death kept her awake most nights just sitting in a living room chair until his safe arrival, as if her mere presence there might be enough to prevent tragedy.

Though my bedroom was at the opposite end of the house, the knock on the back entry door to the kitchen was loud enough to startle me. I curled out of bed and over to my doorway. I poked my head around the corner and looked down the hallway in time to see Mom cross into the kitchen; I heard the back door open.

"Yes, what is it?" she asked the visitor. I scampered down the hallway and peeked into the kitchen.

"I'm really sorry to disturb you so late, Mrs. Connors," the visitor said. And although the figure standing behind the screen door was mostly obscured from view by my mom, I recognized the voice as that of Allison Hoffman.

"Do you know what time it is?" my mom asked in a harsh tone.

"Yes, and I'm sorry, but—"

"What do you want?" my mom said, irritated.

"Well, I'm afraid I have something here that belongs to you." Mrs. Hoffman turned away, drawing my mom's attention to the darkness behind her. Mom pushed open the screen door and leaned her head outside but didn't immediately respond. As I entered the kitchen, her fingers briefly groped for the wall switch, flipping on the porch light.

"Oh, my heavens!" my mom said, rushing outside. I ran toward the screen door, caught it before it shut, and saw my mom bend down over a figure curled up on the lawn. "Bobby!" My mom shook him. He briefly stirred, then resorted to his lifeless status.

A sleepy-eyed Mrs. Hoffman was dressed in a tight pair of red pedal pushers, her blonde hair unevenly brushed and lacking its usual luster. "This was as far as I could walk him before he passed out," she said. "He'll be all right. He's just drunk."

My mom jerked her head toward Mrs. Hoffman. *"Drunk?"* my mom said, shooting daggers out of her eyes.

"Well, I know it's not—"

"Why is my son drunk?" she yelled, then, realizing the possibility of waking neighbors, lowered her voice, but with the same intensity asked, "And why is he with you?"

"Well, I was just—"

"Is this a new method of tutoring?" My mom rose to her feet and boldly approached Mrs. Hoffman. "You get your students all liquored up and then teach them *Romeo and Juliet*? Is that it?"

"No! Of course not! Listen, I had no idea that Bobby was—"

"Hey, what's going on?" my dad asked, joining me at the door. Wearing his bathrobe and slippers, he stepped outside. "Is that Bobby? Is he all right?" He walked over to Bobby's body and knelt down beside him.

"He's drunk!" said Mom. "This woman . . . this . . ." I was pretty sure she wanted to be specific in her description and utter the word *divorcée*, but she didn't. She managed to hold her tongue for a few more beats before blurting out, "This . . . harlot!" I wasn't sure what a harlot was, but by her tone I knew it was even worse than a divorcée. "She got our son drunk!"

"That's not true!" said Mrs. Hoffman. "Look, all I know is your son showed up at my house uninvited when I was about to get ready for bed—"

"Oh, my!" my mom said, putting her hand to her mouth.

"And he was already three sheets to the wind when he arrived.

In fact he stood out on my back patio outside my window and then he started . . ."

"What? He started what?" asked Mom.

Watering the plants? Mowing the lawn? Requesting a tutoring session? None of us could imagine what action of my brother's Allison Hoffman was so reluctant to share.

"He started singing," she finally said.

"What?" my baffled parents asked simultaneously.

"Singing. Sort of . . . serenading me." You could tell she was embarrassed for everyone involved as she picked at her fingernail.

I couldn't help it—I laughed out loud, unfortunately bringing attention to myself. Mom spotted me. "What are you doing up, young man? Go to bed."

I closed the screen door, but remained behind it, not about to leave in the middle of the show.

"Look," Mrs. Hoffman began, "I don't know what provoked Bobby to get intoxicated or to come by my house and do what he did, but you have a good boy here." She gestured toward the lifeless lump on the ground. "I enjoy tutoring him. He's bright, attentive . . . maybe more attentive than I imagined, but I'm pretty certain this is an isolated event."

My mom looked confused. "Robert, please do something about this."

Dad got up and walked over to Mrs. Hoffman and took her hand. "Thank you, Allison, for bringing our son home safely."

"You're welcome. I just hope he doesn't remember too much in the morning." Mrs. Hoffman started off toward her house, but stopped beside by my mom. "I'm sorry if I caused you trouble."

Mom looked convicted, but she didn't apologize for her

words, instead just looked away as Mrs. Hoffman walked past her, fading into the darkness.

"Why don't you go inside, dear," Dad said. "Davy and I'll take care of this." I held the door open for Mom as she walked into the house. Preparing for the worst, I joined Dad beside Bobby, who was still out cold. Then, instead of shaking Bobby until he came to his senses or yelling at him for getting blitzed and humiliating him for serenading his tutor, Dad simply squatted over his oldest son and scooped him up, lifting him off the grass until Bobby was cradled in his arms like a baby . . . a very big baby.

"Get the door, sport," he said in a strained voice. I walked over and held the door open as Dad turned sideways, allowing Bobby's head to avoid colliding with the doorway.

A half-asleep Peggy appeared in the kitchen. "What's going on? Is that Bobby? Is he dead?"

"Drunk," I informed her.

"Well, you're going to punish him, right, Dad?" she said, yawning and following him. "Because that's a really bad thing to do."

"Peggy, go back to bed," Dad said. She turned into her room as I followed Dad into our dark bedroom, where he gently deposited Bobby onto his bed. I crawled into my own and watched Dad slip off Bobby's shoes, unbuckle his pants and pull them off, dropping them onto the floor.

Then my father covered up my brother with the cotton sheet and remained sitting there on the bed for a while, looking down at his son's face. Dad pushed the shock of hair away from Bobby's forehead, revealing the birthmark. He leaned down and gently kissed it. Just like Nancy had done. Except this kiss wasn't fleeting. It was a kiss of entirety, a kiss that not only embodied those moments of love and pride and sheer joy that a father can feel for a son, but one that seemed to dissolve all the times when anger or resentment or disappointment were my father's feelings of choice toward my brother. Unlike Nancy's kisses, this kiss was filled with history, family history, and that's why it would stick. I wished Bobby had been conscious enough to experience it. Then Dad looked over at me and said, "Let this be a lesson to you."

"Yes, sir," I said. "I thought you'd want to kill him."

"So did I. Life's full of all sorts of little surprises."

"Aren't you going to punish him?"

"Yes. But the way he's going to feel when he wakes up tomorrow morning is going to be worse than any punishment I could give him. Good night, sport."

"'Night, Dad."

With that my father walked out of the bedroom and closed the door down to a crack, allowing only the dim glow of the nightlight to slip inside. I looked over at the big flowered curtains over my brother's bed and wondered for the first time why my mother hadn't chosen a more appropriate curtain design for a boy's room. Cowboys and Indians would have been okay, or even some kind of plaid pattern, but flowers? What was she thinking? Once again I tried to discover faces hidden within the pattern, and this time came up with an overly excited clown and a happy Martian. And while looking for more, I fell asleep.

Twenty

DUCK-AND-COVER DRILL

Saturday arrived, and, as Dad had predicted, my brother spent a great deal of the morning kneeling on the bathroom floor, his arms clutching the toilet bowl to steady the spinning room while he barfed his brains out. The late night theatrics had taken a toll on me, leaving my paper-delivery aim less than accurate and my mood that of a cantankerous old man, complaining to myself about everything from early rising squirrels with bad sidewalk etiquette to the sun's slowness in showing itself. After I'd finished my route, I tried to go back to sleep, but the intense, intermittent sound of upchucking kept me awake and gave my own stomach similar notions.

I finally got out of bed and out of the house and ran into Sheena riding her bike around, Sunny bounding along at her side. Before she even took the time to greet me, she said, "Where's your hat?"

"I don't know," I answered.

"I miss it," she said.

"It's been gone for less than a day. How can you miss it?"

"I don't know, but I do. It's like a part of you is missing."

True, it had become as much an identifying feature as my nose, and without it I not only felt a tad naked, but incomplete. Sheena finally let it go, and we rode our bikes over to the Bufords to see if Hank and Amelia wanted to go out to Oakfield to see the tree house. Standing out on the driveway, Mr. Buford was bending over the hood of his yellow Cadillac, buffing the finish with a cloth, using small circular motions. The car sparkled under the summer sun.

"Hi," Sheena greeted him as we rolled up the driveway and hopped off our bikes.

"Hello. Can I help you two?" Mr. Buford asked, straightening up and folding the rag over.

"We were looking for Hank and Amelia," Sheena said. Sunny pranced over to Mr. Buford, who bent over and briefly petted him.

"Good boy. They're out with their momma, shopping for some clothes."

Just then Ron Miller and Vern Borkowski walked by, the latter pushing a wheelbarrow filled with a mound of dirt. They looked over at Mr. Buford. "Mornin'," Mr. Miller said in a friendly tone.

"Good morning, gentlemen," Mr. Buford said with formality, his voice tinged with reservation.

"Say, that's a beaut," Mr. Miller said, checking out the Cadillac as Mr. Borkowski set down the wheelbarrow.

"Thank you," Mr. Buford said.

"I have an old '36 Packard I've restored," Mr. Miller said. "They become like part of the family, don't they?"

Looking slightly less defensive, Mr. Buford leaned on his car, smiled, and answered, "Yeah, this is definitely my baby."

Mr. Borkowski pulled a rag from his back pocket and wiped the perspiration off his brow. "You people love 'em Caddies, doncha?" he said. "Got them white walls and skirts . . . yep, very classy, very classy, indeed."

Sheena and I got on our bikes, but I hesitated before taking off, wanting to see where this might lead. Mr. Buford detected a change in the tone of his visitors and went back to polishing the hood of his car.

"So shiny and not a ding on it," Mr. Borkowski said. "Yeah, you're a lucky man to be able to afford such a nice automobile. Just a word of caution." Mr. Buford looked up at Mr. Borkowski while continuing to buff. "You seem to be leaking some sort of fluid here."

It was easy even for me to see that the considerable water that was puddling along the driveway from beneath his car was simply what remained from the washing he had just given it.

"I believe that's only runoff," Mr. Buford said.

"Oh, I don't know 'bout that. Bring it down to my shop sometime. Fix you right up," Mr. Borkowski said, stashing his rag in his back pocket again. "Otherwise . . . a big leak like that . . . could be dangerous. And you wouldn't want anything to happen to that *baby* of yours now, would ya?"

Mr. Borkowski lifted up on the handles of the wheelbarrow and he and Mr. Miller began on their way again. "Nice meetin' ya, neighbor," said Mr. Borkowski, letting out a quiet, snorty laugh, while Mr. Miller offered a limp wave good-bye.

Sheena and I took off down the sidewalk, but I kept looking back at Mr. Buford. He stood with his hands on his hips and didn't take his eyes off the two men until they were well down the street.

I rode alongside Sheena, the comforting buzz of lawnmowers in my ears and the smell of freshly cut grass — my favorite smell in the world — sweeping up my nostrils. As we were swerving our bikes down the middle of Briarbrook, I heard, "Young man!" At first I didn't see the speaker because she seemed to blend into the thick display of roses that lined the inside of her property, but there was Mrs. Gosweller, wearing a straw hat and work gloves and holding a spade in her hand, leaning forward on her elbow on the crossbar of her gate. I stopped my bike. It was the first time I'd ever seen her in her yard.

"Young man, come over here, please!" She didn't sound very happy about something, although up until then, that was the only way I'd ever heard her sound. I walked my bike over to the fence, and Sheena followed behind me. "What is your name?"

"Davy. Davy Connors. Look, if you're going to call the cops on me for the other night —"

"You *are* the paperboy for the neighborhood, correct?"

"Yes."

"So how would one go about applying for a subscription to the *Trib*?"

"Oh, well, I can get you an order form today, and we can probably start delivering your paper tomorrow."

"Excellent." She turned her attention to Sheena. "And you are?"

"Sheena McGuire, ma'am."

"Nice to meet you, Sheena McGuire," she said as if she were greeting an adult.

"I hope you don't mind . . ." Sheena began.

"What's that, dear?"

"I hope you don't mind, but sometimes I sit out here at night so I can listen to your son play his music. We thought it was you. It's very pretty."

"It *is* pretty, and no, I don't mind. It's a shame about the new neighbors. About their house, I mean. I don't suppose they know who was responsible."

"No, I don't think they do," I said.

"Being different . . . it's not a popular thing to be, is it?"

"I suppose not." I answered, turning my bike around. "Well, we'd better—"

"Mr. Connors?"

"Yes?"

"I apologize for throwing you out of my house in that fashion."

"You mean on my butt."

"Precisely."

"It's okay. You were right. It's your house—I shouldn't have snuck in like that."

"Well, maybe we both learned a little something that evening. And Mr. Connors?"

"Yes, ma'am?"

"You won't forget the order form."

"No. In fact I'll get it for you right now."

"Oh, and Mr. Connors?"

"Yes, ma'am?"

"Don't you find it interesting that the fluorescent green color of your bike is identical to the color of this ghastly line on the sidewalk at the edge of my property?" Mrs. Gosweller was a very perceptive woman.

"I'll see if I can somehow wash that off for you."

"It would be appreciated."

As I walked my bike out into the street and kicked my leg over the seat, I felt recharged, like finally something had turned for the good, like things were looking up. Sheena smiled over at me as she climbed aboard her bike. "Race you around Sleepy Hollow and back to my house," I said. "I'll give you four."

"Wait, I'm not ready," she said.

"One-thousand one . . ."

"Davy—wait," she panicked, struggling to turn her bike around and begin riding.

"One-thousand two . . ."

Finally her long legs began circling with the pedals.

"One-thousand three . . . One-thousand four. Here I come!"

I waited a couple seconds more before taking off after her. She had a good eight lengths on me at the start, but by the time we turned Melzer's corner for the homestretch, I had caught her. As I blew past her I looked back and flashed a cocky face. Her eyes and mouth were both wide open, like the expressions of the faces of Cyrus and his family when they saw the ghosts.

I turned around in time to see Mr. Buford's Cadillac backing out of his driveway directly in front of me, but not in time to do anything about it. Likewise, Mr. Buford had caught sight of me, but only in time to react by stomping on his brakes. The screech of his brakes was followed closely by the sound of my front wheel colliding with his back fender directly in front of those classic red taillights. My bike basket collapsed in an instant, and I was launched like a daredevil out of a cannon, over the twisting handlebars up into the stratosphere.

As I caught a glimpse of my exceptionally shiny reflection on the trunk crossing beneath me, and then the asphalt rushing at me, I realized I had a rather important decision to make. *What is it I can do to make this as painless as possible?* I wondered. No other experience in my short life had really prepared me for this moment. Diving into a swimming pool might have been close, but that wasn't going to help me out in this instance, since I'd never attempted diving into a frozen pool. Clearing the entire width of the car spoke highly of the impressive speed at which I'd been traveling, but the impending impact of the ground seemed sure to negate the athletic significance of that effort. Neither sliding on the side of my face nor landing on my head seemed a viable option.

Then another survival tactic came to mind: Although I was quite certain it would serve no practical purpose in the event of a nuclear explosion, the duck-and-cover drill might just be worth a try here. And so I ducked my head down into my chest, pulled up my knees, and covered my head. I could feel the asphalt strike the back of my arms and roll down my neck, continuing down my spine and across my rear, at which point I believe my body skipped like a flat stone being skimmed across the surface of a lake. But when my body came to a rest twenty feet away from the Cadillac, I was dazed and scraped up, but otherwise, remarkably, okay. Maybe Newton had been at work again.

Mr. Buford rushed over to me. "Oh, Lord! Are you all right?"

I remained on my back for a moment. "I'm sorry. I didn't see you," I said, attempting to sit up.

"Don't try to move. Just take it easy. Where do you hurt?" He noticed a rip in my blue jeans, just below my kneecap where I was already bleeding pretty good. He lightly touched it. "How 'bout your leg? Does it hurt here?"

"A little."

The sound of the collision had drawn other neighbors out of their homes to gather around us. A concerned Sheena came running up. "You okay, Davy?" Mr. Buford continued to search around my arms and legs for a possible break.

"I think I'm all right," I said to Mr. Buford. "I messed up your car, didn't I?"

"Don't worry about that. Let's just make sure you're all in one piece."

With Mr. Buford's help I started to try to get to my feet. It wasn't until I stood up that I saw my father, wearing a look of outrage, run up to us and stiff-arm Mr. Buford out of the way. "Let go of him!" he yelled right in Mr. Buford's face.

Dad took hold of my arm but I tried to shake him loose. "What are you doing, Dad? I'm fine. Let go."

"Why the devil weren't you looking where you were going?" he shouted at Mr. Buford. "You could have killed him!"

I pulled away from my dad. "It wasn't his fault. I wasn't looking where—"

"Of course it was his fault! He shouldn't have been—"

"Dad! Just shut up and leave me alone!"

My father immediately slapped me across my face. Someone gasped. I didn't blame Dad. He was as caught up in the moment as I had been. Still, I felt ashamed. As I limped away in the direction of our house, I could hear Sheena whimpering. My dad stood there in the middle of the street looking embarrassed for a bit longer. Finally he walked over to the other side of the Cadillac and picked up my mangled heap of bicycle parts and hauled it back home.

Twenty-One

A PALMOLIVE SANDWICH, PLEASE . . . HOLD THE KLEENEX

Discipline in our family was doled out almost exclusively by my father in a swift, systematic method. That simple little motion of unbuckling his leather belt and slipping it through his pant loops somehow made the anticipation of the swatting more agonizing than the actual swats themselves. Since most of our indiscretions occurred when he was at work, my dad wasn't emotionally invested in our wrongdoing, so when he did dish out the punishment, he did so without anger. But since this time he was the offended party, I expected the worst.

As I waited for my dad and his brown cowhide belt to arrive, I pulled out my big animation book by Preston Blair, an artist who worked for Disney on movies like *Pinocchio* and *Bambi*. The spine-frayed paperback book was filled with goofy-looking animals: ducks in suits, rabbits in boxing trunks, dancing hippos, and so on. Most examples demonstrated gradual stages in the drawing of a particular character to help teach the correct way to go about developing characters, but I never had the patience. I always skipped right past the intermediary stages and copied the final cartoon. I could just look at a cartoon and, with relative ease, draw a final illustration that had accurate proportions. This seldom failed to surprise and delight me.

It was as though I'd owned this skill from the first time I attempted to draw, an ability that I assumed came easily to everyone. And when I had discovered that it didn't, it made me feel unique, special. But the absolute best part was when I finished a piece of "art" and showed it to my parents, they always responded first with surprise that I was able to copy so well, and then with praise and pride in *me*. It was sort of magical: Do a drawing, get some love . . . do a drawing, get some more love. I would spend a great deal of my later life with pencil and paintbrush in hand, searching for that magic feeling again and again and wondering where it had gone, or if it was ever really there in the first place.

I was copying the image of a dog with a bone in its mouth onto one of the pieces of cardboard that came back in my dad's dress shirts from the cleaners each week when the door opened up and in walked . . . my mom.

"Where's Dad?" I asked.

"He got a call . . . had to go to the hospital for a while," my mom answered in a soft, somber voice.

I had heard the phone ring a few minutes earlier. "Why? Who's there?"

Mom walked up to the end of my bed. "Are you feeling all right? No big pains?"

"My knee hurts a little and my neck's sort of stiff, but I'm okay."

"You know, Davy, you can't just go around telling your father or me to shut up."

"I know. I'm sorry. Who's in the hospital?"

"You're supposed to honor your father and your mother. You're supposed to respect your parents, especially your father."

"But you don't respect him," I said.

"What?" she said, obviously offended.

"You don't respect him," I repeated with a little less gusto.

"Don't be silly. In the first place he's not my father, and secondly—"

"But he's your husband. Aren't you supposed to respect your husband?" I knew it was a bold and disrespectful thing for a kid to say to his mom, and even though I wasn't positive I entirely understood the concept of respect, confusion or lack of knowledge never stopped me from arguing a point.

Peggy appeared at the doorway behind Mom as she sat down on the end of the bed and tilted her head to get a look at the drawing of the dog. "It's true I don't always agree with his decisions or how he feels about a particular subject—"

"Like the Bufords?" I wasn't letting up.

"Yes. Like the Bufords. But I believe in his heart he's always done what he feels is best for this family, and I respect that."

"No, you don't."

"Don't talk back to me, David Connors, or I'll wash that mouth of yours out with soap until you've got bubbles coming out of your ears."

Peggy stepped into the room. "You always say that, Mom, but you never do it!"

"Peggy, please, this is none of your business," said Mom.

"You stood up to Dad," I continued. "I overheard you."

"Davy!"

Peggy crossed her arms. "And he was eavesdropping, Mom. Punish him! Punish him now!"

"Shut up, Peggy," I said.

"See, he did it again," Peggy said. "He told Dad to shut up, and now he told me to shut up. Aren't you going to do anything?"

A weird look came over my mom's face. "Get the soap!"

A beat later Peggy shot out of my room, but I knew my mom well enough to know she was bluffing . . . didn't I?

"Mom—you said Dad scared you and that you didn't care what he thought—you were going to meet with Mrs. Buford again anyway. Doesn't that mean that you don't respect him?"

"Peggy's right—you shouldn't eavesdrop."

"Well, you shouldn't lie. It's a sin. If you were Catholic, you'd have to confess to some guy in a dark closet—did you know that? And you'd have to say a bunch of haily Marys too."

The dumbfounded expression on my mom's face made it clear that I'd wandered a bit too far off course. "When you're older you'll understand."

"I'm old enough now to know that you don't respect Dad and he doesn't respect you, and Bobby doesn't respect Dad. . . . Nobody around here respects anybody else, so why should I?"

Peggy ran into the room tearing the wrapper off a new bar of Palmolive soap. She held it high in the air. "Here it is, Mom! Here's the soap!"

Maybe it was the enthusiasm with which Peggy delivered the line, or maybe Mom was legitimately tired of my insolence. Either way, they were on me like lions on a zebra. Peggy leaned over me with a crazed look, pinning my wrists on either side of my head against my bed, while my mom sat on my thighs, rendering the lower half of my body useless. I locked my jaw while my lips clamped down, my head twisting back and forth to the sides to avoid the oncoming bar of soap that my mother mashed against my mouth. She was much stronger than I'd ever given her credit for.

"Open up!" Mom yelled at me. "I'm not kidding around here, buster! Open your mouth right now!" The force of the soap against my mouth finally split my lips apart, as it pressed against my teeth and seeped through their crevices, serving as a sort of appetizer for the main course. It tasted as nasty as rumored by other unfortunate users of the highly offensive words *shut up.*

"Get him, Mom!" Peggy howled.

I could last no longer. My mouth opened, and the bar of soap slid inside onto my tongue; my teeth clamped down on the bar to keep it from slamming up against my uvula and sliding down my throat—which could result in the Little Rascals' Alfalfa syndrome, where I would release soap bubbles into the air with every word I spoke for days. My mother gave the bar a final twist to assure a flavor sensation before releasing her grasp. I spit the bar of soap out onto the bed, but the damage had been done. The taste was worse than all vegetables combined. Spinach, cauliflower, broccoli, lima beans, and peas—bring them on—they were a hot fudge sundae in comparison.

I popped several tissues from a box next to the bed and crammed them into my mouth in an attempt to wipe the soapy coat off my tongue, but the Kleenex stuck to the inside of my mouth. The taste would not be leaving me anytime soon. It was a horrible experience—a punishment that actually had a good chance of curing me of the crime. I looked over at the two women. My mother looked pained, while my sister gleamed with elation.

As I continued to spit soapy saliva into a handful of dry tissues, Mom walked to the doorway and turned back around. "Sometimes parents are just going to disagree with each other. It's part of life. I don't ever want to hear you disrespect your father or me again! Do you hear me? You're grounded for the rest of the weekend."

"Does that mean I don't have to go to church tomorrow?"

"If you aren't the first one in the car, you'll be grounded for the entire week along with your brother," she said, walking toward the door as I worked at scraping the soap residue off my bubbling tongue with my fingernails.

Peggy couldn't resist having the last word. "Guess you won't be needing dinner tonight, eh, little brother?"

"Peggy, let's go." Mom escorted my sister out the door and closed it behind her.

I felt I had won the argument, but winning had never felt so lousy to me. I wanted to call my mom back in and say, *I'm sorry, and I won't ever say "shut up" again*, and then have her take a look at my drawing and tell me how much she liked it.

Though I still lay wide awake in bed, it was past midnight when I heard the chirping of crickets give way to the familiar sound of my dad's car pulling into the driveway. Bobby had already fallen asleep. My parents' bedroom was right across the hall from ours, and it wasn't long before I could hear them whispering. I sat up in bed to catch snippets of their conversation.

"Heart attack . . . emergency surgery . . . didn't make it." I'd heard enough to know someone had died. I didn't want to interrupt them or have to deal with my dad, but I needed to know who had bought the farm. An uncle? An aunt, maybe?

Immediately I made a short mental list of old people who I hoped it wasn't: Mr. Melzer, for obvious reasons; Grandma Workmeister, who was easily the nicest person on the planet; and my Uncle George, on whom I could play just about any practical joke and live to tell about it. I came up with a longer list of old people who wouldn't cause me to lose any sleep over them if they'd kicked the bucket that night: Grandpa Workmeister, who never had a kind word for me and always made fun of Bobby's birthmark; Aunt Mildred, whose breath was so toxic it could be canned and used as an insecticide; Mr. Feebee, the ancient, gaunt usher at church who wore obnoxious bow ties and always gave me the stink-eye when I'd put my handful of pennies in the offering plate; and Mrs. Chamberlain, my evil music teacher who loved to call on me and my defective vocal cords for solos surely just to amuse herself and cause me embarrassment in front of my peers.

Before I could come up with another name on my hit list, I heard my dad say, "He was such a big man . . . I guess his heart just gave out."

And I knew. Two-Ton Trzcinski had died. He was too young to be on either of my lists, too nice a man to be on God's list. I rolled over toward the wall and let the tears flow down my cheeks onto my pillow. Right then and there, I lost something. I couldn't define what it was, but I could feel it escape from the deepest part of me. I didn't hear my parents say anything else to each other after that. I pictured my mom holding my dad, comforting him like a little kid who'd lost his dog. I couldn't be sure that was the case, but I hoped it was.

A few minutes later my bedroom door squeaked open

farther, allowing a faint light to brighten my wall. As a man's silhouette grew on the wall, I didn't move. The smell of Old Spice settled on top of me, but I didn't turn around. The shadow remained on my wall, motionless, like it was painted on. Part of me wanted to turn right over and sob openly for the loss of Two-Ton and for the loss of the bond that my father and I had once held between us. But I never moved. And before I knew it, the shadow faded, the faint light disappeared, and he was gone.

Twenty-Two

DEATH IS JUST A BOWL OF CHERRIES

I had actually thought about loading the morning papers into my dad's wheelbarrow and pushing it around the neighborhood, but as my mom woke me she said, "After you fold the papers, I'll help you load them into the car." And so it seemed all was forgiven as my mom drove me around the neighborhood streets, me hurling papers out from the passenger's seat. We were halfway through the route when she pulled over to the curb and jerked the gearshift into park.

"Why are we stopping?" I asked.

"Davy, there something I need to tell you."

When I saw the sad expression on her face, I knew what she was about to say and considered telling her so, but instead I listened as she gently informed me of the untimely demise of Two-Ton Trzcinski. And even though I'd already heard the news, and even though I tried to imagine myself smacking a home run at that moment, I almost cried all over again.

Seldom had I seen my father as solemn as he was that morning at the breakfast table. After informing Bobby and Peggy of Two-Ton's death, he had hardly spoken a word until he finally came up with this word . . .

"Church . . . I think I'd like to go to church this morning," he said to my mom.

The three of us kids just looked at each other, amazed, but I think we knew the death of Two-Ton had something to do with his decision. My dad had always admired Richard—his real name—Trzcinski, not only for his ability to entertain, but for his friendship and maybe even for his faith.

"Good," Mom replied. Though my parents hadn't seen eye-to-eye of late, Mom was obviously delighted at the prospect of sitting beside her husband at church, as was apparent by the sudden spring in her step as she collected the breakfast plates.

I dressed before everyone else and walked outside to have a look at the cherry tree, half expecting the leaves on the three-foot tall tree to be wilting or at least turning yellow out of respect to Two-Ton, but they were bright green with new growth. I stood before it, feeling sad all over again.

"I'm sorry," my mother's voice behind me said. I didn't turn around.

"For what?"

"For how badly you have to feel about this."

"I feel okay," I said, still not turning around. She knew better. She was a mom. She gently placed her hands on my shoulders.

"He had such a great attitude, didn't he?" Mom said. "I think he really saw life that way . . . just like a bowl of cherries . . . sweet and fresh and delicious. And he shared that pure joy for life with everyone he met. You couldn't be around him without feeling good. I'd love to be able to do that for people, wouldn't you?"

"I guess." I wasn't exactly sure what it was in Two-Ton that allowed him to laugh so easily, but I, too, had admired that part of him. But I suspected if I didn't already have that particular gift, I would never possess it.

"Maybe in a couple years we'll see some fruit. And we can give it away like Two-Ton did, and maybe somebody will plant those seeds like we did and pass along the opportunity to partake in the sweet things in life."

As usual there was a deeper message somewhere in my mom's words; I just wasn't in the mood to go on a scavenger hunt. "You all ready for church?" she asked me.

"Yeah. Mom?"

"What?"

"It won't be easy, but I'll try harder not to say shut up anymore."

"Good. I'm glad."

As we walked past the bomb shelter and into the house, I said, "Soap really tastes lousy, you know that?"

"As a matter of fact, I do know that," she said.

I can't tell you how great it made me feel to know that my grandma had washed out my mom's mouth with soap. I'm not sure why. Maybe because it made her seem more real, more human. "Really? What kind did you eat?"

"Ivory."

"How was it?"

"Awful. Very lathery."

"No kidding. That's great, Mom. That's really great."

We walked back into the house together, bonded by the same punishment.

As I followed my family into the sanctuary of our community church, there was Mr. Feebee, decked out in his latest lame polka dot bow tie. As he handed me the service program, his deep-pitted eyes met with mine and remorse shot through my body. I actually felt regret for having placed him on my approved list of possible death candidates. Aside from being gaunt and having bad taste in clothing, he wasn't so bad. Truth was, I hardly knew him. But then when, simply to annoy me, he wouldn't let go of the service program once he'd handed it to me, I disliked him all over again.

We paraded down the aisle and took Mom's familiar place on the right side of the sanctuary, in the fifth row of pews. Immediately Mrs. Templeton in front of us turned around and said, "My, how nice, Ruth. You have the whole family here today."

"Yes, it is," Mom replied. And it was. For the moment all the stuff that had divided us seemed irrelevant. I scanned the program to see what the sermon message would be: *Love Thy Neighbor.* It was too perfect—as if Mom herself had conferred with the reverend and convinced him that this would be the ideal sermon for her husband. Surely he'd embrace it, change his ways, and we could all live in peace again.

The choir director took her place at center stage, gesturing for the congregation to stand along with the purple-robed choir. The organist played a simple intro and everyone began to sing "Great Is Thy Faithfulness." Well, almost everyone.

It was the manner in which the silver-hairs in the church would lift their heads high and sing at the top of their irritating falsetto voices that convinced me that hymns were intended for old ladies and not for me, so I basically refused to sing them. Besides, Mrs. Chamberlain had already sealed my insecurity about singing out loud. My silence generally would irritate my mom, but not today. Her husband was standing next to her at his aisle seat, his deep voice singing out strong. Occasionally during the hymn Mom would glance behind her, as if she was looking for someone.

During the second verse I felt a hand on my shoulder. I turned around, and there were Hank and Amelia standing behind me, Mrs. Buford directly behind my mom, and Mr. Buford behind Dad. I smiled at Hank but my stomach felt uneasy. When Mom got a similar tap on her shoulder from Mrs. Buford, they both broke into smiles. Dad wasn't even aware of the Bufords until out of the corner of his eye he caught Mom leaning back over the pew to give Charlene half a hug. He immediately tightened his body, stood up straight, and stared out into the space before him.

At the conclusion of the song, Reverend Smith stepped up to the podium on the altar and said, "The Bible says that God's people will be identified by their love for one another, so at this time please greet each other in that love and in the name of Jesus."

But before he could get all the words out, Dad had curled around the corner of the pew and strode down the aisle toward the back of the sanctuary. I could see the disappointment on my mom's face. Bobby gazed down the aisle with a look of concern.

"Where's your dad going?" Hank asked.

"Don't know," I answered.

Shaking off the obvious awkwardness that he felt, Mr. Buford bent down and shook my hand. "How are you feeling, young man? We had quite a collision, you and me. I'll bet that bike of yours is quite a mess, huh?"

"Yes, it is, sir."

"Any aches and pains?" he asked.

"No, I'm fine, Mr. Buford."

"Good. And don't you worry about my car. It's not flesh and blood, you know. It's just a car. Right?"

"Right," I answered, though my mind was squarely on my dad. Bobby and Peggy greeted the Bufords for the first time. All through the service I wished my dad had stayed. I'm sure my mom felt the same way. I was too upset to even look at Mr. Feebee when the offering was passed and I deposited my handful of change into the plate. And the first half of the sermon was pretty good. Even had some jokes in there that my dad might have laughed out loud at. I wondered where he was and what thoughts might be filling his head. Finally I excused myself to go to the bathroom, hurried down the aisle, through the foyer, and out into the sunlight. I crossed through the parking lot and could see my dad slouching down in the driver's seat of our car staring out the windshield. Bravely I walked over to the car and climbed in the passenger seat.

Dad looked puzzled. "Is church over already?"

"It is for me," I said.

"I don't understand. What are you doing here? Did you walk out early?"

"Yes."

"Well, you can't just walk out in the middle of the service."

"You did."

"Yeah, well, maybe you shouldn't try so hard to be like me!"

He hadn't yelled at me like that in a long time. I bolted out of the car and rushed back inside, feeling certain that I didn't want to be like him, but in some ways I couldn't help it. I couldn't walk back into the sanctuary, not with tears running down my cheeks, so I went downstairs and sat in the stairwell until I heard the organ music start up again indicating the end of the service. Mom was upset with me and asked me where I'd been. I told her I had been feeling sick, which wasn't very far from the truth.

Twenty-Three

TAP, CRACKLE, AND POP

During the school year I could never really enjoy Sunday evenings, knowing that I'd already put off doing my homework all weekend and that I'd have to begin five days of suffering first thing in the morning. But on summer evenings I usually watched *The Ed Sullivan Show* without a care in the world. On this night, though, I had a lot of things on my mind, and when the hour was over, I felt guilty for having forgotten them, even for a moment. My dad had been suspiciously absent from the traditional family viewing of *The Ed Sullivan Show* that night, and my brother, possibly still laying low from his late-night drunken episode, was also AWOL.

As the credits ran, I realized that I had yet to take a good look at the damage I'd done to my bike, so I decided to pay a visit to the garage. Dusk was settling on the neighborhood as I lifted up on the garage door with all my strength, revealing Bobby's old Studebaker. A bare bulb hanging down from a cord wrapped around an overhead beam lit up my brother's feet sticking out the driver's side door, while the intermittent blasts of Chuck Berry belted from the car radio.

"Hey." Bobby's head peeked up over the dash to get a look at his company.

"Hey," I answered. "What are you up to?"

"Thought it was time to do battle with this radio." I walked over to the vacant side of the two-car garage, where my bicycle sat bent and bruised in a heap. Bobby looked over in my direction. "I heard about that. Nice work." I attempted to stand the bike up and straighten out the handlebars, but it was a lost cause. "So is it true that you told Dad to shut up right there in the middle of the street . . . right there in front of everybody?"

"'Fraid so."

"You got some gonads, little brother."

"Got my mouth washed out with soap for it," I said. "But at least I didn't get drunk and spend my Saturday barfing my guts out. You're lucky you only got grounded for a week. What'd Dad say to you about getting drunk?"

"We haven't had that conversation yet. So I'm curious . . . how'd I get home?"

"You don't know?"

"Been sort of afraid to ask."

"Mrs. Hoffman brought you home."

"Oh, shhhh . . ." His voice faded in despair as he slid back down beneath the dash. "I was hoping that was just a dream," his muffled voice said. His head poked up again. "Were you there . . . Were you awake when I came home?"

"Front row seat. Saw the whole show." It took all the will-power I possessed to keep my mouth shut about the serenading, but since I'd recently experienced humiliation myself, I didn't wish it upon anyone. A tool of some sort that Bobby was holding under the dash clinked against metal, and Chuck's guitar riff cut out completely.

"I don't even remember getting into bed," Bobby said.

"That's because you were out cold."

"So how'd I get there?"

"Dad carried you in . . . laid you down on the bed . . . covered you up."

"Man, he must have been pissed off. Did he swear?"

"No," I said.

"Oh, come on—not even a little?"

"No, he didn't swear. . . . He kissed you."

Not a sound could be heard coming from beneath the dash.

"What?" he asked with a softer voice, one tinged with a sense of longing and surprise. It sounded like the equally foreign voice I'd heard while hiding in the Jensens' closet that night.

"On the forehead," I added. "He kissed you on the forehead." It was a difficult thing to say, but I was glad I'd said it. It needed to be said. He needed to hear it. Bobby didn't say another word or make another sound for a really long time. And his head continued to be lost in the shadows below the dashboard. I gently kicked a nearby basketball just to provide some noise to fill the awkward silence.

"What are you going to do about your bike?" he finally said in a stronger than usual voice. "How you going to manage your route?"

"I've been looking for an excuse to quit anyway."

Bobby sat up again. "So you're just going to quit? Just like that?"

"Who's quitting what?" our dad asked from just outside the

open garage door.

I turned around, and there stood our father smoking a cigarette. "The paper route," I said with reservation. "I figured with
my bike all smashed up and all—"

"You're not quitting the route," Dad said, taking a step into
the garage.

"But what about—"

"And your mother will not be driving you around again. You
can ride your sister's bike. She never uses it," said Dad.

I looked over at Peggy's bike leaning up against the wall. "But,
Dad . . . it's pink . . . it's a girl's bike . . . and it has those ribbony
things coming out of the handles. What would my friends say?"

"Your friends are all asleep at that time of the morning.
Besides, if my memory serves me correctly, just before you told
me to shut up, you said the accident wasn't that colored man's
fault at all . . ."

"I'm sorry I told you to shut up," I said.

"The point is . . . you need to take responsibility for what
happened. Have you saved up enough to buy a new bike?"

"No. But I want to quit anyway."

"I didn't raise my children to be quitters. You made a commitment to Mr. Allen. You'll work through the summer. If you still
feel the same way come the fall, you can give it up then. Not
before. Understand?"

"Yes, sir."

Dad looked over at Bobby. My brother had been paying attention, but now ducked his head from view like a wild turkey on
Thanksgiving eve. A burst of music shot out of the radio but then
immediately cut out. Dad turned to go, then reconsidered. He
flicked his cigarette onto the ground and stepped down on it with

a familiar twist of his shoe. He strolled over to the convertible, stuck his hands into his pants' pockets, and jingled the change around for a while. "And what seems to be the problem here?"

"Radio," Bobby said without showing his face.

"On the fritz?" Dad asked.

Bobby felt obliged to sit up into view. "Yeah. It cuts out. Works if you give it a whack or if you play with the heater toggle switch, but it's a little warm these days for that."

"Sounds like you've got some wires crossed," said Dad. "Mind if I take a look?"

"No." Bobby slid over to the passenger side while Dad got in, rolled over onto his back, squeezed down below the steering column, and peered under the dash.

"Hold that flashlight for me, will you?" Bobby aimed a flashlight at the guts of the radio. Dad grabbed a pair of pliers and a screwdriver off the seat and started tapping away. While Dad fiddled with the radio, I walked over to Peggy's bike and batted at the cascading ribbons with my fingertips and squeezed the stupid pink horn that was secured on the handlebar, making it honk several times before Bobby shot me a disapproving look. I could tell he was feeling uncomfortable around Dad in a whole new way. But the mutual hostility that had previously filled any room occupied by both parties at the same time was at least temporarily absent this night.

Maybe Dad was still thinking about Two-Ton, or maybe he remembered how he felt when his first love dumped him, or maybe Mom's words about him pushing everyone away were in the forefront of his mind. Whatever it was that had Dad feeling so amiable, I was happy for it. The car radio crackled, then shot Buddy Holly's voice out. Dad sat up. "Yeah, that's all it was. Just a few crossed wires."

"Thanks," Bobby said. "I didn't know you knew anything about electronics."

"Well, I don't know much. But when I was growing up, we had this old Edison floor model that was always giving us fits. Would short out in the middle of *Fibber McGee and Molly* and just drive my mom up the wall. Your grandpa showed me how to fix it. I guess my dad taught me a lot of things. I suppose I taught him a few too."

That was about as close as my dad ever came to an apology or an acknowledgment that we might have something to offer him.

"So . . . otherwise, how's it running?" Dad asked.

"Good."

"Good," Dad said, stepping out of the car. "Okay, then, I'll see you two later."

As our dad headed out the garage door, Bobby said, "Pop?" Dad stopped and turned around. "I'm sorry about getting drunk and all."

"I know you are, sport. Just don't let it happen again, okay?"

"Okay."

Dad walked out the door and down the drive as if he had no particular destination in mind. I looked over at Bobby who continued to watch our dad as he turned down the walk. I wanted to know what my brother was thinking, but maybe for the first time I realized that some thoughts should remain private.

"You got off pretty easy," I said.

"Like you didn't?" Bobby said. "I can't wait to take a picture of you on that bike."

"You wouldn't."

"Consider it done." Bobby sat down behind the wheel and

turned the radio up.

Sheena and Amelia came by a little later, and I told them I was grounded and couldn't come out to play. Sheena asked me how I was feeling since the accident, and I told her fine. I rolled up my pant leg and showed them my scab. They said they were going to sit outside the Goswellers' gate and listen to Drake play the piano.

When I told the girls that I'd called up Mrs. Gosweller to explain why I hadn't made it back to her place and that I was going over to her house the following evening to deliver the subscription form, Sheena pleaded, "Oh, please, let us go with you."

"I don't know if Mrs. Gosweller would like it," I replied.

"But I want to see him play," said Sheena.

"She's only expecting *me*. Besides it's a business meeting."

"A business meeting? You're giving her a piece of paper," Sheena said.

"Please let us come," Amelia added. "We won't be any trouble."

"I can't promise she'll let you in."

"So we can go?" Sheena asked.

"Fine. Meet me in front of her house at eight o'clock tomorrow night . . . and don't be late." The two girls squealed and hugged each other just like girls are apt to do.

Twenty-Four

ASHES TO ASHES, DUST TO STARDUST

Two-Ton made dying look effortless, as a wildly diverse bunch of people, including my entire family, crowded into the First Presbyterian Church to say their good-byes. Do you agree that if we all lived our lives as ethically as depicted by our friends and family at our funerals, this world would be a much nicer place? Maybe those comments about how wonderful the departed was are not such a bad thing. Could be that it's simply one of the few times when we no longer need to see the sliver in the other's eyes for the log in our own.

As I sat sandwiched between my siblings on that church pew, I was thinking that Two-Ton must have had his share of faults, but the genuine admiration expressed by friends and family that afternoon couldn't be dismissed as being the least bit saccharine.

After a female soloist sang "It Is Well with My Soul," the pastor spoke of how Two-Ton's philanthropic acts were overshadowed by his celebrity status. He portrayed the big man as having an unabashed love for life, for his fellow man, and for his Savior.

Friends lined up in front of the congregation to tell their own personal Two-Ton stories, filled with sweet memories and plenty of laughs. It wouldn't have surprised me if almost everyone in that place could have taken a turn. Even me.

At the end of the service, the puppeteer of Stupid Cat crouched behind the podium and had his mangy feline friend lead everyone in a rousing rendition of "Life Is Just a Bowl of Cherries," while baskets of fresh bing cherries were passed through the crowd. Though I was pretty disheartened that it would be the last time I ever saw Stupid Cat and Two-Ton's wife, Janis, I couldn't remember having a better time at a funeral. As we filed out of the sanctuary, my mom's influence had me imagining that the spirit of Two-Ton that stirred the audience had, without our conscious knowledge, settled on us all like dust—magic stardust, if you will . . . to later be brushed off our shoulders like dandruff or, if we allowed, to be absorbed into our skin like the warmth of the sun on a summer's day, to become a permanent part of us. I wondered which would be the case for my father.

Our family walked silently and uneventfully from the church to our car, and on the drive home, my dad made an unexpected detour. We stopped at a restaurant for dinner. It wasn't the fanciest place in the world, and the food was just okay, but it was a special place, a place where we used to dine out as a family years before, back in the days when we could stand each other . . . in other words, when we were happy.

We all took our places at the semicircle counter of the Choo-Choo restaurant. We ordered our meals, just like we had before, and when the plates piled with hamburgers and fries and chocolate shakes were ready, they were delivered to us atop a Lionel model toy train that *choo-choo*ed its way out of the kitchen on a track that looped the perimeter of the counter and back into the kitchen. And while we ate, we laughed, and we didn't speak one harsh word toward each other, and I concluded the magic dust must be working.

Twenty-Five

FRED AND GINGER DANCE TO "I'VE GOT NO STRINGS"

I didn't tell my parents that I was headed over to Mrs. Gosweller's to sign her up for the paper for fear my dad would make me dress up like Willy Loman. Approaching the Gosweller house, I could see Sheena nonchalantly leaning up against the same iron fence where she once believed Drake had conspired to acquire her soul. Though she had yet to set eyes on the boy, the beautiful, complex melodies that escaped into the warm evening breezes had wrapped themselves around her heart, communicating a sense of safety. Amelia stood in front of Sheena, repeatedly dislocating the Raggedy Ann's arms as she held its hands out to either side and twirled its rag body between them.

"There you are," Sheena said to me. "You're late."

"No, you're early." The carpetbag lay at her feet. "Why'd you bring the bag?"

"I'm considering taking a trip to New York," she said with a smirk.

"You're not going to tell me?"

"No."

"Fine," I said. "You guys promise to be good, right?"

Sheena and Amelia exchanged glances. "We won't embarrass you," said Sheena.

I unlatched the gate and led the two girls down the winding walkway, up to the Gosweller porch. "And don't get mad at me if she says you can't come in," I said, pulling the subscription form out of my pocket.

Just as I began to knock on the front door, it swung open. Behind the crossing diagonal mesh of the aluminum screen door stood Mrs. Gosweller's filtered image, her hands on her hips. She didn't say anything for a moment, just looked all three of us over. "Good evening, David."

"Good evening, Mrs. Gosweller."

"I was under the impression you were coming alone," she said.

"Well, I was and then—"

"Hope you don't mind, Mrs. Gosweller," Sheena interrupted, "but Amelia and I—oh, this is Amelia."

"Hello, Amelia," Mrs. Gosweller said.

"Hi."

"Moving into a new neighborhood . . . not the easiest thing in the world, is it?" Mrs. Gosweller asked.

"No, ma'am," Amelia replied.

"Anyway, the thing is," Sheena continued, "Amelia and I really like listening to your son's music every night, and so we were hoping we could watch him play."

"I'm afraid that's impossible. He only plays the piano at nine-thirty." She opened the screen door only wide enough to allow me to slip through, leaving the two girls out on the porch. "Maybe another time, girls," she said, closing the screen door behind me.

"Well, could we just give him this gift?" Sheena said, shaking the carpetbag.

"You want to give him an old carpetbag?" Mrs. Gosweller asked.

"No. I want to give him what's inside," Sheena said.

Mrs. Gosweller stood there distorting her mouth while she considered the offer.

"I think he'll like it," Sheena added.

"I'm not so certain of that but . . . all right." Mrs. Gosweller opened the door for the girls and they entered the foyer. "Keep in mind, he's not accustomed to company, so the visit will have to be a short one."

Considering that it was still daylight outside, the house was extremely dark inside. Straight ahead of me was the long hallway that I'd snuck down to get a photo of Drake. The shades on the windows in the step-down living room to my left were all three-quarters drawn, allowing only the bottoms of the white lace curtains to allow in light and gently stir with the breeze. The piano at the far corner of the room could barely be made out in the dark.

"Why don't you three have a seat there on the couch?" Mrs. Gosweller said. We stepped down into the room with its hardwood floors and large Persian rugs, and made our way over to a plush red sofa. The smell of flowers that I'd noticed during my first visit was still apparent, and as I looked around, I understood why. There must have been five oriental vases in my immediate scope of vision that held freshly cut flowers: daisies, carnations, chrysanthemums, and some exotic blooms.

"Can I get any of you something to drink—lemonade? A Coke?" Mrs. Gosweller asked.

We all passed on refreshments as I pulled the newspaper subscription form out of my shirt pocket. Mrs. Gosweller picked up a pen off the coffee table and sat down across from us in an old wingback chair. "Is that what you need me to fill out?" she asked looking at the paper in my hand.

"Oh, yeah . . . here." I handed her the slip of paper. I explained how to fill it out, and while she was doing so, the three of us were just sitting there, all wondering the same thing. Finally Sheena spoke up.

"Where is he?"

"Drake?" Mrs. Gosweller asked, as she continued to fill out the form.

"Yes. Is he here?"

"He's behind you, dear," Mrs. Gosweller said, nodding in our direction. We all turned out heads, and there, in the far corner of the room, opposite the piano, was the barely visible figure of a boy seated on an ottoman gently rocking back and forth. The repetition of his movement was so consistent that he almost didn't look real. He looked more like one of those automatons that I'd seen at Disneyland the summer before. Drake's eyes were locked on the floor. Sheena stood up and gazed over the back of the sofa at the boy.

"Is he okay?"

"Drake isn't like other children, dear. He doesn't speak. He doesn't laugh. He spends most his time off in his own little world, rocking back and forth."

"Where's his father?" Sheena asked.

"Out of town. He spends a great deal of time on business trips. It's always a bit of a surprise to me when he does come home." At the time I wasn't sure I knew what she meant by that comment, but I suspect the challenges of such a child must have produced a great temptation for a husband and father to escape it all.

"Isn't it hard for Drake with his father being gone so much?" Sheena asked.

"I'm not sure he even notices."

"Why don't you ever let him go outside . . . I mean, outside your yard?" I asked.

"Drake makes people feel uncomfortable. It's unpleasant. They stare and wonder what's wrong with him. Children ridicule him. Why would I want to expose him to that?"

"So why's he like that?" Amelia asked.

"Some doctors say he was just born that way," Mrs. Gosweller said, pressing the dull end of the pen against her lips. "Something about genetics. Others say it was somehow my fault . . . that I didn't give him enough love when he was a baby."

"But you did, didn't you?" Sheena said.

"I'd like to think so, yes."

"Will he get better?" Amelia asked.

"I hope so, Amelia. I hope someday soon he'll just wake up and be as normal as the next child."

"Like Pinocchio, right, Mrs. Gosweller?" Sheena said.

"I suppose."

"But how can he play the piano like that?" I asked.

"That *is* a mystery. The doctors have absolutely no explanation for it."

"So the angels give him the music," Sheena said.

"We don't take much stock in spiritual matters in this house."

"What do you mean?" Sheena asked.

"Well, Sheena . . . we don't really believe in God."

"Oh." Sheena thought about it for a second. "But if Geppetto never prayed for Pinocchio to become a real boy, Pinocchio never would have become a real boy." As I recalled, Geppetto actually wished on a bright star, but I didn't think it crucial to Sheena's argument to bring it up at that point.

"But *Pinocchio* was just a story, dear," Mrs. Gosweller said.

"Yes," said Sheena. "But God isn't." There was finality in Sheena's voice that left no further room for debate. And for the moment, her confidence made her sound older than Mrs. Gosweller, wiser, more mature. Mrs. Gosweller returned to filling out the form.

Even as a kid I tried to make sense of everything, and the fact that Drake insisted on living in his own little world didn't make any sense to me at all. I wondered if his life made sense to God. Was it his intention to make Drake different from other kids, or was God not up to the task of making Drake normal? It made me think of those people who hung out by the fence at the state mental hospital, beckoning to us when we'd drive to my grandma's house. God couldn't have wanted that life for them. What went wrong? Could something go wrong in my own life to send it off the path of normality? And then again, what was normal anyway? I wondered if I was normal because my skin was white. Were the Bufords abnormal because their skin was brown? Two-Ton was far too fat to be normal, and Mrs. Winklemeyer was too lonely, and Mrs. Hoffman was a divorcée. Maybe there *was* no real normal. And maybe that was a good thing. I wondered if maybe that's what God had in mind all along.

"May I go over and see him?" Sheena asked Mrs. Gosweller.

"You may. But don't expect him to acknowledge you."

Sheena grabbed the carpetbag off of the floor by its leather straps and slowly carted it over to where Drake sat. Amelia followed her. Sheena squatted down next to the boy and tilted her head to try to get a good look at Drake's face, which was tipped down and lost in deep shadows. He didn't stop rocking, and he didn't lift his head to see who his visitor was.

"Hi, Drake. I'm Sheena. And this is Amelia."

"Hi, Drake," Amelia repeated.

"We've brought you something," Sheena said. "Can you see me?" Then she reached over to push Drake's hair away from his eyes. Drake jerked his head away, surprising her.

"I'm sorry, Sheena," Mrs. Gosweller said, "but he doesn't like to be touched."

Sheena looked over at Mrs. Gosweller for the longest time, her eyebrows creating a small vertical crease on her forehead at the sheer incomprehensibility of the concept. Finally in a concerned whisper Sheena asked, "But what if you need to hold him?"

Mrs. Gosweller forced a sympathetic smile. Sheena turned her attention back to Drake, spread open the carpetbag, sank her two arms into its depths, and lifted out the music box with the angel on top. Mrs. Gosweller propped her elbows on her thighs, leaned forward, and cradled a smile in the palms of her hands.

Sheena twisted the key on the music box, pulled out the release lever, and the Brahms waltz began to play. She slid the box directly in front of Drake. Maybe she was hoping that Drake would react in some manner—from something as subtle as ending his endless rocking to something as extreme as breaking out of his trance, leaping to his feet, taking Sheena in his arms, and waltzing her around the room like Fred Astaire with Ginger Rogers. But as the melody continued on, nothing changed. If anything, the speed of Drake's rocking picked up, totally unrelated to the rhythm of the music. I could see by the way Sheena's shoulders kept slouching that she was disappointed in his reaction to her gift.

"It's very pretty, Sheena," Mrs. Gosweller said from across the room.

"I think he likes it," Amelia said with false encouragement.

"So, David, here you go." Mrs. Gosweller handed the subscription form back across the coffee table to me. "Do I need to pay you something tonight?"

"No, you can wait," I said. "I'll come around in a couple weeks to collect."

"Fine."

Mrs. Gosweller stood up, indicating an end to the visit. The music box wound down until the final drawn-out note sounded by pure coincidence at exactly the end of a stanza. "Can I leave the present here for him, Mrs. Gosweller?"

"Oh, Sheena . . . you have a lovely music box there, and I think you should hold on to it."

Sheena was obviously disappointed as she packed the music box back into the carpetbag and stood with Amelia. "It was nice meeting you, Drake," she said to him. The boy continued rocking, having obviously been oblivious to the entire visit. Sheena and Amelia walked over to the couch to join us, and from there Mrs. Gosweller's long arms guided us up the stairs and into the foyer.

"Thank you, David. I look forward to getting my paper. And thank you, girls, for coming by. I know it didn't seem like it—"

A single note on the piano sounded . . . then another . . . then several strung together. But not random notes . . .

The four of us backtracked around the corner, and there sat Drake at the piano, his fingers settling on keys, reproducing the beautiful melody of Brahms's Waltz in A-Flat Major. He had stopped rocking back and forth.

"Oh, my Lord," Mrs. Gosweller said, looking across the room at her son. Apparently she wasn't an atheist after all. We all just stood there, silent, motionless, amazed.

A couple minutes later Drake stopped playing in the middle of a melody line, as if someone had pulled the plug on him. He began to rock back and forth again.

When we made our way to the front door, Mrs. Gosweller turned to Sheena. "I can't thank you enough. As it turned out, I was wrong—you had just what my son needed in that old carpetbag."

"Now do you think Drake would like to keep the music box?" Sheena asked.

"That's very generous of you, but what I think Drake would enjoy even more is if you would stop by from time to time and bring the music box with you—to play for him."

"I would love to do that," Sheena said.

We said our good-byes, stepped off the porch, and walked down to the gate. The sun was setting golden-orange through the trees across the street. I looked down at the fluorescent green line of spray paint on the sidewalk and thought that in some ways it wasn't that different than the spray paint that had covered the Buford's house. I walked home and rummaged through the storage cabinets in our basement until I found a spray can of gray primer. I brought it back over to the Goswellers, got down on my knees, and sprayed a coat of paint that matched the color of concrete, obliterating our line of demarcation between lost and saved souls.

Twenty-Six

SAVE THE LAST DANCE FOR ME

The next few days in the neighborhood went on uneventfully. Mouse and I managed to complete our monster bottle rocket that we planned to launch on the Fourth of July, wrapped it up in newspaper, and stored it safely in the corner of the tree house.

Hank and Amelia's transition into suburban life continued as they got to know the pleasures of Oakfield—including crayfish hunting, card games in the tree house, and glider flying. I considered introducing Hank to the fine art of cap scraping and rocket making, but thought better of it for his sake. If the Bufords came by when Mouse and I were at Oakfield, Mouse would simply walk away, refusing to play with them. He was continually giving Jimmy and me an ultimatum: "It's either them or me," he'd say. "Make your choice." Mouse wasn't exactly a ball of fun to play with, so it was a fairly easy choice to make.

The Little League season had started, and because one of our players moved away, Hank was able to take his place on our team.

Few people seemed to notice that he was colored.

My mom had an appointment with a doctor downtown. I didn't understand why she had to go all the way downtown when there were plenty of doctors in our own town, but she didn't say much about it to me, so I didn't think it was a big deal.

I continued riding Peggy's bike on my paper route, hoping to soon have enough money saved to buy my own bicycle. I was due to collect subscription money from Mrs. Winklemeyer right after the Fourth, and I was sort of looking forward to it. I'd told Sheena about my little dance; she was the only one I trusted not to laugh at me.

I asked Peggy if she could teach me how to dance, and although she initially teased me about it, saying stuff like, "Davy's got a secret girlfriend," she was happy to put on some forty-fives and show me some moves. I was trying to smooth out the clumsy transitional steps in hopes of impressing Mrs. Winklemeyer with my form. *So odd*, I thought: Here I was preparing, looking forward to a visit with a woman whom I had pitied, someone I'd actually held in contempt for looking forward to a visit from me. It made me not like myself very much. I wasn't certain that Mrs. Winklemeyer's radio would be on again or if she'd be in the mood when I arrived, but in case the opportunity did arise again, I'd be better prepared this time.

My dad went back to work. Apparently there was some talk of keeping *Two-Ton's Tree House* with a different host, but everyone knew it would never compare to the original, so that idea was scrapped. So my dad replaced a director on a late-night talk show hosted by Cincinnati's answer to Jack Paar. But this guy, Bernie Starr, was neither clever nor funny nor talented—nor could he interview a guest to save his life. Basically he was everything that

Two-Ton wasn't. Bernie's lack of skills — along with his pompous attitude and irritating laugh — was responsible for falling ratings, and it fell on my dad's shoulders to change that. So for the next week he worked long hours and none of us saw much of him.

Bobby continued his job caddying over at the local golf course where he hung out and played poker after his rounds, blowing his tip money. He told me all about it.

No one bothered the Bufords. No further words were written on their house, and no more rocks were thrown through their windows.

I spent a couple evenings with Sheena, Amelia, Hank, and Jimmy outside the Goswellers' house listening to Drake. But I had trouble enjoying the music. For one thing, it wasn't exactly rock-and-roll. More than that I couldn't stop thinking about what Drake's world must be like. Aside from his gift of music, was his world as horrible as it seemed? Granted there were times I wanted to hide out in my room with the doors closed, away from the world, but eventually I wanted, even needed, to come out to be with people, to share my thoughts, to play, to laugh, and even to be touched by them. The idea of residing alone in any place for too long seemed like a terrifying ordeal.

Twenty-Seven

THE CALM

S ince I refused to be seen riding a girl's bike anytime after
daybreak, I borrowed Jimmy's, baseball cards on the spokes
and all, and rode to town with Sheena to join the hordes of citi-
zens lined up on both sides of Central Road watching the Fourth
of July parade. It was an all too familiar sight: slightly out-of-tune
and out-of-step marching bands, out-of-sync baton twirlers, men
with double chins and receding hairlines riding in convertibles
decorated in red, white, and blue with the names of their clubs
plastered on the side, Mayor Betterman and his family smiling
and waving like they were TV stars, and kids running around
everywhere with American flags and sparklers. And then pulling
up the rear was that group of marchers that I found so intrigu-
ing. Along with veterans from other wars, that shrinking group
of twenty or so vets representing the various armed forces from
World War I proudly marched in brittle fashion down the street.
Their vintage uniforms displayed ribbons and medals, but the
men themselves were stone-faced, like they'd just returned from
the battlefield the week before. As they strode by, people stood
and saluted them.

Those veterans made me think of my father's army hat lying up there on the roof. Maybe someday I'd wear a hat or a medal that indicated I'd done something special. Something that might tell my own kids who I was, what I was about. But I was starting to think I'd rather they got to know me by the way I listened to them or told them I loved them. And I hoped they would look up to me, but not too much, not so much that their own identity became murky, or so much that I wouldn't be able to live up to their expectations of me.

After the twenty-one–gun salute, Sheena and I headed home. We were about five blocks from our neighborhood when Sheena spotted the giant cloud of wind-blown gray smoke rising above the trees from the general direction of our neighborhood. A fire engine with sirens blaring passed us up, heading toward Oakfield.

My first concern was not for the tree house but for the oak tree itself. As far back as I could remember, it had been the friendly giant that had allowed us to play in its arms and rest in its shade, always appearing just as impressive, just as proud, whether standing naked in the bleakness of winter, dressed up in its leafy green summer coat, or shedding its magnificent display of autumn colors. It was a constant that I now feared I'd have to live without. And if the fire had already engulfed the tree, surely the tree house would be gone, and the carpetbag and our treasures would be reduced to ashes. Even if it meant leaving Sheena behind or that some personal chafing might occur, I had to pedal Jimmy's bike faster—I had to know sooner the fate of my playground.

As I raced down Willowcreek I could see a fire truck parked in the empty lot next to Mrs. Hoffman's house on Briarbrook. A dozen or so neighbors were hanging out around the truck as I rode down the dirt pathway and up to the ditch. Two other fire trucks were parked in the field, their hoses shooting generous streams of water, knocking down the remaining flames. I laid Jimmy's bike down in the long grass in front of the ditch where many other neighbors were standing around watching the proceedings. In the middle of the field where the creek meandered through, a circle of charred grass about half the size of the entire field was visible . . . only a few yards away from clusters of green oak leaves swaying in the wind. The tree had been spared, untouched, possibly by sheer luck, but I preferred to believe that the wind had changed directions out of respect to the oak.

About the time I spotted my mom standing with Mr. Melzer, Mrs. McGuire, and others, an out-of-breath Sheena rode up on her bike. "Why didn't you wait for me?" she asked.

"We didn't lose the tree house," I said.

Wearing a two-piece bathing suit that surely elicited an editorial comment or two from my mother, Allison Hoffman stood in her backyard speaking with a fireman holding his fire hat in his hands. Mouse and his dad were standing nearby, within earshot. I strolled over and joined them. "Hey. What's the story?" I asked Mouse.

"Whataya mean?" said Mouse. He sounded strange.

"I was just sunbathing in my backyard, here," we heard Mrs. Hoffman say, "when I heard this *KABOOM!*"

"And then what happened?" asked the fireman.

"Well, I didn't think much of it at first, seeing as it's the Fourth and all. But then when I saw the smoke rising over the field . . . that's when I saw him."

"Who? Who did you see?" Pete Miller asked, joining her and the fireman.

"The little boy," said Mrs. Hoffman. "The little colored boy."

"The Buford kid?" asked Mouse's dad.

"Yeah," said Mrs. Hoffman. "And when he saw me, he took off running. That's when I called you people."

"And we're glad you did, ma'am," the fireman said.

"Can I get you a cup of coffee or something?" Mrs. Hoffman asked him.

"Thanks, I'd appreciate—"

"Whoa—hold on, here," Mr. Miller said stepping up to the fireman. "What exactly are you going to do about this?"

"What do you mean, sir?"

"I mean someone needs to be held responsible, right? Charges need to be filed against this colored kid, right?"

The fireman gave a little smirk and said, "Sir, despite the laws against it, there are dozens of kids in this town who are playing with fireworks today. Just be glad we caught this blaze before any serious property damage occurred."

"That's it? You're not going to do anything else?" Mr. Miller asked.

"Yes, I am, sir. I'm going to have a cup of coffee with this nice lady before I have to supervise a fireworks display at the park tonight."

"But you said it yourself, that colored boy could have burned down this entire neighborhood!"

Mouse's dad continued to squabble with the fireman while I turned my attention to Mouse. "So what happened?" I asked.

"You heard the lady," Mouse answered.

"Guess we can't set off our rocket now," I said.

His unresponsiveness made me suspicious. As I walked in the direction of the tree house, Sheena came up to me. "So how'd it start?" she asked.

"Not sure, but I have an idea." I snuck around behind the fire truck and, when none of the firefighters were looking, sprinted for the tree house. I climbed up the ladder and ducked my head inside. The carpetbag was still there on the floor of the tree house, but the large bottle rocket that Mouse and I had made and stored in the corner was nowhere to be found.

Twenty-Eight

A LADDER TO
THE STARS

It wasn't until we were finished with dinner and Bobby and Peggy had left the table that Mom broke the news to my dad.

"What are you talking about?" he replied.

"I just thought we could do something different this year, that's all."

"But we watch fireworks from our roof every year. It's a tradition, Ruth. We're not changing that." He looked over at me. "Right, sport?"

"I don't know," I said. "It might be fun to see the fireworks up close."

"Whose idea was this?" Dad asked.

"Well, the Bufords—" Mom began.

"The Bufords? What do they have to do with our watching fireworks?" asked Dad.

"Well, I told them that Roosevelt Park was a good place to view the fireworks display, and next thing I knew, they invited us to go along with them," Mom said.

I was so sure Dad would get mad, but he didn't. He just looked away and calmly said, "I see."

"I think we should go," Mom said. "If you'd just give them half a chance, I think you'd see that you'd—"

"Actually I'm a little concerned that the field might still be smoldering," Dad said. "Might flare up. Somebody should really be here to watch the house. Why don't you and the kids go ahead?"

"I don't want to go without you, Rob," Mom said in a slightly desperate tone.

"No. You should really go," Dad said and then got up from the table and walked out of the room. Mom closed her eyes in frustration.

Peggy went off to a Fourth of July party at a friend's house and Bobby said he had somewhere else to be, so Mom and I agreed to ride with the Bufords to our town's fireworks display at the park. Just before I climbed into the roomy backseat of the Cadillac, I showed Mom exactly where I had wounded the back fender. "We really should pay you for the damage to your car," Mom said to the Bufords.

"Nonsense," Mr. Buford said. "I've contacted our insurance, and they'll cover it."

Mom sat up front with Mr. and Mrs. Buford while I rode in back with Hank and Amelia.

Families gathered on three of the four baseball diamonds at Roosevelt Park that shared a common, fenceless, deep center field. The fourth diamond would serve as the launching pad and display area for what I hoped would be a spectacular fireworks show. Along with dozens of other families, we staked claim to our viewing spot by laying out a blanket and lawn chairs. Many folks brought picnic baskets and stuffed their faces with an assortment of food: chicken, sandwiches, chips, and sodas. Kids and grown-ups played cards, tossed Frisbees, read books, swiveled hula hoops around their waists, or just stretched out on their blankets and relaxed, waiting for the sky to grow dark.

While his parents and my mom visited on the blanket, Hank and I sat nearby lighting snake pellets, adding to the scent of sulfur already hanging in the air from sparklers, smoke bombs, and the occasional string of firecrackers.

"This is so nice," Charlene Buford said, taking in the festive atmosphere.

"Yes, it is," Mom said. "It's been years since I've come down here."

"I'm just sorry your husband decided not to join us, Ruth," Mr. Buford said.

"So am I. I just wish you both knew Rob. The real Rob. The one who'll go out of his way to open a door for a stranger . . . the one who won't ever pass a kid's lemonade stand without stopping and paying twice the going price for a drink. And in the winter-time after a snowfall . . . he won't even wait to be asked, he'll just bundle himself up and walk down to Mrs. Winklemeyer's and shovel her drive. And on warm summer nights like this we'll walk around the block and visit with our neighbors. He can chat with anyone about anything. That's something I've always admired about him. That's the Rob I know. And that's the one I hope you'll get to know some day too."

"I suppose it was naïve on my part, but it never crossed my mind that our moving into the neighborhood might divide families," said Mr. Buford.

"But that's okay," said my mom. "It's not like you've done anything wrong. You've just made people think, that's all. And I guess you've made us all take a look at ourselves. Those are scary things, but in the end . . . good things. I love my husband"—I'd never actually heard my mom say that, and it was nice to hear, because of late I'd begun to have my doubts—"but there's something going on in that man's head right now that I don't understand."

She looked over at me and noticed I'd been listening in. "Right, Davy?" I didn't respond. She continued to look my way with a subtle but unmistakable sadness on her face. I wondered if she could detect the same look on mine.

Just then I heard someone yell, "Davy!" Seeking to stake a spot for themselves, the McGuires approached. Sheena broke file from her parents and ran toward us. She held her Raggedy Ann doll in one hand and a box of sparklers in the other.

"Hey, what are you guys doing here?" she asked.

"We thought we'd watch some fireworks," I said.

"Yeah, I know, but I thought you always watch from your roof," Sheena said.

"Well, this year we thought we'd break from tradition," Mom said.

Audrey McGuire, carrying a picnic basket, and her husband, Bill, with an olive green army blanket tucked under his arm, caught up to their daughter. "Oh, hi," Audrey said to the group.

"Hi, Audrey. Hello, Bill," Mom said.

"Hello, Ruth," they both said.

Mr. Buford began to stand up. "That's okay, don't get up," Mr. McGuire said, taking a step in Mr. Buford's direction. "I'm Sheena's dad, Bill McGuire." He reached down and shook Tom's hand.

"Nice to meet you. I'm Tom, and this is my wife, Charlene."

"Hello, Charlene," said Mr. McGuire.

"And this is Hank and Amelia," Mrs. Buford added.

"Hi, kids. Yeah, Audrey mentioned she dropped by your house—something about a welcoming committee," Mr. McGuire said.

"Yes," Mr. Buford said patting his belly. "And I believe your wife is partly responsible for this recent addition to my waistline."

"Chocolate angel food cake—tempts you like the Devil, am I right?" Mr. McGuire asked.

"Precisely," Mr. Buford answered. With that both men chuckled. My immediate thought was, *Why isn't this my father who's standing here joking with Mr. Buford?*

"Would you like to join us?" Mom asked.

The McGuires exchanged a questioning look. "Can we?" Sheena asked her parents.

"Sure, if you don't mind," Mr. McGuire said to the Bufords.

"We'd be delighted," Mr. Buford said, getting to his feet.

"Well, great," Mrs. McGuire said.

Sheena walked up to Amelia and held up the box of sparklers. "Want to play with some sparklers?"

"Can I, Mom?" Amelia said.

"As long as you're careful."

"Here, let me help you out with that," Mr. Buford said to Mr. McGuire. He grabbed the opposing two corners of the blanket, and the two men draped it down onto the grass next to ours. "This looks familiar," Mr. Buford said, referring to the blanket. "Army issue, right?"

"Spent a year in Selfridge Field in '44," said Mr. McGuire.

"No kiddin'!" Mr. Buford said. "I was stationed there the year before."

And so the bonding of the two men continued with war stories of incompetent sergeants, horrendous mess hall food, and practical jokes on fellow soldiers. It was as if they were joined at the hip. And although my dad was not to be a part of it, I felt happy for Mr. Buford. I watched his whole demeanor change: his body loosen, his mouth break into generous smiles and laughter. On this occasion of celebrating our independence, he had not only turned up a comrade in arms but, more importantly, a neighbor.

The purple color of the horizon over the bleacher seats had nearly faded to black. Squatting across from me, Hank struck a match to a snake pellet and looked up with a grin as the flaming black viper of ash grew tall and curled itself up and then over. Amelia and Sheena danced by, waving sparklers, forming dazzling designs alive with silver light.

"They think you burned down the field," I said to Hank.

"Who does?"

"Some of the neighbors."

"I didn't do it."

"So who did?"

He didn't answer. Instead he dumped a few more snake pellets out of their box.

"Was it Mouse?"

"He was there . . . with Jimmy. I just wanted to fly my kite, that's all. And when the kite fell down, Mouse took it and wouldn't let me have it back. He said he'd help me get it back up into the sky." Hank struck a match, held it near a snake pellet, but instead of lighting it, watched the flame burn down near his fingertips.

"He helped you?"

"No." Hank lit the pellet. "He went up into the tree house and came back with this big rocket—"

"Homemade—wrapped in newspaper?"

"Uh-huh."

"That was our rocket," I said. "I helped make it. He lit it, didn't he?"

"He stuck it on the top of the kite. Jimmy didn't want to do it, but Mouse made him stand far away and hold the end of the spool of string. He set the kite on the ground and lit the fuse, and then raised my kite high over his head. The rocket took off . . . took my kite with it. It went across the sky like this"—Hank made an arcing gesture with his hand—"and then, *BOOM!* It exploded. Real loud. My kite blew up in a million pieces, and when those pieces hit the ground, little fires started up everywhere in the field. When I turned around I saw Jimmy and Mouse running away. I just stood there. I wasn't sure what to do. That's when I heard the lady yelling at me."

"Mrs. Hoffman?"

"Some lady in her backyard. She saw me and yelled, 'Hey, little boy! What'd you do?' I just got scared, and so I started running too."

With a loud pop overhead a giant bursting ball of crimson lit up the night sky, its arching streamers showering down toward us and fading into the night.

"Hey, here we go, guys! It's starting!" Mrs. Buford called out. We all headed for the comfort of the blankets. I laid my head down across my mom's stomach, staring up at the blackness. For the next half hour or so, we *ooohed* and *aaaahed* our way through myriad explosions of colors and designs.

With my eyes locked on the black sky, anticipating the next eruption of colors, I kept thinking about my dad. I pictured him hauling the ladder out from the garage and propping it up against the house, climbing to the roof and sitting at the peak, looking out at the distant horizon where the fireworks were exploding over our heads, and wondering why he was alone. I hoped that if he was up there that he wouldn't notice the round object lying in the shadows halfway up the roof. And if he did happen to notice it, I hoped it wouldn't turn his curiosity into investigation and investigation into discovery of the hat . . . his hat that had become my hat, not merely misplaced, but intentionally abandoned.

And although the advice he'd given me in the church parking lot about how I shouldn't try so hard to be like him was sharp and cutting, I believed that holding that hat in his hands, he would still feel hurt, like he had failed me. And the truth, which I was now finally ready to admit, was that he had.

"Every year I watch these fireworks, and I get so caught up in the colors and the spectacle of it all," Mr. Buford said, "that sometimes I completely forget about what the day is supposed to represent . . . whose freedoms are being celebrated." Mrs. Buford reached over to him, rubbed her hand over his shoulder, and smiled.

The grand finale was truly magnificent, with a barrage of explosions of varying sizes and decibels complete with seemingly all colors of the rainbow represented in brilliant array. Spontaneous applause arose from every corner of the park, and then we were all left in the dark to collect our blankets and family members.

"Boy, gets better every year, doesn't it, dear?" Mr. McGuire commented to his wife.

"Very impressive," said Mr. Buford.

"Okay, Sheena, you ready to go home?" her mom asked.

"Oh, let me ride back with Amelia. It's not my bedtime yet."

"Can she, Mom?" Amelia asked with renewed enthusiasm.

"We don't mind taking her home," Mrs. Buford said. "In fact why don't you all come back to our house for some cake and ice cream?"

"Oh, yes, can we, Mom?" Sheena asked.

Mr. and Mrs. McGuire looked at each other. "Yeah, okay," Mr. McGuire said.

Sheena danced around her new friend and let out a giggle. "Good."

"Okay, so we'll see you back at your house then," Mrs. McGuire said, turning with her husband and making her way toward the parking lot.

"Can we have cake and ice cream, too, Mom?" I asked my own mother.

"We really should get home to your father."

"Please?"

"We'll make it a quick one," Mom said.

For Hank and me the battle to file out of the packed parking lot and get home for ice cream only increased the anticipation of the treat. But by the time we actually made it to the road, Amelia and Sheena had both gone to dreamland.

Twenty-Nine

THY NEIGHBOR

W e were just pulling into the Bufords' drive when I caught sight of Sheena's parents walking down the sidewalk in our direction. Mom leaned over the front seat and said to me, "Better wake Sheena up." And I tried to do just that by nudging her and calling her name. And though she'd stir, she was too sound asleep to wake. Mr. Buford pulled the car into the garage, and we all got out as Mr. and Mrs. McGuire approached us.

"She's a pretty sound sleeper," Mom said to Mrs. McGuire.

"Oh, no, she fell asleep?" said Mrs. McGuire.

"Both girls were out like a light as soon as we hit the road," Mrs. Buford said.

"Once Sheena's out, there's no waking her up," Mr. McGuire said.

Mr. Buford reached into the backseat and gathered Amelia up in his arms and carried her toward the front door.

"We'd still love for you to come in for some dessert," Mrs. Buford said.

"Yeah, I can drive you all down the block afterward so you don't have to wake her or carry her home," said Mr. Buford in a soft tone so as to not wake Amelia.

"Oh, well, I don't know," Mrs. McGuire said.

"We should really get back to your father, too, Davy," said Mom.

"Right after we have some ice cream, okay?" I suggested.

"I suppose it won't hurt to just let her sleep in the car," said Mr. McGuire.

"Just a quick bite and then you can go," said Mrs. Buford.

After finally agreeing to leave Sheena to sleep in the car with the garage door open, we all made our way inside the house. The first thing I noticed was that the broken window had been replaced, but the rock that had shattered it was still perched on the windowsill. We all sat around the dining room table, and I wondered if my mom was leery of another foreign object being hurled in our direction. But since the Bufords hadn't had any problems since that episode, I figured it was probably safe after all. Along with chocolate cake, sherbet, and chocolate or vanilla ice cream, we were given additional options of chocolate sauce and whipped cream. I selected chocolate cake with chocolate ice cream, chocolate sauce, and whipped cream.

While Mrs. Buford dished up the ice cream, Mr. Buford turned on a maroon transistor radio that sat on the kitchen counter next to the toaster. I wasn't all that knowledgeable about different radio stations or types of music, but I'd never heard many of the songs that began spilling out of the louvers on that red box. They could best be described as bluesy and soulful. But I could tell Mr. Buford enjoyed it because from the first note of the first song, his head and shoulders nodded along with the melody as he sat down with a bowl of sherbet in front of him. The gentle movement of his body to the music reminded me of how Mrs.

Winklemeyer couldn't keep her body still when she heard the big band sound.

With sporadic pops of fireworks continuing to be heard outside, we were having a great deal of fun inside. Discussion of weighty topics such as neighborhood racial issues were shelved as each of us took turns demonstrating the fine art of whipped cream sculpting. While he was in the process of spraying an additional mound onto his ice cream, Mr. Buford suddenly dropped his spoon into his bowl, turned to his wife, and said, "Well, dear?"

Mrs. Buford glanced over toward the radio, which was playing Sam Cooke's *"You Send Me,"* and said, "Not now, honey."

"I don't believe you can resist, darling," he said, rising to his feet, swaying his hips, and reaching for her hand.

"Dad, please don't," Hank said, obviously embarrassed by his father's behavior.

Mrs. Buford didn't take his hand, but instead turned to a confused audience and said, "I neglected to mention this, but my husband is a little crazy."

"Crazy in love," Mr. Buford said with sort of a dopey look on his face that made his wife laugh.

"What's this all about?" Mr. McGuire asked with a smile.

"You see," Charlene Buford explained, "whenever Tom hears this song on the radio, he feels like we have to dance. He's delusional."

"*You—ou-ou-ou . . . send me,*" Mr. Buford sang along with Sam Cooke, while still waiting for his wife to take his hand.

"Tom, we have company."

"*Darling, you-ou-ou-ou . . . send me . . .* I know. We'll entertain them."

"That's what I'm afraid of," Mrs. Buford sighed.

"Please, go ahead," Mrs. McGuire said, laughing.

"Oh, trust me, you don't want to encourage the man," Mrs. Buford said.

"No, on the contrary, I believe we would like to see this, wouldn't we?" my mom said to the rest of us with a smile.

"Absolutely," Mr. McGuire replied.

Charlene Buford looked up at her husband as he sang along with Sam, "*Honest you do, honest you do . . .*"

Mrs. Buford reluctantly took hold of her husband's hand and stood up to mock applause.

It was just as Mr. Buford tucked his arm around his wife's waist and began to spin her that I first thought I heard voices coming from outside. No one else seemed to hear it. But the second call of "Buford! Tom Buford!" was loud enough to rise above Sam Cooke's voice and turn everyone's head toward the front of the house. Mr. Buford's smile shortened. It wasn't a pleasant voice that called out "Tom Buford!" for a third time. It had an edge to it, the way my father's voice sometimes did when I was in trouble and he was trying to locate me. The couple stopped dancing, and, though Mrs. Buford looked concerned, her husband seemed more annoyed than alarmed by the interruption.

"Davy, Hank, come over here," my mom said. We both stood up and walked around to the other side of the table, away from the window.

"Who is it, Mom?" asked Hank.

"I don't know, sweetie."

Mr. Buford slowly released his wife and walked toward the front door.

"Tom!" His wife called out slightly alarmed, but he continued on his way through the dining room into the adjacent living room and over to the door.

Mr. Buford stood by the screen door and looked out. He paused for a moment, then shoved open the door and stepped out onto the porch like Marshal Dillon stepping through a barroom door.

"Yes? What can I do for you gentlemen this evening?" Mr. Buford said in a deep, strong voice.

Mr. McGuire walked over to the screen door. I broke away from my mom and rushed over to stand beside him. Halfway up the Bufords' walkway stood Pete Miller and his son, Mouse, and Vern Borkowski.

"We want to have a word with your son," said Mr. Miller.

"My son? And why would you want to speak with Hank?"

"We have reason to believe he set that fire in the field today," Mr. Miller said.

I turned back and saw Hank's mom put her arm around his shoulders as they stood against the dining room wall.

"And why do you believe that to be true?" Mr. Buford asked as Mr. McGuire stepped out onto the porch and stood next to him.

"Good evening, Pete," Mr. McGuire said.

"Bill," Mr. Miller returned, surprised to see him there.

"Allison Hoffman says she saw your boy in the field when the fire started up," said Mr. Miller. A few curious neighbors, including the Finnegans and others, began to slowly gather around in the street in front of the house.

"Do I have to be here?" Mouse asked his dad, who immediately shushed him.

Someone turned the dining room light off.

"Well, tell you what," Mr. Buford said. "I will talk to my son, and if he is to blame, you have my word he will be reprimanded. I thank you for bringing the matter to my attention. Now if you'll excuse me, I need to get back to our guests." Mr. Buford and Mr. McGuire turned around to come back into the house.

"We want to see the boy!" Vern Borkowski's slurring voice boomed. "Now!"

Mr. Buford turned back around. "I believe this is my business, gentlemen, and I will take care of it myself."

"No!" said Mr. Borkowski. "You see, that's where you're wrong, chum. That boy of yours could have burned down this entire neighborhood of ours, and that makes it very much our business."

"That's right," said Mouse's dad. A few others in the growing crowd seem to concur. "We're not leaving here till we hear from the boy himself."

A hand on my shoulder spun me around. My mom stooped down in front of me and forced me to look directly into her eyes. "Davy! I want you to go get your father . . . and hurry."

I slipped outside onto the porch past Mr. Buford and Mr. McGuire. I looked over at Mouse, and his eyes darted away. Then I smelled it: the same strong whiff I always got when we'd pull into a gas station and my dad would tell the attendant, "Fill it up with ethyl, please." I hadn't smelled it when we pulled into the driveway. Nobody else mentioned it, so I didn't think too much of it, but I could definitely detect a strong smell of gasoline in the air. I figured it must be coming from Mr. Borkowski's work clothes.

"You men are trespassing on my property," Mr. Buford said. "Now, I'm going back into my house, and when I do, I suggest you all leave immediately or else—"

"Or else what?" Mouse's dad asked. "Are you going to call the police?"

I crossed the lawn, stopping on the sidewalk, to gaze down the street toward my house.

"Go ahead and call them," Borkowski said. "I'm sure they'll be anxious to question your son about arson."

As I stood there, feeling as though my feet were momentarily useless, I wanted to follow my mom's orders but my instincts led me elsewhere. I took off down the middle of the road in the opposite direction.

Headlights behind me on Willowcreek forced me to swerve off the road and onto the sidewalk. Just as the car passed me, it stopped, and out the passenger side a voice called, "David?" Mrs. Gosweller sat behind the wheel of her Oldsmobile. I stopped beside her. "What's all the commotion about back there?"

"They're trying to blame the fire in the field on Hank. I gotta go." I raced on down to Mr. Melzer's house, while Mrs. Gosweller's car turned around. I ran up to Mr. Melzer's unlit porch, opened the screen door and rapped my knuckles on his front door. "Mr. Melzer!" I knocked harder. "Mr. Melzer! It's Davy!"

The porch light came on overhead and a voice inside said, "Hold your horses—I'm comin'." The door opened up, and a sleepy Mr. Melzer dressed in a sleeveless white T-shirt, boxer shorts, and white socks looked dazed and perturbed. "David. What time is it?"

"You gotta come quick. There's a bunch of people in front of the Bufords' house."

"Who? What do they want?"

"It sounds like they're looking to start trouble. It's Mr. Borkowski and Mr. Miller. They think Hank started the fire, but he didn't. Mouse did. Just come down there, okay?"

"All right. Just let me throw something on. I'll be right down there."

I closed the screen door and ran back down the block. When I arrived at the Bufords, the porch was vacant, and Allison Hoffman and Dorothy Merriweather had joined the outskirts of the mob, which was becoming more vocal and more menacing by the moment.

"Bring the boy out or we're coming in after him!" Borkowski shouted toward the front door.

"This is our neighborhood—not yours!" yelled another voice I didn't even recognize.

I ran around to the back of the house and entered through the kitchen door, startling Mrs. McGuire as I did. My mom met me in the dining room where the light had been turned back on.

"Where's your father?" Mom asked me. I didn't answer at first. "Davy?"

"I don't know," I said.

With his back to the front of the house and the crowd outside, Mr. Buford sat at the dining room table, defiantly scooping up the last of his melted ice cream, spooning it into his mouth, and pretending nothing was wrong. Obviously concerned, his wife slowly approached the table and stood across from him, still holding on tight to Hank.

"Listen, Tom . . . Hank says he didn't start the fire. So if he didn't do anything wrong, maybe it would be best we just let them talk to him."

Mr. Buford stared straight ahead. "This is not about Hank. I will not be intimidated by these people, Charlene."

"Let's go, Buford. We're getting tired of waiting!" a voice

outside shouted.

Mr. McGuire walked over to the table. "Listen, these guys out there . . . Borkowski, Miller . . . I know them and basically they're all mouth. I think I can reason with them . . . so with your permission, that's what I'd like to do." Tom Buford didn't say anything at first. But as Mr. McGuire turned to go, Mr. Buford grabbed him by the sleeve.

"This is not your battle," Mr. Buford said.

"As long as I live in this neighborhood, it *is* my battle."

Mr. McGuire headed for the door with Mr. Buford on his heels. "Be careful, Bill," Mrs. McGuire called out. The two men walked out onto the porch.

"Show us the boy," Borkowski belted out again, the majority of the crowd adding their support and encouragement. Mr. McGuire held up his hands to quiet the group.

"Everyone, please . . . just calm yourselves down. You're all making a mountain out of a molehill here. The boy has done nothing wrong."

Pete Miller yelled back, "Nothing wrong? In all the years I've lived here, never once has anyone burned down that field and threatened our homes."

"That's right! This neighborhood was a safe and peaceful place to live until this family moved in," Borkowski said.

"And we never had to worry about our children's safety on their bicycles until now!" Mrs. Merriweather said.

Upon hearing this, my mom rushed from my side and burst out onto the porch. "Dorothy, if you're referring to David's accident, I already told you that it was his own fault. Everybody just go back to your homes. It's late. Go to sleep."

"Not until we see the boy!" Mouse's dad shouted, igniting the gang again. I dashed out onto the porch for a closer look at the action. My mom immediately pinned me against the wood siding at the back of the porch.

"Go back inside," she said.

"Hello . . . Good evening, everyone," I heard Mr. Melzer say.

I peeked around my mom and saw Mr. Melzer stroll up behind the middle of the group and walk toward us, dividing the crowd in half.

Making a point to make eye contact with everyone, Mr. Melzer continued with his greetings. "Vern . . . Pete . . . Hello, Ruth."

"Evening, Joe," Mr. McGuire said.

Mrs. Buford slowly walked out onto the porch while Mr. Melzer continued to patiently acknowledge us all. "Bill, how you doing? . . . Tom . . . Davy." Mr. Melzer gave me a wink, and I felt certain things would now be okay. "Well, seems you've all decided to throw a Fourth of July block party, but no one thought to invite me," he said. "I feel somewhat slighted."

"Just trying to get better acquainted with our new neighbors, Joe, that's all," Vern Borkowski said.

"Well, I've always found flowers and candy make a better first impression than threats," Mr. Melzer said.

"Nobody's threatening anyone here, Joe. We just want to ask the boy some questions," said Pete Miller.

A bottle rocket whistled into the air over the street and exploded into a sparkling crown of red diamonds. Mr. Melzer turned to the crowd. "Come on, folks . . . it's the Fourth of July, for crying out loud. I don't know about you, but this day reminds me that we are free, right? And I don't think we're supposed to use that freedom to judge or to condemn anybody else, are we?

So whataya say, Pete, Vern . . . the fire's been long out. The party's over, folks. Let's just call it a night, okay?" Mr. Melzer said, gesturing the crowd to disperse.

Mr. Miller stepped right in front of him. "Not until we get some answers."

"Dad, let's just go home," Mouse finally said.

"Maybe you should listen to your son, Pete," Mr. Melzer said. "Could be he knows a heap more than you give him credit for."

"What's that supposed to mean?" Mr. Miller asked.

Mrs. Finnegan spotted Hank peering out from behind the living room curtains. "There he is! There's the boy!" The crowd all moved closer for a better look.

Tom Buford shot forward, against the porch railing, stopping the progress of the crowd. "All right! That's it! That's enough! Now listen to me and listen good! We may not be the family you people hoped would be your new neighbors—"

"You're darn right!" a voice called out from the back of the crowd as a rock sailed in Tom's direction, smacking against the woodwork behind us. Mom grabbed me and pushed me through the open screen door, as she followed closely behind. I turned back and stared out.

Mr. Melzer spun around hoping to spot the culprit.

"—but I am telling you that despite how you may feel about us—" Mr. Buford went on as a second thrown rock crashed through the dining room window, causing the rest on the porch to take cover.

"I'm calling the police," Mom said to Mrs. Buford, as she headed for the kitchen telephone. "Don't move, young man," she said to me.

I could hear Mr. Buford finish his thought. "—despite the

threats made against us, and despite the difference in the color of our skin, this family of mine is here to stay!" A larger rock shattered the living room window.

"Stop it!" Mr. Melzer yelled to the crowd. "Stop it right there! The next idiot who throws a rock deals with me!"

Still half-asleep, Amelia strolled into the living room from the hallway. "Oh, Amelia," Mrs. Buford said, walking over to her daughter and picking her. "It's okay, honey, let's go back to bed." Mrs. Buford took Amelia back to her room.

As my mom picked up the kitchen phone and dialed the police, Hank began taking small steps toward the front door. Though his expression didn't indicate that he was crying, several lines of tears streaked his cheeks revealing the truth. "What are you doing?" I asked him.

"I didn't do anything wrong," said Hank.

"I know."

"So I'm going out there, okay?" he said.

"I'll go with you," I said.

With that we both slipped out the screen door and onto the porch. "There he is!" someone shouted. Mr. Buford turned around and immediately wrapped his arm around his son, shielding him from the assembly. The neighbors gathered right up close to the porch railing. Mom and Mrs. Buford rushed out onto the porch and stood behind Hank and me. Everyone grew very quiet.

Reluctantly Tom Buford knelt down beside Hank. "Hank . . . Were you out in the field when the fire started today?"

Hank hesitated before nodding his head, yes.

"I already told you he was there — Allison said so!" Mr. Miller said.

Allison Hoffman moved closer to the front of the crowd.

"Hank, did you start the fire?" Mr. Buford asked.

Hank looked over at Mouse, who once again looked away. "No," Hank said.

"He's lying!" Borkowski said. "Allison saw him! There she is! Just ask her!"

"It's true," Mrs. Hoffman said. "I saw him in the field when the fire started, but—"

"There! There's your proof!" said Mr. Miller. The crowd began its unnerving buzz.

"If my son says he didn't start the fire, he didn't start it!" Mr. Buford said.

"That's not good enough for us," Borkowski said. "Don't you see he's lying? They all lie."

"Hank?" Mr. Melzer said, walking up onto the porch and confronting Hank. "Were you *alone* in the field when the fire started?" For some reason Hank just looked down at the porch floor.

"Tell them, Hank," I said.

"Was there somebody else there with you, son?" Mr. Buford asked.

"Yes," Hank said.

"That's not true! The lady said he was alone," Borkowski said.

"But maybe I didn't see the whole thing," Mrs. Hoffman said. "Sometimes you don't know the whole story." I swear she looked my mom's direction and forced a grin.

"Who was with you, Hank?" Mr. McGuire asked.

To a certain degree I understood why Hank wouldn't answer. He didn't want to implicate anyone, knowing he needed all the friends he could get in the neighborhood. He just stared down at his Keds.

"It's okay. You can tell us, son," Mr. Buford said.

Still Hank kept silent.

"You see there," Mr. Miller said. "The boy started the fire by himself. His silence tells the truth."

"The truth?" Mr. Buford roared. He stood up and started down the steps. "Is that why you've all gathered here at my doorstep like some lynch mob? To find out whether or not some li'l colored boy started a fire out in a field?" Standing on his front lawn surrounded by the accusers, Mr. Buford's chest puffed out. "Or did you drop by with other intentions, looking to discredit our name, to drag it through the streets, and string it from the nearest tree as your personal form of suburban vigilante justice? You're not here for any truth!"

"We're here because there's a disease in this neighborhood!" Mr. Miller boldly announced like a self-proclaimed prophet, turning his attention to the crowd. "And you people know it! A cancer is spreading through this neighborhood, and if it's not stopped right here, it will destroy all of us."

"And you know what this cancer looks like, do you, Pete?" Mr. Melzer asked.

"It's as plain as black and white," Borkowski said, stepping up to Mr. Melzer.

"Is that right?" Mr. Melzer said. He scaled the three steps onto the porch and scanned the crowd. "Most of you know there was a time when this neighborhood was my land. Where you now park your car, where you rest your head at night, where your children play . . . healthy, rich green stalks of corn grew in straight rows."

"Yeah, yeah, Joe, we know all about it—so you grew some

corn. What's your point?" asked Mr. Miller.

"My job wasn't to grow the corn, but to manage it. But the bugs had their own ideas, and diseases tried to kill the harvest and the worthless weeds grew up around the crop, sucking up the soil's nourishment. They all did their best to keep the sweet taste of corn from reaching dinner tables. But with patience and care and the help of the good Lord, they could not destroy this land back then, and I'm sure not going to let any of you destroy this neighborhood now!" Mr. Melzer's gaze ended on Mr. Borkowski.

"Funny, I never would have taken you for a nigger lover, Joe," Borkowski said.

"Is that with an *e* or an *a*, Vern?" Mr. Melzer asked.

"What're you talkin' 'bout?" asked Borkowski.

"When Tom here and I started painting over all the hateful words on these walls," Mr. Melzer said, "we got a kick out of the fact that whoever's handiwork it was, they had some problems with their spelling."

"Guess you don't need a passing grade in spelling to live in the suburbs, do you?" Mr. Buford said. "Just a can of spray paint from that body shop of yours to mark your territory like some mangy, no-'count dog."

"Why, you uppity brown—!" Mr. Borkowski lunged toward Mr. Buford, his fist squarely connecting with Mr. Buford's jaw, sending him over backward into an evergreen shrub. Mrs. Buford screamed.

"Dad!" yelled Hank.

Never in my life have I felt such a surge of anger overtake me. Without considering the consequences, I hopped up onto the railing and leapt off, landing on Vern Borkowski's broad back, locking my legs around his thick waist and my arms around his filthy, grease-streaked neck, knocking him off balance and down onto all fours on the grass.

"Davy!" I heard my mom shriek.

As the back of Borkowski's huge blue torso twisted, he thrust his right elbow back toward me, connecting with my rib cage, sending me flying off. Lying on my back on the damp grass, I watched as the shadowy feet and legs of the concerned crowd immediately circled above me like trees. I lifted my head to see Borkowski rise to his feet in slow motion like a wounded bear, turn around, and look down at me, his face full of rage. As he took one long stride in my direction, a large, swift shadow of a man silhouetted by the porch light crossed in front of me. The figure hauled back and slugged Vern Borkowski on his bulldog face, sending him sprawling backward onto the ground.

"If you ever touch my son again, I swear I'll kill you," my dad's voice rang out. My father turned around and extended his hand down to me. I grabbed hold, and he pulled me up and close to him, wrapped his arms around me, and, without reservation, held me tight and kissed my forehead.

"Are you all right?" my mom asked me as she joined us.

"He's got a gun!" someone shouted. My dad quickly turned around, tucking me behind him and faced Borkowski, who was now on his feet, holding a gun pointed at my dad. Though I'd seen hundreds of guns on TV westerns, this was the first one I'd seen in real life, and it was terrifying, especially since it was aimed at my father by a drunken idiot.

"What the devil you doin', Vern?" Mr. Miller asked.

My dad gave me a gentle shove into my mother's arms, and she guided me back up onto the porch. I knew Mr. Borkowski was a dangerous man, but I hadn't expected this.

"Come on, Vern. Put the gun away. Go sleep it off," my dad advised, stepping toward him. Borkowski defiantly aimed the gun just above my dad's head, and fired it. The shot rang out, followed by my mother's scream.

"Don't be foolish, Vern," Mr. Melzer said. "Put that thing away."

Borkowski took a couple steps toward Dad. My mom was squeezing my arm.

"You think you're some kind of tough guy, don't you?" Borkowski said to my dad. "Some hotshot, white-collar dude."

"Knock it off, Vern," Mr. Melzer said.

"You talked so big. Said you'd fight this thing right alongside us. You even held that spray can in your hand just like the rest of us, didn't you?"

My fears were confirmed and it hurt. "Oh, Rob, no," my mom said, disappointed.

"You just didn't have the guts to use it, did you?" Vern said.

"No, you're right. I didn't. But that doesn't make me any less guilty than you. Because I wanted to use it." Dad turned and looked over at the Bufords. "Because I wanted to make it clear to these people that they were not welcome here! Not in my neighborhood! Not by me." My father looked over at Mom and me. "I said it was about investments and property value, but I was deceiving my family . . . fooling myself. I thought I knew what was best . . . but I was wrong." He looked back over at the Bufords. "And I am sorry. Very sorry."

The look on Mr. and Mrs. Buford's face made it clear that they forgave my dad.

"This family does not belong here, and you people know it," Borkowski said, now pointing his gun at Tom Buford.

"Stop it!" Mrs. Buford screamed. "Someone stop him!"

My dad walked up next to Mr. Buford. "You're not going to shoot anybody, Vern. Because this man is not the enemy," he said, calling Borkowski's bluff. Acting as though it were no more than a cap gun, Dad stepped between Mr. Buford and the pistol.

"Rob!" my mother yelped.

"And you're not the enemy either, Vern." My dad gently poked Vern in the chest. "In here . . . this . . . this is the enemy." Dad turned back toward Mr. Buford and put his hand on Tom Buford's shoulder. "And this is your neighbor."

"These people are not my neighbors!" Borkowski said.

"Then who is your neighbor, Vern?" Mr. Melzer asked.

"Whataya talkin' about?"

"We're called to love our neighbor," Dad said. "So who is your neighbor? Who is a neighbor to the Bufords? Is it the person who threw the rock through this window? Is that who it is, Pete? Maybe it's those responsible for vandalizing their house with spray paint—or is it someone who helped him whitewash over the racial slurs? Who is the neighbor to the Bufords? Is it those of you who turned out tonight to badger and harass their family? Or are their neighbors the ones who welcomed them into this neighborhood with gifts and open arms?" My dad looked over at my mom and at the McGuires, then back at the crowd. "So which ones are really neighbors?"

And though it was most likely a rhetorical question, Allison Hoffman's voice broke the silence, "The ones that showed kindness and mercy."

"Then maybe we should all"—Dad looked directly at me—"*go and do likewise.*"

And there they were. The very words that I'd found tangled

up in the tree.

"What's wrong with you people!" Vern yelled out. "You're not going to listen to all this choirboy babble, are you? The colored boy—he almost burned down your houses today!"

"No, he didn't," a woman's voice from the back cried out. The crowd turned, and Mrs. Gosweller, walking hand in hand with Drake, parted the crowd like the Red Sea. She followed Mr. Buford directly up the front steps and onto the porch, addressing the group. "For those of you who don't know me, my name is Meredith Gosweller, and this is my son, Drake. We live in the house with the iron fence around the front and the wooden fence around the back. My son looks out the through the back fence every day, and he watches the other children play. Today he saw exactly who was responsible for setting the fire."

"This is ridiculous," Pete Miller said. "Why should we listen to him?"

"Yeah, the boy's obviously a retard or something," Borkowski added.

From what little I knew of Drake, I was certain he didn't have the ability to pull this off. I considered speaking out myself, but my word was only based on what Hank had told me and no one was about to believe Hank.

"It doesn't matter who set the fire," said Mr. Melzer. "There's not one of us here who hasn't made a mistake . . . made a bad choice. But if you want to tell us, son, go ahead," Mr. Melzer said to Drake.

Drake's eyes were fixed on the floor of the porch, his right hand curled up and tapping hard against his pant leg. His eyes, set deep in their sockets, showed no sign of looking elsewhere anytime soon.

"Who was it Drake?" Mrs. Gosweller asked. Drake's head began to tilt upward extremely slowly, the porch light beginning to define his sharp features. Drake's gaze stopped precisely upon Mouse. Mouse stared back but couldn't stand it another moment.

"Dad, I'm sorry!" Mouse blurted out. "I was just foolin' around. I didn't know Hank's kite would blow up like that. I'm really sorry." Mouse broke away from his father's side and raced through the crowd and down the street toward his house. Obviously feeling foolish for his allegations and defeated in the cause, Mr. Miller slowly turned toward Mr. Borkowski.

"Give me the gun, Vern."

"You're going to listen to—"

"Give it to me now!" Pete Miller demanded.

Mr. Borkowski reluctantly handed the gun over to Mr. Miller. My father walked onto the porch and up to my mother and me. She circled her arms around him and kissed him on the cheek. My dad turned to Mr. Buford and shook his hand. "Welcome to the neighborhood," said Dad.

Allison Hoffman stepped up onto the porch and approached my mom, and they exchanged a hug. Many neighbors, including Borkowski and Pete Miller, began retreating back to their homes, while others climbed the porch steps and introduced themselves to the Bufords.

"You people make me sick!" Vern Borkowski called out in the direction of the house as he headed toward the sidewalk. I stood next to Hank, and we kept our eyes on the drunken bulldog. He paused at the curb, pulled a big crooked cigar out of the front pocket of his overalls, straightened it out, and crammed it into the side of his mouth. "You're all making a big mistake here.

You'll see." He dug a pack of matches out of his pants pocket, lit his stogie, and called out one final battle cry. "You people will never be my neighbors!" Everyone on the porch was so busy getting acquainted that no one was still paying attention to Mr. Borkowski except me.

It was such a casual gesture on Mr. Borkowski's part: He simply flicked the lit match from his hand onto the ground and turned to walk away. A burst of flames shot up from the curb. I stood speechless for a moment as the foot-high blaze became a ribbon of fire, quickly spreading to the end of the Bufords' driveway and immediately beginning to stretch itself right up toward the garage.

"Hank! Look!"

Hank spotted the fire and called out, "Dad! *Dad!*" The second panicked yell got his father's attention along with most the others as they turned to see the flames, now streaking halfway up the drive toward the garage where the Cadillac was parked.

"Sheena!" Audrey McGuire screamed, as her husband and Mr. Buford bolted past neighbors, sprinting off the porch and around the corner of the house. Slightly confused by the full nature of the emergency, my father and others lagged behind. As I rounded the side of the house I stopped on the driveway, just short of the river of fire and looked to my left in time to see the flaming fuse streak into the open garage, beating Mr. Buford and Mr. McGuire to the Cadillac, where a rag crammed into the open gas tank was visible. Flames leapt up the side of the tire toward the rag as Mr. Buford grabbed the back door handle, jerked it open and dug Sheena's limp body out of the back seat into his arms, and in one swift motion turned and handed her off to her father. The two men ran out of the garage toward us as the rear half of the car was swallowed up in flames.

With sirens blaring and tires squealing, two police cars skidded up to the curb, which flickered with dying flames. Mr. McGuire rushed Sheena into the waiting arms of her mother, and she began to stir. The rest of us watched in shock as the Cadillac was engulfed in a swirling blaze of hot orange. Someone yelled, "Get back!" and a moment later, *kaboom!*—the gas tank exploded, debris blasting out of the open garage door in all directions.

As I ducked down, my parents shielded me from the blast. "Davy, are you okay?" my dad asked. Physically I was fine, but emotionally I'd been overwhelmed. I buried my face in my father's chest and began to cry.

Bending over and breathing heavily, Mr. Buford shaded his eyes from the brilliant inferno, which was no longer limited to giant flames wrapped around the remains of his *baby* but now included his entire garage.

The crowd of neighbors had grown, most of them milling around the end of the driveway and spilling out onto the street. Accusations were hurled back and forth, resulting in the police handcuffing an uncooperative Mr. Borkowski and taking him away in a patrol car. I wished all the neighbors would go home. I wished I were lying in my bed, staring at the curtains, and uncovering friendly faces.

Out of the corner of my eye, I could see Sheena some ten feet away from me, wrapped up tightly in her own parents' arms. She squinted at the bonfire, still perplexed as to what had taken place. Then she looked over at me. Maybe I should have been embarrassed that at my age I was crying and being consoled by my parents, but I wasn't ashamed—I *wanted* to remain in their hold. The world was full of Borkowskis—unpredictable, dangerous, evil men with whom I wanted nothing to do. I preferred the reassuring comfort and security of people who had loved me from the moment I was introduced to them and who currently clearly expressed that love, not with words, but with actions. And that was more than enough for me.

Thirty

A GAME OF DOMINOES

With a gentle shake of my shoulders, a kiss on my cheek, and the words *It's time* whispered by my mom, I woke at five-thirty in the morning to prepare for my newspaper route. The last thing I felt like doing was beating the sun out of bed and riding my sister's pink bike with the colored streamers around a neighborhood that felt like it no longer belonged to me.

I entered the bathroom with the intention of stepping into my body of clothes *du jour*, only to discover a stack of clothing on the toilet seat, layered in no particular order and with no instructions anywhere in sight. I stared at the stack for a while, unsure how to approach this new process of dressing myself. I'm happy to report that it was not that difficult. In fact I caught on almost immediately.

When I entered the kitchen, I was relieved to see that my entire world had not been turned upside down overnight, as my milk and donut were there on the table patiently waiting for me. But so was my father. Wearing his PJs, he was seated with his elbows leaning on the kitchen table, drinking a cup of coffee. "Good morning," he said.

" 'Morning. What are you doing up so early?" I asked.

"Oh, I don't know. I was having some problems sleeping, so I finally gave up. How'd you sleep?"

"Okay." It wasn't until I sat down across from my dad that I noticed the army hat on the table. And he noticed that I had spotted it.

"Found it up on the roof last night," Dad said picking up the cap, kneading the top and running his fingers across the brim trying to return some shape to it. I think he might have been hoping for a good explanation as to how it ended up there, but when I stuffed the end of the long john into my mouth and didn't offer one up, he slid the olive green hat with the medals across the vinyl tabletop to me. "Guess you need to remember to watch out for those big gusts of wind."

I took the hat in my hands and flipped it over.

"It's not there," my father said.

"What?"

"The card. It's not there. Was it left over from Gospel Flight Day?"

"Yeah. I found it attached to a balloon that got caught up in a tree."

"Did you tell your mom?"

"No."

"Did it make any sense to you?" he asked.

"No."

"You didn't look up the verse, did you?"

I was ashamed to have to say, "No. No, I didn't." I set the hat back down on the table.

"Didn't spark your curiosity?" he asked.

"Not enough, I guess."

"Well, it got my goat. Got it pretty good," Dad said. "I just had to see exactly what it was referring to when he said, 'Go, and do thou likewise.'"

"So you looked it up?"

"I did. I recommend you do the same." He took a long drink from his cup. The hat remained on the table. "So how long you been wearing that hat now?" Dad asked.

"It's been a couple years at least."

"Don't you think that's a long time to be borrowing someone's hat?"

"I thought you gave it to me," I said.

"It was just a loan."

"So you want it back?"

"If you don't mind."

"Okay. But why?"

"Well, for one thing, you're not very responsible with it, and also . . . I don't know . . . I guess because I want it to always be around to remind me of a time in my life that meant a lot to me."

"When you were in the army?" I half-asked.

"No," he said without further explanation. My dad asked me how my ribs felt after getting elbowed by Mr. Borkowski the night before. I asked him how his hand felt after slugging Mr. Borkowski in the face, and he said it felt better than he expected. It was the nicest conversation I'd had with my father in some time, and I left the kitchen table to go on my paper route feeling better about life.

As I started out, it was apparent that the previous evening had taken its toll on me, evidenced by an extended yawn exiting my mouth as I passed Spencer's house. The dog was being his usual noisy, obnoxious self as I rode up, but when I flung the paper in his direction, he quieted down and just followed its flight path with his eyes until it landed, skidding along the grass. This was new behavior. I had to stop the bike to watch. Spencer ran over to the rolled up newspaper, gently secured it between his jaws, and pranced around the corner of the house with his tail wagging in the air. Maybe he'd heard as well that attitudes were going to change in the neighborhood, that we all were going to treat each other better, so he decided to give up his nasty disposition and put on a spirit of kindness and cooperation.

The Bufords' garage was still smoldering from the fire as I rode past. I tried my best not to think about how close Sheena came to dying. She was my best friend, and I'd almost lost her. This time when I saw her, I'd tell her how happy I was that she was pulled from the car before it burst into flames.

I passed Mr. Melzer's house and didn't see any sign of the old man. It was a late evening for him as well, so I hoped his early morning absence from the porch was simply a result of exhaustion rather than his receiving a one-way ticket home in the middle of the night.

As I delivered each house's paper, I considered each family's role in the drama that took place the night before: the heroes, the villains, and the extras whose roles were not as well defined.

Mr. Melzer's passion for fairness drove his words, while Mr. Buford spoke with courage, determination, and character. I thought about Hank's decision to step out onto the porch and face the less-than-amiable mob. I doubted I would have had the same guts. I was impressed how the McGuires and my mom never backed down from the fight. Both Mrs. Gosweller and Drake boldly stepped out in public, risking further ridicule. And Mrs.

Hoffman and my mom found a common ground that superseded book covers and wardrobe choices, one that had existed all along without their knowledge.

And then there was my father, whose act of heroism wasn't displayed as much in his coming to my aid by impersonating John Wayne and decking Vern Borkowski as it was in exposing his vulnerability, expressing his weakness of prejudice and doing something I never thought him capable of—changing, admitting he was wrong, and asking for forgiveness. That apparent dropping of his guard, that show of weakness on his part could not have made me admire him more, because in that weakness he showed great strength. The heroes outnumbered the villains by far on the evening of the Fourth of July, leaving me with a sense that my neighborhood would never be quite the same again, but that it would survive.

I couldn't help but wonder about those words *Go, and do thou likewise.* In a sense the Scripture quote *was* intended for me after all, but only in that I needed to hear those words from my dad. They brought back the father who made sense to me. But in the truest sense, I had been used. I was another gust of wind, blowing the message in the direction of my father, and thankful to have been so.

My mother had told me there are no accidents in life and that even those moments that appear to be filled with sadness and despair and frustration and uncertainty hold a purpose. So was it a mere coincidence or something else that made my father come to that decisive moment in time, standing on the Bufords' porch defending their cause?

If it weren't for the combination of my brother sharing with me his resentment toward my father and my own confusion and disappointment over my father's actions, I never would have hurled my army hat onto the roof. And if my mother had not insisted on the two of us going with the Bufords to view the fireworks display, my father would never have found himself alone on the rooftop, and he would never have spotted my hat and picked it up and discovered the index card tucked inside. If it were not for that particular swirl of wind that set that balloon free of its clothespin, or the second blast of wind that caused the balloon to tangle in that tree branch, my father would never have read those words, *Jesus said unto him, "Go, and do thou likewise."* If Sheena had not bought me that glider, and we hadn't flown it that day, and the robin hadn't landed nearby, I may have never even spotted the withering balloon. The branch of the oak tree had to support my weight, and I had to choose to tuck that card into my army hat instead of stashing it into my pocket or throwing it away or tossing it into the carpetbag or giving it to Sheena. Was it actually a choice at all, or was the suggestion whispered into my ear by Newton or someone else? And who planted the original seed in my mother's heart to start a Gospel Flight Day in the first place? All the dominoes had to line up spaced at perfect intervals. The stars had to be perfectly aligned for my father to read those words. And the events that had transpired leading up to the moment he eyed that verse on the roof had to prepare and then produce exactly the right condition in his heart for him to have even considered tracking down a Bible and looking up the Scripture to understand the context in which the words *Go, and do thou likewise* were spoken by Christ.

I considered telling my mother about how all these events led up to my father's receiving the Scripture and having his change of heart, but after all, she was the one who claimed that attaching a return address to the card would show a lack of faith on our part—the fact that we would need confirmation of positive results would only suggest that we doubted God's sovereignty. And she was right. I was the one who had lacked the faith. She had no need of knowing the outcome. It was in God's hands from the start. My mother's faith was strong enough to have not even copied down the entire message of the passage—just enough to intrigue a desperate heart, and eventually convict a broken one.

As I tossed the morning news into Mrs. Winklemeyer's yard, a strange feeling came over me. I can't explain it very well. It was the kind of feeling I got when I suspected someone was hiding something from me for my own good. I remembered that hers wasn't among the many faces of neighbors I'd seen the night before. There was movement on Mrs. Winklemeyer's roof. At first I thought it was a scavenging squirrel, but upon closer inspection, I recognized it as a cat, pacing back and forth along the crest of the roof, meowing. It may even have been Mr. Bergen, but it was too dark to make out details. I continued on my route but couldn't stop thinking about that cat and wondering why it would be up there.

About an hour later, as I rode back toward my house, I noticed an ambulance parked in front of Mrs. Winklemeyer's house and a couple neighbors standing on their front lawns staring toward the house. I parked the bike in my garage and walked back down there. Her front door was standing wide open, and several paramedics continued appearing and disappearing through it. I stood near the ambulance and just watched. The sun was just now rising, shedding enough light for me to recognize that it was in fact Mr. Bergen who continued to meow and walk the peak of the roof. My first thought was a stupid thought: I pictured

Mrs. Winklemeyer spinning around in her dress, maybe practicing dancing in the hopes that when I came back that night to collect subscription money we could have another dance . . . and then falling down, maybe breaking her wrist, grabbing it—or maybe it was her leg or hip.

Just then two paramedics filed out of the front door carrying an oxygen tank and a couple medical bags. As they set the equipment in the back of the ambulance, I could hear the younger of the two say, "She took all the cats with her . . . except that one on the roof." They both glanced up toward the roof where Mr. Bergen continued to pace.

At first I thought maybe they were talking about a vacation or that Mrs. Winklemeyer had moved away in the middle of the night or something. Then the younger man continued. "What kind of person takes her own life on the Fourth of July and poisons all her cats to boot?"

I thought I would pass out.

"A crazy old lady—*that's* what kind of person," the older paramedic said.

"She wasn't crazy," I said to them, now bending over to catch my breath.

They looked over at me, then at each other, and stopped loading their equipment.

"I'm sorry—what?" the first one said.

"She wasn't crazy!" I yelled this time. "Take it back! You didn't even know her. She wasn't crazy! Take it back right now!"

"Okay . . . okay, kid. Calm down," the older one said, approaching me. "She wasn't crazy. You okay now?"

He tried to put his hand on my shoulder, but I jerked away, turned, ran back to my house, hid behind my garage, curled up into a ball, and cried.

Thirty-One

PRIDE AND PREJUDICE

On Saturday morning Dad, Bobby, Mr. Melzer, and I gathered in front of Mr. McGuire's house with other neighbors wearing tool belts and wielding sledgehammers and crowbars. Together we walked down the sidewalk to the Bufords, stopping at the end of their driveway. Streaks of sunlight shone down through the burned-out garage roof as Mr. Buford, with his back to us, and Hank retrieved any salvageable items, laying them out on the driveway. Mrs. Buford caught sight of us through the dining room window and stepped out of the front door and approached us. "What's this all about?" she asked out of earshot of her husband.

"We want to help," Dad said.

Mrs. Buford looked us over. "He doesn't particularly like help . . . even if he needs it."

"Just the same . . ." Mr. McGuire said.

Mrs. Buford glanced over her shoulder at her husband as he stood with his hands on his hips glaring at the burned-out walls, still oblivious to our presence. "I don't know. . . . He's a very proud man."

"Stubborn, you mean?" my father said.

"Like your basic farm mule," she said. "Wait here."

She walked up the driveway and into the garage, circled around the other side of her husband and spoke to him, pointing in our direction. He slowly turned around and caught sight of us. With a perturbed expression he turned back around to his wife and began an animated debate.

"Boy, he *is* stubborn isn't he," Bobby said to Dad and me. "Doesn't remind you of anybody, does he, Davy?"

"Yeah, I get it," Dad said with a grin.

Mrs. Buford wasn't backing down. Mr. Buford turned around toward us again, took a slow deep breath, and all at once let it out. He reluctantly walked down the drive and met us. "I hear you want to help," he said.

"Yes, we do," Mr. Melzer said.

"On one condition," he said.

"What's that, Tom?" Mr. McGuire asked.

"That nobody works harder than I do. I won't put up with that."

My dad looked around at everyone. "Fair enough."

We all walked down to the garage. "Okay . . . anything that's not either burned to a crisp or melted, I'd like to stack over here," said Mr. Buford.

I'd hoped Pete Miller might show up with his flatbed loaded down with lumber, but I'd grown old enough over the last few weeks to realize that wouldn't be happening.

Thirty-Two

PRANKS FOR THE
MEMORIES

Unlike Two-Ton Trzcinski's funeral, there was no service for Mrs. Winklemeyer at a church. Instead her sister Louise, who came in from Indiana, had the Dubonet Brothers Mortuary handle all the arrangements. My mom said I didn't have to go to the memorial viewing if I didn't want to, but I felt like I owed it to Mrs. Winklemeyer to show up. A small, stuffy room with no windows and long, heavy, deeply gathered purple drapes that dragged on the carpeted floor held the open casket containing Mrs. Winklemeyer's body. A spray of long-stemmed roses draped down from the closed portion of the casket. There were a handful of flowers from friends or relatives. Four rows of about ten folding chairs each with a middle aisle held only ten people, mostly neighbors.

When it came time to walk up to the casket, I told my mom I'd rather not see Mrs. Winklemeyer that way, and she didn't say anything like "Don't be silly." Instead she said, "That's fine." Maybe she recalled the Great-uncle Frank experience, or maybe things were just different now.

Peggy, Mom, and I sat there next to Sheena and her mom while cheesy organ music played in the background and a short, sour-faced guy in a baggy suit, possibly one of the Dubonet brothers himself, stood up front and said a few words on behalf of Mrs. Winklemeyer. You could tell he didn't know a thing about her, because he read bland information concerning her life off a sheet of paper—he might as well have been reading her obituary out of the newspaper. It couldn't have been more depressing if the little weepy-eyed girl and her weepy-eyed cat were hanging on the wall watching the proceedings. As I sat behind Louise, I wondered if she knew her sister at all, and her love of music. At the end of the grim little man's speech, he asked if anyone wanted to say anything about Mrs. Winklemeyer. No one did. I wanted to get up and tell everyone how nice she was, but I just couldn't do it. I'd have to tell them about how she talked me into dancing with her, and I was afraid that might make her seem a bit odd to some people. And she *was* a bit odd, but it was that peculiar nature that I ended up liking about her. I couldn't help but think that Mrs. Winklemeyer deserved a better send-off than what she got that day.

Mom, Peggy, and I went back to the Winklemeyer house for food after the service. It was strange sitting in her living room without either Mrs. Winklemeyer or her cats around. It was morbid, I know, but I couldn't help but compare her service to Two-Ton's and wonder which type of funeral I would have when the time came. I was hoping for Two-Ton's, but it wouldn't have surprised me if it ended up more like Mrs. Winklemeyer's. I was doing okay until Mr. Bergen walked into the room and rubbed up against my pant leg. Then I had to leave.

Thirty-Three

THE INFAMOUS BOOGER PROMISE

From my view at the tree house window, I could just make out a portion of Mrs. Winklemeyer's rooftop. As much as I tried to concentrate on other topics, my thoughts kept going back to that night when the two of us danced to Glenn Miller. What bothered me and scared me the most about her death was that when she was dancing all over the place, I couldn't remember seeing anyone happier. Not even Sheena at Chuck Wagon Days when she won that giant stuffed panda by sticking her dime onto the tiny dish.

Everyone at the memorial kept saying stuff like "She seemed happy" or "Who would have thought she'd do such a thing?" Something as simple as a song made her happy. There must have been other little things in life that she got a kick out of. Why couldn't she have just strung them all together and been happy? I didn't know much about loneliness. I was almost never alone, but I'm guessing that even with all her celebrity cats, it was that loneliness that pushed her over the edge. Cats can only give you so much love before they start thinking about themselves again. Maybe that's why she had so many: in hopes that enough small doses of love could add up. But I was pretty sure it didn't work that way.

I think when it came right down to it, she needed what everybody needs: a permanent dance partner. Someone who would listen to her and share her love of swing music, felines, and tea served in petite portions.

This may sound peculiar, but for the next few minutes I sat up there in the tree house, closed my eyes, and tried to make myself feel as sad as Mrs. Winklemeyer must have felt. I considered all the horrible things that could happen in my life, possible tragedies. If I hadn't recalled the duck-and-cover drill, my crash into Mr. Buford's car could have easily resulted in my being crippled, destined to be pushed around in a wheelchair for the rest of my life, spoon-fed by my mom, and wearing diapers like a baby. Or what if a routine medical checkup revealed a rare disease in my eyes and within a week I was rendered totally blind and could no longer enjoy the sunrise or the smiles on the faces of the people I loved? Or what if my mom's visit to the doctor was the beginning of a terrible disease and I lost her? I attempted to wrap my heart around that possibility, to feel that void, that intense sense of abandonment, to have to endure that substantial a loss. I worked myself down into a considerably deep well of sadness and sorrow over these hypothetical scenarios—enough to produce real tears, real grief. And when I tried to imagine what it must have felt like to sustain those feelings over a period of time, I think I began to understand the place Mrs. Winklemeyer must have been in just before she decided to leave Mr. Bergen and the rest of the world behind.

I heard Sunny's jingling collar down below and, moments later, footsteps on the ladder. I quickly wiped my tears with the bottom of my T-shirt. Sheena popped her head in. "Hey," she said, holding a flattened brown paper bag in her hand.

"Hi," I said.

She crawled into the tree house and sat on her knees opposite me. "You okay?

"Fine. What's in the bag?"

She handed me the paper bag, and I reached in and pulled out a long white feather. "It's nice. Thanks. Where'd you get it?"

"Don't get mad, okay? When my mom and I were over at Mrs. Winklemeyer's house for her dealeo . . . her memorial thing."

"Yeah?"

"Well after it was over and you went home and Mom was in the kitchen with some other women cleaning up, I was alone in the living room."

Suddenly I got it. "The stuffed bird? You *plucked* the bird?"

She nodded. "I took the glass off of it and was going to take the whole thing, but I figured somebody'd miss it, so I just pulled one feather out of the bird's wing, and then put the glass back on. No one saw. Nobody knows. Just you."

I held the feather up to the window light. "Why did you do that?"

"Because I thought you might want something to remember her by. But you can't have it."

"What? Why not?"

"Not unless you promise me something."

"What?"

Sheena grew sad as she tried to get the words out. "No matter what and no matter when . . . next week, next year, twenty-four years from now . . . you need to promise me that you will never . . ." Her eyes began to glaze over like she was going to cry.

"Never what?"

"That you will never even think about it."

"Think about what?"

"You know . . ."

I didn't know. "No, what?"

"You know . . . think about doing what Mrs. Winklemeyer did."

I didn't say anything at first. Her concern for a frame of mind that I might possess sometime in the future was spooky and more than a little unnerving. I never thought more than a week in advance about anything, except maybe Christmas or my birthday. That kind of concern was also something that kids just don't have for each other. And even if they did, they certainly wouldn't express it. I felt like I was talking to someone else, my parents maybe, but even they hadn't said much to me about the tragedy since it had happened. My mother's only words to me on the subject were that it was wrong, what Mrs. Winklemeyer did. That it was a sin in God's eyes. I couldn't quite figure that one out. She said it was a sin because God gave us this life and only he should determine at what point to end it. But that was the sensible explanation. I'm guessing there was nothing that made much sense to Mrs. Winklemeyer in the end. I wondered if she felt like she did anything wrong. And maybe it *was* wrong—I didn't know. But I knew this—I couldn't picture God telling Mrs. Winklemeyer that it was wrong. I could only picture him welcoming her home with open arms.

"Why would I do that?" I asked Sheena.

"I don't know, but you need to promise me."

"Okay, okay—I promise," I said.

"*Booger promise* on it?" she asked.

Now I'm guessing you could go your whole life without learning the details of exactly what the booger promise was as a method of pledging or swearing or affirming an oath. But you need to understand and grasp the level of courage and commitment that was involved for Sheena to propose the booger promise in the first place. The reason you've never heard of the booger promise is because Sheena made it up. She developed this creative ritual mostly because she was squeamish when it came to the blood promise, the common method for a kid to seal a deal. I believe the blood promise originated as an Indian custom or at least was dramatized as such on TV westerns. But instead of slicing our fingers open with a large tomahawk to produce the necessary blood, the kid promiser and kid promisee would each pick a scab, swab a drip of blood onto their fingertips, and unite those fingertips in a solemn pledge.

Of course there were other methods of affirming one's vow: locking pinkies, or crossing one's heart, or the ever-popular and overly used swearing on your mother's grave, but these were never very binding. The booger promise was exceptionally binding. The intimacy of Sheena's booger promise made the blood promise look like a limp handshake.

So here is the booger promise, so secretive a vow that I've never mentioned it to another living soul until now. I hesitate to fully explain the details partly out of respect to Sheena, partly because I don't want to gross you out . . . once again. Suffice it to say the covenant involved picking . . . exchanging . . . and consuming. Yes, it was crude and nasty and surely inappropriate behavior at any age, but that's not what's important here. What is important is that through the promise, Sheena expressed a feeling of compassion toward me that surpassed any I'd ever received from anyone before. And I found that I loved her, not in a way that a kid loves another kid, or the way adults do, but in a profound, spiritual way that reached down to places deep within my heart, places that were not simple.

So we did booger promise on it. Right there up in the tree house. And I will never forget it again.

Thirty-Four

THE MORE THINGS CHANGE

At least a week passed before I could bring myself to stop throwing the morning paper onto Mrs. Winklemeyer's driveway. I considered asking Mom if we could adopt Mr. Bergen, but then I realized that I wasn't that fond of cats and I would never have been able to replace Mrs. Winklemeyer in Mr. Bergen's eyes. Mom would have said no, anyway. As it turned out, Mr. Bergen got lucky and was adopted by the McGuires. At least that's what you wanted to hear, right?

Mouse finally gave up the idea of not playing with Hank and Amelia, and actually started becoming less of a jerk.

One night when the entire family was sitting down at the dinner table, my dad produced an object concealed inside a plain brown paper bag and handed it to my mom.

"What's this?" she asked.

"You have a choice," he said.

Mom opened the bag and slid out a bottle of burgundy. She looked puzzled.

"We can either open it up now and have it with dinner," Dad said, "or it can be the first bottle to take up residency in our new wine cellar."

"Oh, honey," she said, leaning over and hugging Dad.

My father looked over at Bobby. "I've decided to call Nikita's bluff."

"Good move, Pop," Bobby said, without looking back at him.

I'd like to say that I finally got that Schwinn Black Phantom bike. I'd like to tell you that Mrs. Gosweller was so grateful to me for exposing Drake to the neighborhood that she surprised me one day, when I came across the bike standing up in front of her gate with a big red bow and my name on it. Or I could tell you that Mrs. Winklemeyer so appreciated that night I danced with her that she left me a hundred dollars in her will to be used specifically for the purpose of buying the Black Phantom. But the truth is, Jimmy got a new bike for his birthday, and so I bought his old one off him for five bucks. I immediately replaced the seat. I wish I could tell you that one of the other scenarios was true, but I don't lie anymore like I did when I was a kid.

But if I did lie, I'd tell you that things got better for me, that the worst was over. If I could continue this story using my own imagination instead of the truth, I'd relate how my brother fell in love again several years later, this time with a beautiful, loyal woman, and how they had three beautiful kids together and lived happily ever after. And I'd write about how this experience with my dad bonded us together so that we never drifted apart again. I'd share with you how Mr. Melzer quietly died in his sleep just as his wife, Margaret, did. If I was the author of my own story, I'd tell you that bigotry was an issue that the Bufords never had to deal with again, and that one morning Drake woke up and was a real boy, and that Mouse was cured of his fits of exaggeration. And the best story line would depict ways in which the guardian angels who watched over Sheena and my mom continued to protect them throughout the rest of that year. But apparently the will of God has little to do with my own will, my own desires. C. S. Lewis wrote, "History is a story written by the finger of God," and he was a guy who knew something about tragedy.

That child I told you about in the beginning . . . well, there was a reason he disappeared, a reason I chose to leave him behind. Maybe you know about it. Maybe you don't. Stories are funny things. They only appear to have beginnings and endings.

Under a perfect summer sky Sheena and I took turns winding up the red plastic propeller until the pink rubber band beneath the plane's slender belly had sufficiently double-knotted. With her Raggedy Ann doll at her side, she looked over the frames of her pink cat's-eye sunglasses and secured the propeller in place with her left hand, while holding onto the body with her right. Her tongue protruding out of the corner of her mouth, she eased the plane back over her shoulder and pitched it forward, releasing it to the wind. Like the beating of wings, the propeller whirled and the airplane immediately caught a gentle updraft, rose, and banked left. Its wings leveled and the balsa bird glided straight toward the upper limbs of the great oak as if it were returning to the nest.

etc.

bonus content includes:

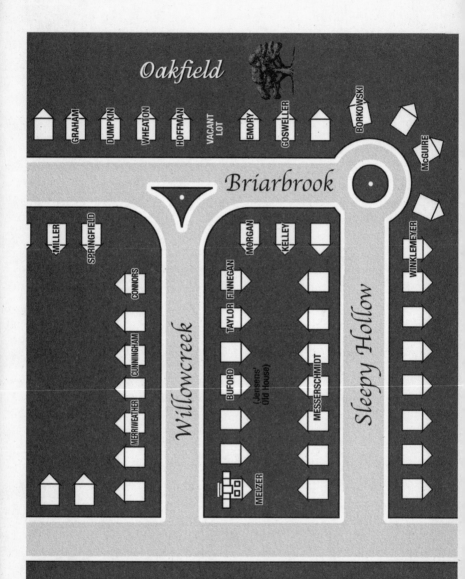

READER'S GUIDE

1. When Gospel Flight Day—or Balloon Day, in Davy's words—is unexpectedly cut short, Davy is concerned about how his mother and Sheena viewed the proceedings: "While they saw the breath of God come down and blow those twenty-five balloons free to find his seekers, I simply saw a freak dust storm roll on through." Do you ever sense your own lack of faith while the faith of others around you appears to be strong? How is Sheena's faith similar to Ruth's?

2. Do you think that Davy's faith grows during the course of the book? Davy mentions that he was a poor Sunday school student and only remembers a few classic stories. He says that he found it "unnerving that God would pick out three ordinary people and not only speak to them but give them employment." He worried that one day God might speak to him. Later, Davy wonders if God is listening to his prayers, and hopes for a clear sign that he is. Does he get that sign?

3. When Davy tells the story of the phantom Good Humor man to Sheena, she immediately knows what Davy has already concluded: that the Good Humor man was an angel sent from God. A recent survey indicated that

approximately 75 percent of Americans believe in angels. As a child did you believe you had a guardian angel(s)? Do you still? Was there any particular time when you were convinced that a guardian angel came to your rescue?

4. Initially Davy describes his dad as his hero. Yet he clearly sees the differences between his father and the father in his favorite TV show, *Father Knows Best*. What are some of the causes for his change in perception of his father? How does Bobby's assessment of their father affect his opinion? Do you remember a time in your own life when one of your parents became more human, more flawed than you had once perceived? Do you believe that Davy regains respect for his father by the end of the story?

5. Why do you think Davy was so bothered by the friction between his brother and their father?

6. We aren't ever privy to exactly why Robert is prejudiced against the Bufords. Could it be that he doesn't even know why, that he is simply following the tenor of the times? Why might Ruth have been prejudiced against Allison Hoffman? Name some of the other characters and their specific prejudices. What are some current prejudices that some people seem to follow without thinking?

7. Both Ruth and Jimmy show the courage of their convictions, Ruth by confronting her husband and Jimmy by standing up to Mouse. Why does Ruth choose to fight this particular battle with Robert? Why do you think Jimmy braved Mouse's wrath? Although he denies having much courage in the narration, Davy has a few moments when he also decides to take a stand. Name some of them.

8. Have you ever found yourself in a position similar to Mrs.

Merriweather's at the welcoming committee—wanting to do the right thing but believing it's just not in you? What is the purpose of the story Mr. Melzer tells Davy about his pet dog, when the young Joe went along with his peers at the cost of hurting a friend (in this case, the dog)? How does Davy apply it to his own circumstances?

9. Why do you think Mr. Connors took back the army hat from Davy? What did that army hat symbolize?

10. When Davy first sees the Bufords' house covered with graffiti, how does he feel? Why? Are his feelings justified? Why do you think he went immediately from his parents' discussion about it to tell Mr. Melzer? Do you think Mr. Melzer's reaction to the news was what Davy expected?

11. Why do you believe Davy didn't help Mr. Melzer paint the house?

12. When Davy was troubled, why did he regularly turn to Mr. Melzer—rather than his parents—for advice? In what way were Robert and Ruth's good parenting intentions to blame?

13. If you've read *The Reluctant Journey of David Connors*, you no doubt saw many correlations in *The Summer the Wind Whispered My Name*. Can you name them all? What item first appears out of the carpetbag in *Reluctant Journey* and what is its connection with the final gift that Sheena gives to Davy? What significance did the booger promise hold over David's actions in *Reluctant Journey*?

14. Davy reflects on how all the series of events had to fall into place for his father to receive the Scripture about loving his neighbor and to act on those words. Similarly the adult David quotes C. S. Lewis: "History is a story

written by the finger of God." Do you believe that to be true in Robert's case?

15. It bothered Davy—or at least the adult David—that his parents didn't tell him they loved him. He mentions that parents back then used a sort of code to say, "I love you." How did Davy's parents show that they loved him? Do you think that parents still use codes to express love to their children? Did yours?

THE WAY THINGS
WERE IN 1960

THE NEIGHBORHOOD PAPERBOY

Twelve-year-old Benjamin Franklin is believed to have been the first paperboy in the United States. In 1718 he delivered copies of the *Boston Gazette* for his brother, James, a Boston printer. Prior to that time, newspapers were mailed.[1]

A CATHOLIC RUNNING FOR PRESIDENT

In an address to Southern Baptist leaders in 1960, John F. Kennedy felt compelled to defend himself as it related to holding the office of president:

> I believe in a president whose views on religion are his own private affair, neither imposed by him upon the nation or imposed by the nation upon him as a condition to holding that office. . . .
>
> But let me stress again that these are my views—for, contrary to common newspaper usage, I am not the Catholic candidate

for president. I am the Democratic Party's candidate for president who happens also to be a Catholic. I do not speak for my church on public matters—and the church does not speak for me.

Whatever issue may come before me as president—on birth control, divorce, censorship, gambling, or any other subject—I will make my decision in accordance with these views, in accordance with what my conscience tells me to be the national interest, and without regard to outside religious pressures or dictates. And no power or threat of punishment could cause me to decide otherwise.

But if the time should ever come—and I do not concede any conflict to be even remotely possible—when my office would require me to either violate my conscience, or violate the national interest, then I would resign the office; and I hope any conscientious public servant would do the same."[2]

FALLOUT SHELTERS

In 1949 President Harry Truman made it publicly known that the Soviet Union had detonated its first atomic bomb, and Americans had to come to terms with the idea of nuclear war. During the next decade the U.S. government concluded that it could not shelter every American citizen from a nuclear war, and from 1958 on, the Office of Civil Defense promoted home shelters and published manuals showing Americans how to build them. Over 100,000 Americans built their own backyard fallout shelters during the Cold War.[3]

THE WIFFLE BALL

Tired of getting in trouble for breaking classroom windows when he and his friends were playing baseball at his Fairfield, Connecticut, schoolyard in the early 1950s, David A. Mullany decided to change the equipment. At first he tried a tennis ball and sawed-off broom handle, but this still resulted in some property damage. But when Mullany found a plastic practice golf ball in his father's golf bag, it triggered the idea that ultimately became the Wiffle ball. With help from his father—a former industrial-league (semipro) pitcher—and a friend in manufacturing, a working ball was created using a slotted-hole design . . . after many trial and error experiments. To this day Mullany says, "I have no idea why it works. We've never had the ball tested."

Mullany's father produced a batch of Wiffle balls, and they were displayed at a local diner. These sold out in a couple of weeks, which led to a contract with a rep in the toy business. Because of its practicality when it came to safety and convenience issues, which included the fact that no gloves were needed to play the game, Wiffleball became an overnight sensation, particularly in the suburbs.

Today Mullany's sons, David J. and Stephen, run Wiffle Ball Inc., a privately held company.[4]

13 GHOSTS

Movie producer William Castle was known as the king of ballyhoo for the various gimmickries he'd come up with to promote his horror films. In one case he promised to provide life insurance policies just in case anyone died of fright during the viewing; in another, random theater seats were electrically charged to stimulate additional audience response and potential panic; in yet another, ticket buyers were assured that a nurse would be on duty in the lobby for those who couldn't deal with the unrelenting horror. For *13 Ghosts*, Castle "invented" a cardboard and acetate ghost viewing device that enabled the audience to see the images of ghosts in the movie. He called it Illusion-O. The hype always surpassed the inevitable cheesiness of the actual effects, but that didn't stop kids from packing the theater in hopes of a payoff as thrilling as the ad campaign promised. Castle's most successful movie was *Rosemary's Baby* in 1968.[5]

DIVORCE

Ruth's discriminatory attitude toward divorce wasn't that unusual for the times. In 1960 the number of divorces per 1,000 married women was 9.2 compared to 17.7 in 2004.[6]

THE GOOD HUMOR MAN

Youngstown, Ohio, candy maker Harry Burt created a smooth chocolate coating that was compatible with ice cream in 1920. There was just one drawback: It was a mess to eat. Then his son suggested copying the company's own lollipop, Jolly Boy Suckers, and putting the ice cream on a wooden stick.

The new product was called a Good Humor bar (from a belief at that time that one's temperament—or humor—was related to the sense of taste), and to sell it, Burt amassed a fleet of twelve trucks, driven by men in white uniforms. The trucks had a distinctive bell to announce their presence and were an immediate success. In 1930 the Good Humor Corporation went national; in 1961 it was sold to Unilever. Good Humor trucks were discontinued in 1976, in favor of grocery store distribution.[7]

THE COST OF LIVING IN 1960[8]

Average cost of new home	$12,700.00
Average cost of new car	$2,600.00
Average salary	$4,700.00
Weekday newspaper	$0.15
Gallon of gasoline	$0.25
Can of beef ravioli	$0.30
Loaf of bread	$0.20
Flour, per 5 pounds	$0.49
Eggs, per dozen	$0.49
Butter, per pound	$0.67
Oranges, per dozen	$0.89
Men's oxford shoes	$12.95
Ladies' nylons, per pair	$1.15
Milk, per gallon	$0.49
Electric can opener	$8.88
McDonald's hamburger	$0.15
Candy bar	$0.05
Postage stamp	$0.05

1. Lisa W. Foderaro, "Men and Women Replacing the Paperboy of Old," *The New York Times*, March 1, 1992, http://query.nytimes.com/gst/fullpage.html?res=9E0CE4D8113EF932A35750 C0A964958260&sec=&spon=&pagewanted=print.
2. John F. Kennedy, "Address to the Greater Houston Ministerial Association," Houston, Texas,

September 12, 1960, http://www.jfklibrary.org/Historical+Resources/Archives/Reference+Desk/Speeches/JFK/JFK+PrePres/Address+of+Senator+John+F.+Kennedy+to+the+Greater+Houston+Ministerial+Association.htm.

3. USHistory.com, "Cold War: Fallout Shelters," http://www.u-s-history.com/pages/h3706.html.

4. Cliff Gromer, "50 Years of Wiffle Ball," *Popular Mechanics*, December 2003, http://www.popularmechanics.com/outdoors/adventures/1278131.html?page=1.

5. http://www.horron-wood.com/archives03.htHorror-wood Webzine. "Archives from the Crypt" "The William Castle Story" (February 2003) by Ron Waite.

6. Maggie Gallagher, "Everything You Always Wanted to Know About Marriage But Were Afraid to Ask Stephanie Coontz," *National Review Online*, February 23, 2006, http://www.nationalreview.com/comment/gallagher200602230759.asp.

7. Unilever Ice Cream, "Good Humor History," Ice Cream USA, http://www.icecreamusa.com/good_humor/history/.

8. Data compiled from the following websites: http://www.thepeoplehistory.com/1960s.html, http://www.foodtimeline.org/foodfaq5.html#mcdonalds, and http://www.ssa.gov/OACT/COLA/AWI.html.

etc.

ACKNOWLEDGMENTS

A big thank you to all of my friends and family for their continued support of this little passion of mine. Thanks also to Jill Grosjean, without whom I'd still be writing for a slightly dispirited audience of one; to Jamie Chavez for making sense of my words and encouraging me to "kill my darlings" for the sake of the story. Thanks to Rick and Mar, the best cheerleaders anyone could hope to have on their side; to Graham for his helpful critique; to Kris and Arvid Wallen for their patience, talent, and willingness to allow me to share in the process; to Reagen Reed for her excellent copyediting; and to Shelley Ring and everyone at NavPress for their hard work. Thank you, Susan, for every smile and every day. And thanks to the One who continually sails balloons over my head with the message that his mercies are new every morning.

ABOUT THE AUTHOR

D on Locke is an illustrator and graphic artist for NBC's *The Tonight Show with Jay Leno*. He also writes screenplays, short stories, plays, and novels. Don's pastimes include oil painting, songwriting, playing softball on his church team, and losing at golf to his brother, Rick, on a regular basis. His best work has resulted in two sons, Morgan, 27, and Graham, 25. Don resides in Southern California with his wife, Susan.

Other Great Reads from NavPress!

The Reluctant Journey of David Connors
Don Locke
ISBN-13: 978-1-60006-152-3
ISBN-10: 1-60006-152-4

On a cold winter night, David Connors contemplates a leap off a skyscraper, hoping to end the pain of his crippling alienation from his family and his anger and resentment toward God. But his attention is strangely drawn to a nearby bundle half-buried on the snowy ledge. Experience the power of the unexpected with this humorous tale of grace and redemption.

Storm Warriors
John Nappa
ISBN-13: 978-1-60006-172-1
ISBN-10: 1-60006-172-9

Somewhere off the coast of England, Lionel Lukin and his family fight for their lives. Caught in the crosshairs of a violent storm, their small ship is quickly slipping beneath the crashing waves. Lionel is miraculously washed to shore, only to discover that his wife and son are lost at sea. Inspired by real-life rescues that took place in the nineteenth century, *Storm Warriors* shares a compelling story of personal tragedy to heroic triumph.

A Minute Before Friday
Jo Kadlecek
ISBN-13: 978-1-60006-051-9
ISBN-10: 1-60006-051-X

When an old friend leaks an Ivy League secret, Jonna must confront the dark forces that run deep within the city. What she discovers is more shocking than all of the stories she's ever reported combined. Will she be able to withstand—and expose—the truth?

To order copies, visit your local Christian bookstore, call NavPress at 1-800-366-7788, or log on to www.navpress.com. To locate a Christian bookstore near you, call 1-800-991-7747.